THE DRAGO
BO

CW01498925

ᴛʜᴇ Pᴏʀᴛᴀʟ

BOOKS BY CAREN J. WERLINGER

NOVELS:
Looking Through Windows
Miserere
In This Small Spot
Neither Present Time
Year of the Monsoon
She Sings of Old, Unhappy, Far-off Things
Turning for Home
Cast Me Gently
The Beast That Never Was

SHORT STORIES:
Twist of the Magi
Just a Normal Christmas
(part of *Do You Feel What I Feel? Holiday Anthology*)

THE DRAGONMAGE SAGA:
Rising From the Ashes: The Chronicles of Caymin
The Portal: The Chronicles of Caymin

COMING SOON:
The Standing Stones: The Chronicles of Caymin

THE DRAGONMAGE SAGA
BOOK II

THE PORTAL
THE CHRONICLES OF CAYMIN

CAREN J. WERLINGER

CORGYN
Publishing

The Portal: The Chronicles of Caymin
Published by Corgyn Publishing, LLC.

e-Book ISBN: 978-0-9960368-7-0
Print ISBN: 978-0-9960368-8-7

E-mail: cjwerlingerbooks@yahoo.com
Web site: www.cjwerlinger.wordpress.com

Cover design by Patty G. Henderson
blvdphotografica.wixsite.com/boulevard

Cover photo: Questions of Light Photography
www.questionsoflight.com

Book design by Maureen Cutajar
www.gopublished.com

"That is the trap of the otherworld.
It allows you to get lost in what might have been."
Caymin

CARMIN'S MAP
OF ÉIRE

CONTENTS

Shadows

Deep in a cave, a slender woman rose from her bed. Rubbing her arm, she neared the fire and flicked a hand to bring the flames to life. The dancing light threw shadows against the rock walls. Nearby, nestled in a depression in the cave floor padded with many skins, a solid black shape lay. One eyelid opened, revealing a yellow eye.

"What is it, Ailill?"

The woman shook her head. *"I do not know. I am restless."*

An enormous black head rose on a sinuous neck, and the edges of scales gleamed in the firelight. *"Your old wound pains you. I can feel it."*

"Yes." Ailill rubbed her shoulder again, kneading the muscles. Her eyes and mouth were marked by fine lines and her dark hair glinted silver in places. She sighed a sigh that was weary with age and time. *"Do you feel it, Riona? The weight of all we have seen and done?"*

"We did what we had to do. It was war."

Ailill turned to look at her companion. *"And it is coming again."*

The great black dragon laid her head on the rock floor of the cave next to Ailill. *"What have you seen?"*

1

Ailill shook her head. *"It is not clear."* She unfurled a scroll, holding the parchment so that she could read by firelight. *"He wrote of a girl and a white dragon. The time is drawing near. Somehow, they will meet."*

She rested a hand on the dragon's jaw. *"All is shadows. I can see that they have left Inishbreith, but beyond that, nothing. What I can see is that they will be hunted and tested in ways they are not prepared for. I wish they were not alone. They are but cubs themselves."*

The dragon sighed, and sparks flew from her nostrils. *"What choice did we have? Whom would we ally with if we were there? Our presence would only put them in more danger."*

"You are right," Ailill said. *"They are the only ones who can do what must be done."*

"They are strong and true. They will not fail."

They sat looking into the fire for long heartbeats. Ailill fingered a crystal hanging from a leather cord around her neck.

"It is out there, somewhere. I feel it calling to me in the deep places of the night." Ailill's voice was heavy with trepidation. *"If it is found, all we fought for will have been for naught."*

"No," said Ríona. *"We bought the world a thousand winters of peace. That was not for naught. But... you are right. I, too, have felt it. Like a thing alive. It wants to be found. If it calls to us, it must to others as well. If it is unearthed, the world will be torn asunder."*

"We must help them to find it first." Ailill tilted her head as she considered. *"If it is to be found, mayhap we can ensure it is found by Caymin and Péist."*

"But how? Even we do not know where it was hidden."

"There may be clues to be found in the scrolls here." Ailill frowned. *"Have we been neglectful? Content to retreat to this land to lick our wounds and forget the world we left? Or were we just blind to think that our part in it had ended, and we would never need be troubled with that world again? Either way, we must try to help."*

"It may be that we can guide them from here." Ríona nudged her head closer, and Ailill obliged with a scratch on the ridge above her eyes. *"We will call to them and pull them to us in spiritwalks. In the spirit realm, we may be able to teach them what they must know."* She paused. *"Should we tell them all?"*

2

"No. There is no need to burden them with all we know." Ailill leaned against the dragon, drawing comfort from her nearness. "*I fear the days of dragons and mages are coming to an end, even here.*"

A low rumble came from Ríona, echoing within the cave. "*Two-legs will reap what they sow. If they permit a world with no magic, no connection to the earth, no balance among the life forces, they will have to live with the consequences.*"

"*Those are the shadows I cannot see past. If humans do not act now to restore balance in the world, it will be too late.*"

Ríona closed her eyes. "*It may already be too late.*"

CHAPTER 1

To the Enemy

With the coming of dawn, Caymin crawled out from under the shelter of the dragon's wing. She shivered in the cold damp of the morning, and was joined by a crow, who flapped her wings to land on the girl's shoulder. Together, they made their way to the top of a hill. Below them, sheep huddled on the hillside, but there were no signs of dwellings or other two-legs. In the distance, they could see cliffs rising from the mist that covered the surface of the sea under a sky tinged with pink and purple.

"*There is the land of Gai's clan,*" said Caymin.

Beanna fluffed her feathers. "*But will they be friend or foe?*"

"*That is what we will have to see.*"

Caymin limped back down the hill to where the white dragon lay. Péist opened his eyes as a man crept out from under his other wing. Garvan straightened his monk's robes and looked up at Péist who stretched his long neck to the sky.

"I'm going to pray before I break my fast," Garvan said, scratching his beard. "Don't wait for me."

They watched him disappear over the same hill Caymin and Beanna had climbed a moment before, while Caymin retrieved a woven bag and pulled out some smoked fish and meat, along with a few of the roots she had harvested from Inishbreith before they left. She passed some of the meat to Beanna.

"Are you rested?" she asked Péist.

"Somewhat. The flight here was tiring, with Garvan's extra weight."

"Do you need to hunt again?"

"I will soon. There is nothing on this rock but sheep." Péist picked at his teeth with a talon. "Their wool catches in my throat."

"I am afraid sheep is all you will have until we get to Éire," Caymin said.

"And when will that be?" Beanna asked.

"I do not know."

When Garvan rejoined them, he ate hungrily. He pointed to the south, where two other small islands could now be seen as the mist cleared. "These three islands are the last points of land this side of Éire. No humans live on them now, only sheep left to graze and breed, but the humans come over in boats in spring and autumn, before the sea gets too rough, to gather the sheep." He looked at Péist. "Until you're ready to show yourself, you can hunt among these islands."

"Eating sheep is not hunting," Péist grumbled.

Garvan chuckled. "I'm afraid your choices are limited out here."

He led them all back to the crest of the hill that shielded them from the mainland. "All the land you see here is under the control of clan Eoganacht."

He glanced at Caymin, and she realized she was unconsciously touching the scars that ridged the side of her face. She immediately lowered her hand.

"I know they raided your village and killed your father, but there are answers to be had there. See that tower?" He pointed to a place where a round tower could be seen rising above the cliffs. "That is one of their outposts. Péist will only be able to fly at night, or they'll see him. Even then, a white dragon will be easy to spot."

"If Péist carries us there," Caymin said, indicating a stretch of cliffs well north of the tower, "can we approach them on foot?"

Garvan nodded. "Aye, but we'll want to be wary. If they think we're a threat to them, they'll lock us up before we can speak to anyone and we won't learn what we need to. We should rest today, and then tonight, we fly back to Éire."

The endless water rippled below, tiny points of light reflecting the moon and stars back from the waves. Silently, great white dragon wings soared over the water, catching currents of air and riding them closer and closer to Éire.

Péist came to ground in a remote stretch of grassland above the cliffs. Caymin unstrapped herself from the saddle while Garvan slid down off his back. Beanna wriggled out of her sling tucked against Caymin's belly. She flew to a thistle bush and flapped her wings.

"We can walk from here," Caymin said, untying her bow and quiver from Péist's saddle and slipping them over her shoulder.

"*I do not like this,*" Péist said with a growl. "*I do not want to leave you unprotected.*"

"You and I will remain connected, no matter how far apart we are," Caymin said. "If I am in any trouble, you will know and can get there quickly. But it would be best not to let them know we have a dragon in our midst in the beginning. Not until I know whether they will help us or no."

Garvan patted the sword hanging from his belt and said, "I promise, I'll protect her."

Péist lowered his head to look him in the eye. "*You had better, holy man.*"

Caymin drew herself up. "You both forget, I do not need protecting."

Péist raised his head and glared toward their destination. "*That remains to be seen.*" He shielded his voice from Garvan. "*Come with me.*"

Caymin walked a short distance away, and Péist lowered his head again to touch her face with his muzzle.

"*I do not like leaving you, little one.*"

"I know," she said, pressing her forehead to his. "It will not be for long. As soon as we know whether Gai's clan will help us, we will move on. In the meantime, rest and rebuild your strength. We may need to flee, and I will need you to be ready." She backed away. "Go now, while it is still dark."

Péist fanned his wings and allowed the wind blowing in from the water to lift him off the cliff. Caymin watched him fly back in the direction of the small islands far out on the sea.

Beanna flew to her shoulder. "Shall we see what we will see?"

Walking as quietly as possible, the trio made their way south. Caymin was able to keep up with Garvan despite her scarred leg. The day was beginning to brighten when Garvan suddenly pulled Caymin to the ground. They heard voices nearby, and soon after, saw a band of five warriors tramp by, all armed with spears, swords strapped to their belts. The cloaks they wore all bore one insignia—a blue wolf with red eyes, holding a yellow sword—the same image woven into the cloak that Caymin wore.

They followed the band from a safe distance and hid behind a hedge of blackthorn to watch the warriors approach a sentry guarding an entry through a stone wall. The stones were stacked taller than two men, and the gate was broad enough to allow four men to pass shoulder to shoulder. The sentry, armed as the other warriors were, questioned them briefly and then let them pass through a small door set into the massive gate.

The wall extended left and right, gradually curving out of sight as it encircled the buildings within. Outside the walls were fields, half of them nothing but stalks, while the others were filled with men and women harvesting.

"They're on alert," Garvan whispered. "The men we followed were probably coming off night patrol. They won't be eager to let strangers enter."

"Gai told us, before he was called back here, that their clan had been battling another. His father was captured and being held for ransom, but I do not understand what that means."

Garvan pulled her down to sit beside him. "It means Gai's clan will have to pay a small treasure to get their king back. This could give us the opportunity we need to bargain with them."

Caymin looked at him in bewilderment. "What do we have to bargain with? We do not have a treasure."

Garvan smiled grimly. "You have a dragon."

"Stay!"

The sentry barred their way, leveling his spear at them. Garvan pulled back his monk's hood.

"Pray, grant us entrance," he said. "We've traveled far and are weary."

The sentry eyed them suspiciously. He jabbed his spear at Caymin. "You, too. Off with your cloak."

When Garvan gestured for her to lower her hood, the sentry stepped back, a look of repulsion on his face as he took in her scars. "What happened to you?"

When she simply looked at him, he glanced at Garvan. "What's the matter with her?"

"She's deaf and dumb," Garvan said, laying a fatherly hand on Caymin's shoulder. "The scars are from a fire. She was burned when she was but a babe."

The suspicion on the sentry's face lessened a bit. He made her turn around. "Where'd she get that cloak?"

"One of your warriors took pity on her. That's what her mother told me before she died and left the lass in my keeping." Garvan bowed his head. "I am but a poor man of God and have no means of caring for a child. I was hoping she might find a place here. She's a good worker."

"I don't know," the sentry said, looking over his shoulder.

"May we petition your lord directly?"

The sentry barked a laugh. "Would that you could."

Caymin looked up at Garvan and rubbed her stomach.

"She's hungry," said Garvan. "Might we enter and look for a bite or two to eat?"

The sentry hesitated, eyeing Caymin and her scars. "Oh, go on then."

He stepped aside, opening the small door.

"God bless you," Garvan said as they passed through, Caymin limping more than usual.

"*That was well done,*" said Beanna from atop the wall where she had observed the entire exchange.

"*Keep watch,*" said Caymin. "*Let me know if you see Gai.*"

She looked around in wonderment as they walked through the village enclosed within the stone walls. In the distance, built into the far portion of the wall, was the largest building Caymin had ever seen, taller than a tree. She saw more warriors on a walkway built into its upper levels, standing guard.

People were stirring, cooking over fires in front of their dwellings. Like the fortress, most of these were built of stone, but with thatched roofs. The villagers watched the strangers with open curiosity, some with expressions of revulsion at the scars marring the right side of Caymin's face, while others took pity and offered a bit of bread or cheese.

Garvan accepted with a blessing and thanks.

"I have never been in the midst of so many two-legs," Caymin muttered as she shoved a bite of cheese into her mouth.

"You'd best not be calling them two-legs while we're here," Garvan muttered back. "In fact, you're not supposed to be talking at all. I'd feel better if we had our weapons."

"We had to hide them. The sentry never would have let us enter with weapons." Caymin looked around. "Most of these people are not armed. I can protect us if need be."

Garvan stopped and nodded toward a stone building with a wooden cross affixed to the roof. "A church. Stay here and let me go talk to the priest there." He glanced at her. "Stay to yourself and, remember, you're the ghost-child again. You can't speak or hear."

Caymin pulled her cloak back up over her head and sat out of the way against the wall. This place felt... strange. It wasn't just the presence of so many two-legs; it was the absence of trees or plants. She dug her fingers into the soil and felt nothing. No hum of life, no power. It felt dead. With a shiver, she brushed the dirt off her fingers.

9

"*Do you see anything?*" she asked as Beanna perched on top of the wall above her head.

"*I see many things. Do I see anything useful? Not yet.*" She hopped along the wall. "*Wait. I see a man carrying a hawk on his arm. Did you not tell me their mage has a hawk that is bonded to him?*"

"*Yes. It was the hawk who brought the message to Gai that his father had been captured. Is the man you see the mage here?*"

"*I do not know. Mages look like other two-legs, but... wait. He carries a staff. I think it is he. He is coming in this direction.*"

Caymin glanced up. "*We must stop talking now or he may hear.*"

Beanna flew away, flitting to another nearby rooftop where she could keep watch.

Caymin sat with her head bowed, her cloak pulled low over her head while she watched the people milling about. She spotted him—a small, thin man, striding away with his staff in one hand. The hawk was no longer with him. She listened, but heard no unspoken conversation between mage and hawk. She felt Péist's unrest as he waited anxiously on the island.

She was just considering whether to warn Beanna to be on the lookout in case the hawk attacked from the air, when the hawk suddenly landed in front of her.

"*Greetings,*" said the hawk.

Caymin blinked. "*Greetings.*"

The hawk tilted his head as he regarded her. "*You dried me and fed me when I brought a message to young Gai.*"

"*I remember, Lorcan. I am Caymin.*"

"*My mage wishes to meet you, Caymin.*"

"*How did he know I am here?*"

"*We felt you. Will you come?*"

Caymin looked around, but there was no sign of Garvan. This village wasn't so big that she wouldn't be able to find him later. "*I will come.*"

Lorcan spread wings that tip to tip were nearly as long as Caymin was tall. He thrust into the air.

"*The crow may come as well.*"

Beanna flew down to Caymin's shoulder. *"The crow was going to come whether the hawk gave permission or no."*

Caymin smiled. They followed Lorcan as he flew from rooftop to rooftop, leading them to an unassuming stone cottage, thatched like most of the others. The only thing that made this cottage different from the others was the small garden of herbs outside its door. Lorcan swooped through the open door. Caymin hesitated for a moment and then followed.

Standing inside near the fire was the man Caymin had seen. Slight of stature, he turned as she entered. Lorcan perched on a stout tree limb that had been dragged inside and propped in a corner. The mage's staff leaned against the hearth.

"I am Eachna." The mage approached, taking Caymin by the chin and turning her head so that he could see her scars. "You are Caymin."

He smiled when she tugged her chin from his grasp. He gestured toward a stool near the hearth. Caymin sat, and Beanna flitted over to a table where she could keep an eye on Lorcan and the two-legs. The inside of the cottage was sparsely furnished with a table and shelves stacked with many bowls and jars. Bunches of dried roots and flowers hung from the rafters—much as Enat's cottage used to be.

Caymin studied him. He was clean-shaven, with short-cropped hair the color of a sword's blade. "How do you know me?"

He didn't respond immediately, but bent toward the fire where he had a kettle sitting. He poured hot water into two cups. As he worked, she felt a push into her thoughts. Without thinking, she cast a protective spell, but the intrusion continued as if she had done nothing. Alarmed, she tried again, to no avail. Against her wishes, she saw images of the mages she had trained with—Enat and Neela making potions, Ivar teaching her how to use a sword, the other apprentices she had learned with.

When the image of Péist formed in her mind, she stood, knocking her stool over.

"Stop!"

"I apologize." He glanced up at her. He didn't look sorry. "That was rude."

11

He held out a cup. She watched him angrily for several heartbeats before righting her stool and accepting the cup.

"Why did you do that?" she asked as she sat.

"Why couldn't you stop me?"

Caymin felt the heat rise into her cheeks, as she had been thinking the same thing. She wondered if he could have cast some type of spell to nullify her magic within his house.

He scrutinized her, but there was no further pushing into her thoughts.

She took a sip of her drink, realizing only after she swallowed that he could have poisoned it or put a sleeping potion in it. She waited, but nothing seemed to be happening.

"How do you know me?" she repeated.

"Gai spoke of you. And Lorcan and I felt you when you arrived."

"I do not understand."

"Your magic. It's powerful."

Caymin blushed again and looked down into her cup. "Not so powerful. I could not stop you pushing into my thoughts."

"You've been in a place of power."

She stared up at him. Had he indeed read her thoughts again without her feeling it?

His smile did not quite reach his eyes. "You've never had to use magic outside a place of power, have you? It's not so easy."

She realized he was right. Enat had warned her when she was first brought to the mystical forest to be trained that using magic would be easier there because of the power of the forest. From there, she and Péist and Beanna had fled to Inishbreith, which had power even greater than that of the forest. When she had used magic on their journey, Péist had had to bolster her power with his own.

"Your magic is like an aura around you, but you've yet to refine it, to learn to control it. If you're here, you left the forest much earlier than you should have." He narrowed his eyes as he studied her. "I wonder why that was?"

She said nothing, but suspected he already knew the answer to his question.

He turned back to the fire and said, "You're probably curious to know how Gai is."

"You said he told you about me."

He shrugged. "It's more what Gai didn't say rather than what he did."

"What do you mean?"

"He's been... different since he returned." Eachna reached forward to stir the fire. "You changed him."

"I? How?"

Again, Eachna didn't answer. Instead, he said, "Gai told me of the cloak you wear, the cloak that was taken from the warriors who attacked your village and killed your family, leaving you to burn." He eyed her curiously. "Your arm and leg are burned as well."

Caymin said nothing, only looked at him.

"You accused him of being a murderer."

Caymin flushed furiously. "I was wrong to accuse him so."

"Were you?" Eachna tilted his head to stare at her again. "Is that why you're here? To tell him you were wrong?"

"*Caymin.*"

She turned to Beanna just as a shadow darkened the doorway. Her mouth dropped.

"Gai."

CHAPTER 2

Ḥaro ⲦꞅuⲦḥⲋ

Enat groaned and sat up. Her head pounded with every beat of her heart, but she closed her eyes and tried to center herself, to pull up her power. A weak ball of flame appeared on her palm, glowing a pale green in the darkness of the hovel in which she was being kept. With a grim smile, she let the flame go out.

The potion Angus was using to deaden her power was losing its potency. Every time they forced it down her throat, she was able to fight the effects off more quickly—not that she wanted to use magic against them. Not yet.

As for the more crude ways Angus had been trying to get information from her—she couldn't suppress a shudder at the thought that he would most likely try again soon. The pain of the beatings was almost more than she could bear. The only thing that bolstered her resolve to stay was the look of horror in Diarmit's eyes when Angus tortured her. The boy was seeing firsthand what his master was capable of, and Enat couldn't bring herself to abandon him—not if there was still some hope he might come around.

Someone raised the bar bracing the door, and daylight poured into the darkness as the door was opened. She shaded her eyes with one hand, squinting to see who it was.

"Eat."

Diarmit squatted before her, holding out a bowl. She let her hands tremble weakly as she accepted it.

"Thank you."

He eyed her, unable to hide his revulsion as she sat there in filthy clothing in this hovel that stank with the smell of the clay pot serving as her toilet. "Why don't you just tell him what he wants to know?"

She blinked up at him as she forced herself to eat the gristly bits of meat swimming amongst the barley. "You know I can't do that. He would destroy everything I hold dear. Including you, Diarmit."

He shoved to his feet, surprisingly agile for such a big boy. "Don't say that! Don't talk to me like that. He's not destroying me. He's training me."

She looked up at him. "Training you to be like him? Cruel? Heartless? That's not who you are. You're so much better than that."

He turned away. "I'm not."

"But you are. When you're ready to see that, I'll be here. We can leave together."

He looked at her, his eyes wide as he backed away. "I can't."

He closed and barred the door, leaving her in darkness again.

She let her head rest against the wall behind her and, as she had done a thousand times over the last six moons, offered up a prayer to the gods and goddesses that Ivar and Neela had been able to get the younger apprentices safely home. Their training would have to wait until this war was over. If the things she had seen in her spiritwalk came to fruition, they couldn't take a chance on children being caught in an attack on the forest.

As for Una and Niall, it grieved her that they had not had the chance to earn their staffs, but perhaps the forest would grant them that opportunity one day. She could only hope that they had also made it to safety.

It had not been an easy decision to leave her beloved forest and follow Diarmit when they set him free.

"We can't keep him captive forever," she'd argued.

"I could," Ivar growled, his hulking silhouette throwing a bear-like shadow as he paced. "This is lunacy."

"What will become of you?" Neela had fretted.

"I'll allow them to capture me," Enat had said simply. "Then I can keep an eye on Diarmit, and mayhap learn what it is they intend. And you both must stay away. If my vision comes true, you can't defend the entire forest with only two of you. We'll have to trust that our protections will hold."

Her lightness of tone had belied the heaviness in her heart as she prepared to leave. The hardest decision had been to leave her staff hidden. She couldn't take the chance of it falling into Angus's hands. She whispered one more prayer that someday, Caymin would find it and would know what to do with it. Everything rested on that.

Gai sat at the table and watched her, his face impassive. Caymin, for her part, thought him much changed. He was taller, but just as pale and just as beautiful as he had been. He wore an embroidered tunic of a rich blue and a ring of gold around his slender throat. She still did not understand exactly what role a king or his family played, but she found herself feeling humbled before him.

"You've changed your hair," he said.

She reached up to finger the thin red braids hanging to her shoulders. "Yes."

"You look like Méav."

She flushed. "No. I will never look like Méav. But this was easy to do myself."

Eachna sat silently, watching the two of them.

Gai tilted his head as he regarded her. "Why have you been by yourself?"

Caymin opened her mouth, but then closed it again, considering where to begin. "Much has happened since you left the forest."

"Pray, tell us." There was just a hint of his old sneer in his voice.

"It was Diarmit. The one who attacked Fergus, the one who injured Péist."

He looked as if he didn't believe her. "Diarmit. That dolt."

"He is not. He was pretending to be slow and stupid, but he is very powerful. There is a priest in his village who has power, and is using both magic and the fear of the Christ to control people. He wanted—"

She stopped abruptly.

Eachna leaned forward a bit. "He wanted what?"

Caymin looked from one to the other. "Is your father still held captive by another clan?"

"Yes," Gai said, his eyes narrowed. "My brother, Flann, is leading our clan while we try to gather the tribute we need to ransom my father."

"What if I could help you to get your father back, without paying the ransom? Would your father be willing to pledge his warriors to help us?"

"To help with what?" Gai glanced at Eachna who looked just as puzzled.

"There is a war coming. I have seen it." Caymin shivered at the memory. "Enat and the others, being attacked by the followers of this monk. We must stop it."

Gai sat back. "You came here, to the people who attacked your village, to ask for our help."

Caymin nodded as he stared at her, his face a mask.

"Is this why you left the protection of the forest before you had your staff?"

"No, it isn't," Eachna said when Caymin didn't answer.

"I had to leave when Péist began to hatch. Timmin attacked me. He wanted to control Péist for himself."

Gai's brow furrowed as he tried to remember. "I thought Péist was a worm-like creature. The one who warned you when the northmen were invading the forest?"

"He was, but... he is more."

No one said anything for many heartbeats. Gai and Eachna looked at each other in bewilderment.

"Timmin was First Mage," Eachna said. "I don't understand. Why would he jeopardize his position? What is this Péist?"

"*Should I tell them?*" Caymin asked Beanna who had been sitting silently through this exchange. She saw immediately that Gai and Eachna had heard.

"*It is why we came here,*" Beanna said.

Caymin took a deep breath. "He is a dragon."

Gai laughed, but stopped when he saw she was serious. "A dragon."

She nodded. "Timmin said we needed to fight the followers of the Christ who are attacking the old ways and restricting us to only a few places of power. He wanted to use Péist to attack them and drive them from Éire."

Eachna rubbed his face as if rubbing sleep away. "You have a dragon."

"We are bonded to each other."

Gai stood and paced. "So, you and your dragon would help us get my father back, and in return our clan would pledge to help defeat this priest and his horde to protect the forest?"

"Yes."

Gai whirled, and his eyes were dark as coals. "Why would I help you? The elders or any of you? You never trusted me. We're a clan of murderers, remember?"

Before Caymin could say another word, he stalked out. Caymin stared after him in dismay.

Beanna ruffled her feathers. "*Well, that did not go as planned.*"

Out on the island, Péist waited in agitation. He was tired of eating sheep. The silly things actually ran headlong off the bluffs when he appeared. All he had to do was fly down and scoop them out of the water. But prey was prey, and he needed to eat. To be ready.

He was lying in the sun on the west side of the island, away from any on the mainland who might be looking toward these rocks on the water, when he felt Caymin's consternation at whatever had happened where she was.

"*Do you need me?*" he asked, gathering himself, ready to leap into the sky.

"*Not yet. This did not go well. Let me see if I can repair the damage. I will call you if I need you.*"

"*I do not like being so far from you, little one.*"

"*I know. I told Gai and Eachna about you, but it is not yet time to reveal your presence.*"

With a burst of smoke from his nostrils, he huffed his displeasure, but he stretched out in the sun again. The autumn sun was warm, and the breeze coming off the water was gentle as he lay there, listening to the sea birds calling and waves washing against the rocky coast. He let himself drift into a restful trance, still alert enough to hear his mage if she should need him.

A distant voice called to him, a voice he had heard before. He let himself be pulled deeper into his trance. All was black as night as he passed through into a world he had visited many moons ago when first he arrived on Inishbreith.

When the darkness lifted, he stood on a hill overlooking a wide, green valley, surrounded on all sides by high mountain peaks. Dragons of every hue flew or walked about down below him.

"*Greetings, young Péist of Caymin.*"

He turned to find an enormous black dragon beside him. "*Greetings, Ríona of Ailill.*"

Standing next to the dragon was a two-leg female, not much larger than Caymin. Her eyes were kind as she inclined her head.

"*You are Ailill of Ríona,*" Péist said.

"*I am.*"

Péist looked around, quivering with joy at the sight of others of his kind. "*Why have you called me here?*"

"*We must speak with you,*" said Ailill.

Péist lay, his front feet tucked under him. "*About the war that is coming?*"

"*Yes. That and other things. About the last dragon war.*" Ríona settled into a like pose.

"*What do you know of the last war?*" Ailill asked, sitting and leaning against Ríona.

"Only that it was over a thousand winters past, and that you both fought."

"Éire, indeed the entire world, was much different then," said Ailill. "All beings then knew the power of magic. It was as the air we breathed. Two-legs kept the feasts of the gods and goddesses and all revered the mother earth and the things she gives us. The clans were smaller and each had its leader, but none were so powerful that their petty battles amounted to more than a brief skirmish here and there."

Riona rumbled from deep in her chest. "It was a time of abundance. Dragons roamed most of the known lands, and two-legs respected our wisdom. Their leaders came to seek our counsel."

"Then what changed?" Péist asked. "How did it change?"

Riona and Ailill exchanged a glance. "One clan leader, Aolu, began to gather power," Ailill said, fingering a dark crystal hanging around her neck. "For the first time, clans began to band together under him, and he thought to challenge the role of dragons and dragonmages. One of our kind, Scolai, took umbrage with Aolu."

Péist perked up. "I have heard of this Scolai. He was mage to Tuala."

"Yes," said Riona. "They subdued Aolu and his clan quickly, but they did not stop there. After they controlled all of Éire, they turned their attention to the lands east of Éire. Scolai and Tuala grew to like power and thought all the lands should be ruled by a dragonmage and dragon. Two-legs, naturally, did not agree, and thus began the last great war."

Péist looked out at the dragons roaming about below. "Did all dragons and mages join Scolai and Tuala?"

"No," said Ailill. "But many did, even some of the unbonded dragons. They agreed that two-legs, who live for only a heartbeat compared to us and cannot see past the ends of their noses, had no right to rule themselves. They considered us much better suited to rule. Rather than living in harmony with two-legs, they sought to subjugate them to our will. Those of us who disagreed were forced to go to war against our brothers and sisters."

"The dragons and dragonmages here now, are they all the ones who opposed Scolai and Tuala?"

"No. When the war ended, we had to find a way to make peace amongst ourselves, or we would have died out completely," Riona said. "We are but a fraction now of the numbers we were before."

Péist felt the weight of their sorrow. Ríona raised her head and looked down on the valley. Péist looked up at her, towering far above him, and he felt very young.

"But, are you not mating? Have there been no young dragons? No cubs, like me?"

Ríona's great head slumped to the ground. Ailill laid a hand on her companion's brow.

"You were not old enough to be shown this on your last spiritwalk with us on Inishbreith," she said. *"Because we can live for eons, dragons may mate with only one other, and each may only give birth to one cub."*

Péist paused. *"I do not understand. In the forest, males and females mate, and the females give birth or lay eggs. How then do dragons each give birth?"*

"Dragons are not like other creatures," said Ríona. *"We are born male or female, but it does not determine which other dragon we will mate with. All are born with one seed within us. One that may replace us upon the earth. When we meet our mate and bond, we each fertilize the other's seed, but the young dragon may be held in our bodies for ages before coming into the world. That way, we may decide which will give birth first. A young dragon is tiny and helpless, as you were when we had to leave you in the forest where you would one day bond with Caymin."*

Péist stretched his neck, scanning the valley and the dragons below with renewed interest. "Are the ones who created me still here?"

Ailill shook her head. *"No. One of your sires was killed in the war, and your other sire died of his grief soon after giving birth to you. Of the ones left among us, most had already given birth. We lost many of our young dragons in the war, before they had a chance to find their mates and give birth. Only a very few young have been born to us since we came here."*

Péist turned his back on the valley. He didn't want to look at other dragons anymore.

"Do not grieve, little one." Ríona reached out to nuzzle him, though she couldn't actually touch him. *"For many of us who have bonded with a mage, that bond is as deep as any we would have with a mate, and we never choose to find a dragon mate."*

Péist sat silently.

"There is one other thing," Ríona said. *"When I spoke with Caymin while you were on Inishbreith, I told her that the two-leg who was there, the monk, must be*

silenced. No two-leg other than dragonmages may know of the existence of Inishbreith. Yet, he travels with you. Even now, he is among other two-legs."

"Garvan gave us his word to keep our secret and pledged his sword to our cause. He has been honorable and has given us no cause to doubt him."

"He was alone on an island with a dragon and mage who could kill him at any time. Of course, he seemed honorable. He will be different now that he is back among his own kind. They always are. He must be silenced."

Péist bowed his head. He did not need to speak with Caymin to know what her response would be, and it echoed his own. *"You left me alone to fend for myself for over a hundred winters. My mage was likewise orphaned and left to the care of her badger clan."* He raised his head and glared at Ríona. *"We have had to learn to make our own judgments of others—whom to trust and how much—and we will not kill wantonly simply because we are told to by those who have hidden away from the world and abandoned us."*

He heard their voices calling after him as he roused himself from his trance-state. Back on the island, all alone, he stretched his neck upward, keening his grief to the skies.

Caymin sat at Eachna's fire as Beanna searched for Garvan. She pushed to her feet and limped to the door. There was no sign of them. Péist was blocking her. She knew he was agitated and angry about something, but she couldn't tell what it was.

Eachna sent a servant to bring three bowls of stew from the kitchens. While they waited, he filled a pipe with crushed leaves and lit it with a flick of his finger.

"Come and sit," he said. "They'll be here soon."

With a frustrated sigh, she came back to the fire.

Eachna sat and watched her through the haze of smoke from his pipe. "I told you that Gai spoke of you. More than any of the others. He told me of the badgers rescuing you from the fire and raising you; how you could speak to them. But there was something else, something about you that troubled him, something he wouldn't tell me."

Caymin squirmed. "I accused him of things he did not do."

"No." Eachna squinted. "It wasn't that. It was something he was too ashamed to tell me about, but it affected him greatly."

Caymin knew precisely what Gai hadn't revealed to his teacher—the day he had shot a pheasant for sport and Caymin had made him feel the poor bird's pain before she healed it. But if Gai hadn't spoken of it, neither would she.

The silence stretched on for many heartbeats before Eachna said, "Did you know that Enat and I were apprentices together?"

She twisted around to look at him. "I did not. She never spoke of you."

His mouth twitched. "I'm not surprised. She never liked me much. Thought I was arrogant."

"Are you?"

He laughed. "Aye. I suppose I am. It helps to be arrogant here."

She tilted her head. "Is that why Gai is arrogant?"

"Gai's arrogance is a shield."

"A shield against what?"

"Against being hurt."

Caymin was forcefully reminded of Enat saying exactly the same thing to her more than once.

"His father is a hard man with no time for a gentle soul like Gai. His brother is little better. Gai was used to being brushed aside and ignored, always trying to prove himself to a father who takes no notice, but he was different when he returned from the forest. There was something about you, and I've been puzzled. Until now. I think I understand."

She frowned. "You understand what?"

He watched her, his expression inscrutable. "Your strength comes from within. It couldn't be burned out of you. It couldn't be beaten out of you. No matter the damage to your exterior, your core is solid. Your roots reach deep into the earth and cannot be shaken. Not so with everyone. Some are like beautiful trees, perfect to our eyes, but hollow and brittle inside, their roots shallow, searching for sustenance. Gai wants to be like you, to be true to himself no matter what others say or think, but he doesn't know how."

Caymin listened, though she didn't want to. "I have hurt him."

"Aye, you have. You of all, who spoke no words for many winters, should understand the power they have. With the right words, you could have helped him to heal, to grow stronger from within in the belief of his own goodness. Instead, you accused him of being like his father, and your words cut as surely as an axe, exposing the emptiness within. He stands on a precipice between good and evil, and I fear you have the power to push him over the edge."

Caymin's eyes stung with tears.

Their conversation was interrupted by the servant, delivering their meal. Eachna accepted the bowls and dismissed him. Just as the servant left, Beanna flew through the door with Garvan on her tail feathers.

"Here you are! I've been—" He stopped short as he realized Caymin wasn't alone.

"Garvan, this is Eachna, the mage here."

Garvan inclined his head as Eachna beckoned him to the table. He put herbs into three cups and filled them with water from the kettle.

"Come and eat."

They sat together. Garvan prayed while Caymin set some pieces of meat aside for Beanna, and Eachna did the same for Lorcan. The birds joined them at the table.

As they began eating, Garvan regarded Eachna. "How is it a mage and a priest are both here in the same village?"

Eachna smiled—a not altogether pleasant smile, Caymin thought—and said, "King Dughall believes in magic. He's seen enough of it not to doubt, but he is a pragmatic man. He knows the Christians are gaining ground, and he figures it's better to have one of their priests here where he can keep him under his thumb."

He eyed Garvan in turn. "And how is it a monk is traveling with a dragonmage and dragon?"

Garvan turned to Caymin. "He knows?"

"I had to tell him. Gai was here as well."

"Well..." He paused to eat a few bites, and Caymin wondered if he would keep his vow of silence on the existence of Inishbreith. "I was caught in a storm off the coast. My boat was damaged, and I was injured. Caymin and Péist saved my life and nursed me back to health."

Caymin breathed a sigh of relief. "Did you learn anything? Did the priest here know of any gathering of the followers of the Christ?"

"No, but I think that makes more sense now, knowing there's a mage here." Garvan shrugged. "They wouldn't count on help from this clan. They'll be looking for allies elsewhere, in clans and places where there are no more mages."

Caymin turned to Eachna. "When can we talk to Flann about an alliance?"

Eachna considered. "You haven't been back to the forest since you had this vision of war?"

"No. We had to flee when Timmin attacked us, and we have not yet returned. I had the vision after we left, so I have no way of knowing how the forest is."

Eachna took a drink. "I think it would be wise for you to go and see what has actually happened there. I don't think we can convince Lord Flann to mount an alliance when we don't know the threat is real."

Caymin opened her mouth to argue, but Garvan cut her off. "He's right, Caymin. I believe you saw what you did, but this Lord Flann is going to need more to justify risking men's lives."

"What about the king?"

Eachna smirked. "They won't harm him. They want their ransom. He's been held captive this long; he'll keep a bit longer." He tipped his cup toward the monk. "Garvan is welcome to stay with me while you and Gai go to check the forest."

"Gai?"

He pursed his lips. "This journey will give you both time to say what needs to be said."

CHAPTER 3

Forgiveness

Darkness was falling as Caymin made her way through the village contained within the stone wall. Eachna and Garvan walked her through the gate.

"Bring Gai to meet us as the moon rises," she said once they were beyond the hearing of the sentry.

"Where will you be?"

She pointed. "Far enough to be out of sight. Speak without speaking, and we will hear you."

"Take care, young Caymin," Garvan said. He placed his hand on her head as his lips moved in silent prayer.

"Are you asking your god to protect us?"

"I am. I know you don't believe, but you've a good soul. God will recognize that."

"Thank you."

She left them, making her way through the wild country outside the fortress wall. Beanna flew around her. Caymin called to Péist, asking him to fly to them. While she waited, she found the place where they had hidden their weapons. She collected Garvan's sword, gathered up her bow and quiver, and hung her knife on her belt. She hunkered down in the shelter of a hillock and tried conjuring the elements. Surely such basic magic couldn't be that difficult.

She closed her eyes, drawing her power up as she had been taught and found it sluggish, unwilling to do her bidding. She tried harder and, with a pop, a ball of fire appeared in her palm.

"*What is wrong?*" Beanna asked as she alighted on Caymin's knee, watching the white flames flicker.

"*Earlier today, Eachna was probing my mind and I could not put up a shield charm. He told me something I have never thought of. I have never tried to do magic other than in a place of power like our forest or Inishbreith, or with Péist's power to add to my own. I am weak, as I was when Enat first brought me to the forest to learn.*"

"*You are like a fledgling, flapping her wings until they are strong enough to fly.*" Beanna clicked her beak. "*Your magic will grow again. I told you when you first claimed your name that we all felt your power. That has not changed, little one. You must simply learn to look deeper within yourself for your power.*"

Caymin felt Péist before she saw him. He glided in on silent wings, landing near her. She rushed to him and threw her arms around his neck as he hummed his pleasure at seeing her again.

"*I did not like being apart from you,*" she said.

"*Nor I from you.*"

She pulled back. "*Something has been troubling you. You blocked your feelings from me. Why? What has happened?*"

Péist hesitated. "*It is too much to tell. Let me show you.*"

He placed his brow against hers and showed her all that had occurred with Ríona and Ailill. She gasped and dropped to the ground.

"*I did not know how dragons produced young, or where you came from,*" she said. "*You had two fathers?*"

"*Yes, and the one who gave birth to me chose to die rather than live without his mate,*" Péist said bitterly. "*He did not care enough to see me safely grown.*"

They sat in silence as the stars wheeled slowly overhead.

"*I was alone in the forest for so long, from before I could remember, and it was simply the way things were.*" Péist lay down beside her. "*But it feels different now. I felt your sadness at knowing that your father had been killed in the raid on your village, and your mother captured, but I could not truly understand what you felt until I learned that the ones I came from are both dead.*"

Caymin laid her hand on Péist's leg. His grief was almost enough to drown her. Beanna fluttered to his neck, perching there to look down at him.

"*I am sorry you never knew the ones who hatched you.*"

"Thank you, Beanna."

Péist roused himself from his thoughts. "*How went it with the two-legs? Will they help us?*"

"*We are to go to the forest first and see what has happened there.*"

A sliver of moon rose above the hills. Voices signaled the approach of Gai and Eachna. They topped a rise, both carrying packs and wearing travel cloaks against the night's chill air, and stood with their mouths open.

"I didn't really believe it," Gai said, descending the hill to stare up at Péist.

Péist lowered his head to fix Gai with his piercing gaze. "*Do you believe it now, young Gai?*"

Gai stumbled backward, tripping over his sword. "You can speak." He turned to Caymin. "He can speak."

"*Of course I can speak. Whether you can hear me is up to me.*" Péist raised his head to look at Eachna who remained up on the hill.

Eachna bowed. "*It is an honor to meet a dragon. I never thought to have the opportunity.*"

"*Greetings, mage.*"

Caymin handed the sword to Eachna. "Can you bring this to Garvan?"

She hoisted her bow higher on her shoulder and climbed onto Péist's saddle. "*We should go. We will need to fly under cover of night.*"

"Fly?" Gai's eyes widened as he looked up at Péist again.

Caymin fastened her tethers and held a hand out to Gai. "Fly."

Hills and rivers passed below them in shades of gray as they flew through the night.

"*How are we to get into the forest?*" asked Gai, speaking without speaking as the wind made it impossible to talk aloud unless he shouted.

"*If the magical protections are still in place and bar you from entry, I can fly in,*" Beanna said from where she lay tucked in her sling.

"*But that will not help us,*" Caymin said. "*I have thought on this, and...*"

Péist glanced back at them. "*You are thinking I may be able to fly in?*"

"*Yes, like Beanna. The borders of the forest are protected, but are the treetops? Did the mages who placed the protection ever envision a dragon and dragonmage flying there?*"

"*I suppose we'll find out.*" Gai leaned over a bit to watch the terrain below. "*Tell me more of what happened after I left.*"

Caymin provided more detail of Diarmit's betrayal and Timmin's attempt to force Péist to do his bidding.

"*He tortured you?*"

Caymin nodded. "*He used a curse—I have never felt such pain, and I do not wish to again.*"

"*When did Péist transform into a dragon?*"

"*When Timmin attacked me, Péist was already in his khrusallis, beginning his transformation from worm to dragon. He started to hatch, and we had to flee. Ríordán and Osán helped us.*"

"*The giant elk?*"

"*Yes. They were the only ones strong enough to carry Péist's egg by then. He emerged from the khrusallis before we got to the borders of the mystical forest. His wings were not strong enough then to fly. We had to walk to the edge of the land.*"

"*Why? Where did you go?*"

Caymin realized she had said too much. "*We flew to an island where he could grow and get stronger without two-legs seeing him.*"

"*How much longer do you think to keep him a secret?*"

Péist glanced back again. "*Not much longer.*"

"What will happen when people realize we've a dragon in our midst again?"

Caymin laid a hand on Péist's neck. *"We do not know."*

"We are drawing near," Péist said.

Up ahead was a dense forest—the first time any of them other than Beanna had seen it from the sky. Péist descended, flying low over the trees. He aimed for a clearing large enough for his wingspan, but— there was a jolt and he rose again.

"I cannot get through."

He climbed and circled, trying again in a different spot.

"We can feel it," said Caymin. *"The magical protections are intact."*

"Is that a good thing or not?" asked Gai.

Péist set down outside the forest where a dense mist formed a wall between them and the trees.

Beanna fluttered free of her sling and landed on a nearby bush. *"What now?"*

"I do not know." Caymin looked to Gai. *"How do we enter?"*

Gai strode into the mist and emerged again a short while later. *"It won't let me in."*

Beanna flew to Caymin's shoulder. *"I will fly in and see if I can find any of the elders."*

"I also will fly around the borders of the forest to see if perhaps there is another way in," Péist said.

Caymin nodded. *"We will wait here."*

She and Gai hunkered down, chilled from the cold flight through the damp night air. They set their weapons and packs on the ground.

"Do you think we can chance lighting a fire?" he asked through chattering teeth.

She snugged her cloak more tightly under her chin. "We did not see any other humans near here. I think we might."

They gathered fallen wood. She hesitated as they both readied to ignite it. She did not want to fail at this, not with Gai watching. Concentrating hard, she drew her power. Even though they were outside the forest boundary, its proximity made it easy to find her center and conjure the fire.

The flames crackled greedily at the dry wood, and they huddled close, trying to warm themselves. An uncomfortable silence filled the air between them.

Caymin chanced a sidelong glance at Gai, at the fire chasing shadows across his face. He met her gaze.

"I am sorry—" they both said at the same time.

Caymin took a breath. "I came to your clan because I was told I needed to forgive. We need your father and brother as allies if we are to defeat this monk that Diarmit serves." She paused. "But there is more. I also need to ask your forgiveness. I was wrong about you. I accused you of being like your father. I should not have done that."

"I understand why you did it," Gai said softly. "I'm ashamed that my father's warriors were responsible. I've tried asking my brother about it, but if he knows, he's not saying to me." He bowed his head. "I am truly sorry about what happened—to you and your family."

"We were both babes when it happened. It was no more your fault than mine."

Gai smiled and, as always, it seemed to her that he became beautiful when the hard contours of his pale face softened into a smile— perhaps because he did it so infrequently.

"I hope the elders and apprentices are safe," he said.

Caymin turned a stony face to the forest. "As do I."

They sat in silence as they waited, staring into the fire, each lost in thoughts and memories. Something began to worry at the back of Caymin's mind, a nagging feeling that there was something... something she should have remembered. She sat up straighter and listened.

"Do you feel or hear...?"

She got to her feet, turning in place to look around her.

Gai watched her. "What is it?"

"I do not know..."

She walked off into the night. Gai jumped up and ran after her.

"Where are you going?"

"I do not know," she repeated, but followed the voice that whispered to her, annoying as a gnat in the summertime.

They walked through the trees outside the magical protections of the denser forest, Gai a half step behind as Caymin kept adjusting her course. At length, she came to a tree, an ancient oak tree that had been splintered by lightning long ago. The trunk stood, rising higher than Péist's neck could stretch, but the lightning had killed the tree when it struck, destroying the treetop.

"What is it?" Gai asked as Caymin circled the tree.

"I am not certain, but something here calls to me."

She stepped closer, pressing an ear to the tree. She laid her hands on the trunk. *"I am Caymin of Péist."*

For long heartbeats, nothing happened. Gai listened as Caymin stood there, her hands maintaining contact with the tree. A sharp crack reverberated through the air, and a small opening appeared in the trunk. It was wide enough for Caymin to insert her hand into the hole. She frowned and reached deeper until her entire arm was within the tree.

"There is something here."

She withdrew her arm, a long stick held in her grasp.

"It is Enat's staff," she breathed, holding it reverently.

"Are you sure?" Gai asked, stepping closer.

Caymin nodded. Her eyes shimmered with tears. "What has happened to her? Why was this left behind?"

"More important," said Gai, "why was it hidden here for you to find?"

As if in answer to his question, the staff glowed white as Caymin held it. "I think I know."

She called to Péist. *"We have found something. Come back to us."*

While they waited, they went back to extinguish the fire and gather their things. Péist landed with a thump.

"What have you found?"

She strode to the mist still shrouding the enchanted forest. Holding the staff before her, she walked into the mist and paused.

"I am Caymin of Péist. In the name of Enat, mage and protector of this forest, I ask you to permit us entry."

The mist parted. She turned to look back at them. "We have found a way in."

Caymin breathed deeply as they walked. She'd almost forgotten the hum of life and power in this forest. Everything around her, the very earth upon which they trod, felt alive. It gave her some consolation to know that this power was intact.

Behind her, Péist struggled to push through the trees. *"This was not this difficult when we fled."*

She looked back at him. *"You have grown. You were not this large when we left. We walked for days to leave the forest."*

"We do not have time for this," Péist grumbled. He crashed into a clearing large enough for him to partially spread his wings. *"Climb on my back."*

Caymin and Gai both scrambled up. Gai again wedged himself between two of Péist's spikes while Caymin tethered herself to the saddle. Péist crouched and leapt skyward. With a few strong flaps of his wings, he was able to rise over the treetops. The sky was just beginning to lighten in the east. The forest passed below them in a blur as he soared toward the village. Caymin scoured the gaps in the trees as they passed over, looking for any sign of those she had left behind.

"Droc? Cuán? Are you here? Beanna, meet us at the village."

As the mage elders and their apprentices were the only two-leg inhabitants of the mystical forest, there was only the one village. Caymin's hopes were dashed as Péist landed, and they saw that it was deserted except for the chickens, who squawked and ran from them. She and Gai climbed down. The door to the meetinghouse stood open. The central fire pit was long cold.

"I must hunt," Péist said. *"I have flown two long journeys since last I ate."*

"Please do not hunt the giant elk," Caymin said. *"They got you safely out of harm's way when you were in your egg."*

Péist inclined his head and gathered himself. Caymin and Gai shielded their heads from the buffeting of his wings as he took off again.

"Look around here while I check Enat's cottage," Caymin said.

She carried the staff with her as she hurried through the forest to Enat's dwelling, a bit removed from the others, as Enat had always preferred her quiet—at least she had until she took in the badger-girl, Ash.

Caymin smiled as she entered the cottage, remembering how strange it had all seemed back then, after having been raised by badgers for eight winters after she was burned and her village destroyed.

No sooner had she thought it, than she heard grunts and the scuffling of badger feet approaching the cottage. She ran outside and fell to her knees to greet them.

"Broc! Cuán! Oh, it is so good to see you."

Broc climbed up into her lap to nuzzle her cheeks while the younger badgers crowded around with whickers of happiness. Cuán blinked up at her.

"How is it that you are here, little one? Where have you been?"

Caymin sat on the ground and held Broc tightly while she caressed the sleek white stripe on Cuán's head. *"I will tell you everything, but first, I must know what happened to Enat and the others."*

Before the badgers could speak, Beanna arrived with a loud caw. *"Greetings."*

"Greetings to you," Broc said.

"There is no sign of any two-legs anywhere," Beanna said. *"The four-legs I encountered said there have been no invaders or strangers in the forest."*

Caymin turned to the badgers. *"Tell us."*

"It is true," said Cuán. *"There have not been any strange two-legs in this forest. Your elders decided to leave before that could happen."*

He was interrupted by Gai's footsteps as he ran to the cottage. He stopped abruptly at the gathering of badgers surrounding Caymin.

"Greetings," he said as he dropped down next to them. *"There was nothing in any of the dwellings. The boys' and girls' cottages are empty, as are Ivar's and Neela's. The scrolls and books in the meetinghouse are all gone. Everything is empty."*

"All the scratchings are with us," Broc said.

Gai looked at her. *"The scrolls?"*

"Yes. They wrapped them in cloth to protect them, and we have them safe in our sett, where we kept the worm's egg."

Caymin glanced at him. "Cuán was just telling me that they decided to leave before invaders arrived."

The boar chuffed. "Enat came to us, told us of their plan. She said Ivar and Neela would take the young two-legs back to their clans."

"What about Una and Niall? The two older apprentices?" asked Caymin. "They did not earn their staffs yet."

"They would have gone through their trials at the next new moon," Gai said. "At Samhain."

"They could not wait," Broc said. "Enat was sad about that."

"What happened to Enat, then?"

"She had captured the other young two-leg, Diarmit, when Timmin attacked you, little one."

Cuán growled. "He was a traitor, to you and to the forest. But Enat insisted they could not punish him without violating their own code of honor. She planned to let him escape, and to follow him back to his master." He blinked his small eyes. "And she planned to let them capture her."

"What?" Caymin looked at them in alarm.

Broc nuzzled her again, trying to calm her. "We also did not think it a good plan, but she told us that it was the only way she could stay close enough to protect him. She still believes he can be turned to the good."

Caymin and Gai shared a dark glance. One of the young badgers pawed at the staff.

"Is this her stick? She told us she left it for you to find. She said you would need it."

"We did. It was the only way for us to enter the forest, as we never earned staffs of our own."

Gai thought. "Did she tell you where she was going? Where Diarmit would take her?"

"No." Broc whickered. "She did not know."

"Mayhap she left something in her dwelling to help you, little one," said Beanna.

Caymin went to the cottage and pushed the door open. She peered into the dark, cold interior. She stepped inside and, with a flick of her hand, ignited the peat stacked in the hearth. The others followed. The badgers' long claws clicked and scratched on the flagstones as they sniffed. The air was slightly musty, but smelled of the dried herbs hanging from the rafters. Beanna flew to the stone mantel.

Enat's bed was undisturbed, as was the one Caymin had used. All was neat, orderly and empty.

"Look."

Gai pointed to a small scroll of parchment lying on Caymin's bed. She picked it up. Unfurling it, she read so all could hear.

"*Dear Caymin, if you find this message, then you have found my staff. I know that you will want to come after me, but I am not your priority at this time. Diarmit has confessed that, when he has gathered sufficient followers, Angus plans to try and take the forest, but we do not believe he will do so just yet.*

Unless you have been able to gather allies, you and Péist alone cannot take on Angus and his forces. Nor can Ivar and Neela protect the entire forest themselves. They will stay nearby while I follow Diarmit to ensure he does not come to harm. Remember, your priority is to protect the forest and its creatures, not to find me. If the day should arrive when it is time to seek help, remember the spell Méav placed on the knife she gave you."

She rolled the parchment up again and tucked it into her belt.

"*What now?*" Beanna asked.

"*Let us eat and discuss it,*" Caymin said. She and Gai retrieved their bags containing food and brought them to the fire. She handed out bits of meat to the badgers and Beanna, while Gai shared the cheese and bread he had.

"*Has there been any sign of Timmin since we left?*" she asked.

Broc looked up from her meal. "*No. He has not shown himself. Enat did not know if he was still within the forest. But you should be on your guard against him, little one.*"

Gai glanced at Caymin. "*We know the forest is safe for now, and the protections are intact.*"

Caymin nodded. "*Yes. I think the next thing we should do is speak with your brother about rescuing your father. Then, we will have allies to help us go after this Angus and rescue Enat.*"

A loud crash announced Péist's arrival. The badgers cowered as his enormous white head darkened the door, his snout sniffing.

"*That is the worm?*" Cuán asked, his fur on end.

Broc crowded close to Caymin. "*I called him the ugliest cub I had ever seen.*"

Caymin laid a calming hand on her back. "*Yes. That is Péist. You last saw him when he was in his egg.*"

Péist fixed them with one green eye. "*I have not forgotten that it was you who hid and guarded my egg when I was vulnerable.*"

Beanna clicked her beak and flew to land on Péist's snout. "*He is just a worm with wings and fire now.*"

He responded with a snort that sent sparks flying into the cottage. "*With one burst of flame from my jaws, I could burn the entire forest.*"

Beanna opened her mouth in perfect mimicry of a yawn. "*Yes. You are mighty.*" She shuffled her feathers and settled there on his nose.

"*Let us rest here today,*" Caymin said to Gai. "*Tonight, under cover of darkness, we will return to your clan and speak with your brother.*"

Caymin limped along beside Garvan as they followed Eachna through the dark village to the fortress. Péist, she knew, was just over a hill, staying out of sight until she called for him. Enat's staff was safely secured to his saddle. She had not thought it wise to bring it with her into the village. She didn't trust Eachna and his clear disdain for Enat.

Gai had gone on ahead to wake his brother and ensure he was alone in their father's rooms.

"I think it would be best not to speak with him in front of others just yet," Eachna had said when they returned during the night and told him the forest was safe. "You might not want them all to know you've a dragon, and we don't want to back Flann into a corner in front of his warriors. He won't react well."

Caymin didn't understand what that meant, but had to trust that Eachna knew Flann well enough to know how best to approach him.

She stared in wonder as Eachna led them through the fortress. They passed through an enormous room with many long tables with benches on either side. The flagstones were strewn with rushes, and several large dogs scoured the floor under the tables for any scraps of food remaining from the evening meal. She gave them a reassuring word as she passed.

As they walked around the large fire pit in the middle of the room, she saw that the walls were hung with shields. At the far end of the room was an elaborately carved chair behind which hung a large tapestry woven in the pattern of the wolf holding a sword—the same image woven into her cloak. Draped over the back of the chair was the pelt of a wolf, its teeth bared in a silent snarl.

"The shields were taken from the vanquished," Eachna said in a low voice. He pointed with his staff. "The king's chair."

She paused when she saw mounted above the tapestry a pair of enormous antlers, as wide as two men lying head to foot.

"Giant elk," she said in a strangled whisper.

She looked up into the shadows overhead. A few hawks watched them from the beams that supported the roof. She hurried to catch up to Eachna.

Eachna led her up a wooden stair to an upper level. He stopped before a closed door and knocked.

"Enter."

He opened the door and stood back to let Caymin and Garvan precede him into the room. Gai stood near the window where he had pushed open the wooden shutters while a chair nearby was occupied by a man she assumed must be Flann. She never would have guessed him to be Gai's brother. Where Gai was slender and pale, with his dark hair and eyes, Flann was thick and muscular, with a face that looked to Caymin to be red with fever and hair the color and texture of straw. His pale eyes glittered as he looked them over.

"Is this a jest?" he said. "You tell me we have a way to rescue the king, and you bring me a monk and this cripple?"

"My lord," Eachna said with a small bow, "this girl is mage-born. She can help. The monk is Garvan, and he has valuable information as well."

Flann pushed to his feet and circled Caymin. She turned in place, facing him defiantly. Flann laughed.

"Pray, tell me how this runt can help us."

"Enough of this."

Flann whirled around, looking for the source of the voice. Caymin smiled as the tower in which they stood shook with the impact of Péist's arrival. White talons gripped the window ledge and one eye peered in at them, its vertical pupil contracting. Flann swore and fell backward, his eyes bulging as his mouth gaped.

"Do not insult my mage, you-who-would-be-king."

Flann pointed and his mouth moved, but no words would come.

Gai smirked. "The runt has a dragon, brother."

CHAPTER 4

The Dragon Revealed

The doors to the hall were thrown open so that Péist was able to fit his head through them. Flann and his warriors were gathered around one of the tables with a large sheet of parchment spread out on it. Eachna, Garvan and Caymin were seated at the center of a bench, across the table from Flann.

The warriors whose backs were turned toward Péist kept glancing nervously over their shoulders. Outside, the entire village had gathered, maintaining a respectful distance from Péist's spiked tail, which he twitched occasionally. The constant murmur of their voices carried into the hall.

On the parchment was a detailed map of the region, including the fortress of clan Mruad.

"We don't know where they're keeping him," Flann was saying. "But it's a fair guess they're holding him in their tower."

"Not the dungeon?" asked one of the warriors.

Flann gave the man a withering glance. "He's a king. If they're holding him in their dungeon, it's not ransom they'll be getting from us."

Another of the warriors pointed toward Péist. "'Tis not ransom they'll be getting at all."

There was laughter all around the table.

Flann smiled. "True enough."

He pointed to the area south of the fortress. "Here are their crops. If they're like us, most has been harvested, but not all. If we approach from here and threaten them with burning their fields, their warriors will have to come out and meet us." He looked around toward Péist. "Once they've been drawn away, the fortress will only have a small force left behind to guard it. Easy enough for a dragon."

He gestured to Caymin. "Do you see any problems with this plan?"

The warriors watched her curiously.

"Why were you fighting that clan to begin with?" she asked.

Flann blinked and looked around. "They were attacked by clan Briuin the summer before. They lost nearly all their crops that year."

"So they were hungry."

"That doesn't mean they can take our livestock and crops," one of the warriors said angrily. "Then we'll be the ones to go hungry."

Caymin tilted her head. "We can get your father back without destroying their fields. Threaten, but do not burn. Give them no reason to raid you again."

Flann's ruddy face flushed a deeper red. "They must be punished!"

"*And where will it end?*" Péist asked, speaking so they could all hear. "*My mage is wise. You would do well to listen to her. We can accomplish our goal without leaving them no choice but to raid other clans to feed themselves.*"

Gai, who had stood silently near his brother said, "We'll threaten, no more. As long as it draws them away from the fortress as we're planning."

Flann gave his brother a harsh look. "We march at dawn day after tomorrow. Use this time to gather supplies."

Péist withdrew his head from the doorway so that the assembled warriors could leave to begin preparations.

As the warriors dispersed, Flann was surrounded by a few men, their heads together.

Caymin said, "Lord Flann, I would have a word with you."

He looked at her in clear irritation but turned back to the table as the warriors reluctantly left. Péist's head reappeared in the door as Gai and Eachna also stayed behind. She glanced up at Garvan as they all sat again.

He gave her an encouraging nod. "Go ahead, lass."

She drew herself up. "We have one further condition to helping you."

Flann frowned. "And what would that be?"

"I wish to know why your warriors raided my village and what happened to my mother."

Flann's eyes narrowed. "How do you know—?"

"Her cloak," Gai said. "The night the village was burned, that cloak was taken from one of our warriors by... by her rescuers."

Caymin realized Flann did not know she had been rescued by badgers and silently thanked Gai. It seemed best to have some secrets when dealing with him.

"How long ago?"

"Ten winters past."

Flann threw up his hands. "I've no idea who we were attacking ten winters ago."

"My lord," Eachna said, "it may be that Urard will remember, or may have recorded the events."

Garvan looked from Eachna to Flann. "Who is this Urard?"

"He's our scribe," said Gai. "He records the history of our clan and our deeds."

Flann shrugged. "You may ask him, but I make no promises that he can tell you anything."

He pushed up from the table. "I've preparations to make."

Gai stood also. "I'll take you to him."

Péist withdrew his head again, shielding his voice so only Caymin could hear. *"I grow tired of these two-legs milling about, staring at me. I am going to fly where I can be alone. Keep our link open so that I may hear what is being said, little one. If you need me, I will be here in three beats of my wings."*

42

Caymin's mouth gaped as she looked around Urard's room, situated in the eaves of the fortress's tower. There were narrow vertical windows all round—Gai told Caymin that archers might come up to use these in the event of an attack—but the room otherwise was filled with Urard's scrolls and books. Shelves upon shelves were filled with them, sheaves of parchment and tightly furled scrolls. The floor was littered with droppings and regurgitated bones from the owls and hawks who flew freely in and out of the unshuttered windows. Several were perched on the rafters in the darkness under the thatched roof.

Urard himself reminded Caymin of a gray heron that used to fish in the stream near the badger sett. He was very thin and had an unusually long neck with a prominent knob in front that bobbed whenever he spoke or swallowed. His hair was long and gray and wispy. His eyes were mildly crossed, and he had a long, hooked nose that nearly touched the scrolls as he sifted through them and held them close, looking for the information he sought. A few unlit candles sat scattered about the room, but he carried his scrolls to the windows, using what daylight came through to help as he peered at his own writing.

"I've got it here somewhere," he muttered.

He leafed through a different stack of pages, his claw-like fingers stained with ink. On the tables lay mounds of feathers, their quills waiting to be sharpened for writing. Apparently, the birds' mess was worth it to Urard in exchange for having a ready source of discarded feathers.

From the back of a chair, Beanna peered up at the birds of prey watching her from the rafters. She fluffed her feathers to make herself appear larger. *"I am companion to the dragon."*

Caymin grinned and tapped her shoulder. Beanna hopped up to nestle into the crook of her neck.

"Here it is!" Urard waved a sheet of parchment. He spread it on the table and lit a candle. Leaning close, he ran an inky finger along the lines of miniscule writing. He read to himself as his finger traced down half the lines on the page. "Yes, yes indeed."

"Indeed what?" asked Gai.

Urard blinked up at him and looked around as if he'd forgotten there were others there. "Oh, I was reading about the campaign of that winter. King Dughall heard rumors that the clans to the east were making alliances. He sent our warriors out to eradicate any villages not loyal to clan Eoganacht." He stood upright and rocked back on his heels, nodding. "Yes. I remember when they returned."

"Did they return with captives?" asked Caymin.

He glanced at her and then looked more closely as he noticed her scars. "Yes," he said, almost absent-mindedly.

Eachna made an impatient noise. "Do you have a record of what they brought back?"

Urard turned to him, looking highly insulted. "Of course. I record everything."

He flipped through his sheets of parchment, pulling out the one he sought, and handed it over to Eachna. "Of course, there's no way to know which of these unnamed villages any of these captives came from."

Eachna scrolled his finger down the page. "The captives are listed by male or female and age." He glanced up at Caymin. "Nothing else. No names or other description."

Caymin's hopeful expression faded. "I do not know her name anyhow."

Urard looked from one to the other. "Sorry, but whose name?"

Gai laid a sympathetic hand on Caymin's shoulder. "Her mother was taken captive by our warriors. We were hoping to learn what happened to her."

"Traded," Urard said brightly.

Caymin's head snapped up. "What do you mean?"

Urard bent over again, his nose nearly touching a different page as he read, "Traders from the north purchased all the captives in exchange for gold and weapons." He pointed to Gai. "That torq you wear around your neck was made from their gold."

"All the captives were traded to the northmen?" Caymin asked.

Urard nodded, rocking back and forth on his feet. "Yes, yes. King Dughall didn't want any of them going back to join with our enemies."

"I'm sorry, lass," Garvan said.

She blinked hard as tears stung her eyes. "It was unlikely I would find her."

They descended the stairs from the tower. Down below, the village was a beehive of activity as everyone prepared for the journey to rescue the king. Women and girls prepared and packed food; men sharpened weapons while the boys pretended to be warriors.

"Come back to my dwelling and we'll eat," said Eachna.

Caymin shook her head. "I wish to be alone with Péist for a while."

She made her way toward the gate. One sentry stepped forward to challenge her, but another guard elbowed him and mouthed something. They stood back to let her pass. Outside the walls, wagons were assembled and being loaded with supplies for the campaign.

"*Where are you?*" she called as she climbed a small hillock.

Péist appeared in the sky, and she heard startled exclamations behind her. When he landed, she strapped herself to the saddle.

"*Take us where we may be alone.*"

Péist took to the air and flew north to an isolated area near the cliffs. He landed, and Caymin slid down. She sat in the grass, looking out over the endless water. Péist nestled beside her.

"*I heard, little one.*"

Caymin wiped her cheeks. "*My village was attacked and my father killed for no reason. Simply because they might be friendly with some other clan.*" She sat silently for several heartbeats. "*I will never find her. There is no way to know which northern tribe she was traded to.*"

They sat side by side, their faces turned to the wind blowing in from the sea.

"*Do you trust these two-legs?*" Péist asked.

Caymin snorted. "*It seems every time I trust a two-leg, I am fooled. So, no. I do not trust them. But we need them.*"

At last, Flann and his warriors were assembled and ready to march. Most of them wore thick leather pads over their chests. Even Gai wore a leather breastplate and helmet. Flann, Gai, and a few others were mounted on animals Caymin had never seen.

"They're horses," said Garvan. "Not as practical as oxen for pulling the wagons, but much faster and nimbler in battle."

The horses bucked and kicked when Péist appeared. The warriors astride them had difficulty getting them under control.

"They know I could eat them," Péist said with a huff of smoke. As if to prove his point, he lifted his head and let go a blast of flame.

With neighs of terror, the horses spooked and took off with their riders.

"Enough!" Flann bellowed, yanking his own horse's reins viciously as it sidestepped under him.

Nearly all of the village and surrounding clansmen had gathered to see the dragon.

"Best if you mount and fly ahead," Eachna said, hiding a smile. "You and Gai will be able to maintain contact from a distance."

Caymin tethered herself to the saddle, and Péist spread his wings. With a few strong flaps, he was airborne as the people below cheered. Beanna lay snugly inside her sling against Caymin's belly. Péist circled, flying higher and higher. The air became colder and thinner as they continued to circle.

"We will appear to be no bigger than a bird from up here."

Caymin leaned over where she could see the long line of warriors followed by their wagons. *"These same warriors will be the ones to help us against Angus and his followers. Let us hope we can get their king back with no bloodshed."*

They arrived at the outer reaches of the territory of clan Mruad under cover of darkness. Péist landed at some distance from the main force so as not to spook the horses and oxen again. Beanna flew to a nearby tree where she could keep an eye on things. Flann and his warrior chieftains walked out to meet Caymin. Gai followed.

They climbed a hill that gave them a distant view of the Mruad fortress. Small points of light could be seen along their walls and scattered at farms and dwellings lying outside the walls.

One of the chieftains, a large, burly man named Lasair, pointed. "All of that ground is what remains of their fields. Their last cuts of barley, hay and wheat. If we spread out and light our torches, they'll have to come out to meet us."

He turned to Caymin and Péist. "Then if you fly around to their fortress from the other side, while their attention is diverted to us, you should be able to find the king and rescue him."

Caymin checked her tethers and made sure her quiver was within easy reach, her bow securely fastened to the saddle. "Remember, we only want to threaten, not give them a reason to retaliate."

Lasair and Flann shared a dark look and turned away to divide the men and begin spreading them out along the fields to the south and east.

Gai stepped over to Péist and Caymin. He took the golden torq from around his neck and held it up. "Take this to convince my father that you are an ally and have come to rescue him. He may not believe a dragon wants to help."

Caymin leaned down to take it and threaded it through her belt. Gai stepped back as Péist spread his wings and took off. He flew a wide arc around the Mruad fortress and found a hill well to the north where they could watch for the torches.

"*You are troubled, little one,*" said Péist.

Caymin busied herself stringing her bow and did not reply immediately. "*My power has been less since we left Inishbreith. Eachna told me it was because I was not in a place of magic, and I realized he is right. Since we arrived here, this is the first place I have been that is not a place of power.*"

"*But we are together. Remember the strength it took for us to pass the test in the firechamber on Inishbreith. We must be strong for each other. If we have doubts, it will weaken us.*"

Caymin laid a hand on his neck, taking comfort from his warmth. *"I have no doubts when I am with you."*

They waited and before long saw tiny lights appearing in the distance, strung out along the periphery of the fields. Péist quivered.

"We will not kill unless we have to," Caymin said, her own nerves making her tremble.

"Agreed. I can frighten them with my fire without burning their dwellings."

"I think you will frighten them just by letting them see you."

Before long, more torches appeared as the Mruad marched from their fortress to meet the Eoganacht. They waited until the line of torches was more than half the distance across the fields.

"Now."

Caymin nocked an arrow, and Péist flapped into the air. He gained enough altitude to glide in silently. He circled the tower. Startled screams sounded from below, and some of the remaining warriors shouted warnings from the walls. Arrows whistled by. Caymin did not know if arrows could pierce Péist's scales, but she threw up a shield spell just in case.

"King Dughall! We have come to bring you back to your clan."

Péist spoke so that all could hear as he continued to circle. He belched a line of fire, aimed well over the heads of the warriors still shooting at them, but it was enough to make most of them run for cover. Caymin scanned the windows of the tower. Figures appeared in several of them, but she could not tell if one was the king.

"Dughall," Péist called again. *"We have come from your fortress with your sons and warriors. Show yourself that we may rescue you and be gone."*

He landed on the side of the tower, like a woodpecker on a tree, his talons gripping stone and ledge as he and Caymin peered into windows.

"There."

Caymin spied a man cringing against the far wall of a room. His straw-colored hair and beard marked him as Flann's father.

"Quickly," Caymin shouted. *"Come with us. Flann and Gai have sent us to rescue you."*

The man whimpered and cowered, his eyes fixed only on Péist.

An arrow snapped as it hit Caymin's shield charm and bounced off. She looked up to see two warriors on the top rampart of the tower, shooting down at them. She drew her bow and fired but, as Péist changed his grip on the wall, her arrow flew wildly. They each shot again, their arrows whistling past her head. She took more careful aim and fired, catching one of them in the shoulder. He cried out and disappeared from sight. The other warrior withdrew.

"Enough of this," Péist growled. He tore at the window opening, sending stones clattering down below as he enlarged the window enough to swipe one foreleg into the room. The door of the room burst open, and three warriors rushed in, brandishing swords. Péist gave them a fearsome growl as Caymin conjured a ball of flame and flung it in their direction, forcing them to leap aside. With wild yells, they backed out of the room.

Péist grasped Dughall with his talons and pushed off, flying away to the north and then circling around to where Flann and Gai waited.

When Péist landed and released Dughall, he lay curled in a ball, his arms over his head. Beanna flew to Caymin and perched on her shoulder.

"Sire." Flann knelt next to his father and touched his arm.

Slowly, Dughall loosed his arms and looked around. He stared up at Péist and Caymin. "How is this possible?"

"We will tell you all," Caymin said. "But for now, we must withdraw."

Dughall got to his feet and took in the scene around him. He straightened his twisted tunic back into place and demanded a drink. Someone produced a wineskin, and he drank deeply. As he looked down at the scene below, Flann pointed out the positions of the two clans.

"Lord Flann," Caymin said. "We have rescued the king. Call your warriors back."

"No," growled Dughall. "Burn everything."

"You cannot," Caymin gasped, but Flann bellowed the order, which spread as quickly as the flames across the fields. Within a score of heartbeats, the fields were burning. Shadows ran back and forth behind the line of flames but, inexorably, the Mruad were pushed back as the fire spread through the remaining crops.

Caymin and Péist could only watch as the scene was obliterated by smoke. She glanced at Gai, but he looked as stricken as she was.

"Shall I do the same to the lands of this fool?" Péist asked.

Dughall and Flann whipped around to look up at the dragon, who arched his neck and glared down at them.

"Let us think on it as we fly back," Caymin said. She grasped Beanna and tucked her safely in her sling.

Deliberately buffeting them with the draft of his wings, Péist took off, flying into the night.

CHAPTER 5

Che Bloodstone

S it, lass," Garvan said as Caymin paced around and around Eachna's cottage.

"I cannot."

Péist crouched outside as dawn broke to a misty rain. His tail whipped in agitation equal to Caymin's own. *They will return soon. We must decide what we will do.*

Eachna's eyes followed her movements as he puffed on his pipe. "This was not entirely unexpected."

Caymin whirled. "But why? We had rescued him. He could have called his men back, and we could have left with no damage done."

Eachna smiled an unpleasant smile. "You don't know Dughall. He'll want them punished for daring to abduct him."

She paused and glared at him. "We will not be used so."

He sat back and studied her. "Then you have some decisions to make."

"What do you mean?"

"Sit," Garvan said again, scooting a stool toward her.

She threw herself down and fumed as Eachna deliberately added crushed leaves to his pipe and lit them. Up above, Beanna sat on a rafter, keeping her distance from Lorcan.

Peering at her through the smoke, Eachna said, "You already know how desirable a connection to a dragon is. Timmin was willing to hurt you to get Péist. I can promise you, by the time Dughall gets back here, he'll have figured out how he wishes to use you in exchange for an alliance. Everyone you meet will want something from you. A promise of help, your allegiance, control over a dragon. Something. You and Péist need to understand that and know where you are willing to pledge your loyalties."

Caymin stared at him for many heartbeats. She looked to Garvan who nodded sympathetically.

"He's right. You and Péist are unique and will be highly coveted by many—and all for their own reasons. Your goal is to stop this Angus and his invaders before they can destroy what you hold dear, but others will have their own goals."

One of Péist's eyes stared in at them. *"Who, then, can we trust?"*

Eachna looked at him. "None."

Caymin's shoulders slumped.

"That's not entirely true," Garvan said gently. "I promised you my sword and my loyalty. And I'll hold true to that to my dying breath." He looked expectantly to Eachna.

Eachna sighed, a stream of smoke issuing from his nose, making him look like a dragon. "I am sworn to obey my king, but my loyalties go deeper than that. The power of the ancient forests, the mages I studied with, the future of magic in Éire—these are all on the edge of disappearing from this land forever. I'll help you in any way I can."

Caymin frowned as a sudden thought occurred to her. "When will they be back here?"

"They won't march through the night now they've got the king back," said Eachna. "The earliest they'll be back is late tomorrow."

Caymin got to her feet. "We will return."

Garvan stood also. "Where are you going?"

"Stay here." Caymin held out an arm for Beanna. "We must think before we face Dughall again. We will be back on the morrow."

She climbed up and tethered herself to the saddle as Beanna wriggled into her sling. Péist spread his wings, scattering the villagers who stood gathered around. With a great leap, he was airborne.

"Where are we going?"

"Have you the strength to fly us back out to one of the islands?" Caymin tightened her cloak against the cold mist as Péist flew.

"Yes, but why?"

"We have need of the counsel of those wiser and older."

Péist hunted as dusk fell. Caymin and Beanna sat huddled near a fire as they listened to the bleating of the terrified sheep. Girl and crow shared a meal of smoked meat as well as some bread and cheese.

Caymin raised her head. *"I feel sorry for the sheep, but he must eat."*

Beanna bobbed her head. *"They are being raised for two-legs to eat. They are going to be eaten by someone."*

When he returned, Péist nestled down near them. Overhead, a few stars lent their faint light behind incoming clouds. Out over the endless water, a fresh storm brewed. Flashes of lightning forked from cloud to cloud.

"The rain will be here soon," Péist said. *"You will need to shelter under my wing, little ones."*

"We will."

He looked down at her. *"You mean to go on a spiritwalk."*

"Yes. I think we need to go together. To speak with Ríona and Ailill." She stroked Beanna's back. *"Will you keep watch for us?"*

"I will. If I see anything, I will call for you."

Caymin settled against Péist, and he covered her with his wing. Beanna huddled nearby where she could see a wide arc around them.

"I have never done this without a potion or by accident," Caymin said.

"I have," said Péist. *"Stay with me and I will lead you."*

She let herself settle into a trance, linked with Péist. She was vaguely aware of the first fat raindrops spattering against the filmy membrane of his wing. Together, they walked into a familiar mist, trusting it would lead them where they wanted to go.

When the mist parted, they were standing on the hill they had both visited previously, overlooking the broad valley where dragons roamed. The sky was dotted with more dragons soaring.

"*Well met, Péist.*"

A slight woman was standing near them, her head bowed.

"*Greetings, Ailill.*" Péist placed his jaw against Caymin's shoulder. "*You have not met my mage, Caymin.*"

"*Greetings.*" Caymin stared at her, the only other dragonmage she had seen. "*Where is Riona?*"

"*She is hunting. She will join us if she can.*"

Ailill sat on the ground. Caymin and Péist did the same.

She eyed Péist. "*I thought not to see you again after our last talk.*"

Péist snorted sparks. "*I stand by what I said that day. Garvan has been faithful to us. We will not harm him simply because we are told to.*"

For long heartbeats, Ailill stared at the pair of them, her face impassive. At length, she sighed. "*What troubles you?*"

Caymin glanced at Péist and said, "*We did as we were instructed and went to Gai's clan to seek an alliance. We agreed to rescue their king in exchange for their help in pushing back the monk who is threatening the mystical places—the one I saw in my spiritwalk when we were on Inishbreith—and stopping the war that looms.*"

Ailill studied her as she spoke. A grim smile played upon her face. "*I can guess, things did not go as you had planned?*"

"*Their warriors drew the other clan from their fortress so that we could get to the tower and rescue the king. After we did, they could have retreated, but the king gave the order to burn their fields. Rather than opting for peace, he chose a path of retaliation.*"

Ailill tilted her head as she regarded Caymin. "*And this sits ill with you?*"

Caymin's eyes flashed. "*My village was attacked, my family torn apart by this same thirst for violence. It is unnecessary and only fuels the desire for vengeance.*"

Ailill lowered her gaze. "*War often requires that we do what is necessary, not what is pleasant.*"

"*We will if we must, but this was not necessary.*" Péist shifted. "*We suspect by the time the king and his warriors return, he will have new conditions for pledging his clan's help with our cause.*"

"And you wish to know if we ever had to swear allegiance to another."

"Yes."

An enormous shadow darkened the sky over them as Ríona soared in. The earth shook as she landed. She folded her wings and extended her neck, her gold eyes sharp as she gazed at them.

"Greetings, young ones."

Both Caymin and Péist inclined their heads. Ailill turned to her companion.

"We were just speaking of swearing fealty to another."

Ríona's lip curled, revealing gleaming fangs. "I heard."

Caymin glanced from Ríona to Péist and back again as the younger dragon raised his head and met his elder's eye.

"So the young one who thinks he knows all is back to ask our counsel now?"

Péist arched his neck, and sparks flew from his nostrils.

Ailill laid a calming hand on Ríona's shoulder. "Hush, old friend. We left them to grow without us, trusting they would be true to the path laid before them. Part of that is not repeating the same mistakes we made. If we can aid them in this, we must."

Ríona glared at Péist for several heartbeats before breaking eye contact. She circled in place and settled. The only sign of her continued agitation was the twitching of her tail.

"Very well. Allegiance. It is tricky to know when, if ever, to pledge it."

Caymin leaned forward. "Eachna, the mage of the Eoganacht, told us everyone we meet will want something from us. We cannot fight Angus alone, but how are we to know whom to make alliances with?"

Ailill sighed. "You must understand the difference between making an alliance and pledging your fealty to someone. You may make alliances with any who may aid your cause—just as you attempted to do with the Eoganacht. You rescued their king in exchange for their pledge of help in confronting this Angus and his forces. If, however, this king requires a pledge of fealty, you must be wary. He will undoubtedly try and use the power of a dragon and mage to his advantage against his enemies. You will be honor-bound to do as he commands."

"In the world of two-legs," said Ríona, "it is best for dragons and their mages to remain neutral."

"*Did you do this?*" Caymin asked. "*I thought the last war was fought because many dragons and mages had pledged their fealty to Scolai and Tuala.*"

Ailill and Ríona looked at each other. "*We did not remain neutral,*" said Ailill at last. "*And that was our biggest error in judgment.*"

It was Caymin and Péist's turn to share a bewildered glance. "*We do not understand.*"

Ríona inclined her head, and Ailill said, "*Scolai did not just ask us to pledge our fealty. He demanded we seal it in blood.*"

Péist and Caymin listened raptly.

"*Before he made his thirst for power known to all, Scolai argued that we were too scattered in the event of any kind of threat to magic or our kind, like the threat mounted by Aolu. He said the blood pact we made would enable us to be called instantly, no matter how far away we were.*" Ailill scowled as she spoke, her fist tightly gripping the stone hanging around her neck. "*We were such fools.*"

Ríona touched her foreleg to her mage. "*Do not dwell on it. We were all deceived by him.*" She fixed her yellow eyes on the two young ones. "*We each gave a few drops of our blood to enable this charm of his. But it was not what we thought.*"

"*What was it?*" Péist asked.

Ailill closed her eyes. "*The blood was absorbed by a stone Scolai had enchanted, the Méarógfola–the Bloodstone. That stone contains the blood of nearly every dragon and mage that lived at the time. And it gave Scolai and Tuala power over us.*"

"*How?*" Caymin's heart was filled with dread.

"*Because our pledge of fealty–and Scolai's spell–was sealed with blood,*" said Ríona, "*it cannot be broken. It compels us to obey the holder of the Bloodstone.*"

Péist curled his lip. "*Do you mean to tell us that anyone who holds this Méarógfola has the power to command dragons and mages?*"

Ailill nodded sadly. "*Yes. It was our greatest shame and our worst fear. In our blind trust of another mage and dragon, we gave them power over our will.*"

Caymin gaped at them. "*But you fought them? How could you if you were sworn to fealty by this Bloodstone?*"

Ríona lowered her great head so that she was eye to eye with Caymin. *"We did terrible things under the power of that stone. We killed and burned and destroyed. All non-magic folk lived in terror of us. Only by getting the stone from Scolai could we be freed from its hold over us."*

"How did you do that?"

"One much like you. She was a young girl who was mage-born. She had not earned her staff, but she had such purity of heart, such goodness, that we decided to trust her with an impossible task."

Ailill laid a hand on Ríona's brow, scratching absently. *"She stole the stone from Scolai."*

"How?" asked Péist. *"And what did she do with it?"*

"We do not know the answer to either question," said Ailill. *"We never saw her again. We knew when the Méarógfola was no longer in Scolai's possession. It was as if waking from a horrifying spiritwalk. We were finally free to fight against him and those who were still loyal to him without the coercion of the Bloodstone."*

Caymin frowned. *"This was all a thousand winters in the past, yet you have been speaking as if the stone still holds power over you."*

"It does." Ríona blinked and her vertical pupil contracted to a slit. *"If it is found again, the one who holds it will wield power too great to imagine. He or she will be able to summon us—all of us whose blood is encased by the stone—and we could be used again as instruments of war."*

"You would be brought back to our world?"

It was Ríona's turn to close her eyes. *"We would. It was one of the reasons we retreated to this land, so that we could do no more harm."*

Péist growled, a low rumble from his chest. *"Are there any dragons now living who are not under the power of the Méarógfola?"*

Ríona opened her eyes. *"Very few. And of them, only you are bonded to a mage."*

Caymin and Péist sat in stunned silence as they realized the implication of these revelations.

Caymin asked in a strangled voice, *"What was the girl's name?"*

"Aine."

Ailill held a hand out to them as she began to fade, her voice coming as if from far away. *"You must learn from our past and never allow yourselves to be used as we were used. Swear fealty to none. And if you can, you must find the Méarógfola and destroy it once and done so that it can never be used again."*

Beanna was hopping about, pecking at them as they woke from their spiritwalk.

"I have been trying to wake you. What was happening?"

"Why?" Caymin crawled out from under Péist's wing. In the not-too-far distance, a scrub tree was blackened and smoldering. *"What did that?"*

"Skyfire." Beanna flew to her shoulder. *"The storm—it was drawn here by you and the worm."*

Péist roared to the sky.

"What is wrong with him?"

Caymin looked around in despair. *"We are more alone than we thought we were. And if we do not succeed, there may be much more at risk than we knew."*

CHAPTER 6

Allies No Longer

E achna entered his dwelling and closed the door. "He refuses to meet with you privately. He's planning to have all of his chiefs and warriors assembled in the hall when you're presented so that he can thank you for rescuing him."

Caymin sat, freshly bathed and wearing a new tunic and leggings that Eachna had procured for her.

"You'd best not stand before the king looking like a beggar," he'd said, eyeing the holes in her old leggings from her time in Péist's saddle.

Péist, who felt he was magnificent enough as he was, remained outside the stone walls surrounding the village, listening through their connection—"*I grow weary of being surrounded by curious two-legs,*" he had said.

"He does not mean only to thank us, does he?" Caymin asked now, watching Eachna shrewdly.

"No, lass, he doesn't." Garvan braced his elbows on the table.

"He thinks by addressing you, a child of simple background, in front of all, that he can intimidate you into swearing fealty to him."

Eachna filled three cups with one of his herbal teas and set a plate of bread on the table. "I tried to convince him that it was not likely you would do it, but he's already seeing the victories he can win with you and Péist leading the way."

"*We will not be used in such a manner,*" Péist said so they could all hear.

"We know that," said Garvan. He glanced at Eachna. "We've an idea to discuss with you. Given that you can't count on Dughall for aid, you're going to need help from other places. I think I should try to find Angus and join him. As a fellow monk, he's likely to welcome me. He'll not know of my connection to you. I may be able to help Enat if she's still with them. At the very least, I may be able to learn of his plans and get word back to you."

Caymin opened her mouth to protest, but paused. "Why would you do this? Do you not want the followers of the Christ to spread?"

He shook his head. "Not by violence." He looked around—at Eachna, at Beanna, back to her. "I'm thinking there's room for both in this world."

She nodded. "It may be helpful to have someone we trust there with Angus. And I would rest easier if I knew Enat had help."

Beanna flapped to the table, waddling over and picking at a bit of bread in front of Caymin. "*I could go with him, and then I would be able to bring messages to you, little one.*"

Caymin looked to Garvan. "She is offering to go with you. To carry messages if needed." She stroked Beanna's breast. "But Diarmit knows you."

"*He knows the talking crow from the magical forest. He does not know one crow from another where he is now. I will be careful. And if Enat is there, I will be able to tell her what has been happening since we parted.*"

Eachna whispered a translation for Garvan.

Caymin was torn. Beanna was the first creature to have befriended her when Enat brought her to the mystical forest.

"*It is a generous offer,*" said Péist.

"*Where will you go from here, little one?*" Beanna asked, cocking her head as she looked up at Caymin.

"Péist and I have decided our best hope for finding help without the Eoganacht is to seek out those who were apprenticed with me. We will begin with Méav, as I have a means of finding her. She may know where the elders are. We will go from there."

Eachna nodded. "Very well. I'll work from here to try and gather support from those with power who live in this part of Éire." He held out a crystal, hung from a leather cord. "I've enchanted it with a seeking spell. All you need do is press it to your lips and speak your name to enable the spell. Then it will always give me a way to find you. I'll be able to join you when it's time."

He held it out to her.

"*No!*" cried Péist, shielding his voice so that only she could hear it, but she needed no warning.

"I cannot." She watched his face darken as if a mask had been pulled down over it. "I know you mean well, Eachna, and I thank you for trying to help, but Péist and I may have to go places we cannot tell others of, and I cannot be bound to you by any charm. If we have need to summon you or tell you where we have gathered, I will ask a bird to fly to you with a message."

Eachna stared hard at her for several heartbeats and then stood. "Very well. It's time."

The assembled warriors sat on either side of the long tables, with the chieftains sitting at the high table in front of the king's chair. Flann and Gai, she noticed, sat with the chieftains while Dughall was ensconced in his chair, dressed in a brilliant crimson tunic embroidered with gold thread. He wore a thick gold torq around his neck like the one Gai had worn. Above his head snarled the dead wolf.

Péist consented to fly in so that he could be present for the audience with King Dughall. As before, both doors of the great hall had been opened so that Péist could look in from where he crouched outside the fortress.

Caymin entered, unarmed but for the knife at her belt, as she followed

Eachna up the middle of the hall, between the tables, until they stood before the king. Eachna bowed.

"*Do not,*" said Péist, but only to Caymin. "*A dragonmage bows before no one.*"

She was nervous, her heart beating fast in her chest, but she stood as tall as she could and met Dughall's gaze. Only his eyes reflected his displeasure, and she could tell he was re-evaluating his estimate of her.

"My king," said Eachna formally as he straightened. "This is the dragonmage, Caymin, and her dragon, Péist. It was they who rescued you from the Mruad."

It seemed ridiculous to Caymin, as Dughall knew very well who had rescued him.

Eachna stepped back, leaving Caymin standing alone before the king. Dughall rose and beckoned her forward. She felt self-conscious as she limped up the two steps to where he stood.

"You and your dragon have my thanks," he said so that all could hear. He held up his hands. "A token of my gratitude."

A low murmur of approval rippled among those assembled as he slid a smaller torq of gold around her neck.

"Thank you," Caymin said, though she did not like the feel of the thing. It was cold and heavy and felt as if she was wearing a collar like the ones she had seen around the necks of the oxen as they pulled the wagons.

"What else would you ask as your reward?" said Dughall as he resumed his chair and the hall quieted.

Caymin saw his plan at once. He knew very well why she and Péist had rescued him, but rather than offering to help her, he was going to make her ask so that she would appear to be beholden to him. She thought quickly.

"In your absence," she said, "your elder son, Lord Flann, pledged your clan's aid in helping us to prevent a war with a monk who is leading a band of his followers against those places that are still strongholds of magic. We have kept our end of the agreement by rescuing you with not a single life lost from among your clansmen."

She twisted to look back at the warriors behind her and caught

Gai's eye briefly as the warriors nodded and murmured again. She turned back to the king.

"We ask you now to honor your son's pledge. Come with us to prevent more bloodshed and protect the places of power that have guarded over Éire for ages beyond memory."

Dughall's pale eyes narrowed as he regarded her. She had put him in an untenable position, and he knew it. She had learned enough to know that all of Flann's actions in his father's absence were a reflection of the king. Either he disavowed his own heir's promise of aid and dismissed her and Péist's efforts in securing his rescue, or he pledged his clan's forces in a way that made him appear to be subservient to a girl and dragon.

"Clan Eoganacht will help you," he began. Another buzz of low voices broke out behind her. "But..." The room became silent once more. "We ask only your pledge of fealty to the Eoganacht in return."

He and Caymin stared at each other. Behind her, the warriors no longer made any effort to keep their voices down. She heard snatches of "dragon" and "victorious" and "conquer".

"We cannot do that."

Immediately, all chatter ceased as Péist spoke for the first time so that all could hear. Dughall looked over Caymin's head to where the dragon peered in at him.

"As the only dragon and dragonmage left in Éire, we cannot be loyal to any one clan. We will be protectors of all, looking over all."

This time when the voices murmured, the sound was angry, like hornets. Dughall's ruddy face burned redder under his thatch of light hair.

"You won't swear fealty to the Eoganacht?" he asked. He rested his hand on the pommel of the sword at his side, a simple gesture, but Caymin felt a shift in the atmosphere inside the hall.

She drew herself up. "We cannot. As Péist said, no clan can claim the fealty of the last dragon and mage."

Only Dughall's eyes moved as his gaze flicked to some place behind her. He had, she suddenly realized, expected this response and had prepared for it. She turned to find a score of armed warriors now standing around the hall, situated to be able to intercept her. She returned her gaze to the king.

"You would thank us for saving you with a show of force?"

He smiled unpleasantly. "I would have this alliance for the sake of my clan."

She tilted her head. "Then you leave us no choice but to look for allies elsewhere."

She spun to descend the steps she had climbed moments before, but half the warriors who had stood made to block her way while the others approached Péist with ropes and spears in hand. She was certain there were others outside the hall doing the same thing.

Forgotten was her recent doubt about being able to do magic as she saw the threat. Without thinking, she summoned her power, flinging her hands out to the sides. Warriors and tables alike went flying.

Outside, Péist roared. There were sudden screams and yells as his white talons ripped at the door to the hall, tearing stones apart to create an opening big enough for his head and forequarters to enter. With one breath, he threw a burst of flame at the roof overhead. The dry thatch ignited immediately.

Caymin found her path to him blocked by the warriors who were picking themselves up off the floor. With another burst of fire, Péist scattered them as they dove out of the way. Caymin ran through the flames and out to where she could climb up onto his back. She saw Gai running toward them. Hesitating for just a moment, she held out a hand, and he leapt, scrambling up behind her. Péist spread his wings, burning the ropes that tethered him, and flung himself into the sky.

They circled once, watching the smoke billow as the villagers ran about like ants. Péist wheeled in the air and headed to the cliffs.

A soft misty rain fell as Gai paced. Far below them, at the base of the cliffs, the sea crashed against the rocks, sending plumes of water into the air. All about was agitation, but Caymin felt calmer than she had since they had left Inishbreith.

Gai looked from her to his own hands, raw and burned in places, his tunic pocked with scorched holes as well. "Why aren't you burnt?"

"*A dragonmage cannot be burned by the dragon she is bonded to,*" Péist answered as Caymin quickly folded Gai's hands in between hers, closing her eyes to heal his burns.

"But you could be burned by other dragons? If there were any?"

She opened her eyes and inspected his hands, whole and unblemished now. "Yes. I would have to throw up a shield. Dragons have inner lids to protect their eyes from dragonfire. Their scales are not vulnerable to flame."

"*But our wings are.*"

She turned and looked to Péist. "*You are uninjured?*"

"*Yes. Their spears and arrows did not find their mark.*"

Periodically, she called out with her mind and, before long, Beanna found them, bringing Eachna and Garvan with her. They were out of breath and fell to the ground, panting. They dropped the packs they carried.

"Well, you left things in a right fine mess," growled Eachna.

She regarded him calmly. "What would you have had me do? Let him try to force us to swear an allegiance to his clan? Let them ensnare Péist!"

With an expression of distaste, she pulled the torq from around her neck and dropped it on the ground.

Rather than answer, Eachna rounded on Gai. "And you! What were you thinking? He'll consider you a traitor now. You realize that?"

"Aye." Gai scowled, but his expression slowly turned into a bitter smile as he pulled his own torq off and looked at it. "Better a traitor who can think for myself than a weakling he's forever ashamed of."

Garvan twisted around on the ground to look at Péist. "I daresay they'll remember you."

"*As they should.*" Péist closed his eyes and lifted his head skyward. "*Those puny two-legs, thinking to put their ropes on me and make us their captives.*"

Caymin laid her hands on him, checking for herself that he was not injured. "Can spears and arrows go through your scales?"

He opened his eyes and gazed down at her. *"I do not know. Probably, in certain places, or fewer dragons would have died in the last war."*

Eachna threw up his hands. "What now?"

"Now," said Garvan, "Beanna and I go to find Angus and you do what you can from here." He pointed to the packs. "We brought food and water skins for all of us."

"I have something for you," she said. She went to where the staff was still tied to Péist's saddle. Pulling it loose, she stood before him. "You gave me your vow once, pledging your sword and your aid. Will you now promise to bring this to Enat? It looks like an ordinary stick, and it will be in your hands. Carry it as if you need it to walk. None may know it is hers until you are able to return it to her."

"That shouldn't be hard as I did have a broken leg." He accepted the staff. "I give you my word, I'll protect this until I find Enat."

Eachna laid a hand on his shoulder. "Remember the things we practiced."

"What things?" Gai asked.

Eachna smirked. "Just a few things that should help if this Angus is as shrewd as I suspect he is."

Caymin turned to Eachna. "Will Dughall let you come back?"

He shrugged. "I'll tell him you lied to me, and I had no idea you intended to refuse him. I need to stay close so we know what he's planning. He could be more dangerous than Angus now."

She sobered at this thought. "I did not mean to make another enemy this day."

Garvan barked a laugh. "I daresay you'll have plenty of enemies before this is through." He peered at her. "What about you?"

"Now we search for those we know will help." She looked at Gai. "Will you go with us?"

He opened his mouth, but didn't respond immediately. "You want me to go with you?"

"Of course we do."

He beamed. "I will."

She reached to her belt and pulled the knife from its sheath. Laying it in her palm, she whispered, "Méav."

The knife blade glowed a faint blue and wobbled on her flat palm. Slowly, it began turning until its tip pointed north.

"I will never get used to that," Garvan breathed.

She looked to the north. "We go that way."

While Garvan prepared his pack, Caymin and Péist said their farewells to Beanna.

"Look after the two-leg," Péist said. *"And yourself."*

Caymin could not see for the tears that filled her eyes as she stroked Beanna's breast. *"I will miss you sorely. Help him bring Enat back to us."*

"I will. You and the worm take care. Word will spread quickly now that there is a dragon in Éire, and others will be looking for you. I do not want to have to come rescue you as well."

With a gentle tug on Caymin's ear with her beak, she flew off to join Garvan.

"Where is it?"

Enat lay gasping, her wrists secured to a post by leather straps so tightly wrapped that they bit into her flesh. Angus's last blow felt as if it had broken a rib, and she couldn't take enough air into her lungs to answer.

He knelt beside her and yanked her head back by her hair. Leaning near, he hissed into her ear, "Your staff. Where is it?"

She blinked back the tears that blurred her vision to look into eyes that were hard and black. She managed to give a weak cackle. Infuriated, he drew his fist back and punched her in the cheek.

She couldn't help a cry of pain, but panted, "Even if I knew where it is now, it wouldn't do you any good. You didn't earn the right to use it. Do you think it wouldn't know that it was in the hands of a usurper who wants to use it to do evil?"

With a last vicious kick, he left her lying in the dirt. Everything went dark for a time.

When she came to, it was to find Diarmit gently dabbing a salve on her bloody wrists, untied now. A poultice lay on her bruised cheek.

"Be careful he doesn't see you doing this," she whispered.

His eyes when he looked at her were frightened. "Can't you just tell him? Then this would stop."

She allowed her eyes to close again. "But it wouldn't. He'd only want more. Are you ready to leave?"

"Why do you keep asking me that?"

"Because one day, you will be."

He pushed to his feet. "I can't. He'd kill me first."

"I could protect you."

Diarmit scoffed. "You can't even protect yourself. Look at you." He went to the door. "I can't."

Alone again, Enat rolled over and struggled to summon the power to heal her own injuries. It was taking nearly all the power that was coming back to her to keep her body going, but she had to. She had to be ready. She'd seen... in a spiritwalk, just a couple of nights past.

Caymin was coming.

CHAPTER 7

TOGETHER AND APART

The rain continued to fall and, though it made Caymin and Gai miserable to be wet and cold, the mists and clouds helped to obscure them as they flew. They had briefly debated flying around Éire to stay out over the sea but, with the additional protection offered by the weather, they had opted to fly as straight a line as they could.

Periodically, Caymin held the knife in her palm. She had to take care the wind of Péist's flight didn't blow it out of her grasp, but the blue blade pointed their way, and they adjusted their course accordingly.

The cold worsened as night fell early.

"We must land and get dry and warm," Caymin said as she shivered uncontrollably.

"And I must hunt."

Péist soared over a remote stretch of forest and landed in a clearing large enough for him. Caymin and Gai dismounted, stiff with cold. The rain here had stopped, but all was wet. Péist left them to go hunting while they gathered fallen wood and used magic to force a fire. They dried their sodden cloaks with another spell and pulled food from the bags they had packed.

"You think Méav will help us?" Gai asked as he tore a chunk of bread and handed a piece to Caymin.

"I hope she will. She told me before she earned her staff that she had a vision of us fighting side by side, and she was sure we would meet again." She chewed thoughtfully. "What do you know of her clan?"

"They live along the north coast of Éire. Some are fishermen; some are traders; those farther inland are farmers."

Caymin's face fell a bit. "They are not warriors?"

"I imagine they are when they've need to be." Gai shifted closer to the fire, prodding it magically to keep the wet wood burning. "They've had more contact than my clan with those from Gwynedd, Britannia, and Caledonia, and I imagine some travelers from the north."

Caymin looked up at this. "Like the northmen who invaded our forest?"

Gai nodded. "From what Urard told me, they've come to Éire several times, sometimes to invade and take what they want, sometimes to trade peacefully."

Caymin felt his gaze as she stared at the fire.

"I know what you're thinking," he said.

She said nothing, only frowned at the flames.

"It's not likely any northmen we meet would know aught of your mother," he said gently.

She glanced up at him. "What do you know of your mother?"

Gai's dark eyes glittered in the firelight. "She was from a clan to the south. The pairing was arranged as part of a treaty between the clans. I'm told I look much like her. Urard says she wrote poetry and sang songs. I never knew her."

They sat huddled by their fire, both lost in thought, until Péist returned from his hunting. His white scales gleamed in the darkness.

"What did you see?" Caymin asked.

"I saw fires and smoke of two-leg dwellings in the distance, but not near us."

"Are we near the coast yet?"

"Not yet. I saw no endless water."

He settled, offering them a wing for shelter from the dripping branches overhead. "How close do you want to fly?"

"Let us rest for part of the night, and then fly on until morning. I think Gai and I should walk then to find Méav. There is no need to alert her people to your presence immediately."

"Are there islands nearby where I can wait as I did when you went to the Eoganacht?"

"I believe Ivar's maps showed some islands to the north," Gai said. "But we do not know exactly where Méav is."

Péist snorted his displeasure. "Soon, all will know of us, little one. We cannot keep this secret much longer."

Each time they encountered a scattering of human dwellings—hardly big enough to count as villages, according to Gai—Caymin hung back and let him approach the villagers. Most of the people thereabouts knew of the mage named Méav, but only a few had actually met her. They pointed the way farther north, and the two young mages trudged on, following the blue glow of the knife.

Caymin wore her bow over her shoulder, and kept her cloak on, as the days remained cold. Gai did the same with his cloak, partly for warmth, partly to cover the richness of his tunic, despite the holes burned into it.

"I wasn't planning on fleeing with you, was I?" he mumbled as he looked down at himself the first time a shrewd old man tried get Gai to pay for information.

He kept his sword strapped to his belt, and they both carried the bags of food Eachna and Garvan had brought them.

Along the way, Caymin reached out to any four-legs and birds they encountered, asking them as well if they knew of Méav. While many had felt her power, none knew her current whereabouts.

Caymin kept contact with Péist as he flew, staying in remote stretches of land that had no two-legs. He refused to fly out over the sea until she was closer to the coast.

The sky cleared and, overhead, a quarter-moon rose on their third night.

As they sat near their fire, eating, Caymin glanced over at Gai. "Have you ever fought? In actual battle? With your father's warriors?"

He shook his head. "Only sparring and training. We were preparing to fight to get my father back from the Mruad if we couldn't ransom him, but... no."

"Could you kill?"

He looked deep into her eyes, and she knew they were both remembering the day he had shot the pheasant for no reason.

"I have killed on the hunt," he said. He diverted his gaze back to the fire. "I suppose I could kill in battle. If I had to. You?"

She thought for a bit. "I do not know. I think I wounded one of the warriors the night we rescued your father. I do not know if I could kill."

"You'd better know before you get into battle, little badger."

Caymin and Gai both jumped to their feet at the sound of the voice speaking from the darkness of the surrounding trees. As one, they filled their hands with balls of flame, ready to defend themselves.

"Méav!" Caymin cried as a hooded figure stepped into the firelight, bearing a staff.

Méav tossed back her hood and smiled. "Greetings."

"How did you find us?" Gai asked.

She joined them at their fire and accepted some cheese and bread. "I felt... something. There's been a feeling of unrest recently. In the trees, in the earth. I've been listening, thinking it might be you. Then, today, an owl came to me and I knew."

"We have been searching for you." Caymin offered her a water skin and waited as she drank.

Méav looked much as Caymin remembered her, her black hair braided into small strands, with piercing blue eyes and a strength that had always made Caymin think of the goddesses of the tales sung round the fire. Méav caught her glance and grinned. She reached out to finger Caymin's red braids.

"You look a proper warrior now, little badger."

Caymin blushed. "I do not know if I will ever be a warrior."

Méav regarded her. "Something has changed you since I saw you last. You are different."

Caymin nodded. "I am. We have much to talk about."

Méav glanced at Gai. "Apparently, we do. How did you come to be traveling together?"

Before they could reply, Caymin felt Péist's approach and, without warning, he soared over them, blocking the moon from their view before he landed.

Méav leapt to her feet, her staff glowing as she held it at the ready. She could only stare up at Péist as he approached.

"Greetings, Méav," he said.

Her mouth opened but no words came out. Caymin stepped to him and laid a hand on his jaw as he lowered his head to her.

"This is what we must talk about. Méav, this is Péist."

Méav found her voice at last. "Péist? The creature from the forest? The one you and Ronan found."

"Yes. He was a cub then, and we bonded. I did not know he was a dragon until Timmin tried to wrest him from me."

Méav's mouth gaped as she continued to gaze at the white dragon standing before her. "I need to sit down."

They all sat around the fire, Péist settling as near as he could get.

"So, tell me." Méav couldn't seem to help glancing past Caymin to Péist.

"A war is stirring," Caymin said. "Timmin wanted Péist to lead us against the followers of the Christ and drive them from Éire, and he was willing to hurt me to get him. That is why the elders forced him to leave the forest. And then Diarmit—"

"Diarmit," said Méav. "The slow, stupid one?"

"The twit was only pretending to be slow and stupid," Gai cut in.

Caymin nodded. "He had been trained by a monk with power. His name is Angus, and he is using magic when it suits him, but pretending to be a leader of the Christians. I saw, in a spiritwalk, his followers attacking the forest, attacking the elders. I thought to gain allies from Gai's clan, but..."

She glanced at him.

"My father and brother betrayed the agreement they made with Caymin and Péist," Gai said bitterly. "Not that that was unexpected, but now Enat and all the elders have left the forest—"

"Wait!" Méav held up a hand. "The elders are gone? How do you know this?"

Caymin sighed. "There is much to tell you. Péist and I had to flee when he was in his egg and Timmin was trying to steal him. When we saw the war that is coming, we returned. I went to Gai's clan, but their mage, Eachna, sent us to the forest first to see if it was safe. The protections are intact. We found Enat's staff where she hid it, and were able to enter. She left a message that she was going to follow Diarmit and try to protect him."

She suddenly found her throat too tight to go on. Péist nuzzled her.

"*Do not despair, little one.*" He focused his green eyes on Méav. "*We have come in search of you.*"

Méav sat, digesting all they had told her. "Do any others know of these events?"

Caymin raised her face, swiping at her eyes. "Only Garvan, a monk we saved on the sea. He has pledged to help our cause and has gone to try and find Angus and join his forces so that he may send us information when he has it."

Méav looked around at all of them, her mouth open slightly. "A dragon, a monk and two mage-born without staffs... and we're supposed to stop a war."

Péist raised his head and huffed a few sparks, making Gai jump aside. "*Well put. We are more than enough.*"

Caymin and Gai trailed along behind Méav as she led them to her dwelling.

"I'm sorry it isn't large enough to accommodate you, Péist," she had said, inclining her head. "It is not so very far. You can safely stay here, I think, and be close enough to the little badger should she need you."

Péist had lowered his head to look her in the eye. *"I understand why my mage thinks so highly of you."*

Gai had grinned as Caymin felt her face go hot and busied herself with her pack.

She had to trot to keep up with them as Méav strode along, using her staff as a walking stick.

"You carry no other weapons," Gai noted.

"I do when I've need," she said over her shoulder. "But most of the time, this is sufficient."

Through the trees, a light beckoned, leading them to a stone cottage much like Enat's. Light shone from inside where the windows were unshuttered. Méav pushed the wooden door open and held it for them.

"We have visitors," she said.

Near the fire, a woman straightened and turned to them. Caymin still had a hard time judging human ages, but this woman appeared to be about twenty winters, close to Méav's age. Her hair, catching the firelight, was red—not fox-red like Caymin's own, but the deep red of autumn leaves. Her skin was pale and soft, like fresh milk.

"You must be Caymin," she said, smiling.

Caymin could only nod.

"This is Séana," said Méav. She nodded in their direction. "This is Gai. They were both apprentices with me."

"Welcome," said Séana. "You must be weary. Take off your cloaks and sit near the fire."

She poured cups of hot tea for all of them as Méav hung their cloaks and got a plate of oatcakes.

Caymin looked around and saw the trappings of a mage's cottage, bunches of dried herbs and flowers hanging from the rafters, jars of salves and potions lined up on shelves.

"You have made your life here," she said.

"Aye." Méav took Séana's hand briefly. "We've made our home here. I travel when needed to heal those who are sick or tend to an injured animal. Those about know where to find me, but we prefer to live apart from others."

Caymin flushed again as she watched Méav and Séana together.

The warmth of the cottage felt good after the cold, damp night, and the oatcakes—the first Caymin had had since she and Péist had fled the mystical forest—were delicious.

She suddenly felt very tired facing yet another telling of all that had happened, and so she sat, listening as Gai and Méav told all, filling in only where necessary.

Séana exclaimed and looked up at mention of Péist as if she expected him to land on their roof at any moment. "There's a dragon in Éire? A real dragon?"

Méav grinned. "You'll meet him soon enough. But for now..." She turned to Caymin, but Séana laid a gentle hand on her arm.

"Not tonight. The poor thing is falling asleep where she sits. This can wait until the morrow."

She got up and went to a wooden chest where she pulled out two folded sleeping mats. She laid them out near the fire while Méav retrieved extra blankets.

"I'm sorry it's not a proper bed," Méav said. "But it'll be warm and softer than the forest floor."

"This is fine, thank you," Gai said.

All Caymin could do was nod. She lay down, suddenly feeling as if she couldn't keep her eyes open. The last thing she remembered was Méav pulling a blanket over her.

Clouds scudded across the sky, temporarily obscuring the moon as it rode through the night. Péist had finished hunting and was flying for the joy of it. His night vision allowed him to watch the heat of four-legs and some winged ones below, all fleeing, as if they could outrun him. He felt Caymin as she slept and knew that she was safe.

He found an isolated place to settle and clean the blood from his talons. When he was finished with his ablutions, he lay down and tried to let his mind settle into the trance-state that was most often his sleep. He would never admit it, but he missed Beanna. The crow, though she constantly nettled him, had been a faithful companion since he had hatched from his *khrusallis*.

As he lay there, his feeling of isolation and loneliness grew. He was tired of being left behind, hidden as if he were something to be ashamed of. He belonged with his mage. He felt truly alone. He was truly alone. The only dragon in this realm. The others, though they existed somewhere, were far away. His sires were dead. He and Caymin had been tasked with the impossible. If the Méarógfola had been hidden away for a thousand winters, how were they supposed to find it? And why should they? If none had found it in all this time, what was the likelihood they would now?

Too restless to sleep, he took to the skies. He was a dragon, not an ox to be ridden and then put to pasture when it served two-legs. With a roar, he unleashed a fountain of fire into the night.

"I do not care if every two-leg in Éire sees me. I am a dragon!"

CHAPTER 8

WOLF VISION

Caymin woke, not sure at first where she was. Then she heard whispered voices and remembered.

"She's just a wee thing. Her scars make me want to weep."

"Don't. They've made her strong."

"How old is she?"

"No one knows," Méav replied. "Enat guessed she was ten winters when she came to us, so going on twelve now."

"Twelve!"

"Shhh. We'll wake them."

"But so young."

"You weren't there. She's powerful. The night she claimed her true name, the entire forest trembled with it. She's destined for great things."

"And..." Séana hesitated. "You would follow her into war."

"Aye. I would."

They lapsed into silence, and soon Caymin heard their breathing, slow and steady. All was quiet when she rose from her mat. Gai lay on his side, sleeping soundly. In the glow from the embers, she saw Méav and Séana lying together in their bed. Silently, she opened the door and stepped outside. Her breath puffed out before her in the cold night air as she stole through the trees. All around her winged ones and four-legs paused their own hunting to mark her passage.

She knew Péist was flying; his agitation had broken through her sleep, and she felt it also.

"All is well, little one?"

"Yes. I cannot sleep. Keep flying."

She knew he shared her anger, her frustration that they had been tasked with doing what those far older had failed to do. On and on she walked, breathing in the biting air and listening to the night sounds. A pale sliver of moon watched over her as she went, wishing she were still living with Broc and Cuán and the other badgers in their sett, wishing Enat had never come to find her, and that she had never gone to the mystical forest to be trained as a mage. But then... She paused to look up at the moon. She never would have bonded with Péist.

She came to a small knoll and sat at the base of a twisted yew tree, hugging her knees to her chest. Her anger bubbled inside her as she contemplated the possibility of flying away with Péist to some distant land where they could live in peace, just the two of them.

She leaned back against the tree, her hands resting on its roots as she imagined how it would be if they were free to do as they wished. Slowly, like the distant but ceaseless noise of the waves when they were on Inishbreith, she became aware of the tree. She closed her eyes and felt... vague images of growing under the protection of other trees long gone now; of two-leg wars fought many ages ago, spilling blood on this soil; of hundreds of winters growing on this spot, sending its roots out deeper and wider.

She found herself walking through a heavy mist. She stopped, not wanting to go where the mist was leading her. All around her, the fog swirled, pushing her onward like so many hands. When the mist cleared, she gasped in horror at the scene before her.

A swarm of humans were cutting down a vast forest, leaving only the stumps behind as branches were hacked off and tossed onto enormous bonfires while teams of oxen hauled the trunks away. As far as she could see, the land was dotted with stumps. Beyond the noise of the men and the oxen, there were no other voices—no birds, no badgers or foxes or rabbits or deer. She crouched and dug a hand into the earth. Even it was silent.

Her cheeks were wet with her tears when she opened her eyes. She gasped as she saw that she was not alone. Sitting before her was a wolf. His eyes glittered, and something else glinted at his neck. She sat motionless as he regarded her.

"*Greetings,*" she said at last. "*I am Caymin.*"

"*I know who you are. I am Mactíre. You are with the* Ceann Bán."

"*The white one? Yes. His name is Péist.*"

"*I know that as well.*"

Caymin frowned. "*How do you know us?*"

"*Why do you weep?*"

Caymin had forgotten she was. She wiped her face with her sleeve. "*I have seen horrible things.*"

"*Things to come?*"

"*Mayhap.*"

Mactíre tilted her head. "*And you are here to stop this?*"

"*We are going to try.*"

Caymin looked up and saw dawn brightening the sky to the east. "*You did not say how you knew us—*"

When she glanced around, the wolf had disappeared. With a heavy sigh, she got to her feet and made her way back to all that awaited her.

She was nearing the cottage when she encountered Séana carrying two buckets of water from a nearby stream. Caymin hurried to take one from her.

"Thank you," Séana said. She set her bucket down. "Sit with me."

Caymin sat beside her on a large boulder jutting out of the earth. Looking at her in the breaking daylight, she saw that Séana's eyes as they probed her were like the sea, gray-green. She sat, staring into those stormy eyes as she waited to see what Séana wanted.

Séana's gaze flicked down to the knife at Caymin's belt. "The blade Méav gave you?"

"Yes." Caymin pulled it from its sheath and handed it to her.

She held it, running a delicate finger over the blade. "She spoke more of you than any of the others. She told me you were orphaned and raised by badgers."

"I was."

"She also said she had a vision that she would be fighting at your side." Séana raised her eyes to Caymin's.

"She told me. The night of her first trials."

Séana blinked rapidly and looked again at the knife in her hands.

"You are Méav's mate?" Caymin asked.

Séana smiled. "I suppose I am." She glanced up again. "I love her. As do you, I think."

"I do." Caymin looked at her solemnly. "Do you have power?"

Séana shook her head. "No. Not like you and Méav and Gai. I know a bit of healing and herbs, but I've no magic in me."

Caymin frowned. "But you have seen things."

Séana handed the knife back. "I've had spiritwalks where I've seen the battle that is coming."

"Can you see who is fighting?"

Séana shook her head again. "I can't. I only see the fighting."

Caymin stared at her. "And it frightens you."

A slanting ray of sunlight glinted on the tears filling Séana's eyes. "Yes."

"Have you spoken to Méav of this?"

"No." Séana took a deep breath.

"Would you have us leave without her?"

Séana tilted her head to study Caymin more closely. "You would do that?"

"Yes."

Séana wrapped an arm around Caymin's shoulders. "I think Méav is right to admire you so. And she would never be happy leaving those she cares about to their fate without doing what she could to keep them safe."

She stood and reached for her bucket. "Let's break our fast. I've a dragon to meet today."

They hadn't gone ten steps before the earth shuddered under their feet. Tree branches snapped as something enormous moved through them. Séana dropped her bucket as Péist's great white head lowered to her level.

"*Greetings.*"

Méav and Gai were both awake by the time the odd trio returned to the cottage. Méav smiled.

"I see you've met Péist."

Séana could only nod.

Caymin turned to him, speaking aloud so Séana could hear. "You have hunted?"

He, also, spoke so that all could hear. "*I have.*"

"I've porridge for us," Méav said, going back inside to dish out four bowls.

They sat outside so that Péist could be with them. At least, most of him could. His hindquarters and tail were shadowed by the trees surrounding the cottage. Caymin took his saddle off so that he could stretch out more comfortably.

"Do you know where the other apprentices are?" Gai asked.

Méav shrugged as she ate. "I know where they came from, but I've no idea where they are now. Fergus lives not a day's journey from here. He'll be easy to reach. Daina and Niall are also from the north, but further to the west. Cíana and Una live in the south of Éire."

"What of Ronan?" Caymin asked.

"*He is the one who was with you the night we bonded?*" Péist asked.

"Yes."

Méav frowned. "He's been wandering. He sends messages now and again, but the last one was over a moon ago. At that time, he was in Connacht."

Gai looked up from his bowl. "What of Ivar and Neela? Enat wrote that she asked them to stay away. Do you know where they are?"

Méav shook her head. "I've not heard."

Gai set his empty bowl down. "This is mad. How are we to reach everyone when we don't know where they are?"

They sat in silence for a bit.

"Is not Samhain to be celebrated soon?"

They all turned to look at Péist.

"He's right," said Méav. "Night after tomorrow. Everyone, no matter where they are, will be celebrating."

"Can you reach them in some way?" Séana asked.

Méav's eyes narrowed as she thought. She raised her gaze to Caymin. "Aye. I think we can."

Caymin paused with her spoon halfway to her mouth. "What are you thinking?"

Méav smiled. "We'll need to think on it a bit. In the meantime, I can send a message to the ones who live nearby and try to get them here before Samhain."

She closed her eyes and sent out a call. In a few heartbeats, two hawks and an owl responded.

"Thank you."

She chose the older of the two hawks.

"Why not this one?" Gai asked, stroking the fluffy breast of the owl.

Méav looked to the sky. "It's going to storm later. If she's caught in the wet, the owl will be grounded until her feathers dry. The other hawk was just fledged this spring. He's not yet strong enough to fly through the wind."

She went into the cottage and returned a moment later with a small, rolled piece of parchment. She tied it to the hawk's leg.

"Take this to Fergus. Then see if you can find any others with power nearby. Safe flight."

The hawk spread his wings and flew off.

Méav turned back to the two young ones. "Now, you haven't had a proper lesson, either of you, since you left the forest. We're going to fix that."

Péist curled up to go into his trance and rest while Caymin and Gai brewed potions.

"What are you—?" Gai started to ask as he saw the potion ingredients

Caymin had laid out.

Caymin's cheeks burned scarlet, and she shifted to try and hide her potion from him.

"No need to be embarrassed," Méav said. "If he'd ever had to put up with the pain and bleeding, he'd be making this potion quick enough. And you'll be needing it every moon now."

"You've forgotten how to do this," Méav said a while later, wrinkling her nose as she dipped a ladle into Gai's cauldron. "You added the beetle wings too late. You're supposed to add them as soon as it begins to bubble."

She turned to Caymin's potion. "And you didn't stir the correct length of time. See? It's too thick. It won't work properly."

She waved her staff over both cauldrons, magically emptying them. "Again."

By the time Péist stirred, they had correctly made three potions and two batches of salve for a pox that had broken out among the children in the region.

"This will help tremendously," Séana said happily as she used a flat stick to push the salve into squat clay pots. "Thank you both. It would have taken me several days to make this much."

Gai's grumpiness vanished when Séana smiled at him. His pale cheeks colored as he cleaned up.

Caymin grinned until she heard Péist, speaking so only she could hear, say, *"I would not laugh, little one. You did not see the look on your face when Méav told you your last potion was perfect."*

Scowling, Caymin carried her cauldron back into the cottage as the first raindrops of Méav's predicted storm began to fall. Outside, she heard Péist's laughter rumble up from his chest.

"What's wrong with him?" Méav asked, looking in alarm back out at the white dragon spouting smoke from his nostrils.

Caymin glared in his direction. "Nothing."

Garvan crouched behind a hedge of rowan, watching as Beanna flew down into the valley below where there was a large encampment of people. The camp was situated inside a curve of the river Sionainne. He knew this river well, having fished it farther to the north when he was a boy.

Several beehive huts, built of rock, dotted the valley floor, while other dwellings appeared to be hastily constructed of wood and daub, with crudely thatched roofs.

Beanna flew from tree to tree, gradually drawing nearer. He watched as she joined a small flock of crows who were picking at a garbage heap, looking for edible scraps of food. From what he could see, none of the humans paid the slightest attention to the birds.

He sat down and pulled some smoked fish from his own provision bag and gnawed on it as he waited. After five days' walk, his food supplies were half gone, even eating sparely. He chewed slowly, trying to make the bit of fish satisfy his growling belly.

He'd been careful about which farms and villages he approached since taking his leave from Caymin and Péist. The last thing he wanted was to leave a trail of suspicious people who would remember the lone monk who'd been looking for Angus. To most, he was a wandering hermit on a pilgrimage, limping along with his stick. Beanna had taken to the trees when he was with them to avoid arousing more curiosity.

Most of the folk he encountered had been willing to share a meal with a holy man in exchange for a blessing on their crops or livestock or children. By listening, he'd gleaned bits of information about the monk who was preaching a holy war against the ungodly. None of the simple farmers and sheepherders he met wanted to be seen as ungodly to a monk, but he spied more than one bonfire site being prepared for Samhain night.

When he was done eating, he closed his eyes to wait for Beanna's return. The flapping of her wings woke him.

"Is it Angus?"

Though he couldn't hear Beanna, she could understand most of what he said, and they had worked out a system of clicking her beak to answer his questions.

One click to signify yes.

"Did you see Enat?"

Two clicks.

"What of the boy, Diarmit?"

One click.

"He's there, then?" Garvan looked through the hedge. "Should you take a message to Caymin? Show her where they are?"

Beanna clicked her beak twice with a shake of her head.

"You're right. Not until we find Enat. I may need you to help with that."

He took a deep breath and shouldered his bag. "May as well see what we're dealing with."

Beanna flew off to watch his progress from a distant tree as he made his way down the hill toward the encampment. Though there was no wall, like that around the Eoganacht fortress, he was met by sentries who halted him.

"Who might you be?" asked the taller of the two, a man simply dressed in a rough tunic and leggings.

"A wandering monk. Garvan is my name. I heard of Angus and his holy war. I want to pledge myself to his work."

The other sentry, a squat man whose face was covered by a patchy beard, laughed. "A lame monk. Some help you'll be."

The first sentry stepped aside. "Let him go. It's not for us to decide."

Garvan heard their continued laughter behind him as he limped into camp. A few others paused to watch him curiously. He was surprised to see several families, the children playing in the dirt outside the squalid dwellings.

He nodded as he passed and made his way toward the center of the encampment, where the largest of the stone dwellings stood. Here, more men stood guard.

As Garvan neared, they raised spears to bar his way.

"I'm looking for Angus."

"And who are you?" asked one of them.

"I'm Garvan. I come to offer my aid for his cause."

A voice from within said, "Let him pass."

The guards shifted to let Garvan enter. He tripped over his walking stick, hitting his leg where it had broken. The men behind him laughed as he gritted his teeth against the throbbing pain.

It took a moment for his eyes to adjust to the darkness of the interior of the building. Sitting at a table set with candles laid out around a large parchment were three men. The two on either side stood, but Garvan's gaze was fixed on the one in the middle. He remained seated, so his stature was hard to judge, but his dark eyes burned with a fire that marked him as Angus.

Garvan inclined his head.

"Garvan, is it?"

"Aye, Brother Angus. I'm a simple monk, but I've heard of you and your cause. I come to pledge myself to it, if you'll have me."

One of the other men barked a laugh. "A good warrior he'll make. Going to poke the heathens with your walking stick?"

"Silence." Angus rose and came around the table. His head barely came to Garvan's chin, but those eyes burned into his. Garvan's heart pounded as he dug his fingernails into his palm, forcing himself to focus only on the pain in his leg as he and Eachna had practiced. He tried to keep his face blank while Angus probed his mind. Eachna had predicted he would need to pass this test.

After several heartbeats, Angus stepped back with a nod. "You are well come, brother. I'm sure we can use you."

He turned back to the table. Garvan could now see that the parchment was a map. Angus pointed.

"Where have you come from?"

Garvan indicated the west. "I have been wandering, but most recently was in the territory of clan Eoganacht."

Angus's expression darkened. "Ah, yes. Dughall, the Wolf of the West. Consort with the devil. We'll deal with them when the time is right."

Garvan quickly scanned the map. It had marks farther to the east, as well as the northeast. "What are your plans, Brother Angus?"

Angus smiled and called to one of the sentries. "Take our newest brother and find him something to eat and a place to sleep."

With another small bow, Garvan turned and limped after the sentry. They wended their way through the encampment to a small hut composed of equal parts stone and stick. Inside were four sleeping mats.

"You'll share with others here," said the sentry gruffly. He pointed to another hut with a fire burning in front of it, a large kettle suspended over the flames. "You can get something to eat over there."

"Thank you, brother."

Garvan shrugged off his pack and rolled his shoulders. Looking around, he spied a crow, perched on the roof of a nearby beehive hut, cawing to the skies like all the other crows. It tilted its head and clicked its beak as it watched him. With a grin, he ducked inside his own new home.

CHAPTER 9

Samhain Flight

hold it steady."

Méav walked around behind Gai as his hands trembled with the effort of his spell. Caymin stood nervously in a rocky streambed as Gai held the water back on either side of her. The current pushed against his wall of magic, trying to rejoin with its other half and swirl back into the empty space at Caymin's feet. Her eyes darted from side to side, watching the water threatening to douse her.

They all jumped as a familiar voice said, "Now, that's a sight."

Distracted, Gai turned, and the water came rushing at Caymin, knocking her off her feet as she whirled in the eddy caused by the two halves of the stream crashing together again.

Niall reached in and plucked her out by the neck of her tunic. She sputtered and coughed as he set her back on dry ground. He was laughing so hard he fell down beside her. When she could breathe again, she chuckled with him.

Méav and Gai came over and offered them each a hand. Caymin, sopping wet, said, "We do not have to practice more, do we?"

"Not today." Méav tugged on a few of her wet braids. "Come, let's get you dried off and see what this one has been up to."

She draped an easy arm around Niall's shoulders, though he stood taller than she. They led the way back to the cottage, she with her staff, he with a long spear in hand.

"Sorry," Gai mumbled. "I shouldn't have lost my concentration."

Caymin grinned through chattering teeth. "I needed a bath, but hot water would have been welcome."

Séana clucked in a motherly way when she saw them. She found a dry tunic that hung past Caymin's knees. "This will have to do. Go change into this, and we'll wash yours while they're nice and wet."

Méav introduced Niall, tousling his hair. "I do believe you're getting some sun."

Niall shook back his hair, which was as white as the moon, matching his eyebrows and lashes. Even his eyes had no color, being such a light blue that only the pupils shone.

Caymin changed quickly and joined the others around the hearth. Gai passed her a cup of hot tea—its warmth welcome as she continued to shiver.

"Fergus sent word he'd come when he could," Niall was saying. He sipped his tea, eyeing both Caymin and Gai. "I'm guessing the reason you summoned us has something to do with these two."

Méav hid a smile. "Yes and no."

A quizzical look crossed his face. "What does that mean?"

The light coming in through the cottage door was suddenly extinguished as Péist lowered his head to peer in.

"It means, mage, that it has to do with more than those two."

Niall jumped to his feet with a cry as the others laughed. He looked around at them and sheepishly picked up the cup he had dropped in his panic. "I take it you've things to tell me."

Séana took his cup from him and refilled it. "Sit down. We've much to tell you."

Méav nodded her head in Péist's direction. "You remember Caymin's white worm when we were in the forest? Well, he isn't a worm any longer."

Niall shifted to sit facing the door where one dragon eye continued to look in at them. He pointed at Péist. "The day Timmin attacked us. This is why?"

Caymin nodded. "Yes. Péist was in his egg by then, but Timmin wanted him. For a war. A war against the followers of the Christ."

Péist snorted, blowing sparks into the cottage.

"Stop that!" Méav said, jumping up to stamp them out.

"*My apologies,*" Péist said. "*But the thought that I would have consented to do as Timmin wanted...*"

"And yet," said Séana, "we are facing a war against them anyhow."

"*This is true.*"

Niall looked from one to another. "What are you talking about?"

Méav sat back down. "First, tell us what happened in the forest after Caymin left it."

"Enat was in a fury," he said. "She had Diarmit tied up and confined to the boys' cottage with one of us standing guard over him day and night. That was the first we knew of this monk he served. There was only Una and me from our group, and Cíana and Daina left from the younger apprentices. Ivar and Neela were still reaping. They didn't return for maybe a fortnight after you left with the elk."

"Peist began hatching as we left the forest," Caymin said. "We had to stop while he did, and then he needed to hunt before we could move on. I thought Timmin would come after us again, but he did not."

"Well, as soon as Neela and Ivar got back with new apprentices, they had to decide what to do with Diarmit. They argued a lot, but Enat convinced them to let him go." He glanced to where Méav's staff leaned against the wall. "They decided to send all the rest of us home until the danger is past. Daina and I came north. I don't know where the others are."

Méav laid a hand on his shoulder. "I know you would have taken your trials tonight. 'Tis a bitter thing."

He shrugged her hand off. "So why haven't we been called back to the forest?"

"Enat followed Diarmit," Caymin said. "She left her staff behind for me to find, and left a message that she intended to let them capture her so she could learn their plans."

"You jest!" Niall looked at the solemn faces around him.

Their silence told him it was no jest. His face fell.

"I'd hoped you sent for me to tell me I was to take my trials tonight after all."

"No." Méav's tone was sympathetic. "We summoned you because we need to contact all the magic folk we can to put our own force together to combat this Angus."

Niall sat up straighter. "All of us?"

"As many as we can gather," said Gai. "We thought my father and his warriors would help us, but now we must use Samhain night as a way to reach as many as possible."

"Why can we not do both?"

The humans all turned to look at Péist.

"Both what?" Méav asked.

"The mystical forest where Caymin and I bonded is not so far from here. It is not yet midday. We have a mage with a staff to let us enter. I can fly two or three of you at a time, and we could all be there before sunset."

Niall's mouth gaped. "You mean, I could take my trials tonight? Earn my staff?"

"It would mean flying during the day. Two-legs will see us."

They all looked at one another.

"We could do it," Méav said slowly, pondering. "If we brought what we need for tonight's ceremony with us. We've no idea what the elders left behind."

"The power of that forest would aid us in our quest," Caymin said.

Méav nodded. "Aye. It would."

Séana stood. "What are you sitting around for? We've a lot to do."

Overjoyed at Caymin's return, the badgers milled around, licking and nuzzling every bit of her they could reach as she lay on the ground hugging them.

When Péist had flown in with Caymin, Méav and Niall, Méav had gained them entry to the forest. Nothing had changed since the last time

Caymin had been there with Gai; the village was empty, with no sign that any of the elders had returned. Méav walked Niall into the forest and gave him instructions for preparing himself for his trials. She returned alone and joined Caymin and the badgers as they watched the skies anxiously, waiting for Péist to return with Gai and Séana.

"*How long can you stay this time?*" Broc asked from where she lay curled up against Caymin's thigh.

"*I do not yet know.*" Caymin cuddled one of the young badgers while she traced a loving finger along the white stripe on Broc's head. "*We will know more after tonight.*"

Cuán looked up at her. "*How do you think tonight will be different than other nights?*"

"*All those with power will be celebrating Samhain this night,*" Caymin said. "*We are hoping we can reach out to them, like a spiritwalk, calling them to our cause.*"

"*How can we help, little one?*"

Méav turned to them. "*If you could keep watch over us, it would be most helpful.*" She looked around with a frown. "*We will have to be deeply under the influence of our power tonight to reach out to all. Niall will be alone in the forest.*"

Caymin shifted. "*You are worried about Timmin.*"

Méav met her gaze. She reached under her tunic and pulled out a deep green stone. "*The jade you enchanted for me. It has been warm against my skin ever since we entered the forest.*"

Caymin looked around in alarm. "*That means an enemy is near.*"

The badgers bristled and growled.

"*We chased him off once,*" said Broc. "*We can do it again.*"

"*You caught him by surprise before,*" Caymin said. "*He will be ready for you this time.*"

She looked at Méav. "*You are a full mage now.*"

"*But I am no match for Timmin. He was as powerful as Enat when he was here.*"

Cuán whickered. "*Others will help as well. The elk, the winged ones.*"

"*Yes,*" said Caymin. "*I can call to all of them and ask if they will help keep watch tonight.*"

Méav nodded, looking to the sky again. *"I think that would be wise. It is their home we are protecting as much as ours."*

They gathered on the sacred hill, only the light of the stars to guide them, as the new moon hid her face. The birds of the forest kept watch over Niall as the forest itself guided him on his trials. Osán and Ríordán, the giant elk, paced the perimeter of the circle. Caymin watched the skies anxiously.

Péist had returned weary and hungry from his second flight with Gai and Séana, but he had insisted on leaving the mystical forest again to hunt.

"All here have worked to protect us. I regret that I had to hunt among them when first I emerged from my khrusallis, but I will not now. Méav will be able to open the forest protections for me when I return."

The badgers, having hunted early, were also standing sentry, keeping an eye out for danger.

Méav carried a pouch with ashes collected from the fire at Lughnasadh. She'd found it in the meetinghouse. "This must have been one of the last things they did before they left."

A sense of heaviness and foreboding weighed on them. The last Samhain, the only one Caymin had ever kept in the company of other humans, had been a time of celebration, though Caymin remembered it differently.

Overhead, a silent moving shadow blotted out the stars.

"He is back." Caymin pointed.

Méav raised her staff and whispered words. A heartbeat later, Péist landed in the clearing. He folded his wings and bowed his head to the elk, who had instinctively bolted to the edge of the forest upon his arrival.

"You helped save my mage and me when I was in my egg. You protected us and carried us to safety. We cannot ever repay that debt, but we pledge ourselves to your aid if ever you should need it."

The elk stepped out of the trees, Ríordán's magnificent antlers each broad enough for Caymin to lie upon, and tentatively approached.

"It was our honor to do what we could," said Osán. "Though we did not know when we departed that it would be a dragon who would emerge from that egg."

Péist tilted his head as he eyed her. "You carry life within you."

Ríordán nuzzled her as she said, "Yes. The first I have carried for many winters. We lost our last young one to two-legs when he left the boundaries of this forest."

Péist turned to Caymin and shielded his voice from all but her. "I feel your melancholy, little one. What is it? Is this not what you wanted?"

"Yes. This gathering is what we must do, but I cannot help but remember last Samhain. I saw my father and spoke with him. The only time I can remember doing that."

Péist lowered his head. "I know you would like to do it again, but do not part the veil on this night. We must focus on our task and I have a feeling of... unease."

Caymin looked up at him. "What do you mean?"

"I cannot explain. I have seen nothing untoward, but still... there is a feeling that not all is right. We must be on our guard."

Méav summoned everyone to gather round the prepared bonfire. The humans positioned themselves at the compass points while the badgers spread out around the clearing and the elk paced the perimeter. Méav reached into the pouch and grasped a fistful of ashes. Sprinkling them over the wood, she chanted words of power, asking the spirits of the forest and the gods and goddesses to guide them in their quest on this solemn night. She nodded to Caymin and Gai, and they all produced balls of flame in their palms. Péist crouched beside Séana. She laid a hand on his neck as he belched a small burst of flame, joining the others as they ignited the bonfire.

The flames danced into the night, throwing undulating shadows across the clearing. Séana uncorked a bottle and took a drink. Making a face, she passed the bottle to Caymin who hesitated.

"What is it?" she asked, taking a tentative sniff.

"Poitín," said Méav. "But I've added a bit to it to aid us tonight." She reached over and tipped the bottle toward Caymin's mouth. "Take a big gulp."

Caymin did as she was told and grabbed her throat as the poitín burned its way down her gullet. She felt her insides were on fire, and she tried to catch her breath as Méav and then Gai also drank. Almost immediately, Caymin felt as if her feet no longer touched the ground. Séana began to chant a song that echoed within her head, and she felt her body swaying, though she did not consciously do it. All gathered around the fire clasped hands, Caymin and Séana's together clasping one of the spikes ridging Péist's neck. As Séana's song continued, Caymin closed her eyes and let her spirit wander.

She saw faces, multitudes of faces gathered around fires just as they were doing. Most, she could not reach, but there were those—those with power who were open to her—and to them, she called out.

"We need you. Gather all who are willing to fight to protect magic and the old ways and join us at the mystical forest at the next new moon. Spread the word to others."

As she moved from fire to fire, she felt those with power rise up to meet her. They, in turn, moved on to other fires, like ripples in a pond when a stone is thrown in. Someone familiar was at her shoulder. She turned and saw Cíana, her golden hair rippling, a smile on her face.

"I will join you as soon as I can," Cíana said before fading into the darkness as Caymin moved on.

Samhain bonfires dotted the darkness like stars, each pulling her onward, spreading the message as her mind reached out to touch those who were open on this sacred night. In the distance, she could hear Méav and Gai doing the same. Each fire she approached, she searched for Enat's face, but she didn't see it.

"Caymin."

It was barely a whisper. She stopped and listened. It came again. "Caymin."

She turned and saw her father. He held out a hand, smiling and beckoning to her. She stood, torn. She looked over her shoulder at the fires in the distance, waiting for her.

"I'm waiting, too, daughter. Come to me."

The sound of his harp made her whirl. He sang a song, a distant, forgotten memory that suddenly came back as if it were yesterday—her mother holding her and humming in her ear as her father plucked the harp and sang.

Somewhere in the background, she still heard Séana's chant, but her father's voice became stronger the closer she drew to him. Slowly, he backed away, beckoning her to follow. He led her through green fields dotted with spring flowers. Vaguely, she wondered why those flowers were blooming when winter was nearly upon them, but his music lured her on and on. Gradually, all became dark again. He reached out and parted a veil beyond which there were no fires. His eyes, the color of a summer sky, crinkled as he laughed.

"Come, Caymin."

She moved toward him and had nearly reached the veil when something grabbed her from behind. Struggling, she pulled against the something as her father waited, calling and holding the veil for her.

She gave a great cry as she was wrenched away from him, hurtling through the night toward a blinding light. She landed in a heap. Dazed, she looked up to find Péist and the others hovering over her. Broc stood on her chest, her nose pressed to Caymin's.

"What happened?" Caymin asked faintly.

Broc jumped down, and Séana helped her to sit up.

"You tell us what happened," Gai said, his face white, his hands shaking.

"We thought we'd lost you, little badger." Méav's face, too, was drawn.

"*You frightened us,*" said Péist.

She saw that dawn was breaking in the east. "How can it be morning? We only just drank the poitín and went into our spiritwalks."

"Méav and I returned from our spiritwalks half the night ago," Gai said. "We couldn't wake you."

Caymin rubbed her forehead. She felt ill. "I was moving from fire to fire, reaching out to those with power. And then I saw my father. He came for me, played his harp and sang for me. He was leading me..." She gasped. "He was leading me through the veil. I nearly went with him. Something pulled me back."

"That something was Péist." Méav heaved a great sigh. "He was the only one who could reach you."

Péist nuzzled her, and Caymin felt his distress.

"But that was only a little while ago."

"No, it was not. It was a battle that lasted half the night."

"How is that possible?"

Méav held out a water skin, and Caymin took a tentative sip, afraid her stomach might reject even that.

"It was Timmin," Méav said.

Caymin choked. "You saw him?"

"No. He never showed himself." Méav scowled. "But I felt his power pushing into your mind. He knew how to reach you. How to draw you to him."

"But he is here? In the forest?"

Méav nodded. "I think he is. Somewhere."

"Niall! Is he safe?"

"Be easy," Méav said. "He passed his trials. He's earned his staff. He's standing guard at the village."

"Do you think you can walk?" Séana asked.

Caymin nodded. "I think so."

She turned to the badgers. *"Thank you for keeping watch over us. Go get some sleep."*

Cuán raised his face to her. *"You are sure, little one?"*

"I am sure. I will see you later. Go now."

The badgers trundled off, and the small band of mages began the trek down the hill while Péist soared in low circles overhead where he could keep an eye on them.

"If Timmin shows himself, I want to be there to greet him."

Back in the village, Niall met them, proudly holding his new staff.

"I am happy for you," Caymin said, running a finger along the holly. She felt a tremor of power in the wood. "Are you not leaving to begin your life as a full mage?"

"Not yet. Not while the forest is in danger." Niall glanced over as Péist glided into the village and walked toward them. "I couldn't have done it if it hadn't been for you and Péist."

"If it were not for us," Péist said, *"you would not have had to leave the forest in the first place."*

"Not true," said Méav. "Angus had designs of his own long ago, or he wouldn't have sent Diarmit here. The forest was in danger with or without you."

"I think we all need to eat and rest," Séana said.

She unpacked some smoked venison and oatcakes, passing them out while Gai told Niall what had happened during the night.

Caymin sat silently off to one side while the others discussed their thoughts on how to flush Timmin from wherever he was hiding. Séana came to sit beside her.

"What troubles you?"

Caymin could not meet her eyes. "He knows my weakness. He used it and nearly got what he desired."

"No." Séana wrapped her arms around her and held her tightly. "'Tis not weakness to miss your family. To want to see them. Don't ever think that way."

"*She is right, little one,*" Péist said from where he lay curled up. "*If ever we lose that, we lose something vital. If we lose that, what are we fighting for?*"

CHAPTER 10

MAGE AND MONK

E nat struggled to sit against the rough stone of her hut. Her head was still groggy from the double dose of his potion Angus had forced down her throat to dull her mind for Samhain. He was taking no chances that she could connect with others on a night filled with power.

She tried to quell her despair, reminding herself that she had allowed this to happen for a reason. She kept her eyes shut as she centered her power, trying to heal her own injuries from Angus's latest round of questioning. He was determined to get his hands on a staff and gain entry to the mystical forest—she shuddered to think what he wanted to do to it, or to what purpose he would use the additional power he would gain there.

A cut on her cheek stung, and her eye was nearly swollen shut, but she focused her energy on healing her abdomen. She was fairly certain his kicks and blows had induced some bleeding. What she really needed was one of her potions to stem the bleeding and replenish her blood.

As if he'd heard her silent plea, the door opened and Diarmit slipped inside. He knelt beside her.

"Here, drink this." He held a bottle to her lips, tipping some of the liquid it held into her mouth.

She choked a little, but got most of the potion down her throat. "I remember," she rasped, "when you thought this potion was beneath you. Thank you."

He sat back on his heels.

Her one good eye focused on him. "You don't look good."

He barked a laugh and immediately glanced toward the door to see if anyone had heard. "You should see yourself."

Enat waved a hand dismissively. "Are you ready to leave?"

Diarmit bit his lip. "Even if I were, you can't travel."

It was the first time he'd spoken so. She sat up straighter. "What is Angus planning?"

He shook his head. "I'm not sure, but he's got every available man sharpening swords or making bows and fletching arrows." His eyes when he looked at her were frightened. "He'll be marching soon."

Voices outside made Diarmit jump. He went to the door and listened for them to go.

"Diarmit, I'll be ready when you are."

With one last shake of his head, he cracked the door open and crept out.

Enat settled back against the wall again, feeling the potion at work. A sudden noise startled her. There, in the narrow window built into the wall, sat a crow.

"Greetings, old friend."

Enat burst into tears. Beanna fluttered down from the window to Enat's knee, tilting her head as she watched helplessly.

"I am sorry, Beanna. You do not know how happy I am to see you." Enat wiped her face. "How did you find me?"

"I saw the traitor and followed him."

"No. How did you know where I am?"

"Caymin found your staff and your message."

Enat gasped. "Caymin is here?"

Beanna tore a bit of bread loose. "She and the flying worm are in Éire. As is Garvan."

101

"Who is Garvan?"

"A holy man whose boat was broken on the endless water. Caymin and Péist saved him and healed him. He has pledged himself to our cause. He is here now, learning what he can of this Angus and his plans. He and I traveled together."

Enat closed her eyes. "I had almost given up hope."

Beanna clicked her beak. "Never give up hope, Enat. All will be well. Péist is flying Caymin and young Gai in search of Méav."

Enat's eyes snapped open. "Caymin is traveling with Gai?"

Beanna fluffed her feathers and settled as if she were on a clutch of eggs. "There is much to tell you."

Gai and Méav were seeing to the weapons Ivar had left behind—polishing and sharpening swords and spears, repairing bows, making new arrows—while Caymin, Séana and Niall went to the planted clearing that had not been harvested.

"We're going to need more than eggs and chicken if we're to be here for a moon or more," Séana had pointed out reasonably as they gathered the eggs they could find while the village chickens squawked and scratched. "We should see if there's aught left to gather."

Many of the root vegetables were still good, as were about half of the apples on the trees. The beans had withered, and most of the cabbages had been eaten by rabbits and deer, though there were some whole enough to harvest. The barley, wheat and oat stalks had dried out, but were still standing. Some had been grazed, but most was waiting to be threshed and gathered.

They worked for days, storing most of the food in the cold cellar and grinding some of the grains into flour to bake with.

Péist flew over the forest, keeping watch over them and rarely letting Caymin out of his sight. "I do not trust Timmin. He will try again to lure you from me."

The only time he left her was to hunt, which he continued to do outside the magical boundaries of the forest. Now that Méav and Niall could allow him to re-enter, leaving was not a problem. He brought enough meat back to share with the two-legs so that they had no need to hunt. Some they made into thick stews that warmed now that the weather had turned frosty, some they smoked and cured to save for when they would be forced to travel.

Nearly a handful of nights after Samhain, they were gathered around the hearth in the meetinghouse, sharing a meal, when a voice hailed them from outside.

"You in there!"

They jumped up and ran out to find Ronan standing there, grinning at them through a thick beard. After a flurry of slaps on the shoulder from Méav and Niall, he turned to greet the others. He didn't try to hide his surprise at seeing Gai.

"You're back, are you?"

Gai gave him a tight-lipped smile. "Obviously."

Caymin knew Ronan still half-suspected that Gai had been the one to attack Fergus the first night they took their trials.

"You do not know," she said.

He turned to her. "I don't know what, little badger?"

The others hid their smiles as they glanced at one another. Ronan looked at them, perplexed.

"What don't I know?"

His question was answered a heartbeat later as Péist dropped from the skies with a loud thump to land with his forelegs braced on either side of Caymin. With a cry, Ronan jumped back, lifting his staff, which immediately glowed red in his hands.

Caymin leapt between them, holding her hands out. "Stop! This is Péist."

Ronan's mouth opened and closed like a fish several times. "Péist. The worm." He looked to the others as if expecting them to burst into laughter at the hoax, but Méav nodded.

"Not a worm any longer."

Péist lowered his head. *"You welcomed me to your fire the night we met. The night I bonded with my mage. I thank you, Ronan."*

Ronan could only utter a kind of whimper. "I need to sit down."

"Come in by the fire," Séana said. She wrapped her arm around his shoulders and guided him inside as he kept twisting to look back at the white dragon crouching outside the door.

A short while later, Ronan's mouth gaped open again. "You mean Diarmit was the one all along? He attacked Péist and Fergus? And Enat was daft enough to let him go and try to protect him? What was she thinking?"

Méav shrugged. "She's Enat. She looks for the best in everyone."

Ronan snorted. "Even when it's not there."

"She saw it in me," Gai said quietly. "When no one else did."

An embarrassed silence followed his words.

"You're right," Ronan said at last. "My apology to you, Gai."

Their eyes met.

"You only thought what everyone else did," Gai said.

"But we were all wrong," said Méav. "You more than proved yourself when you stood up to your father and brother when they failed to honor their agreement with Caymin and Péist."

Faint patches of scarlet colored Gai's cheeks.

Ronan turned to Caymin. "So you haven't had any word from this monk who went to join Angus?"

"No."

His bearded jaw worked back and forth. "You're sure you can trust him? What if he joins this other monk and tells him of you?"

"We do not believe Garvan will do that," said Péist from where he lay, listening to the conversation. *"He gave us his word and has given us no reason to doubt him."*

"That's a lot of trust," said Ronan stubbornly.

Caymin tilted her head. "This is too big to do alone. We must trust one another or we will fail."

"Fair enough," Ronan conceded with a nod. "So what's the plan?"

"We think Angus and the followers he's gathered will march on this forest sooner or later," said Méav. "But they may attack other places of power on the way here. We've reached out to all we could on Samhain. Hopefully, they're preparing and on their way to us now."

"We've been readying weapons," Niall said. "Mages will enter the forest from all directions and, we don't know which direction Angus will come from. We should distribute weapons to various places in the forest so we have them available wherever we may need them."

He pulled out one of Ivar's maps of the forest and pointed. "We know the invaders from the north came in here, from the lake. Angus might do the same."

Ronan pointed to other likely places. "Here and here. But it took us two days' walk to get there when the invaders came last time."

"Caymin and I can fly the weapons to those places," Péist said. *"We can get them all done in one day."*

Méav smiled. "Whatever followers Angus has gathered to him, it can't beat having a dragon."

Despite the nature of their mission, the time alone together was joyous for Caymin and Péist.

"We have not been alone together for so long," Caymin said as she spread her arms wide, her face raised to the skies as Péist swooped over the treetops.

"Far too long." Péist rose into the air, twirling as he let loose a blast of flames and flew through them.

They delivered a mix of swords, spears, bows, and quivers of arrows to the designated places. The sun was just nearing the far horizon as they dropped off the last of the weapons.

"Take us to the stone circle."

Péist obliged, flying to the clearing where stood the ancient stones that fairly trembled with power of their own.

He landed in the center of the circle, the stones standing like ancient sentries—covered in lichens and moss—throwing long, crooked shadows in the slanting rays of the sunlight.

"Why did you want to stop here?"

Caymin paced the interior of the circle, her arms spread as she absorbed the vibrations of power within it. *"You and I are at the mercy of events taking place around us, and over which we have no control."*

Péist crouched, his wings furled and his legs tucked under him. "*You are speaking of Dughall and his clan?*"

"*Yes. And more. I was told I had to forgive, to seek allies among those who I considered enemies. We did that, and they turned on us. Timmin is still out there, wanting to use you.*"

She sat down against his side. "*You and I must decide what path we will take, and how far we are willing to go to achieve it.*"

"*Others will want to use us toward their ends.*"

"*We already saw that with Dughall. Others will be the same.*"

Péist lowered his head to rest his cheek against her shoulder. "*Have you thought of what happens if we are successful against Angus?*"

She leaned more heavily against him. "*You mean, do we only fight to protect the mystical forest or do we try to drive them from Éire entirely?*"

"*As Timmin would want.*"

"*We have only been among two-legs for a short time, but the tide of the world is changing from what it was. Enat has told me many stories from when she was young, and it is not like that any longer. The followers of the Christ are many, and not all are bad people. Look at Garvan.*"

Péist closed his eyes as he soaked up the last of the weak sunshine. "*But can there be a truce in which both sides are willing to allow the other to exist in peace?*"

They sat in silence for a long while as twilight wrapped itself around them. Péist opened one eye.

"*Something else troubles you.*"

"*The others look to us for leadership, but they are so much older. How can we be their leaders?*"

"*We must, so we will. But there may come a day when we can no longer support what they want.*"

Caymin woke in an unfamiliar bed, listening to Méav and Séana's breathing from the bed that had been Neela's. The boys had all taken up their former beds in the boys' cottage in the village. Caymin had wanted to go back to Enat's cottage but, after Samhain, Méav had insisted it was too far away.

"We need to stay close," she'd said.

"Timmin?"

"Anything," said Ronan when they debated it again after his arrival. "If anyone else gets through the forest's protections, we may only have a short bit of warning. We need to be together."

Caymin had turned away. Séana came to her.

"What is it?"

"You and Méav will want to be alone at night."

Séana wrapped her in a hug. "What we want is to keep you safe." She'd kissed the top of Caymin's head and released her.

Caymin reached up now to touch her head where Séana had kissed her. She knew from her spiritwalks that her mother and father had held her, had loved her, but she had no memory of being hugged and kissed like that. Sudden tears stung her eyes.

Silently, she got out of bed and added some peat to the fire to ward off the early morning chill in the cottage. She let herself out the door and went to the latrine. Péist, she knew, was off hunting. She could feel him in the distance. Overhead, the stars were just beginning to fade as the sky to the east began to lighten.

She made her way to the meetinghouse and magically lit the fire there. Likewise, she lit a couple of candles on the long table and pulled some of the scrolls from where they had been returned to the shelves. She was looking for any information she could find on the last dragon war, but there had been very little about that war here. She wished she could have brought some of the books and scrolls she and Péist had found in the dragon caves on Inishbreith, but with Garvan's extra weight, they had had to leave all behind.

A sudden gust of wind made her candles gutter as the door opened and Gai entered.

"You couldn't sleep, either?" he asked as he joined her at the table. She shook her head.

He pulled one of the candles near and waved a finger, making the flame twirl and dance. "Remember when this was hard to do?"

She watched his face in the flickering light. He bit his lip as he stared at the flame.

"What is wrong?" she asked.

"I keep thinking about how things were a winter ago. We were all here, learning as we should have been. The elders were together, not scattered all over Éire. There was no war looming over us."

He raised his gaze to hers. "Are you frightened?"

"Yes," she said. "I have no wish to fight, but I will to protect the places of power." She regarded him. "Are you?"

He dropped his gaze back to the candle. "Yes."

It was strange to hear Gai, the boy who had bragged the most about using real weapons and sparring with his father's warriors, admitting he was frightened of the pending war.

As if he sensed what she was thinking, his mouth twisted. "You think I'm weak."

"No!"

"My father would say I am. He would say I'm not worthy of being his son."

"Enat would say only a fool glories in fighting." She tilted her head. "I think you must be more like your mother, and I think that is a good thing."

Gai blinked rapidly. "I wish I could remember her."

"Do you ever see her in spiritwalks?"

He shook his head.

She sighed. "That is the only time I have seen my mother or father. I wish I could remember more of them."

They both jumped as something heavy hit one of the shuttered windows. Caymin stood ready to cast a protective spell as Gai went to the window. He jerked the shutter open to find an owl sitting on the ledge, shaking her head.

"Ivar is on his way."

The owl spread her wings and took off silently into the dawn twilight.

Péist flew over the forest, flapping his wings in a slow rhythm as the cold night air offered no updrafts for him to soar on. The hunting had been good, and he would not need to hunt again for three or four days. As he flew, his keen gaze scanned the terrain below. As always in the dark, his eyes adjusted to detect shapes emitting heat. Four-legs, small and large, moved about in the forest while winged ones—probably owls—hunted.

He banked and made for the periphery of the forest, scanning for any activity beyond its borders. They had vague information that Angus, when he came, would be coming from the south, but they had no way of knowing if he had allies who might come from other directions.

All was quiet as he flew along the forest's edge. He was just preparing to turn and fly back toward the village when his attention was diverted to a band of two-legs approaching the forest. The others were nowhere near enough to intervene. He hesitated a moment, considering whether to send a warning to Caymin, but now... he had the element of surprise.

He dove, gathering flame in his maw, ready to loose it at them, when suddenly he heard, *"Stay! We are friends of Caymin!"*

With a mighty effort, he beat his wings to break his dive, buffeting the two-legs with the force of his wind. Circling, he landed in front of them.

A female two-leg stepped forward, her gold-colored hair catching the light of the waxing moon. *"I am Neela, one of the elders of the forest. We saw those who called to us the night of Samhain and have come to help."*

A large male two-leg, most of his face obscured by black beard, stood beside her, holding a sword aggressively pointed in Péist's direction while his other hand grasped his staff. Behind them, the other two-legs, perhaps a score or more, cowered, holding to one another as they stared up at him in terror.

Neela spoke again. *"You are Péist."*

"I am."

She looked up at him in wonder. *"Enat told us she was certain you were a dragon, but never did we think to see dragons in Éire again."*

The male shifted.

"This is Ivar," she said.

Péist lowered his head. "*Caymin has spoken well of both of you.*"

"*She is here?*"

"*With Méav and her mate, as well as Gai and Niall and Ronan. They will be happy to see you.*"

Ivar dropped his sword, but only a little. "*Where are they?*"

"*At the village.*" Péist lifted his head. "*If you will permit me to fly back through the forest's protections, I will tell them you are coming.*"

Ivar lifted the sword again. "*The forest is still guarded? Then how have you been getting in?*"

"*Méav, Ronan or Niall allow me passage.*"

"*Niall?*"

"*He earned his staff on Samhain. Méav helped him to prepare.*" Péist huffed impatiently. "*Are you going to question me until daybreak?*"

Neela laid a hand on Ivar's arm. "*Stop, Ivar. He is bonded to Caymin, and Enat risked all to save him.*"

Ivar scowled but lowered his sword. Neela raised her staff and whispered words as the wood glowed white in the night. She and Ivar waved the others through.

"*I will tell them to expect you,*" Péist said as he lifted off.

By the time Péist got back to the village, he found the others awake and gathered. "*You know?*"

"*An owl brought a message that Ivar was coming,*" said Caymin.

"*Not only Ivar. Neela is with him as well as several other two-legs.*"

Méav stood. "*Neela is with him?*"

"*Yes. They should be here by midday.*"

She dropped back down to her seat and closed her eyes. "Thank the gods and goddesses."

Péist backed away as they began talking. He shielded his voice from all but Caymin. "*Come with me.*"

She followed him into the outskirts of the forest.

"*Why is Méav so relieved to have them here?*" he asked.

Caymin glanced back at the others. "*I think it is because we are all so young, barely more than children to two-legs.*"

"*Though I was here as a worm for over a hundred winters, I have had less than one as a dragon. We are young.*"

"I think that is also what worries Riona and Ailill."
"Young or old, we are here and they are not."

"My brothers and sisters, God has called us to be his mighty arm, to wipe out the idolaters and heathens from Éire!"

Garvan listened from the back of the gathered crowd as Angus went on, repeating much the same message he delivered every second or third evening when the day's work was done. The torches burning around him added to the maniacal expression that lit his features. What was new was a large embroidered banner depicting a wolf holding a cross.

"God has spoken to me!" Angus went on. "He has appointed me his voice in this wilderness. I am the Wolf of God! We must see that all in Éire are brought to see him as the one, true God!"

There were shouts of agreement from the assembly, and Garvan mimicked their nods of approval at Angus's message.

"He speaks to me even now!"

Angus went rigid, then his arms thrashed about and the torches were extinguished. A few people screamed in the unexpected darkness. A brilliant column of fire suddenly rose up, with Angus standing in the midst of it. More people screamed and yelled and then, they all fell to their knees.

While everyone's attention was focused on Angus, Garvan stole away from the others to where Beanna sat perched on top of one of the stone beehive huts. Glancing around first to make sure no one else was watching him, he lifted the bar off the door and peered into the dark interior as Beanna fluttered down to the window in the stone wall.

"Enat?"

A light flared in the darkness as Enat conjured a ball of flame and held it in her palm. "Garvan?" her voice rasped. "Beanna told me you would come."

He had to crouch to pass under the low lintel, wrinkling his nose at the stench that hit him. Enat sat, her hair matted, her tunic filthy. Her eyes filled with tears as she looked at him.

"I never thought to find a friend here," she whispered.

He set the staff down and knelt beside her, offering her a drink from the water skin hung over his shoulder. With a flick of her hand, the flame moved to float in the air as she gulped some of the water down. She laid her hand over his.

"Thank you."

Beanna flapped to her knee, tilting her head as she clicked her beak. Enat stroked her breast.

"Thank you both."

"Caymin and Péist send their greetings," Garvan said. He scanned her frail body, doubting that she would be able to offer much resistance to Angus, with or without her staff.

She must have read the hesitation in his eyes, because she reached for the staff lying on the ground. At her touch, it glowed white, dazzling in the darkness of the hut. She closed her eyes, seeming to drink in energy from the staff much as she had drunk water a moment ago.

"Are you well enough to fight your way out of here?" Garvan asked.

She nodded and opened her eyes, letting the staff go back to being plain wood. "I am, but we'll need to choose the right time." She took another drink. "Do you know Angus's plans yet?"

Garvan shook his head. "From his preparations, it'll be soon. He's got wagons loaded, weapons stockpiled. The Wolf of God is down there, setting himself on fire and stirring them all up as we speak."

"The Wolf of God?"

"That's what he's calling himself now." He chuckled. "I have to admit, a few moons ago, I would have been on my knees as well, watching his magic tricks."

Enat eyed him shrewdly. "Why aren't you there? Why are you doing this?"

Beanna clicked her beak again, and he smiled. "They saved my life. They didn't have to, but they did. A girl and a dragon. And they've shown me that magic can be used for good. I don't see it as incompatible with a belief in God. I've sworn my service to Caymin and Péist, and I'll die before I break that oath."

"Have you seen the boy, Diarmit?"

"Beanna pointed him out to me," Garvan said. "He hasn't paid me any attention, so I don't think he's recognized Beanna from any of the other crows here. He won't be able to sound any kind of alarm."

"We have to take him with us when we go."

Garvan sat back, frowning. "When we go, we'll need to be moving quickly. We won't have time to force a petulant boy along with us."

"He's scared, Garvan." Enat held his gaze. "He is ready to leave Angus, he just doesn't know how. Promise me you'll try."

He stared into her eyes for a long moment before nodding. "I'll try. But if he refuses or hesitates, we're leaving without him."

CHAPTER 11

Escape

For a while, life in the forest felt almost as it had before, except with more apprentices. The people who had come with Ivar and Neela took up the leftover beds in the boys' and girls' cottages, while Ivar moved in with Neela, leaving his cottage for several of the others. Méav and Séana joined Caymin in Enat's cottage along with another woman named Fiona.

Not everyone who had answered the plea for help had magic. Most had some, though not all had earned their staffs. They had some training and could make potions and work simple spells, but their power was limited. Accompanying them were non-magic folk who believed in power and wanted to fight to help protect it.

Ivar and Neela seemed generally pleased with the state of the weapons and the work that had been done to make them ready in various parts of the forest.

Once they were over their shock at seeing a dragon in their midst, all had accepted Péist's presence with some amount of awe, certain he would ensure their eventual victory. Or nearly all. Ivar continued to eye him balefully.

They spent much of their time sparring—something even Caymin quickly saw was badly needed, as most of those who had come to help had even less skill with weapons than she. Ivar wandered among them as they practiced with staffs, spears, and fake swords. Neela guided those on the archery field. Caymin and the other recent apprentices were the most accomplished and so acted as sparring partners for the others. Caymin still could not fend off an attack with a staff or sword, but she persevered as best she could, picking herself up again and again.

"*You are a dragonmage,*" Péist said with a growl as he watched. "*Why are you permitting this humiliation?*"

Caymin dusted herself off and grinned in his direction. "*It is good practice for me. I may have to fight hand to hand.*"

"*You will not. We will be together.*"

"*But will we? There may be times when we need to be in different places.*"

Péist huffed his displeasure, sending a plume of smoke skyward.

The evenings were spent communally with everyone pitching in to prepare meals. Fortunately, the newcomers had come loaded with as much food as they could carry. Péist continued to hunt for all of them, bringing entire deer carcasses back after he had eaten his fill.

Following the meal, Ivar usually spread out his maps, strategizing as to where the invaders would most likely try and enter the forest. He used small stones and crystals as representatives of the various factions, moving them about his map.

"Why would he attack in the winter?" asked one man who had accompanied them.

"Probably because no one would expect him to attack in winter," said Ivar. "Yes, it'll be cold, but it'll be easier to get the wagons over frozen ground than the soft mud in the spring. He won't wait. I wouldn't."

Neela looked around. "We haven't had word from Angus's camp yet that they're on the move, but we should probably send small parties out to keep watch where Caymin and Péist have already stashed weapons."

"Who do we have in Angus's camp?" Fiona asked.

"Enat is there." Neela pursed her lips. "She'll send word when she can."

"Will she?" Fiona looked doubtful. "Hasn't she been there for several moons? Do we even know if she's still alive?"

Caymin stood, bristling. "She is. I know it."

Neela laid a hand on Caymin's shoulder. "Enat is canny. And she should have allies there now. She'll find a way."

"We would know if she were dead," Péist said.

Ivar scowled toward the door of the meetinghouse. "Why is he here?" he muttered.

"Why should he not be here?" Caymin challenged him. "Why are you so hostile to him?"

Ivar's black brows knitted together as he frowned at her. "I'll tell you why. Because his kind was responsible for the last great war."

Caymin drew herself up. "You mean my kind as well. It was dragons and mages who started the war."

They glared at each other for several heartbeats.

"Very well," he said. "Since you said it first, yes. Your kind."

"But it was also our kind who stopped it," Péist reminded them. *"Angus is a two-leg mage, with no bond to a dragon, who is starting a war, yet we are not looking at all of you as if you were the cause. Dragons and their mages are no different. Some grew hungry for power and tried to force their will on all. Others disagreed and fought them."*

"He's right," Neela said. "Péist has saved us in the past, and he's on our side now. We must trust him."

Ivar's lips disappeared behind his bushy whiskers as if he was holding back the words that longed to burst forth. He turned back to his map.

Caymin limped out of the meetinghouse and strapped herself onto Péist's saddle. *"Let us fly."*

Péist spread his wings and leapt into the night. They soared over the forest.

"He is right, little one," Péist said. *"Scolai and Tuala did start the last war."*

"And you were right. Dragons and mages like Ríona and Ailill stopped it."

"Still, Ivar has reason to distrust us. And he would distrust us even more if he knew of the Bloodstone."

They flew, both enjoying the silence after days of nothing but talk. The night was overcast with only a dim glow of the moon from behind the clouds.

"If this war is coming, I wish it would get here," said Caymin. *"I am tired of the waiting."*

"I, too, am restless. But I think, once it is here, we will wish it were not."

By the time the moon waxed to full, the small village in the forest was overflowing with people come from various directions, magic and non-magic folk together.

Daina and Fergus arrived with a large band of people from the north and west, and some days later, Cíana and Una did the same from the south. Fergus brought news.

"I've taken a mate. She's heavy with our first child, too far along to come with me." The grin on his face faded a bit into a dazed stare. "By the time I get back to her, I should be a father."

"But you should be with her," Caymin fretted.

He smiled again. "She's got women about her who can help. And I'm where I'm meant to be."

Being reunited with her first two-leg friends felt almost as happy for Caymin as when the badgers had arrived at the forest, but her happiness was tempered by the fact that Enat, Beanna and Garvan were not there and had not sent word.

Their reunion was cut short by the news they brought.

"As we traveled, we heard tidings of Angus and his followers," Una told Neela and Ivar. "We saw them. There must be hundreds. We had to skirt wide to get round them on our way north."

"But they weren't marching yet?" Ivar asked.

"Not yet."

As he had when they went to the Eoganacht, Péist grew weary of being gawked at by the newly arrived who were first terrified and then delighted to learn they had a dragon on their side.

"I feel as if I am going to step on one of them like a beetle. I will stay at

the circle of stones. It is large enough for me to move and close enough that I can be here in a few beats of my wings if you need me."

As soon as they could, Cíana and Daina pulled Caymin into the forest where they could speak.

"You have grown," she said to them. "How has it been, being back among your families?"

They glanced at each other.

"Different," said Daina. "More of the people around us are Christians now, so my mother warned me to be careful about using magic. Mostly, I've just made potions and remedies for the ill. I've had little chance to practice anything else."

Cíana nodded. "I as well. We've not as many Christians among us, but without a staff and all my training, I can't do very much." She fingered Caymin's braids. "You've changed."

Caymin blushed. "I grew weary of people flinching when they see my scars. If they think I am something to be feared, I may as well look it."

She looked from one of them to the other. "Tell me what happened after we left."

"We didn't know what to think when Enat brought Diarmit back, all tied up," said Daina. "It was still a half a moon before Ivar and then Neela got back with the apprentices they had reaped. Poor things. They'd barely got here when they all had to go home."

"Niall said the elders argued about what to do with Diarmit," Caymin said.

Cíana nodded. "They did. Ivar wanted..." She glanced at Daina. "Well, we're not sure what he wanted, but he didn't want to let him go. In the end, Enat convinced them that they couldn't harm him, no matter what he'd done. They decided to let Enat follow him to see what she could learn before this priest could attack." She reached for Caymin's hand. "But tell us about you."

Caymin told them of the elk carrying her and Péist's egg until he began to hatch, of their journey out of the forest. She told of flying to an island to let Péist grow and get stronger, and of her spiritwalk where she saw the coming war.

Daina looked at her, her eyes wide. "You really saw it?"

"I think I only saw what might be, to give us time to stop it."

She did not tell them of her most recent vision of the forest being destroyed, but that image became more real with every band of people who arrived to help. What she hadn't anticipated was the drain these extra humans put on the forest's resources. A system that had been harmonious with the rhythm of the forest when there were no more than a score of two-legs living there was suddenly wildly out of balance.

Though the newcomers were respectful of not cutting any trees or branches, the demand for food and peat for fires soon outstripped what was available.

"*I cannot hunt for myself and all of these others as well,*" Péist told Neela as she tried to ration what food stores they had.

By day, while Péist rested from his nights of flying, Caymin often took refuge in the badger sett, curling up with Broc and Cuán and the others.

She lay with her head resting on Broc's warm body. She could feel the movements of the cubs growing inside her. "*You will give birth soon.*"

"*Yes. I worry that I will be with the newborn cubs when you have need of us.*"

Cuán nuzzled her. "*You will take care of our young. The rest of us will do any guarding that needs to be done.*"

The sett had been expanded as the younger cubs who had come to the forest with them had found mates among the badgers already living there. Their small clan had nearly doubled in the time they had been in the forest.

"*The energy of the forest has changed,*" said Broc.

Caymin sat up. "*It has. There are too many two-legs here now.*"

"*It is sad that the two-legs who come to protect the forest may be the ones to destroy it.*"

Walking back to the village, Caymin's heart was heavy as she thought about Broc's words. She passed small encampments of newcomers, living in hastily constructed shelters with fires burning in front of them.

She sought out Neela who was going through the food stores with Séana.

"How many days' worth of food do we have?"

Neela sighed as she looked at the shrinking stockpile of food. "Even with what people have brought with them, we've not enough to keep everyone here fed for more than another moon."

"I was thinking..."

Neela turned to her. "What were you thinking?"

Ivar and Neela called a meeting. Everyone gathered in the center of the village, as the meetinghouse was now the bedding place for as many as could fit.

"It's time to disperse all of you to various points around the forest, or just outside," Ivar said. "We'll assign a mage to each band as much as we can, so that those with a staff can leave and enter as needed."

He handed out gold tokens, the remnants of Gai and Caymin's torqs, now melted and divided into small pieces.

"Take these," Neela said, giving each group a map. "They'll point you to the weapons that have been hidden. Go to the villages and farms outside the forest. Explain to them what is coming and ask for their help with food and supplies. They may not have magic, and they've never been in the forest, but they feel its presence. If they resist, remind them how many times they've asked us for help when they or their animals were ill or injured and that we were the ones who turned back the invaders who came here a summer ago. Tell them that when Angus and his warriors get here, they won't look kindly on any who've trafficked with magic. We must band together."

She held up a parchment and called out names of people, putting a mage in charge of most groups. People found their places and began to organize.

"What about us?" Una asked as she, Daina, Gai and Ciana gathered with the newest mages.

Méav, Niall, Ronan and Fergus stood with their staffs. Caymin saw Una eye Niall's staff resentfully as Ivar joined them.

"Come with me," he said.

He led the small band aside and spoke in a low voice. "Caymin came to us with an idea. Rather than sitting about, eating up all of our food until we have to attack the forest we're sworn to protect, we're going to take the fight to Angus."

The others looked at one another in surprise.

"So nine of us are going to take on Angus and his warriors?" Fergus asked.

"Not nine," said Séana. She stood among them with a sword belted to her waist. "Twelve with Neela, Ivar and myself."

"And Péist," Caymin said.

Méav grinned. "Aye, let's not forget the dragon."

"Angus won't expect such a small group to take him on," Neela said. "And we suspect, if he's pretending to hate magic and the old ways so much, he's not revealed to his followers that he himself has power. Diarmit may be the only one to know. When we meet them, he'll either have to fight without magic or show himself for what he truly is."

Ivar nodded. "That may cost him."

Neela looked around at all of them. "You're the youngest among us, but the ones we want with us. There's no shame, though, in opting not to do this. If you'd rather go with one of the other groups to wait for the fight to come to us, we understand."

The young ones all glanced at one another. "I don't see anyone leaving," Niall said.

Ivar nodded. "Good. Get packed. We leave at dawn."

As the group dispersed, Gai turned to Caymin, his face troubled. "Even if he couldn't change my father's mind, I thought Eachna would be here with some of my clan."

She reached out for his arm. "They may yet arrive. But I am glad you are with us."

They got to their feet to go pack food and supplies when Caymin suddenly whipped around.

"Péist!"

Péist lay with his snout tucked under one wing as he curled up in his trance. He twitched as his mind roamed while his body recharged in preparation for the upcoming journey.

In his trance, he soared over green fields in search of prey. In the distance flew a bird. As it drew near, it became larger and larger until he saw that it wasn't a bird at all. It was a dragon. A brilliantly crimson dragon, brighter than a sunset sky. Nearer and nearer it came, bugling a welcome.

Overjoyed at the sight of another of his kind, Péist flew in spirals, dancing in the air with the red dragon. He didn't know how he knew she was female, but he did. Together, they tore through low-hanging clouds, dragging trails of vapor after them. They trumpeted into the skies, breathing plumes of fire and plunging through the heat in tandem.

Without warning, the crimson dragon banked and soared out over the endless water. Péist followed. Folding her blood-red wings tight to her body, the other dragon fell from the skies, arrowing into the water with barely a splash.

Péist heard her calling to him, urging him to follow. He soared tight circles above where she had entered the water, where she was waiting for him—another dragon, here in this realm, one he could perhaps mate with. And still, he hesitated, his wings twitching, pulling in, allowing him to plunge through the air, only to flare out and up again just before he hit the water. He *felt* her just there, under the surface, waiting for him.

But something else called to him... a voice far, far away. He turned. He loved that voice and the two-leg it belonged to, more than anything. Again, he circled, listening to the call of the dragon waiting for him, but the voice in his head was becoming clearer, louder. Reluctantly, he arced away from the place where the scarlet dragon had dived into the water and flew back toward land, toward Caymin. With one last glance back, he saw the red dragon's head break through the waves.

He flew fast now, over fields, over forest. Inside the stone circle was what looked like a snow-covered hillock. Péist was surprised to realize he was seeing himself lying in a heap, with Caymin and Gai shouting at him. He tried to join his body and wake, but... he couldn't. He was stuck, outside and apart from all of them. Caymin knelt at his head, her hands on him, her eyes closed, her body rigid, as she summoned her power and pulled him... pulled him back to her.

It was like being dragged through a darkness so thick that it choked off breath, squeezed until he was sure he would burst from the pressure and then, suddenly, he gasped, drawing deep breaths into his lungs.

He opened his eyes to see Caymin crying as she wrapped her arms around his neck.

"Do not cry, little one."

"I thought I had lost you. That you would not come back to me. What happened? Where were you?"

Péist slowly raised his head. *"I do not know. I was resting, and then a red dragon came to me, led me out over the endless water and wanted to me dive under the surface to join her."*

Gai dropped to his knees beside Caymin. *"You saw another dragon? Is there another here?"*

"I do not believe so. I cannot explain, but I do not think she was here."

"Timmin."

Caymin and Péist both stared at him.

"What do you mean?" Caymin asked.

"He used a vision of your father to try and pull you through the veil on Samhain," Gai reminded her. He looked at Péist. "I think he used a vision of this dragon to pull you into the otherworld."

"What is the otherworld?"

Gai looked from one of them to the other. "You don't know what the otherworld is?"

Caymin shook her head. "We had no one to tell us of these things. The badgers never spoke of it."

"Well, Eachna studied everything he could find on it. He says no one knows for certain, but the old ways teach that the Portals to the otherworld were mostly under water—lakes, rivers, seas. There, the gods and goddesses ruled and used water as the way in and out of this world. And not just gods and goddesses, but other magic creatures as well."

"What would have happened to me if I had entered the endless water with the dragon I saw?"

Gai shrugged. "I don't know, but I think your body would have stayed here while your spirit was trapped in the otherworld."

They were silent for a moment, considering the implications of what might have happened.

"He is using what he knows of us. Your longing for your family. Mine for other dragons. He is using our weaknesses."

Caymin bowed her head at his words.

Gai laid a hand on her shoulder. "I don't think it's weak to want those things, but it does give Timmin an opening to use against you, a way to lure you."

Caymin raised her head, her eyes hard. "We must work harder to block him. We cannot let him separate us from each other."

Through the slit windows of her stone hut, Enat saw the snowflakes coming down in the moonlight. She dug her staff out from where she had hidden it under the dirt and waved it to create a barrier through which no light would pass. Within her magical shelter, she conjured a fire—just enough to warm her without using too much energy.

A black shadow darkened the window. Enat lowered the shield long enough for Beanna to fly through. The crow dropped a large piece of bread in Enat's lap.

"Thank you, old friend," Enat said as she tore a piece off and chewed. *"Is it to be tonight?"*

"Yes." Beanna hopped onto Enat's knee. *"Garvan said to tell you to be ready. He believes the snow will cover our tracks quickly."*

"What of Diarmit?"

"I have been keeping watch over him. I know where he sleeps, but there are other two-legs in there."

"We will have to lure him away from them."

Beanna tilted her head, looking at Enat with her bright eye. "I have thought of that. We know now that he can speak without speaking. I can call to him."

Enat considered. "But what if he runs to Angus?"

Beanna clicked her beak. "Enat, you have sacrificed enough for this young two-leg. If, as you believe, he wants to leave but is frightened, this will be his opportunity. If he chooses to stay and raise an alarm, we must leave him behind."

Enat sighed. "You are right. The choice is his now."

"Garvan will come in a while to unlock your door. Be ready." With those words, Beanna flew away as Enat released her shield and extinguished her fire.

Enat sat, waiting. She shivered, but not now from cold. Her staff she kept grasped in her hands as she closed her eyes and listened, extending her mind out beyond the walls of her hut. Angus had removed her guards long ago, believing her so broken and frail that there was no need for more than a bar across her door. She detected no others moving nearby.

When she heard the scrape of wood against wood, she held her staff at the ready. The door creaked open.

"Enat?" Garvan whispered. "'Tis time."

She got to her feet, and he wrapped a thick woolen cloak around her shoulders. Across his own back he carried a loaded pack. He led the way through the encampment, staying to the shadows.

In the distance, figures could be seen moving around fires. Snow fell thickly, muffling their footsteps and covering them almost immediately. Garvan paused on the far side of an enclosure holding several oxen.

"Beanna is going to the boy now," he whispered. He turned to look at her. "But we're not delaying if he won't come."

She nodded. "Agreed."

Long heartbeats passed as they waited. Enat peered around the corner of the enclosure. The oxen shifted restlessly.

"Do not fear," she reassured them, and they settled.

Beanna appeared, flitting from hut to hut. A human shadow followed her.

"*Wait,*" Diarmit called to the crow. "*I must speak with you.*"

Onward Beanna led him until he came around the corner of the enclosure. Garvan snatched him, clamping a hand over his mouth and twisting one arm behind his back. Diarmit struggled until he saw Enat. His eyes grew wide at the sight of her standing there with her staff.

"Listen to us," she whispered. She laid a hand on Garvan's arm. "Let him go."

"If you yell, I swear by all that's holy, I'll break your arm," Garvan breathed into Diarmit's ear.

Diarmit's eyes flitted around wildly, but he nodded. Garvan carefully released the hand over his mouth. Diarmit twisted around to look from Enat to Garvan and back again.

"What are you doing?" His eyes landed on the staff. He pointed. "Where did you–?"

"We don't have time for questions," Enat said. She stepped near. "I told you I would take you from here. From Angus. You've seen what he's really like, Diarmit. His cruelty, his thirst for power. The choice is yours. Come with us."

"You... you would really take me back? After all I've done?"

"Aye. But you have to decide now."

Diarmit stood there as snow settled on their shoulders. "What'll the others think?" he asked.

"Better question is what will Angus think when he finds Enat gone?" Garvan hissed. "Do you not think he'll suspect you?"

"Diarmit," Enat said. "You've made mistakes. We all do. And you'll have to atone for them, but atoning is better than continuing down a wrong path, a path you'll regret."

Still, Diarmit hesitated, looking back toward the encampment.

"Now, boy," Garvan growled. "What's it to be?"

Diarmit turned back to them. "I'll go with you."

Garvan grabbed him by his cloak. "Come then."

"But my things..." Diarmit pointed back toward his hut.

"No time," Enat said.

Beanna hopped along the edge of the top rail of the enclosure. "*We must leave now.*"

She flew toward a distant patch of forest. Garvan pushed Diarmit ahead of him, and Enat followed.

No sooner had they stepped out of the shadows than a voice hailed them. "Halt! You there!"

They broke into a run, but Enat, so weakened, could only run partway before she stopped, panting. Behind them they heard more men shouting and the pounding of footsteps.

"Go!" Enat said, turning to face their pursuers.

Garvan stepped up beside her, his sword drawn. "We're not leaving you. I promised Caymin I would bring you back."

The men bore down on them, brandishing swords and spears. More men, roused by the shouting, came running.

Enat leveled her staff, which glowed red in her hands, and shot a spell at them, knocking three of the men into the air.

Behind them, another band of warriors sprinted in their direction. She aimed her staff again, and the gate of the enclosure splintered as if kicked by a giant. The oxen, panicked, broke free, trampling all in their path. The warriors were forced to scatter.

Garvan picked Enat up and ran with her, but the men from the encampment regrouped and pursued them, rapidly closing the distance.

"Stop," Enat gasped. "You cannot outrun them. Set me down."

Garvan, heaving for breath, did as she asked. Diarmit joined them as they faced their pursuers.

"Stop her!" cried one.

He pushed through the others, skidding to a halt when he saw the trio standing there.

"Angus," Diarmit whimpered.

"You," he fumed as he caught sight of the boy. "After all I've taught you, all I've done for you, you betray me? You Judas!"

His gaze moved to Garvan. "And you traffic with magic? A monk? Traitor to God, traitor to all that's holy." He focused on Enat standing beside them. His face became livid as he saw her staff. "Where did that come from?"

He raised his sword. "Take them!"

Enat whirled her staff in the air, and a blinding wall of snow rose between them. "Run!" she shouted. Together, they ran, Diarmit and Garvan each taking one of her arms to help her as the wall of snow shielded them.

They reached the protection of the trees. Enat swept her staff behind them to cover their footprints. The warriors pursuing them stopped at the tree line. Enat waited just a moment to see if they would venture into the dark forest. They milled about uncertainly, peering into the shadows.

"After them!" Angus shouted.

Just as they started to enter the trees, Beanna and several other birds burst out of nowhere, flying at them. With their arms covering their heads, the men screamed and fled as the birds pecked and clawed at them.

Taking advantage of the diversion, Enat, Diarmit and Garvan ran on, deeper into the forest before Enat collapsed, gasping for air.

"Rest," Garvan said as he stood guard, watching for any sign of movement behind them.

A black shadow moved through the trees, and Beanna alighted on a branch near them. *"They are gone. Too fearful to come after you now. We have escaped."*

CHAPTER 12

WOLF'S BANE

Péist flew circles, Caymin tethered tightly to the saddle, while they waited for the others to pass through the forest. Una had shown them on Ivar's map where they had seen Angus's forces, in Laigin to the southeast of a great, long river where it drained into a lough.

"You can't miss them," Cíana had said. "There are hundreds of them."

"*This will take many days,*" Péist complained as they flew. "*You and I could be there by sunrise.*"

"*I know, but I think the plan we have is wise. We keep you a secret for as long as possible, letting the others position themselves to be able to attack. You and I cannot attack alone.*"

Clouds hung low over them, promising more snow. Caymin snugged her cloak more tightly under her chin.

When at last, Ivar, Méav and the others emerged from the boundaries of the mystical forest, Péist rose higher, into the clouds, so that other two-legs would not spot them during the day. The water droplets from the clouds gathered on Péist's scales, each gleaming with a tiny rainbow, but Caymin was soon drenched and chilled to the bone, despite Péist's warmth under her. She conjured a spell to dry and warm herself, with only a small drain on her energy. Péist flew above the cloud layer, where the air was thin and cold, but at least the sun felt warm on their faces.

At nightfall, they landed, depositing Caymin with the others while Péist flew off alone to hunt.

"How was your journey?" she asked Séana as they prepared a hot meal. "Did you encounter any who challenged you?"

"No. We saw farmers watching us pass, but they didn't question us."

Caymin looked down at the sword lying on the ground beside her. "You have been trained in combat?"

Séana glanced at her. "Aye. I knew a bit, but Méav has taught me more. She says you're brilliant with a bow."

Caymin felt the heat rise in her cheeks. "I am no good at fighting with a sword or spear."

Séana laughed. "I didn't say I was any good." She brushed her hand over Caymin's head. "We'll all do what we must when the time comes, won't we?"

There was little chatter as they ate. Light snow began falling, sizzling as the wet flakes hit the fire. Ivar decided they could risk setting only magical protections around their camp so that they could all sleep without keeping watch.

"Might be the last night we can," he said gruffly.

So the next few days went. Péist and Caymin flew in advance of the others, trying to keep to the clouds as much as possible.

"*This reminds me of when we were on Inishbreith, searching for other lands to go to,*" Caymin said as they scanned the ground for any sign of Angus and his warriors.

Finally, "*There,*" Péist said on the fourth day. He had dropped just below the layer of heavy winter clouds that blocked any sun from reaching the ground.

A valley far below them looked as if it were covered with ants as small specks moved slowly north. Péist retreated just into the cloud cover, and Caymin was grateful he was white. As they soared over Angus's warriors, they saw many wagons loaded with food and supplies while the people walked—armed men in the forefront while women and children brought up the rear.

From this height, they couldn't tell which was Angus.

"*Do you see Enat?*" Caymin asked.

"*No. And we do not dare to call out to her. If Diarmit knew how to speak without speaking, then Angus probably taught him.*"

They rose higher into the clouds and raced back to their friends. Upon hearing their report, Ivar looked at the sky.

"It's well past midday. Let's make camp for today."

Soon, they were gathered around a fire, sharing a meal as Ivar laid out his plan.

"I don't think they'll expect to encounter any of us outside the forest. Angus probably thinks to find us waiting for him to bring the war to us. If Caymin is right and we're two to three days apart, then they're still to the south of Sliab Bladma. We can cover twice as much ground as they can, so if we can get to those mountains first, we'll be able to see them coming from leagues away. With wagons, they'll probably go round the mountains, rather than marching through the pass."

"Whichever way they choose," Fergus said, "we can spread out and attack so that we seem like more than we are."

"Then Caymin and Péist can fly round from the other side and come at them from behind," Méav said. "They'll be trapped."

"They are not all warriors," Caymin reminded them. "Some are children. I think we should talk about what we are willing to do to stop them. You know Enat would be asking this if she were here."

"They're coming to kill us," Niall said. "To wipe out all magic from Éire forever. What would you have us do?"

Caymin frowned. "I do not see why those with magic cannot live alongside those who believe in the Christ."

Neela laid a gentle hand on Caymin's shoulder. The firelight played on her golden hair as she said, "Angus doesn't want to live alongside anyone he would have to share power with. He doesn't consider those he leads to be his equals. Like Diarmit, they are there to do his bidding."

"Then can we not show him for what he truly is so that they will not follow him, and then let them go back where they came from?"

Ivar scoffed. "You really think they'll just let us be? They are trying to force all to believe in their god. Those who don't, they attack. They've been at it for over two hundred winters, and they won't stop until they've converted all of Éire."

"Then, even if we defeat Angus, where does that leave us?" Caymin asked.

The rest of the small company stared into the fire and did not answer.

With no pots to cook with, hot meals for Enat were not possible, but they were able to roast some of their food in the coals. Diarmit used magic to warm a healing tea, which he handed to Enat.

"Drink this."

Garvan refused to sleep and leave Diarmit on watch, and Enat was still too weak to stand watch for more than a short bit of time, so Garvan was snatching sleep only in small increments, leaving him surly and short-tempered.

Beanna helped to keep watch from various trees, as they remained hidden in the woods they had fled to.

"Do you think they will come back after us?" she asked Enat.

"My guess is that, with our escape, Angus will expect us to send warning to the others, and he'll start north to attack."

"Should we send warning?" Diarmit asked.

Garvan watched their—to him—silent conversation with a scowl.

"Aye, we probably should." Enat looked up at Beanna.

"I am not leaving you," Beanna said with a click of her beak.

Enat smiled and called out. A handsome young falcon answered, flying down to land on her arm. After giving him a message for whoever might be in the mystical forest, she raised her arm, sending him aloft. She watched him fly through the bare tree branches until he disappeared from view.

She turned to Garvan. "Sit. We need to plan."

Garvan squatted down with her and Diarmit. "Aren't we going back to the forest?"

"I think not," she said.

Diarmit looked at her in surprise. "No?"

She smiled grimly. "I think we may be of more use if we stay where we can keep an eye on Angus."

Diarmit's eyes opened wide. "You mean, go back?"

She shook her head. "Not back within their ranks, but if we can shadow them from a distance..." Her eyes narrowed. "I have a feeling the others won't wait for him to get to the forest. They'll come to meet him."

"But... how many can they gather?" Garvan asked doubtfully.

"Not as many as Angus has," Enat admitted. "That's where we may be of more help, if we can be a nuisance, a distraction, pulling his attention in more than one direction."

She took a sip of her tea and sighed. "They won't be able to move very fast, and that will give me time to get stronger."

She finished her drink and stood. "And now, I must find a pool of water to bathe in."

"You're daft!" Garvan said. "'Tis freezing. You'll catch your death, and after all our trouble rescuing you."

Enat chuckled. "I admit, it won't be pleasant. But I daresay, it will be invigorating. Besides, I can't stand to be near myself, and I'm tired of watching you wrinkle your nose when you're downwind of me."

From one of the mountain peaks, the small band of mages watched Angus and his followers as they moved slowly toward the mountains that formed the only feature in this central part of Éire. As they began to circle to the east, following Ivar's prediction, he had a sudden thought.

Turning to Caymin and Péist as they crouched beside the others, he said, "The land to the west is all bogland."

Caymin glanced at Péist. "I do not understand."

Ivar pointed. "If they can't go east, they'll have to go west. The wagons and oxen would be mired in the bogs. The men would have to scatter to find bits of dry land to fight from." He turned to Péist. "If you were to set fire all along the land to the east, they'd have to turn and go round the other direction. That or come through the mountains. I'm thinking they won't chance the bogs. Then we'll be waiting for them here when they come our way."

"But what of the lands I would scorch? What of the two-legs there?"

Ivar frowned. "It can't be helped. We must stop them with the least damage, and this will push them in our direction."

Caymin looked at Péist. "We will burn only enough to make them turn."

She climbed up and strapped herself tightly to the saddle. "What if they see us?"

Ivar smiled grimly. "Let them. It's time for Angus to know there's a dragon in Éire."

Péist spread his wings and hurled himself off the bluff, allowing his bulk to drop into the valley below so as to stay out of sight as they flew to the east. They flew through the mountain passes, catching updrafts where they could, flying past hawks and falcons hunting. Farther and farther Péist flew, out of the mountains. Scanning the terrain below, he picked a spot.

"There. That swath of grassland. I see no two-leg dwellings. If that is burning, then Angus will have no choice but to go far out of his way to go round, or turn back as Ivar said."

He swooped down, opening his mouth and letting loose a blast of flame. He swept along, setting fire to the dry, brittle grass below. In heartbeats, it was burning, sending plumes of black smoke into the sky.

Péist circled, and they watched the flames spread as more and more grass ignited. Pheasants and other grassland birds exploded from their cover, and Caymin's heart caught in her throat as she saw scattered four-legs—deer, rabbits, foxes, martens—all scrambling to escape.

Reading her emotions, Péist said, *"We cannot save them. They will have to fend for themselves."*

"No! We must try."

Caymin called out to them, trying to reassure them but, in their panic, they wouldn't listen. She centered her power, casting a spell to stun them as they raced along the fire line, looking for an escape. It wasn't a spell she'd been taught, nor one she had ever thought of but, in her moment of need, it came to her.

Péist landed, allowing Caymin to loosen her tethers and jump down. She gathered up the smaller animals; she could feel their terror even in their stunned state. Again, she reached out to them with her mind, telling them she and Péist were there to help. She clambered back on Péist's back while he himself picked up as many deer as he could carry in his claws and flew them all to safety. Once out of harm's way, Caymin released the spell and the smaller animals all ran for cover while the deer bounded away as soon as Péist set them down.

Wheeling away, Péist circled far to the south, lighting more fires as he went, so that soon, a half-circle wall of smoke and flame barred the invaders' progress. Using the smoke as a screen, he flew them high into the clouds where they could see Angus's followers, like a dark shadow on the land. They seemed to have halted and were milling about at the sight of the smoke.

Slowly, the dark shadow shifted as they altered their direction, heading toward the mountains.

"What is it?"

Diarmit crouched behind a hedge of gorse with Garvan and Enat, looking at the wall of smoke rising into the sky on the other side of a vast valley. Below them, they could see Angus and his followers shifting their path away from the smoke.

Enat smiled grimly. "It's Péist and Caymin."

Garvan pointed to the mountains. "They're waiting for them. There."

Enat nodded. "I think you're right."

Diarmit turned to her. "You think Caymin and the worm did that?"

Garvan laughed softly. "You haven't seen the worm recently, have you, boy?" To Enat, he said, "Should we try to get to the mountains first? It would be close, but we might beat them there."

Enat shook her head. "I think not. I think we'll be of more use if we bring up the rear, cut them off from retreating once they realize what's waiting for them."

Caymin sat through her turn at watch while Péist hunted far away on the north side of the mountains, out of sight of Angus's followers. She could see them camped below, tiny fires burning. In the distance, the remains of Péist's grassfires still lingered, spread along the horizon like a fiery rope.

All around her, owls and other night animals hunted, but she could feel their heightened alertness. They all knew something was coming.

Footsteps behind her made her turn. Méav sat down.

"How are you, little badger?"

Caymin shrugged. "I do not know. How am I supposed to be?"

Méav leaned in until their shoulders bumped. "Nervous. Frightened. Any number of things." She pulled the jade Caymin had enchanted for her from under her tunic and held it in her hand. "Warm constantly now. The enemy is near. Tomorrow, we won't be sparring. 'Twill be real."

Caymin nodded. "I keep wondering if Enat is down there."

Méav followed her gaze out to the plain below them. "I know. If she is, I hope she's strong enough to protect herself."

Caymin turned to her. "You think they would harm her?"

"I think they might use her as a shield to keep us from harming them."

Caymin hadn't thought of that. "They would do that?"

Méav sighed. "I think we need to be prepared for them to do anything." She gave Caymin a gentle push. "Go sleep. I'll keep watch now."

Dawn found them all silently trying to eat a bit. Gai nervously pulled his sword from its scabbard over and over, checking the edge while Niall and Ronan twirled their staffs, spinning them, gripping them. Daina and Cíana both had bows, like Caymin, along with swords at their belts. Neela likewise held her staff with a bow slung over her shoulder. Méav handed Séana a spear to go with her sword. Caymin had her quiver of arrows strapped to Péist's saddle, within easy reach.

"It's time," Ivar said grimly. "Spread out on either side of the pass. Wait until they're well along before we let them know we're here."

Neela looked at all of them. "Be safe."

Caymin mounted, strapping herself to the saddle before Péist looked back at her.

"Are you ready?" he asked.

"As ready as we can be."

Péist spread his wings and leapt into the sky. He flew low, using the mountains as cover as he flew wide. Angus's followers were already on the move. They were stretched in a long line with the first members of their column climbing into the pass while the wagons were still on the plain below.

Péist wheeled away. *"How long do we wait to let them see us?"*

"I do not know. I think we should wait until the fighting begins, or they may try to turn and run when they see us."

The waiting was an agony as Péist flew circles to the north, out of sight. Together he and Caymin waited for some signal that the fighting had begun.

At last, they heard Neela call to them. *"Now!"*

"Now, we fight, little one." Péist rose higher and prepared to dive over the pass where the others were all gathered.

Caymin nocked an arrow to her bow just in case any of the warriors below thought to fire at them. *"Yes. But we do not kill."*

"Not unless we have no choice."

Péist's acceleration took her breath away as he folded his wings and dropped like a stone toward the would-be invaders. The scene below froze her heart—it looked so like the spiritwalk she'd had on Inishbreith. Ivar had a sword grasped in one hand, his staff in the other, fighting two men dressed in monks' robes while Neela and Méav fought back-to-back, their glowing staffs a blur as they swung and parried, flinging spells when they could. Gai was also fighting sword to sword with a man twice his size. Séana, Ciana and the others were all engaged in battle while scores more of Angus's warriors raced into the pass to assist their comrades. Niall fired arrows, his targets falling while Ronan and Fergus stepped over them to meet the oncoming invaders with staff and sword. Though the mages had the advantage of surprise and terrain, the sheer number of Angus's warriors was overwhelming.

As they neared, Péist's shadow passed over the Christian column. Caymin saw faces raised and mouths open in screams that couldn't penetrate the wind in her ears. Caymin loosed arrows at the approaching Christians, aiming to scatter them as Péist roared fire. They stopped in their tracks, watching in apparent horror as Péist rose in the air and circled to come back at them again. The sight of a white dragon and rider was too much for most of them. They broke ranks and fled back down the pass.

One man, his sword arm raised, stood his ground, watching them approach—not in fear like the others, but with a fierce expression on his face.

Angus. It could be no other. Caymin caught a glimpse of a banner emblazoned with a wolf head. Péist opened his mouth and loosed another stream of fire over their heads. He and Caymin flew through it unscathed. Below them, people dropped to the ground screaming, while Angus alone grabbed a spear and threw it. It arced through the air harmlessly as Péist wheeled and flew back around. Caymin leaned to the side and saw Angus watching her and, even from this distance, she saw the fire in his dark eyes. Suddenly, she understood why Diarmit and others followed this man unquestioningly.

Péist flew them back to the top of the pass. She saw one of Ivar's foes fall to his sword, and the other fled. At almost the same moment, she saw Gai go down. Arrows flew from Daina and Ronan's bows as the few of Angus's warriors still advancing approached with weapons drawn. Péist breathed another rope of fire, not hard enough to reach the people cowering below. Those who were not lying on the ground—wounded or dead, Caymin couldn't tell—began to flee, the last of their courage deserting them. Some stopped to throw spears or shoot arrows toward their airborne attackers, but they were few. Angus didn't try to stop them, but only turned in place, his eyes never leaving the girl and dragon.

Péist and Caymin flew away toward the rest of the column still slowly making its way up the mountain pass, oblivious to the confusion above them, with the wagons bringing up the rear.

"Enat! Enat, are you here?"

Caymin scanned the figures below, but there was no sign of Enat or Garvan, and no response to her call.

At the sight of the white dragon flying toward them, the oxen panicked and overturned the wagons as they kicked and bucked against their traces. The normally placid creatures bellowed their fear and raced back down the mountain, dragging the splintered wreckage of their wagons behind them, leaving a trail of supplies toppled onto the ground as they galloped.

Péist rose higher where he and Caymin could watch the retreat of Angus's force as they fled the mountains back down to the plain below. At last, Angus himself, accompanied by his wolf-head banner, marched back down. He raised a defiant fist in their direction.

"This is not over, dragon and mage. You will be mine."

Péist roared again, in rage this time. He magnified his voice so that all below could hear. *"You dare speak to us? Liar and usurper—pretending to those sheep who follow you that you do not have magic. Go back whence you came, and if you come our way again, be prepared to pay with your life."*

Angus merely laughed in their direction. With a last glance, Péist wheeled in the sky and flew back to the others.

Diarmit's mouth hung open. "A dragon? He really was a dragon?"

Enat looked at him. "You saw the books and scrolls Timmin had been collecting. You knew what he suspected. Why are you so surprised?"

"But..." Diarmit just looked at her. "I didn't really believe it."

She looked at him sternly. "You attacked him, tried to collect him to bring him back to Angus."

Diarmit flushed. "Only because it was something I'd never seen before, and I knew Angus would want it. It was a worm, no bigger than my leg. Just a worm."

Enat shrugged. "Not a worm any longer."

Garvan smiled. "Told you, boy. I felt the same way when they plucked me out of the sea and saved my life. The day I met Péist, I thought I was going mad."

Diarmit turned back to where they could see the tattered remnants of Angus's followers, in complete chaos now, as they fled the mountains. "He will not let this rest. He'll not be content until he owns the dragon now."

Beanna flew to Enat's shoulder. "*That will never happen. The worm is completely devoted to Caymin. They are bonded in a way no one will ever break.*"

They saw Angus marching down from the pass, his wolf-head banner still being carried along behind him.

"Wolf of God, indeed," Enat said, her lip curling.

Garvan turned to her. "What now?"

She considered as she watched the scene below. "I think we should join our comrades, but I'm inclined to agree with Diarmit. Angus will not let this go. I am concerned about what he'll try to do now."

"*I can follow him,*" Beanna said.

Enat turned to her, stroking her sleek breast feathers. "*Are you sure?*"

"*I will learn what I can and rejoin you. Here in the mountains or back in our forest.*"

"*Make sure he does not know you have any connection to me.*"

Beanna nibbled her ear gently and then flew away. Enat and the others stood.

"Let's go say hello to our old friends."

CHAPTER 13

AMBUSh

When Péist landed, scores of bodies were lying about—some still, some moving, as the fallen groaned in pain. Caymin unfastened her tethers and dropped to the earth, looking around in dismay. She went to one of the people writhing on the ground—a warrior of Angus's, a thickly built man wearing monk's robes covered now in blood. He had taken a spear through his chest. The spear had been pulled out, but there was a gaping hole. He was gasping for air, frothy red bubbles on his lips.

She knelt, and he looked up at her, then at Péist. Recognizing her as the dragonmage, he tried to wriggle away from her.

"Stay away from me, you devil!" he gurgled.

"Be still," she said quietly. "I can help you."

Ivar came to her just then and grabbed her arm before she could lay her hands on the man. "We take care of our own first."

Reluctantly, she followed him. As he stepped aside, she saw Méav lying lifeless and bloody, her head cradled in Séana's lap as Séana rocked. Caymin dropped to her knees beside them.

"What happened?"

Séana looked at her through her tears. "She took a sword through her middle. She's dead." She stroked Méav's forehead as her tears dropped into the black hair.

Caymin's own eyes filled as she bent forward, laying her forehead against Méav's chest. Forgotten were the others around them as she and Séana cried together, and then Caymin stilled.

She sat up and laid her hands over Méav's bloody tunic. She closed her eyes and her hands glowed with her power as she sent energy deep, deep into Méav's body, trying to heal the damage there. The cords stood out on her neck and she swayed. Péist came near and pressed his snout to her shoulder, lending his power to hers. The heat in Caymin's hands surged and, suddenly, Méav gasped, her mouth open as she gulped air. Her eyes fluttered open, and Séana froze, too stunned to react. She leaned down and kissed Méav's forehead as Caymin slumped to the side.

Séana looked up and reached for Caymin, grasping her hand as she panted weakly.

Péist nudged her. *"Are you all right, little one?"*

Caymin pushed herself upright. "I will be fine."

"How?" Séana asked, still squeezing Caymin's hand. "How did you bring her back from the dead?"

"She was not dead, but nearly. Her heart was barely beating."

Méav blinked and turned to her. "I was nearly there."

Caymin stared at her. "Nearly where?"

"Through the veil. It waited for me, called to me. I was moving toward it when I felt you pulling me back."

Séana helped Méav to sit up. She reached for Caymin.

"Thank you, little badger," she said as she folded Caymin in an embrace. "We will forever be in your debt."

Caymin flushed. "There is no debt." She left them together and went to where Neela was tending to Gai who was lying in a pool of blood.

Neela glanced up, her face pale and sweaty. "He'll live, but I can't save his arm."

Caymin's stomach gave a lurch as she saw that Gai's left arm was severed above the elbow, only a thin bit of sinew and skin still holding it to his body.

"Let me try."

Neela reached out to stop her at the same moment that Péist said, *"You cannot heal this, Caymin. Even with our combined power, this is beyond us. It would kill you to try. That is not what Gai would want."*

Caymin dropped her hands helplessly. "What can we do?"

Neela tore a long strip of cloth from Gai's cloak and held it ready. "I need for you to cut his arm loose, and then I'll bind this. I must stop the bleeding or he'll die."

Shaking uncontrollably, Caymin drew the knife from her belt—the knife Méav had given her—and winced as she sliced through that last bit of flesh keeping Gai's arm attached. Revolted at the dead weight of the lifeless limb in her hand, she dropped it while Neela tightly wrapped the fresh stump.

Caymin got to her feet and staggered away, retching. Cíana was tending to Ronan who had sustained a flesh injury to his thigh from a spear or sword. Daina's cheek was bleeding while Niall and Una were both limping as they checked on the fallen.

As badly injured as the little band of mages was, there were many more of Angus's warriors lying dead or wounded. Ivar was moving from one to the other, dragging the wounded to where he could prop them against boulders or trees to assess their injuries. He gestured Caymin near and handed her a water skin.

"I've mixed a healing potion in here," he said. "Try to get them to drink. We can't magically heal them all, but we'll do what we can."

She went to the first man she'd encountered. His shortness of breath was worse, but still, he cringed from her as she approached. She knelt and held out the water skin.

"Drink."

His gaze raked her face. "You're even scarred by the fires of hell, you heathen."

Her jaw clenched, but she only said, "I am scarred because invaders raided my village and left me to burn. Now drink. It will ease your suffering."

His face was pale with pain and the effort to breathe. "How do I know it's not poison?"

She tipped the skin up and took a small drink. "It is not poison. It will help."

Grudgingly, he took the water skin and sniffed, still eyeing her suspiciously. "Why would you want to help us?"

"Because we are not like you. We do not wish to force others to believe as we do. We seek only to live in peace, caring for our places and our people. Why is it so hard for us to live side by side?"

He looked at her as if she were asking him why the sun could not shine at night. "Because magic and religion don't go side by side. It's one or the other, and if you don't believe, then you're damned for all eternity."

With a small smile, she said, "Drink."

Hesitantly, he took a sip, tasting the brew. Apparently deciding it was safe, he took a deeper pull. Almost immediately, his eyes began to close. He blinked, fighting sleep, but was soon out. She laid a hand on his chest, centering enough power to stop the bleeding of his impaled lung, but not so much as to heal him entirely.

She tilted her head as she studied him—up close, he was much younger than he had at first seemed. She suddenly wished Garvan were here to talk sense to these men. Looking around, she realized they were all men. Not a single woman had been among Angus's warriors, yet she knew women had been traveling with the wagons.

She went to other injured, offering them the potion. Some of them were grievously wounded, others only badly enough to keep them from running away, but even if they'd thought about it, the sight of Péist pacing back and forth seemed to immobilize them with fear.

The long, weary day passed. Snow fell intermittently. Caymin lost count of how many trips she made to refill water skins. Dusk was falling when Neela came to find Ivar. "How are we going to feed them all?"

Péist answered, *"Their supplies are scattered down below. I will fly down and bring back as much as I can carry."*

Caymin, her arms filled with yet more empty water skins to be refilled, heard him. "I will go with you."

"*There is no need. Stay here and help. I will be back soon.*"

Beanna flitted as silently as she could from tree to tree, trying to keep Angus in sight as he stealthily crept back up into the mountains, taking a rougher trail to avoid the pass he and his men had climbed earlier in the day.

When she'd left Enat and Garvan, she had joined other birds who had flocked to feed on the grain scattered over the valley floor after the oxen galloped away from Péist. Hopping along, pecking at the ground, she'd been able to get close enough to hear when he and his captains regrouped, sharing a jug of some liquid.

"By all the saints," one man said, "did you ever think we'd see the devil born again as a dragon?"

"It spoke," said another. "What did it mean, Brother Angus? It said you have magic."

Angus rounded on him. "You believe that devil over me? Have you learned nothing from your time with me?"

"I'm sorry," the man said, bowing his head. "Forgive me."

"What shall we do, Brother?" still another asked, wiping his mouth on his sleeve as he held the jug out to Angus.

"I need to pray." He waved an arm at them. "Leave me."

They did as he ordered, looking back at him as he paced, his hands clasped to his lips, muttering to himself.

Beanna had made certain she kept him in view as the day wore on. She watched the tattered remnants of his warriors as they returned from the mountains, gathering what they could of their supplies. As the day waned, they lit fires, mumbling among themselves as they kept a wary eye on their leader.

At last Angus stopped pacing, looking back toward the mountains. He waved a hand and three of his warriors ran to him.

"What has God told you, Brother?"

"I must go back."

"What?" the men exclaimed in a chorus.

"You can't."

"What if that devil incarnate snatches you?"

He turned to them. "It's my fault our wounded brethren lie up there at the mercy of that monster. I must do what I can for their souls."

When they started to argue again, he held up a hand, silencing them immediately. "Do you not think I carry God with me as my protector? I can come to no harm, lest He wills it. Do not fear on my account. I want you to gather those you can, comfort them, and wait for me."

He took the banner down from the rod that carried it, draped it around his own shoulders so that the wolf covered his back, and strode off toward the mountains.

Now, as darkness fell, Angus reached a place where he could look down at the mages caring for the wounded. Small fires burned as they heated what food they could. Caymin moved among the others, but Péist was nowhere to be seen.

Beanna perched in a tree, looking down along with him. She did not see Enat or Garvan, and didn't dare call out to Caymin, as she knew Angus would hear. Angus suddenly shifted to watch as Caymin limped away from the fires toward the river that splashed its way through the mountain pass. When Angus moved to keep her in sight, Beanna followed.

Full night was falling as Caymin wearily carried what she hoped would be the last armful of water skins to refill them. All day she'd been doing this, as they constantly needed water for potions, for cooking, and for cleansing wounds. The river that tumbled down the pass was too rough in most places to approach, but she'd found a bridge—a very ancient bridge judging by the moss and lichens growing on the stones—over a pool where the river had been partially dammed. Here, where a thin skim of ice had formed around the edges, she could kneel at the water's edge and fill her skins.

Péist had not returned from his mission to fetch food from down below, but he had stayed in communication with her.

She knelt at the pool's edge, yawning. Gai had not yet awakened, and she did not look forward to the time he did. He was now maimed, just as she was, and she knew he would not take it well. Though humans often stared, Caymin had never been spurned for her burns and scars. First the badgers and then Enat had taken her in; they had accepted her and loved her, but with Gai, it was different. He still judged himself by how his father saw him and, having met Dughall, she knew Gai was right. Dughall would never accept having a one-armed son.

A rock came tumbling down, splashing into the pool and making her jump, but there was no movement. She could feel the winged ones and four-legs nearby, sheltering and very still. None of them would hunt this night, not after the fighting of the two-legs, but the stillness went beyond that. It took a moment for that realization to sink in. She sat up.

Just as she saw a figure move out of the corner of her eye, Beanna burst into sight with a great flapping of her wings.

"Caymin!"

There, on the other side of the pool, stood Angus. Caymin leapt to her feet as Beanna dove at him, but he raised a hand. There was a flash of light, and Beanna fell to the earth at his feet, a limp clump of black feathers.

Caymin cried out, dropping to her knees at the sight of her friend lying dead on the far side of the water.

Another flash of light, and Caymin was stunned motionless, just as she had done earlier to the animals running from Péist's grassfire. She toppled to her side, unable to move anything but her eyes as Angus approached. He tugged the rope belt from his waist and tied her hands and feet so tightly that the rope bit into her flesh. He yanked on the rope and pulled her feet up behind her.

"I thought you would be more powerful," he said, and his voice was like poison, sliding into her head and echoing there.

She tried to call out to Péist, but she couldn't. Somehow, he had blocked that as well.

He squatted next to her, taking in her scars, peering into her eyes. He must have seen the fury there because he laughed.

"Diarmit told me of the worm-creature, but I never dreamed he would become a dragon. Those northmen obviously knew something we do not. Of all the lands that dragons once roamed, they came to Éire looking for one. What led them here, I wonder? What else do they know? Perhaps how to control dragons. We'll see what yours does when you're no longer here. He may be more malleable."

He reached under her arms, lifting her as easily as if she'd been a bird. He hoisted her over one shoulder and walked up onto the bridge. His stunning spell was wearing off. She wriggled against her ropes, but they were too tight.

"Let's see what the dragon does without his mage."

He took her in his arms, held her out over the water, and let go.

CHAPTER 14

Che Portal

The world had gone green and dark. Caymin held a hand out in front of her, and small bubbles trailed her movement. Her braids floated around her head. She looked up and saw, not sky, but ripples of greenish light. Yet, she breathed, she walked. In the distance were mounds, islands. She had no sense of time as she walked but, without her realizing where exactly it had happened, she found herself no longer walking through water, but in a familiar forest. Over that hill, she knew, would be a village—her village. She looked back at the forest, listening... but for what, she wasn't sure.

Caymin's eyelids fluttered open. Someone was singing. A woman. She closed her eyes again and listened. This was a spiritwalk she didn't want to wake from. Her bed was warm and soft, and the voice was soothing, familiar, beloved. The singing stopped.

"Time to wake, sleepy one."

Soft lips kissed her forehead and smoothed her hair. Caymin opened her eyes again to see her mother smiling down at her.

"I've got the porridge ready. Take your brother out and then come eat."

With a last tousle of Caymin's hair, she went back outside to the fire and the kettle hanging over it. Caymin sat up and looked around. The cottage was only one room, with a larger sleeping mat against one wall—empty now—and a smaller one near hers. A redheaded boy was lying there, his thumb in his mouth as he lay sleeping.

Gently, she shook him. "Ian. It's time to get up."

His brow furrowed as he fought being awakened. She smiled and pulled his blanket off. Picking him up, she carried him outside into the cool morning. Sunshine slanted through the trees and, gradually, he woke completely, though he sagged contentedly in his sister's arms. When they reached the ditch that had been dug as a privy, they both did their business and then walked hand in hand back to the village. Some of the men were already out in the fields, scythes in hand as they sliced through the golden stalks of wheat and barley.

Ian brightened. "Do we harvest today, Caymin?"

"Aye. We do." She pointed. "Da's already out there. See him?"

Ian nodded and tugged her hand to hurry her along. They passed other cottages with other sleepy children breaking their fast. When they got to their dwelling, their mother handed them each a bowl of porridge with a bit of honey drizzled over top.

"Eat this now, and then we'll go join the others," she said.

She hummed again while Caymin and Ian sat near the fire to eat.

"Drink," Ian said, pointing to the bucket.

Caymin shook her head at his demand, but reached for the ladle and dipped some water for him. He drank deeply and went back to his porridge. As she leaned over the bucket to dip another ladle-full for herself, she paused. Staring back up at her from the surface of the water was her own face. Absently, she reached a hand up to touch her cheek, smooth and soft, surrounded by softly curling red hair. She frowned, trying to remember....

"Caymin! Time to go harvest. Are you ready?"

"Coming, Mam."

The other villagers made their way to the fields, laughing and talking. Caymin's father paused, leaning on his scythe as he watched them approach. He grabbed her mother around the waist and pulled her close for a kiss.

"Eoghan, stop it," she said, but she was laughing as a blush bloomed on her cheeks.

"Ah, Fionnair, my lass, I can't help myself," he said, smiling broadly. "I've the most beautiful woman in the entire valley." He turned to Caymin and Ian, dropping his scythe and scooping them into his arms. "And you've given me the most beautiful red-haired babies." He rubbed his whiskers against their cheeks, making them both squeal, and then set them down.

He pointed to the swaths of grain lying on the ground. "If you'll tie those up in bundles and carry them to the wagon, we'll get this harvest collected."

Caymin and Fionnair joined the other women and children in getting the grain tied into bundles. Ian dropped more than he actually gathered as he toddled about.

Eoghan came to her and pulled some of her stalks out, scattering them back on the ground. "Don't forget to leave some for the púka, or they'll come after our harvest."

She squinted up at him. "Da, there's no such things as púkas."

Eoghan looked around quickly. He grabbed Caymin by the arm and yanked her down to her knees beside him.

"Don't ever say things like that," he whispered. "Ever."

He went back to cutting. They spent the morning in the fields. Songs broke out periodically as the entire village worked to get the grain cut and gathered. They paused at midday to eat, and then resumed until the sun began to set.

Caymin paused, watching the scene as the sky glowed in the west. She realized she had tears in her eyes and quickly wiped them away.

"Halt where you are!"

Niall peered through one eye, the other swollen shut, as he held his staff defensively, watching three shadows move toward him.

"'Tis I, Enat."

She staggered into the light and fell to the ground, exhausted. Niall lowered his staff and hurried to her as Garvan bent over her, but he raised the staff again as he saw Diarmit. The tip of the staff sparked as he leveled it.

"What are you doing here?"

"Stay, Niall," Enat panted as Garvan helped her to her feet. "Garvan and Diarmit are both allies in this war."

Neela ran toward them. "I thought I heard your voice." She embraced Enat, holding her tightly. "I've missed you so, old friend."

"Old is how I feel at the moment," Enat said, smiling weakly.

"She's still hurting from her time with Angus," Garvan said. "Can we get her to a fire, and some food and drink?"

Neela wrapped an arm around Enat's frail shoulders and led the way into the encampment where there were many exclamations of surprise upon seeing her. Enat looked at all of them, taking in their various injuries as they gathered round.

"You are a sorry-looking lot. And I've never seen anything so wonderful in all my life."

Ivar glared at Diarmit, who shrank back. He reached out for Enat, guiding her to the fire. "Come and sit, tell us everything."

Someone fetched some smoked venison and oatcakes for the travelers as they all sat in the warmth.

"I've been Angus's guest for several moons," Enat told them. "He used a strong potion to block my power, but it gradually lost its ability to work on me. I pretended, though, to still be under its influence so that I might overhear things he didn't realize I was hearing."

Fergus spoke up, frowning at Diarmit, "So why is the traitor with you?"

"Diarmit came to me, at great peril. He brought me healing potions and food. He took care of me as best he could without Angus knowing." She smiled in his direction. "When we were ready to leave, he chose to come with us rather than stay. He has made his stand on our side."

Ivar's attention turned to Garvan. "You're the monk Caymin told us of? Are you sure you're not one of Angus's?"

Garvan smiled at Ivar's aggressive tone. "No. I'm one of Caymin's. And Péist's. They saved me when my boat floundered. I owe them my life."

"Garvan pretended to join Angus," Enat said. "He's been able to keep an eye on me and try to learn Angus's plans at the same time."

Garvan looked around. "Speaking of Caymin and Péist, where are they? We thought they'd be here."

Neela glanced around as well. "Péist went to retrieve some of the supplies Angus's warriors left behind, but Caymin should be back. She went to get water, but that was a long time ago."

Enat got to her feet. "Something is wrong."

No sooner had she spoken than Péist's shadow blotted out the stars.

"*I cannot hear her. I cannot feel her. What happened? Where is she?*"

Péist landed with a crash, dropping the bags of food he had carried back from where the wagons had overturned. He saw Diarmit and pounced, pinning him between his claws.

Péist's lip curled in a fierce snarl. "*Where is she?*"

Enat hurried to them. "Diarmit has been with me."

Méav pointed. "Caymin was getting water. From up there."

Péist heaved himself, partly flying, partly hopping along over the treetops, raining branches down on the humans as they ran upstream. They all came to the pool where the water skins lay on the bank, only a couple of them filled.

"*Caymin!*"

Péist's voice rang through the woods, but there was no answer. The humans gathered silently at the edge of the water. A faint rustling came to them.

"What is that?" Cíana asked, looking around for the source.

Ronan pointed across the pond. "There!"

He sprinted over the bridge and around to where Beanna lay, fluttering her wings feebly. Gently, he gathered her up and carried her back to the others. He held her while Enat laid her hands on the crow.

"What happened?"

Beanna blinked up at her, her eye dull. "Angus. I could not move. He attacked Caymin. Tied her up and threw her in the water."

Péist roared and leapt into the pond, sending a surge of icy water over the banks as he probed the bottom of the pool. He emerged a moment later with Caymin hanging limply from his jaws. Tenderly, he set her down. Enat, Ivar and Neela knelt beside her while the others watched. Ivar cut the ropes binding her as Neela laid her ear against Caymin's chest.

Her eyes shone with tears as she looked up at Enat and Péist. "I can't hear her heart."

Péist raised his head to the skies and keened, a sound that made the hairs stand up on all the two-legs gathered below.

"No," Enat murmured. She laid her hands on either side of Caymin's face. "She's warm, though. I don't think she's dead." She leaned down and laid her forehead to Caymin's. At last, she sat up, a hand pressed to her mouth. "I think she's in the otherworld."

Caymin snuggled up with her mother's arm around her as they sat near the fire, listening to Eoghan plucking his harp and singing. Ian played with a small cloth doll of Caymin's—one her mother had made her when she was Ian's age, maybe two or three winters, but she was too big for it now. People sat at fires at nearby cottages, listening to Eoghan's song—one about Cú Chulainn and his exploits. The song was familiar, but for some reason, in Caymin's mind, it had been sung by a woman. It must have been one of the other villagers.

The village dogs crowded round, lying as close to her as they could get. She petted them, scratching their ears and bellies as they rolled over. They looked at her with their soft eyes, almost as if they were speaking to her.

Overhead, a sliver of moon rose through the trees. Her eyes closed and she yawned, fighting sleep. The fires burned down to ash... Ash. Something about ash....

When she woke, she was in her bed. Something called to her from the dark. She got up and padded out into the night. A whisper came from the forest near the village.

The trees threw faint shadows that rippled over her as she walked and then, suddenly, an animal stepped out of the shadows. A dog. But no… It moved nearer, and she saw that it was a wolf. It occurred to her that she should be scared, but she wasn't. Its eyes gleamed as it watched her, and something shimmered at its neck with a faint green glow. The wolf turned and walked away from her a few steps, glancing back, as if it was beckoning her to follow it.

She walked away, back toward the snug cottage, her home, where her parents and brother lay. With a last look at where the wolf had stood, she saw that it was gone. She crawled into her bed. As she fell asleep again, her fingers searched for a pattern that ought to be woven into the blanket that covered her.

Once back in the encampment, Garvan set Caymin down near a fire while someone added wood to stir the flames.

"*How do we get her back from the otherworld?*" Péist pushed through those who had gathered round her and probed her with his snout, trying to nudge her awake.

Enat shook her head. "I don't know. This is beyond any magic that I know."

Cíana wiped tears from her face. "Did Angus send her there? If we can find him, can we make him bring her back?"

"I don't think so," Enat said. "I think he meant to drown her, and when he threw her into the pond, she went through the Portal to the otherworld on her own."

Beanna, still weak, used her beak to grab Caymin's tunic and pull herself up onto her chest. She settled there. "*Do not dare leave us, little one.*"

Péist's fury built within him until he couldn't contain it. He lifted his head and blasted the night sky with a fountain of fire. "*I will destroy him!*"

He spread his wings and jumped into the air. Enat yelled, trying to call him back. He saw her, a tiny figure far below him, but he knew what he had to do. With a twitch of his wings, he turned down the mountain pass, following the same path he had flown not so long ago, back to the grassy plain below where Angus's followers camped.

He dove, flying low enough to hear their screams. He spoke so all could hear as he swooped over them. *"Where is Angus?"*

When there was no response, he loosed a stream of fire over the camp, eliciting more screams from the two-legs cowering below.

"Where is Angus?"

One man, braver than the rest, ran a short distance away from the others, waving his arms to get Péist's attention. "He is not here."

Péist descended to land in front of the man, who visibly trembled as Péist lowered his head and fixed the man with a fierce gaze. *"Where is he?"*

"We don't know. He told us he was going into the mountains to tend our brethren."

Péist snarled. *"He lied to you. Again. We are tending to your wounded. Angus abandoned them as he abandoned you! He murdered my mage and fled, leaving you to face my wrath without him."*

The man's courage failed him. He fell to his knees, covering his head with his arms. "Have mercy," he whimpered.

Péist whirled, lashing out with his tail, bashing those unfortunate enough to be within reach. He loosed another volley of fire, setting flame to a pile of supplies they had retrieved from their ignominious retreat earlier in the day. People yelled and ran as Péist arched his neck. In his anger and frustration, he snatched an ox from where it bucked and bellowed at the end of its tether. With a great shake of his head, he snapped the ox's spine and sent its limp body flying through the air.

"Angus has lied to you all! He has magic, but in your ignorance, he fooled you into thinking he was leading you in the ways of your god. And you were gullible enough to believe him."

At that moment, Péist understood exactly why Tuala and Scolaí had done what they did. Two-legs were not fit to govern themselves, with their petty gods and their foolish clashes for power and land. Only dragons and their mages had the wisdom to rule properly.

He rose up on his hind legs, his wings open wide, and he roared, *"As it once was, so shall it be again!"*

"Do I have to go? It's so cold."

Fionnair fastened Caymin's cloak more closely under her chin. "Cold or no, the sheep and goats have to graze. Go on, now. Take them out."

Reluctantly, Caymin went outside into the gray drizzle to let the animals loose from their pen. They bleated mournfully, as if trying to tell her they didn't like it any more than she did. She used a long stick to tap their hindquarters and keep them moving toward the meadow. Once there, they spread out. Other children drove their own sheep and goats, along with a few cattle, to the meadow. The children huddled under a pine tree that offered some shelter from the soft rain that continued to fall.

One boy held a bow with a few old arrows, their fletching crumpled, some of the quills missing from the feathers.

"Bardán, where did you get that?" she asked.

His ruddy face glowed. "My da made it for me. Let me have some of his old arrows."

"Can we shoot it?" asked another girl, Grián.

"Aye."

Bardán shot first, taking aim at the trunk of a nearby oak tree. His first arrow flew wide, though the next two struck the tree. Caymin ran out into the drizzle to fetch the arrows. Bardán showed Grián how to nock the arrow to the string. Her arrows all flew wildly, and Caymin again ran to collect them.

"My turn."

"I'll show you," Bardán said.

"I know how." She placed an arrow on the bow and drew the string to her jaw. She did know how to do this. She'd never shot a bow before. Her da didn't own one. When he hunted with the other men, he carried a spear. But somehow, she knew this. She loosed the arrow and, even with the crooked fletching, it struck the tree trunk right in the middle. The other two arrows followed, all clustered together.

"You're really good at this," Grián said in admiration.

Caymin grinned at her. Frowning, she held the bow out.

"What?" Bardán asked as he took it back.

"Nothing." But she continued to frown as she watched some of the others shoot. There was something about a bow… It was like waking and trying to remember a spiritwalk that disappeared like smoke.

"You should get some rest."

Méav laid a hand on Enat's shoulder as she sat between Caymin and Gai, both of them lying motionless.

Enat sighed as she covered Méav's hand with her own. "I will." But she didn't move.

Méav sat down beside her.

"They're so young," Enat said softly. "That they should have lived to see this makes me sad."

"They're both strong."

Enat blinked rapidly. "They'll need to be."

"You couldn't have stopped this," Méav said, reading Enat's mind.

"I can't help but wonder if I could have, if I'd been here all along."

"You did what you thought was best. You saved Diarmit."

Enat looked from Caymin to Gai and back again. "But at what cost?"

Méav nodded down toward the pass. "What do you think Péist is doing?"

Enat shook her head. "I shudder to think what a dragon might do in his grief and pain."

They both sat, watching Caymin as she lay quite still—not even her chest moved with her breath. It was as if she were made of stone.

"How can we reach her?"

"I don't know." Enat bit her lip. "If even Péist can't reach her, I don't know how."

"Timmin."

Enat and Méav both jumped at the raspy sound of Gai's voice. His eyes were open, and he was looking at Caymin.

"What did you say?" Enat reached for his hand.

His gaze flickered to Méav. "Did you tell her about Samhain?"

Méav's eyes widened. "No. I didn't. He's right. At Samhain, we were all under the influence of the potion, trying to reach out to everyone on that night, but Caymin was nearly pulled through the veil. Her father appeared to her, tried to lead her through. We figured it must have been Timmin."

"He tried again. With Péist."

"When?" Méav turned to him. "What are you talking about?"

"Before we left the forest. He was up at the stone circle and went into a trance where he saw a red dragon. It tried to lead him under the sea. We nearly couldn't wake him."

Enat's nostrils flared and her mouth tightened to a thin line. "The otherworld again."

Méav's eyes flashed. "He may not have been the one to drop Caymin in that pond, but he'll be happy enough to have her out of the way."

Gai tried to sit up, but gasped in pain. Enat pushed him back down.

"What—?"

Gai raised what was left of his arm, staring at the bound stump. His face was a mask. Enat reached out to him, but he pulled away from her.

"You could have stayed safely behind cover, using a bow or magic," Méav said to him. "But you didn't. You fought bravely, and you paid the price. As I did." She lifted her tunic to show the red, angry scar on her stomach. "Don't be ashamed. That is a warrior's badge of honor."

Gai's chin quivered, and he turned away.

"Leave him be," Enat said quietly as she got to her feet. "He needs time."

CHAPTER 15

Home Once More

Péist flew as gently as he could, with Enat strapped to his saddle and Caymin cradled in her arms. He altered course as needed to avoid turbulent currents, flying high and then low to find the calmest air. It meant that he had to flap rather than glide, but he did not mind. He kept a slow, steady rhythm of his wings, looking back frequently to make certain they were secure.

There had been a good deal of discussion about whether Caymin should stay near the pond where she had entered the otherworld.

"If she's taken away, will she be able to find her way back to us?" Daina had asked.

"I don't think the Portals to the otherworld are fixed to places in this realm," Enat replied. "Wherever Caymin's body is will have no bearing on whether she returns."

There had been little argument about who should ride with Péist, as Garvan had pointed out that Enat didn't have the stamina yet to walk all the way back to the mystical forest.

"I'll carry Beanna," he said. The crow was still weak and feeble after the spell Angus had used on her.

"We'll follow as quickly as we can," Neela said.

"Angus's wounded will have to go back to their own people now," Ivar said. "We've done what we can for them."

Séana watched them limp away, supporting each other, looking back over their shoulders at the mages who had cared for them. "Maybe they'll think differently now."

"What about Gai?" Méav had asked, watching his gray face as he began moving around the camp. "Should he ride back with you?"

But Gai had settled that argument by refusing to ride. "I'll walk with the others." He looked down at Caymin's still form. "Maybe the forest can bring her back."

"We'll see you soon," Neela said, laying a hand on Péist's shoulder as he took off.

Enat waited until they were well underway before asking, *"What did you do when you went down below?"*

Péist didn't answer immediately. *"Angus has deserted them. They do not even realize how he deceived them."*

"Such is the nature of deceivers. They cast a spell over those who follow—not a spell of magic, but one of easy answers and promises they cannot deliver."

Péist thought on this as he flew. *"I may have hurt some of them in my anger. They are not fit to rule themselves. They do not deserve to live."*

Enat laid a hand on his neck. *"You are probably right, which is why they were such easy prey for Angus. But do not be too quick to put yourself in the role of making such judgments. Some of your ancestors did that. Do not follow in those footsteps."*

"Ivar does not trust me for that very reason. He blamed dragons for the last great war."

"He probably fears you. It is the nature of many beings who have physical size and power to use it over others. He expects you to succumb to the temptation to use your power over two-legs."

Péist turned his head slightly to glance back at her. *"I nearly did down below."*

"I do not think it an accident that you were bonded with Caymin, someone so small and physically weak. Her frailty balances your strength."

They flew on under the stars.

"*Something else disturbs you,*" Enat said. When Péist didn't reply, she said, "*I have not bonded with you as Caymin has, but I've known you since you were a cub. I can feel that you are troubled.*"

"*Why should I not be troubled? My mage is as good as dead to me. I have no others of my kind here from whom I can seek counsel.*"

Enat let him fly on for a while before saying, "*But there is something more. I feel your anger.*"

Péist glanced back. "*Yes, I am angry. I am angry that two-legs are so warlike and gullible. I am angry that my mage and I were left with no guidance. I am angry that we were tasked with the impossible.*"

"*What are you referring to? What is the impossible?*"

Péist wished he had said nothing. Ríona and Ailill had said to tell no one of the Méarógfola, but now... without Caymin, he had no chance of finding it on his own. Nor did he wish to try. He felt lost, more lost even than when he'd been alone in the forest all those winters, waiting for his mage to arrive, though he hadn't known that was what he was waiting for.

In halting sentences, he told her what he knew of the Bloodstone.

"*Gods and goddesses,*" Enat said when he was finished. "*The dragons still live in another realm? And you and Caymin have been able to communicate with them?*"

"Yes."

"*This Méaróg fola exists and could be used if found?*"

"*That is what they told us.*"

Enat was silent for long heartbeats. "*To think what could happen if the wrong person learned of this. Any of it.*"

"*That is what Ríona and Ailill are afraid of.*"

"*But it has been a thousand winters since the last dragon war. It could be anywhere.*"

"*If Angus or Timmin got word of such an artifact, they would stop at nothing to find it. And the world would be at their mercy if they did.*"

"Aye," Enat agreed. "*It would.*"

"Eoghan, we need more wood," Fionnair said as she cut chunks of chicken into a pot.

He looked up from where he had Ian on his lap, letting him pluck the strings of his harp. "In a bit, my love."

"If you want to eat sometime today, I need wood now," Fionnair said firmly.

Caymin grinned as Eoghan gave Ian a kiss on the cheek and set him down. He held out a hand to her and said, "Come, little one. Let's get your mother the wood she needs to keep us fed."

"Da, I'm not little anymore," she chided as he picked up two woven bags and his axe.

"You'll always be my little one," he said, laying a hand on her shoulder as they trekked toward the forest. "I remember when I could hold you in my two hands, you were so tiny."

She smiled and took his hand. The air was sharp and cold, and their breath puffed out as they walked. When they got to the trees, they each took a bag. Caymin gathered dead wood lying on the ground while Eoghan chopped dead branches off standing trees. Caymin could hear the sound of his axe as she wandered through the trees stuffing branches into her bag. If they were too big, she whacked them against another tree to snap them and picked up the pieces.

On and on she walked, gathering wood. She wasn't worried about getting lost. She knew this forest like she knew her own village. She bent down to pick up some more branches and froze. Moving only her eyes, she looked around. There was a badger, just standing there, watching her. She knew of badgers, but had never seen one close up. Her da said they usually hunted at night. This one was out in the day. It didn't seem to be afraid of her. Nor she of it.

She knelt down and held out a hand. The badger trundled closer, nose busily twitching. It nuzzled her palm, letting her scratch behind its ears, grunting contentedly as she did. It lifted its head and looked into her eyes, and she could have sworn they were eyes she knew....

It turned and waddled away, stopping to look back at her. Like the wolf, she had the strangest feeling it was waiting for her to follow.

"Caymin! Caymin, come now," called her father. "We've got to get this back to your mother."

"I'm coming, Da."

When she looked again, the badger was gone. She peered through the trees and listened, but there was no sign of it anywhere. As she carried her gathered wood back, she lifted her hand to her nose and smiled. It smelled of badger.

When Enat opened the protections of the forest to let Péist fly through, he felt her alarm.

"What have they done?"

"There are too many two-legs here now. The forest cannot sustain them without their doing harm."

He flew to the village and landed. She handed Caymin down to those who gathered round, eager for news. Restlessly, he stood guard over his mage while Enat told the others of the skirmish in the mountains.

"So this Angus has disappeared?" asked one.

"It seems so," Enat replied.

"Then we can go home?" asked another.

Enat nodded tiredly. "Yes. If you can wait a few days, the others are on their way back. We cannot thank you enough for coming to our aid. Any of you who wish to stay are welcome. If the threat rises again, we may call upon you to return, but for now, you can all go home."

"On what?" asked yet another. "Our food is thin."

"I will hunt for everyone," Péist said. *"I will bring back enough to feed them on their journey home."*

Enat laid a hand on his shoulder. *"Thank you, Péist. I will look after Caymin."*

Péist watched anxiously until Enat settled Caymin on her old bed. *"Listen for my call upon my return, so you can lower the protections and let me through."*

Enat removed his saddle so that he could fly unencumbered.

164

He felt it, too, as he flew. The forest, normally calm and unshakeable, was agitated. Its energy was disturbed. It felt... wounded.

As he climbed through the protective spells, it was almost like taking a breath of fresh air. The atmosphere within the forest was sick. Why did two-legs have that effect everywhere they gathered in any numbers?

He hunted first for himself, eating ravenously. He then caught and killed three deer, carrying them all back. The sooner the other two-legs prepared the meat and got underway, the better.

Enat parted the barrier for him, and he flew down to deposit his kills. He left the carcasses for the two-legs to cut up and went to see about Caymin.

Cuán hissed as he lowered his eye to peer through the door.

"*I did not mean to startle you,*" Péist said. "*How is she?*"

Broc looked over from where she lay against Caymin's side. "*She is as the dead.*"

"*I know. I do not know how to call her back from wherever she is.*"

"*Tell us what happened,*" Cuán said.

Péist told them what he knew.

"*Is there nothing we can do to help her find her way back to this world?*" Broc asked as she nuzzled Caymin's face.

"*Perhaps now that we are back here, the power of this forest may help us.*"

It was a while before Enat joined them. The badgers greeted her as she leaned over the bed to check on Caymin.

With a heavy sigh, she stacked peat in the hearth and lit it magically. She swung the kettle over the flames and sat.

"*What now?*" asked Péist.

Enat glanced toward the door where he crouched. "*I have been thinking we need help with this. I do not know enough about the otherworld. You told me you have been in communication with—*"

She stopped abruptly as Péist snorted a warning. "*With others who may know more than we. I think it would be good if you could communicate with them again. Ivar, Neela, and the others will have returned before midwinter's day. That will be a powerful night to try again. At the circle of stones.*"

"The last time I went into a spiritwalk there, Timmin tried to lure me into the otherworld."

Enat nodded. *"This time, we'll have help. The badgers and elk will keep watch while the other mages and I stand guard over you."*

Péist stared at her. *"Will they know with whom I am speaking?"*

"No. They do not need to know that."

Fionnair hummed as she combed Caymin's thick hair. Caymin sat, her eyes half-closed in pleasure as the wooden comb Eoghan had carved scratched her scalp each time her mother drew it through her hair.

"I think I'm putting my little one to sleep," Fionnair said, leaning forward to plant a kiss on Caymin's cheek.

"I'm not tired," Caymin said, but she yawned despite her protests.

Eoghan chuckled and bent over to pick her up. She snuggled into his neck as he carried her to her bed. There he covered her and gave her a kiss on her forehead.

She turned on her side to watch her parents back at the fire. Her eyes drifted shut, though she tried to keep them open.

It seemed only heartbeats later that the cottage was on fire. There were screams and yells from outside. When she opened her eyes, she saw her father through the door, fighting warriors with just his scythe. Fionnair ran to him, screaming as the thatched roof overhead burned. Caymin got out of bed, rubbing her eyes and crying as the thatch and rafters from above began to rain fire down on her. Outside, the warriors grabbed her mother as she tried to fight them off. Caymin stumbled outside, crying. One of the warriors backed into her, knocking her over and into the flames just as the walls collapsed.

Caymin sat up in bed, screaming, her arms wrapped around her head.

"Shhhh, shhhh," said Fionnair as she ran over and rocked Caymin gently. "'Twas only a spiritwalk, my little one. It's not real. It's not real."

Caymin cried in her arms, unable to calm herself. Her mother continued to rock her and hum soothingly in her ear until she stopped crying. When at last she sat up, she ran her hands over her face, expecting to feel hardened ridges, but her cheek was soft and whole, and her hair grew evenly.

Eoghan knelt next to her bed. "Nothing can harm you while you stay here with us."

Her mother pushed her back down onto her bed. "We're here to protect you, Caymin. We won't let anything take you away from us."

Péist lifted his head as Garvan appeared, carrying something white on his shoulder. "*You are back!*"

The white something flapped its wings. "*And you have nothing to say to me?*"

Péist stared. "*Beanna?*"

Garvan chuckled. "It's her. She turned white in the days after Angus attacked her."

Beanna held her wings out. "*It is humiliating.*"

Péist reared up a bit, showing his white belly. "*There is no finer color. You look much better now.*"

Beanna clicked her beak at him. She flew ahead of Garvan and through the door of the cottage to Caymin's bed. She walked around her, cocking her head as she pecked gently at her clothing.

"*She does not wake,*" Péist said.

Garvan entered the cottage, ducking his head under the lintel. He knelt next to the bed, taking Caymin's hand in his. "She's still warm."

"Yes." Péist watched with one eye through the doorway. "*Her body is alive, but not her mind.*"

Beanna settled on Caymin's stomach with a rustle of her feathers as Garvan pulled a stool over from the fireplace.

Péist crouched outside. "*You are not leaving with the others?*"

Garvan glanced at him. "No. I'm not leaving. At least not now." He turned back to Caymin. "I've nowhere to go. My superior banned me from my community. And I'm not sure now I could join another, not if they're as close-minded as the people I just left."

He laid a gentle hand on Caymin's forehead. "Does she need to eat or...?"

"Enat says her body is in-between–not dead, but without the needs of the living."

The sound of voices reached them as the young two-legs approached Enat's cottage. Méav and all the others crowded around Péist, peeking in through the door at Caymin.

"How is she?" Séana asked.

"The same. Are you not leaving?"

Ciana shook her head. "We're staying to finish our training and earn our staffs."

He looked at Méav and Séana. *"And you?"*

"We're staying to help you and Caymin," Séana said. "And to help protect the forest in case there are any other attacks."

"What of the people you served?"

Méav shrugged. *"We had not been there long. We will go back some day."*

"Fergus did leave," said Daina. "He has a mate and a baby to take care of."

"How are the injured?"

"I'm fine," said a voice from the trees surrounding the cottage. Gai stepped into view. He wore a cloak draped over his shoulders. "I am the only one still injured, aren't I?"

He looked up at Péist, who regarded him. He'd never paid much attention to the finer features of two-leg faces, but Gai's was a puzzle to him. He was very pale, and his mouth was often fixed and hard, but his eyes... his eyes were soft despite the harsh words that issued from his mouth.

"You are only injured if you see yourself that way."

Enat arrived at that moment with Ivar and Neela.

"Well," Ivar said, avoiding Péist's gaze, "mayhap now we can get back to some semblance of normal life here." He looked at the young ones. "You're all apprentices again. Nearly all." He looked at Méav, Niall, and Ronan. "We'll need your help. Between teaching and guarding, we'll have more than we can handle as we used to."

"I don't want to leave Caymin alone," Enat said. "I've no idea if

Timmin might want to steal her away, but one of us will have to stay with her at all times when I can't be here."

Séana stepped forward. "I can help with that. I won't be much use for anything else."

Neela smiled sweetly. "Oh, I think we can find better uses for you. You'll be helping make potions and salves to trade. We've so little food left, we'll have to trade more than we normally do until the next growing season."

"*I will continue to hunt for all of you,*" Péist said. "*I wish I could bring you more than meat.*"

Enat looked up at him. "*The meat is much appreciated, Péist.*"

She sent a pointed look in Ivar's direction.

"Aye," he mumbled. "Much appreciated."

Péist snorted and a few sparks flew from his nostrils. "*I think it would be best if you and I admit we need each other. We do not have to like each other. It would save time. Of course, since dragons live forever, I have more of that than you do.*"

Ivar glared at him, but the others burst into laughter.

Enat scanned the flat, gray sky overhead. "We should take advantage of the dry weather and dig turf for our fires. The ground will be hard with the cold. We may need to use magic to help, but we need to replenish what's been used up or we'll never get through the rest of the winter."

"You should rest," Méav said. "We can cut the peat."

Enat's shoulders slumped in relief. "Thank you. I'll start a meal for this evening and begin preparing for mid-winter's night."

Péist and Beanna stayed behind with her as Garvan joined the others. Enat set about putting her cottage to rights, grumbling to herself about the mess left behind by those who had been staying there.

"*What preparations must you make for mid-winter's night?*" Péist asked, his head lying on the ground where he could watch through the door.

She glanced at him as she went to the table where several scrolls and books sat. "These were in Timmin's cottage. I've not looked through them carefully, but I think it would be wise to learn what he knew."

"*Do you think he knew of...*" He paused. From the bed, Beanna cocked her head. "*Of what we spoke?*"

Enat shook her head. "I don't know. If he did, he won't rest until he has it." She settled at the table and opened one of the books. "But first things first. We must learn how to bring Caymin back through the Portal to us."

CHAPTER 16

RELUCTANT RETURN

Ailill sat beside the fire in her cave, a cloak drawn about her shoulders. A click of claws on rock behind her roused her from the sleepy trance she had sunk into.

"*Good hunting?*"

"*I have not been hunting.*"

She jumped at the unexpected voice and whipped around to see Péist standing there.

"*Péist, what are you doing here? Where is your mage?*"

"*That is why I am here. She has gone through the Portal to the otherworld, and we cannot bring her back.*"

Ailill jumped to her feet. "*What? Tell me all.*"

Péist sniffed and looked deeper into the cave. "*Where is Ríona? I would rather tell this only one time.*"

"*She is hunting. But she has heard us. She will be here soon.*"

Within heartbeats, the entrance to the cave was darkened by the enormous black dragon as she flew in.

"*Péist,*" Ríona said by way of greeting. "*Why have you come?*"

Quickly, Péist told them all that had happened—the gathering of

171

mages after Samhain, the ambush of Angus's warriors, Caymin's disappearance, and finding her body in the pool of water.

"*And this is why you think she is in the otherworld?*" Riona asked.

"*Yes. She is warm, barely breathing, so she is not dead. Yet, she is not here, in our realm. We do not know how to bring her back.*"

"*First, she must want to return,*" said Ailill. "*Or she never will.*"

"*I have thought about trying to go through the Portal to get her,*" Péist said. "*Timmin tried to lure me through once before. But if I go, will I find her? What does the otherworld consist of?*"

Riona glared at him. "*Timmin tried to lure you into the otherworld?*"

"*Yes. He invaded my mind when I was resting, with a red dragon who tried to get me to follow her under the sea.*"

Ailill frowned. "*How is it you are here now? Who is protecting you?*"

"*Enat and the others are watching over me at the circle of stones to make certain Timmin does not try to draw me through the Portal again.*" He asked again, "*Can I find her if I go through the Portal?*"

Ailill shook her head. "*We do not know for certain, but we do not think so. The otherworld is not like this one. When one goes through the Portal, there are as many realms as there are stars in the sky.*"

Péist's head drooped. "*Then she is lost to us forever.*"

Riona and Ailill looked at each other. "*Perhaps not.*"

Péist raised his head. "*What do you mean?*"

"*It is said that you can be guided through the Portal by one who has been sent.*"

"*Who would that be? Who could be sent to her?*"

Ailill sighed. "*A thousand winters ago, when Scolai and Tuala were at the height of their powers, we told you a young mage-born girl named Aine was sent to steal the Méarógfola and hide it.*"

"*Yes,*" said Péist impatiently.

"*We know she succeeded,*" said Riona. "*Because we were then freed of the Bloodstone's control over us, but there is more.*"

Ailill's expression was somber as she said, "*Scolai wrote that there was another dragon—a white dragon—and a young mage girl, who fought him.*" She grasped the crystal hanging around her neck.

Péist stared at both of them. "*But how can that be?*"

"*We do not know,*" Ailill said. "*But we knew when we saw you, that you and Caymin were the ones. You will do this, because you have done it.*"

"*Somehow,*" said Ríona, "*Caymin will find her way back to you, and then the two of you will find your way into the past, where you will meet Aine, and you will battle Scolaí and Tuala.*"

Caymin sat with her arms wrapped around Ian who snuggled in her lap as the entire village gathered around a huge bonfire. Her father played his harp and sang a song of the gods and goddesses taking daylight away from humans.

Ian looked up at her and whispered, "Do they really take the day away?"

"No," she whispered back. "This is the longest night of the year, and it feels as if the sun won't come back. But it always does."

Across the fire from her, Bardán sat with his family, his mouth stuffed full of oatcakes as he listened. He caught her eye and grinned.

Others took turns singing or telling tales as they kept the bonfire burning through the long night. Ian was long since asleep, his head still cradled on Caymin's thigh as Fionnair wrapped her cloak around Caymin's shoulders and pulled her close.

Caymin's eyes were beginning to droop when she heard the howl of a wolf. She snapped to, instantly alert. None of the others seemed to have heard it. She looked around, trying to see into the darkness beyond their circle of light. There, just for a moment, she thought she caught a glimpse of an old man, his silver beard and hair catching the firelight, but the next heartbeat, he was gone.

She glanced up at her mother and then to her father, but their faces were serene, untroubled by seeing strangers or hearing wolf cries in the night. She shuffled closer, turning her face into Fionnair's shoulder and shutting out everything else but the feel and smell of her mother.

Enat pulled a candle closer as she pored over an ancient text. The writing on the calfskin pages was so faded, and the language so archaic, that it was difficult to make out. She glanced over at the bed where Caymin lay, unmoving, with Beanna settled on her chest, sleeping.

Péist was off hunting. He had waited until he and Enat were alone to tell her of his spiritwalk and the things Ailill and Ríona had told him.

"*That is impossible,*" she'd said when he was done.

"*I do not know what to think.*"

"*But... but the Portal, the otherworld... it allows you to go back in time? If others knew of this, if they went back, the havoc they could wreak. Who knows what damage could be done?*"

"*I, too, have thought of this,*" Péist said. "*They did not know how we did it, only that it was written by Scolaí that he had met and fought a white dragon whose mage was a girl. Who else could this be?*"

Enat rubbed her forehead now as she read. The potential implications of these revelations had given her a headache that would not cease. She had taken a healing potion, and Neela had made a special salve to rub into her temples, but still, the throbbing continued.

A knock at her door made her jump. She opened it to find Gai standing there.

"How is she?" he asked as she stepped back to let him in.

"The same."

He took a seat at the table and pulled her book near as she poured two cups of tea.

"Have you found anything?"

Enat shook her head as she handed him one of the cups and sat back down. "Not yet. Nothing that explains the otherworld or how to bring someone back from it."

Gai swirled the dark tea within his cup as he frowned. "I may have some help for that. Eachna knows a good bit about the otherworld. At least, he seemed to when he was teaching me. I've sent him a message. I hope you don't mind."

Enat gave him a reproving glance. "Eachna?"

"I know you don't like him—"

Enat snorted. "Like him? I could barely tolerate him when we were apprentices."

"Why? What did he do?" Gai watched her curiously.

She glanced at him. "It wasn't any one thing he did. We just never got along. Much like you and Caymin used to be."

She turned to look at Caymin's death-like form. "Still, if he knows anything that might help…"

"Good," Gai said. "Because he sent a message back. He should be here soon."

They didn't have long to wait.

The apprentices were at the meetinghouse, learning to cast an invisibility charm. Outside, the wind howled, rattling the shutters fastened over the windows and making the candles flicker wildly.

"It doesn't really make anything invisible," Neela explained. "It just charms an object so that others see what's behind or around it, as if it were invisible."

Daina sighed in frustration as she tried again and again to make a cup disappear.

"No," said Cíana, shaking her head. "I can still see it, though it maybe looks a bit more like the wood of the table."

Daina rounded on Diarmit. "This is the spell you used the day you attacked us at Timmin's cottage. You made yourself invisible to get away. How did you do it?"

Diarmit's cheeks flushed. "Angus taught me this charm when I was young. He forced me to learn it."

Enat stepped in quickly. "Each of you has learned some spells easily, while others are more difficult. Look." She pointed. "Gai has made his scroll disappear." She reached into what appeared to be an empty shelf and retrieved a scroll that materialized as soon as she touched it. "This is a difficult spell. Which is why you're learning it now, and not during your first seasons with us."

The door burst open, and a gust of wind blew out all of the candles. Neela pushed the door shut while the apprentices relit the candles.

"Like this?" said a voice from the direction of the doorway.

They all turned as one, looking for the source of the voice. With a sweep of his hand, Eachna lifted the charm and stood there with his hawk, Lorcan, on his shoulder.

"Yes," said Enat with a thin smile. "Exactly like that."

Péist lay like a giant white boulder, blocking the entrance to Enat's cottage. He raised his head as they approached.

"*When did you arrive?*"

"*Just now,*" Eachna said.

"*Good of you to lend your aid,*" Péist said, curling his lip.

"*I am here now.*"

Reluctantly, Péist shifted to allow them to enter. Inside, Lorcan flew to a rafter while Garvan stood from where he'd been sitting near the bed, keeping watch.

Eachna dropped his cloak on a chair and leaned over Caymin while Beanna stared up at him from where she still lay protectively on Caymin's chest. She kept a wary eye on Lorcan.

"How long has she been like this?" Eachna asked.

"Not quite one full moon cycle," said Méav. "We've searched our books and scrolls for anything that would help us to bring her back, but we've found nothing."

"No," Eachna said absently as he laid his hand on Caymin's head. "You wouldn't."

Enat bristled. "What does that mean?"

He glanced up. "Only that this sort of thing touches on dark magic." He smiled unpleasantly in Enat's direction. "And you don't teach that sort of thing here, do you?"

"Dark magic?" Séana asked, reaching for Méav's hand.

Eachna straightened and turned to them. "Not all dark magic is used for evil. Some of it is only considered dark because of its potential for being abused. That's why it's not taught or taken lightly." He gestured toward Caymin. "What if you knew how to trap anyone there, wherever she is?"

He turned back to the bed. "No," he said softly, almost more to himself than to them. "We need a guide."

Ivar scoffed, his arms folded over his massive chest, his black hair and beard making him look very like a bear standing on two legs. "What kind of guide?"

Eachna looked up at him. He tried to puff himself up as much as he could, but his head still only came up to Ivar's chest. "A guide who can go back and forth between realms."

Neela frowned. "Where do we find someone like that?"

Eachna reached for his cloak and turned toward the door. "We don't. We ask the guide to find us. Bring her."

He led the way back to the village as the wind continued to moan through the gathering dusk. Beanna and Lorcan flew to a nearby tree branch, gripping tightly as the tree creaked in the wind, to watch as Eachna stacked some dried wood in the fire pit outside the meeting-house and ignited it with a flick of his hand. Garvan carried Caymin, wrapped in a cloak, and set her on the ground near Eachna who gestured to the others to sit around the fire with him.

Garvan and Séana stepped back.

"What are you doing?" Eachna asked impatiently.

They glanced at each other. "We've no magic," Garvan said. "You won't want us as part of the circle."

"You care for her, don't you?" Eachna asked. "You have a connection to her? Then sit. We need everyone."

They all took their places on the cold ground. He did a double take as Gai sat beside him, and his cloak shifted, revealing the bandaged stump of his arm. Eachna opened his mouth but then closed it again. He reached into a pouch at his belt and threw some kind of powder into the flames.

Instantly, smoke rose—dense, thick smoke that at first was formless. Eachna whispered words, his eyes closed, as he held his hands out toward the fire. The smoke began to whirl and twist as if tying itself in knots.

Eachna opened his eyes and frowned as he saw that the smoke was still an indistinct, undulating mass. "We need more power," he murmured.

He looked past the circle and saw that the badgers had crept near, watching protectively.

"*Join us,*" he said, holding his hands out to either side as he continued to chant.

He placed his right hand on Gai's shoulder while, to his left, he and Niall rested their hands together on Cuán's back. The other badgers all settled in place between the humans as they clasped hands, completing the circle as Enat and Méav laid their hands on Péist's neck. The air prickled and sparked with the combined power of all gathered there.

The smoke continued to swirl until at last it took a distinct form.

"A wolf," Neela murmured.

Eachna nodded. "*If you are here,*" he called, speaking without speaking, "*show yourself. We have need of you.*"

They waited, hands still clasped, power still filling the very air. Cíana gasped as a large wolf stepped silently into the firelight. The badgers hissed.

"*Stay,*" Enat murmured. "*He is here to help.*"

Cautiously, the wolf approached to where Caymin lay, stepping over Gai and Daina's joined hands. He touched his nose to her forehead.

"*You are her guide?*" Eachna asked.

"*Yes. I have been trying to lead her back, but she resists.*"

"*Where is she?*" Péist asked.

The wolf raised his head and looked at the dragon. "*She is with her family. Her two-leg family.*"

Enat frowned. "*But they are dead.*"

"*Not in the otherworld. She has gone to a realm where they live, and she is happy there. That is why it has been so difficult to lead her away.*"

He sat, and a green stone glittered at his throat. "*There is something more. I have seen an old man, with white hair and beard. He is there as well.*"

"*With Caymin?*" Péist asked.

The wolf tilted his head. "*Not firmly in her realm—he does not know how to find the one she is in—but I have seen him in my passage through the Portal. He searches for her.*"

The mages exchanged worried glances.

"*How can we help?*" Eachna asked.

The wolf glanced around at all of them. "*With your combined power pulling her in this direction, I may be able to tear her from the otherworld, but it will not let her go willingly. You must all call to her, ask her to return to you, while I go back to lead her through the Portal.*"

With a last nuzzle of Caymin's face, he got to his feet and padded back into the shadows.

Caymin lay on her back in the meadow, watching the blue sky above her as the animals grazed nearby. The air was still cold, with a hint of the snow that lingered in small pockets here and there, but the sun had been out more than usual lately, and its warmth felt good. Even the flowers felt it. She smiled and sniffed a wildflower she'd found at the base of a tree—small and purple. It was an orchid, though she couldn't remember how she knew that.

Voices made her sit up. Bardán and Grián were herding their animals to the meadow. She waved to them, and they ran to join her.

"Are you excited for tonight?" asked Grián.

"Tonight?"

Bardán punched her in the arm. "Imbolc, you goblin!" He rubbed his rotund belly. "Can't wait for the feast."

"We're going to gather snowdrops and blackthorn," Grián said. "Come with us."

Caymin got to her feet, tucking the orchid behind her ear, and followed them into the forest.

"Here!" Bardán ran to a bunch of small, white flowers. He squatted down to cut them.

Caymin spied others. "I'll gather those."

"And blackthorn," said Grián. "We'll need lots of blackthorn, enough for every fire."

Caymin followed the snowdrops, patch after patch, through the forest, where they bloomed in little rays of sunshine that fell through the trees. The blackthorn was tougher, for the sharp thorns made it difficult to grasp the branches without getting stuck. She wondered how to cut it and, suddenly, found a knife at her belt. She pulled it from its sheath and looked at it, turning the blade to catch the light. She'd seen it somewhere before, but where eluded her.

She was busily cutting blackthorn when she paused at the sound of rustling nearby. She looked around. There was the badger again. At least, she thought it might be the same one. It wasn't afraid of her, approaching with its nose twitching and sniffing. She smiled and held out a hand. The badger came near enough for a scratch behind the ears.

The badger turned and took a few waddling steps away from her, looking back to see if she was following. Curious, she got to her feet, carrying her snowdrops and a few blackthorn branches with her.

The badger kept glancing back as if encouraging her, and it led her deeper into the forest. Caymin stopped. She couldn't hear Grián or Bardán's voices any longer. A small whicker at her feet made her turn. The badger had taken a few steps back in her direction, calling to her. Uncertain now, she hesitated, but when she turned to go back, the wolf was blocking her path. She stumbled backward, dropping her flowers. She looked for the knife, but it was gone. She held a blackthorn branch defensively, ready to lash out if the wolf attacked.

It sat, tilting its head as it regarded her. Again, she saw a glint of something at its neck and leaned forward to get a closer look. It watched her with bright eyes. As she stared into those eyes, she forgot to be afraid. She lowered her branch, and the wolf got to its feet and came to her. It, too, nuzzled her, licking her palm, and then nudged her with its body, pushing her in the direction the badger had been going.

With the badger leading the way, Caymin and the wolf walked side by side until they came to a pond. Faintly, she heard something. It seemed to be coming from the water. She cocked her ear, trying to listen, but it was just out of clear hearing.

The badger trundled up to the water's edge, but Caymin held back. Again, the wolf nudged her. She was suddenly afraid.

"No."

She tried to run back in the direction from which they had come, but the wolf snarled and grabbed her by her tunic while the badger did the same with her legging, taking hold and growling fiercely while it dug in with its strong claws. Together, they dragged her into the pond and pulled her under.

Péist stared intently at the smoke wolf still writhing in the air over the flames. It snapped and lunged at something unseen and, a few heartbeats later, Caymin's mouth opened as she grasped her throat and gulped for air. All the two-legs gathered around the fire jumped, startled by her unexpected movement, but Péist reached his long neck across to her, nudging her with his nose.

"*Little one?*"

Caymin sat up. "What happened? How..." She looked around dazedly. "No..."

Her eyes focused on those gathered around. She twisted to see the meetinghouse and village buildings. "How are we all back here?"

"You have been gone," said Enat.

Caymin gaped at the sight of Enat and Garvan, and tears filled her eyes. "You are here." She glanced around again, taking in all who were assembled around the fire. "You," she said to Eachna. "And Diarmit."

Beanna flapped down from the tree, landing on Caymin's knee. "*Little one. We thought we had lost you forever.*"

Caymin stared at her. "*Beanna? But what happened? How did you turn white?*"

"What do you remember?" Eachna asked.

She frowned. "I was... But I could not have been. It must have been a spiritwalk, but the most realistic one I have ever been on."

"You weren't in a spiritwalk, Caymin," Enat said gently. "You have been in the otherworld."

She stared around at all of them. "No."

"What is the last thing you remember from the mountains?" Neela asked.

Caymin thought. "I was gathering water. Near the bridge." She inhaled sharply. "Angus!"

"*He attacked you,*" Beanna said.

"Yes. He bound me and..." Caymin's eyes widened.

"*He dropped you into the pond,*" Péist said.

"But... but it was so real." Her voice was small. "How long?"

"*Nearly a moon,*" said Péist.

She stared. "That is not possible. I was... it has been many moons."

"Time does not move at the same pace in the otherworld," Eachna said. Something moved in the shadows beyond the firelight.

"Mactíre?" Caymin said. The others all turned to look at the wolf, who stood watching them, his fur still wet.

He inclined his head. "*Caymin.*"

"How do you know the wolf?" Cíana asked.

"He was her guide," Eachna reminded them.

Caymin shook her head. "No. Yes. He was there, with me. But we met before." She glanced at Méav. "When Gai and I flew to find you, I met him."

"*I have been waiting for you.*" Mactíre turned his gaze to Péist. "*I have been waiting for both of you.*"

"But this cannot be," Caymin said, pressing her fingers to her eyes. "My family. I had a younger brother. It cannot be all in my mind."

"The otherworld isn't in your mind," Eachna said. "But even if you had tried to find your way back alone, you could have wandered through it forever, from realm to realm, without ever finding the Portal back to this world."

"What's this?" Séana reached behind Caymin's ear. Lying in her hand was a small, purple orchid.

Caymin sat hunched over a bowl of porridge, poking at it with her spoon.

"You should eat," Enat said. "Your body has been without nourishment for a very long time."

"Where is Péist?"

"He is hunting."

Caymin nodded and ate a bit, still keeping her head lowered as she sat at the fire.

"What is it?" Enat asked gently.

Caymin shook her head.

"There's no one here but me," Enat said. "Beanna is also hunting, and the others have all left you to rest."

When Caymin raised her head, her eyes glistened with tears. "It felt very real."

Enat reached out and tenderly touched Caymin's face. "A life where you'd never been burned and your family was alive and together?"

Caymin lowered her head again, and tears dripped into her porridge.

"You heard Eachna. The realms in the otherworld are real. When Angus dropped you into the water, you went where your heart led you. There's no shame in longing for your family, Caymin."

Caymin sniffed and wiped her sleeve across her nose. "There were things there that felt familiar, four-legs mostly. A badger came to me. I think it was Broc. And the wolf. But always, I turned away and went back to my family."

They sat quietly for a moment.

"You said you had a younger brother?"

Caymin nodded. "Ian. And my father was Eoghan, and my mother was Fionnair. I never knew their names."

She met Enat's gaze again. "I am glad to be back here, only..."

Enat smiled. "That world was nice, I'm sure. Nicer than coming back to conflict."

Caymin ate a bit more. "Angus left after he attacked me?"

"It seems so. There's been no word of him."

Caymin gave her a sideways glance. "What did he do to you?"

Enat stared into the fire. "He was... persistent. He wanted my staff. He desperately wants to have a mage's full power. He forced a potion on me that dulled my mind and my magic, but eventually, I was able to resist more and more."

Caymin eyed her closely. "He did not only use a potion."

Enat met her gaze. "No. He did not. Diarmit came to me, tried to help as much as he could."

"I am glad."

Enat shifted on her stool. "Péist told me of your ability to communicate with Ailill and Ríona, and of all they've shared with you."

Caymin's head snapped up. "All?"

Enat nodded. "He told me of the Méarógfola."

"Why would he do that?"

"He was alone with that knowledge while you were away. He wasn't sure how to proceed without you."

Caymin bit her lip. "He is not hunting. That is, he may be hunting, but he wanted to be away from me."

"I don't think—"

"He told you he was leaving to hunt. He did not tell me. He is angry with me."

Enat was quiet for long heartbeats, the only sound the fire snapping and crackling in the hearth. "I think perhaps he is hurt that Mactíre was able to lead you back from the otherworld while he could not."

Caymin set her bowl down and stood. "I need to go see Broc and Cuán."

Enat looked startled. "Don't you think you should rest?"

Caymin snorted. "I have been asleep for almost a moon. I do not need more rest."

CHAPTER 17

A Very Old Friend

Caymin lay on her side in the darkness of the sett, caressing the new cubs as they nursed. *"I am sorry I was not here when they were born."*

Broc whickered and nuzzled Caymin's face. *"Cuán told me of the night you were brought back. We have all been afraid. You were dead to us."*

Caymin lay silent.

"Was it so much better, where you were?"

"It was..." Caymin paused. *"Having my family was a happiness I have never known, at least not since I was old enough to remember, but I was simply a two-leg cub. I was not a dragonmage. I did not have an entire land looking to me to stop a war. I was not tasked with–"* She sighed. *"Life was simple. You were there."*

"Was I?"

"I did not know you by name, but you appeared to me over and over, always trying to lead me... now I know, you were trying to lead me back here."

Though Caymin couldn't see Broc's eyes, she knew the badger was watching her. *"And still, I resisted coming back."*

"I do not think any could blame you for wanting a simple life where bad things had not happened to you. If I could go to a place where I had not lost

cubs to sickness and wolves, I might go. But then, I would not have found you."

Caymin smiled. "No. That is the trap of the otherworld. It allows you to get lost in what might have been." She frowned in the dark at her own realization. "But it is not better than what is here."

Broc sniffed the air. "They wait for you."

Caymin sat up. "I know. I must go." She leaned forward to press her forehead to Broc's. "I will return when I can."

Caymin crawled out one of the tunnels, shivering in the cold air after the warmth of the sett. Darkness had fallen, and there was no moon. She did not need light to know where she was going. She strode through the forest, touching trees and bushes as she went. All was different from the last time she'd been here with Gai. Enat said the people who had come to protect the forest had upset the balance within it, but it was healing.

On she walked until she came to the circle of stones. She was unsurprised to find Péist there, along with Mactíre. The two of them sat, as still as the stones, waiting for her. She walked the perimeter of the stones, casting a spell to block any from hearing what they said. When the spell was complete, she sat on the ground, completing a circle within the circle.

For long heartbeats, they sat, none speaking, until Mactíre said, "It has been a thousand winters since we have gathered thus."

"But how?" Caymin asked. "How is it that you know us?"

Mactíre shifted to lie down. "What do you know of Scolaí and Tuala and the Méarógfola?"

Péist said, "We know that Scolaí and Tuala enchanted the Méarógfola and so coerced the fealty of all who had given blood to it. We know that a mage-born girl named Aine stole it, and..." He paused for a moment. "It is written that a white dragon and dragonmage fought them."

Caymin's mouth gaped for a moment. "How do you know of this last?"

Péist arched his neck to look down upon her. "Not all of us have been sleeping for a moon."

Her cheeks burned at his rebuke.

"What you say is true," said Mactíre. "This is why I have waited a thousand winters for you to come."

Caymin stared at him. "How is that possible?"

"I was there—I will be there—with Aine, when you come to us. I have been under a spell of her making, waiting for you."

"How did you know we were here?" Péist asked.

Mactíre looked up at him. "I do not know precisely how, but I was awakened when a dragon returned to Éire."

"But I have been here for a hundred winters," Péist said.

"Not as a dragon."

"Only as a cub," Caymin said. "Until you hatched from your egg."

Mactíre's tail twitched. "I only awakened a few moons ago. I do not know what changed, but it woke me from the spell I had been under."

"Inishbreith," said Caymin. "We had to fly to Inishbreith. You had to go into the firechamber."

Péist looked down at the wolf. "We are all here together. What happens now?"

Mactíre got to his feet and padded over to sit before Caymin. He lifted his chin. "The stone I wear. It is for you."

Caymin reached around his neck and untied the leather cord holding the stone. She held it in her hand, an uncut emerald. She felt the power thrumming in it. "What is it enchanted with?"

"It is your tether."

She looked up at him. "My tether? To what?"

"Not to what," Mactíre said. "To where. And when. And whom. When you are strong enough, we must all go back through the Portal."

Péist snorted sparks. "We almost did not get Caymin back from the Portal. Why would we return?"

"It is the only way to go back to where you are meant to be. If you have something from a specific time or place, you can safely travel through the Portal to your destination."

Caymin touched a finger to the stone lying in her palm. "And what is our destination?"

"That stone will take us to Aine."

The sparring yard was filled with the sounds of people yelling, swords clanging, and arrows thumping targets. Caymin found Eachna sitting, watching from a small knoll. She sat beside him.

"Buffoon." Eachna gave her a sideways glance. "Not you. Him." He tilted his head.

Caymin followed his baleful gaze to where Ivar and Garvan sparred with swords, teeth bared in fierce grins through their beards, faces shining with sweat despite the continued cold weather, as they enjoyed the challenge of being evenly matched.

"He thinks because he's large, he can bludgeon everything into submission." His lip curled as he watched them. "He uses magic the same way. He has no appreciation for subtlety."

"I do not understand."

Eachna turned to her. "You know you can't physically overpower most people, so you've learned to outthink them. Do you think Ivar could have handled Dughall the way you did? It would never have occurred to him to use his own words against him."

"I still had to fight my way out of the king's hall," Caymin reminded him.

"Only because he tried to trap you. And the dragon did more damage than you did."

Down below, Méav and Niall sparred with staffs, as did Cíana and Daina. They were much improved since the last time Caymin had seen them fight. Over at the archery range, Diarmit, Ronan, and Una practiced. The others had grudgingly accepted Diarmit's presence among them. At a far target, Gai practiced with spears, throwing one after another.

"You're not the only one fighting with a disadvantage anymore," Eachna said without looking at her.

"I never meant for any of this to happen."

"But it did. Because of you."

Caymin's face fell.

"You all fought. Gai lost an arm. You were nearly lost forever. Angus is gone and his legions scattered, and they never made it anywhere near this forest." He turned to her. "So what was it all for?"

"Do you not believe in fighting evil?"

He scoffed. "Evil? Or inevitable? I believe in accepting reality. The Christians are spreading, whether we like it or no."

She had no response to that.

He returned his gaze to those below. "His father will never accept him back now. Not like this."

"His father is without any sense of honor," Caymin snapped. "His opinion means less than nothing."

Eachna turned slowly, an unpleasant smirk on his face. "And yet, Gai would give anything for his father to say he's proud of him."

Caymin clenched her jaw, recognizing the truth in Eachna's words. After her own recent experience with her family, even if it wasn't real, she knew the power of wanting to please her parents.

She pushed to her feet and left. Wandering through the village, she heard voices coming from the meetinghouse. Peeking in, she saw Séana grinding something with a mortar and pestle as Enat and Neela stood over two cauldrons. Without saying anything, she backed away.

She felt restless. When she was with other two-legs, she wished to be alone, but when she was alone, she wished for company. The company she missed, she realized, was Péist's. They had spent only moments together since their talk with Mactíre a few days prior. When she questioned him, Péist said only that he had to hunt, or that he was tired. She still felt her connection to him, but it was as if from a great distance.

She thought about going to the sett, but she didn't even want to be around the badgers. Scowling, she went to Enat's empty cottage, dropping onto her bed. No sooner had she settled, than Beanna flew in through the window, landing on Caymin's stomach.

She rustled her white wings and settled herself. "*I have not seen much of you since you woke.*"

"*No.*"

Beanna tilted her head, fixing Caymin with one black eye. "*Nor have I seen much of the worm. Where is he?*"

Caymin looked up at the underside of the thatched roof. *"I do not know. Probably at the stone circle resting. Enat cast a protective spell there to block Timmin from intruding into his sleep."*

Beanna rose up and down slightly with Caymin's breathing.

"At one time, you and Péist were as one," Beanna said. *"I chose to go with you, to help you if I could, but it was difficult."*

Caymin frowned. *"Why was it difficult?"*

"Because I felt I had lost my friend."

Caymin sat up, catching Beanna as she slid from her stomach to her lap. *"Why would you feel you had lost me as a friend?"*

"You and the worm shared something I could not. It left me feeling as if I was an interloper."

"You never said anything."

"What could I say? You and the worm are bonded as you and I never can be. I thought nothing could disturb that. It seems I was wrong."

"It is not that our bond is broken..."

Beanna hopped down from Caymin's lap, waddling along the bed to where a small purple flower lay at the edge of the feather-filled mat. She picked it up with her beak and dropped it next to Caymin.

"Then why does it feel as if half of you is still in the otherworld?"

Caymin stared down at the orchid for long heartbeats. At last, she swung her legs over the side of the bed. *"I must go find Péist."*

Péist lay inside the protective confines of the stone circle. He could have rested anywhere within the forest, but the power of this place drew him. It felt as if it were trying to speak to him. Timmin had encroached upon him here once before, but it hadn't happened since. Whether Timmin had not tried again or whether Enat's spell was keeping him out, Péist didn't know and didn't care.

Enat had been the only one to seek his company in the days since Caymin had awakened. Of course, the fact that he huffed smoke and curled his lip when two-legs tried to approach might have put them off.

He'd tried the same thing with Enat, but she had ignored his display, settling herself on the ground with her back resting against one of the towering stones while she began weaving a new basket of reeds.

When she pretended not to notice the snarl and the puff of smoke, Péist had turned his back on her. Still, she sat there, silently weaving her reeds. The basket was half-done when Péist shifted to sneak a glance at her.

"Are you ready to talk?" Enat asked, keeping her eyes on her weaving.

"What is there to talk about?"

She smiled—an expression that mystified him. When Caymin had first done it, he'd thought she was snarling. When he'd tried it, she had laughed at him. He had decided that dragons were not meant to smile.

"Oh, we could talk about how lonely you are. Or we could talk about how angry you are. Or we could—"

"I do not want to talk."

Enat shrugged. *"Fair enough. But I have missed your company these many moons. I never got to spend any time with you as a dragon, only as a cub."* She glanced at him. *"You are very handsome."*

He huffed, and little geysers of steam puffed from his nostrils. *"I am a dragon. Naturally, I am magnificent."*

Enat chuckled. *"And so modest."*

"Modesty cannot obscure the truth. Dragons are magnificent. But..."

"But what?"

"But you are right about the other things."

"She is lonely, too, you know."

"She does not act it."

"She does and she does not."

He watched her for a moment. *"I do not understand."*

Enat's mouth twitched again. *"Caymin is entering a difficult age for two-legs. She is probably as confused by her feelings as you are."*

Péist raised his head to look at her. *"Then how are we ever to be as we were before?"*

Enat lowered her basket. *"Be patient with her. She will sort her feelings out in good time."*

Péist thought on that conversation now, as he stretched out in the meager sunshine slanting down from between clouds. He missed having a warm, snug cave all his own as they'd shared on Inishbreith. He missed sharing that space with his mage.

He felt her before he heard her, huffing and stumbling as she climbed the hill and approached the circle. He quickly curled up and kept his head tucked under one wing, but he opened an eye, watching through the filmy expanse of his wing as she struggled to drag his saddle into the circle. At last, she dropped it to the earth and fell to her knees, gasping for breath. The emerald swung forward from where it now hung around her neck. Still, he did not move.

She sat, breathing heavily, watching him. At last, she said, *"I know you are not sleeping."*

Slowly, he pulled his head out from under his wing and turned to her. She got to her feet and approached.

"Are you still angry with me?" she asked.

He looked down at her, so small, so fragile, and felt something hard and cold inside him begin to soften. *"I am not angry with you."*

She blinked up at him. *"Then why are you hiding up here?"*

"I am not hiding. I simply prefer my own company lately."

"Because you are angry with me."

He rested his head on the ground. *"I told you, I am not angry."*

She sat beside him. *"Then what are you?"*

He said nothing for many heartbeats. He didn't know how to explain the loss he'd been feeling.

"Do you remember," she said, *"when you learned that your sires had both died? That those you came from were no more? If you had had a chance to go to a place where you could be with them—spend time with them, get to know them—would you have done it? Even if it meant you had to go without me?"*

He shifted his head to see her more clearly. *"Yes. I think I would have."*

"That is what it was like for me. I found myself in a place where they were alive and we were together, where none of the bad things here had happened. It was nice."

"Were you happy there?"

She frowned as she scratched a finger through the dry winter grass. *"Yes and no. I was happy for bits of time, but there was always something pulling at me."*

Péist snorted. *"Yes. The dog."*

Caymin's mouth twitched. *"No. Not just Mactíre. Many things felt odd. Broc came to me."*

"But not me."

"No. And I am not sure why." She looked into his eyes. *"I am sorry I did not come back to you sooner."*

The thing inside him that had begun to soften now felt as if it was breaking. *"I thought I had lost you."* He closed his eyes. *"I think dragons who lose their mages must go mad at the thought of living forever without that companionship. I do not know if I could have gone on without you."*

Caymin flung herself forward to wrap her arms around his neck. *"I have missed you."*

"And I you, little one." He tucked his chin around her, pulling her more tightly to him.

They stayed like that for a long time. When at last Caymin sat up, she gestured to where she had dropped the saddle.

"Can we fly?"

"It is daylight."

"I do not care," Caymin said. *"Most must know of us by now, and those who do not, should."*

Péist trotted over to the saddle and crouched so that she could hoist it into position and fasten the straps. She used magic to help lift it.

"Why did you not do that to carry it?"

She stopped and stared up at him. *"I did not think of it then."*

Péist rumbled deep in his chest. Caymin climbed up and fastened her tethers.

"Should we send a message to Enat so that she can let us back through the forest's protections?" Péist asked.

"We are a dragon and dragonmage. We should need no permission but that of the forest."

Péist turned within the circle of stones, loosing a volley of fire as he did so. Caymin opened her arms and summoned their combined power.

"Hear us," she called. "Know that we pledge our lives to your protection. Grant us the freedom to come and go as needed."

The air shimmered, rising from the circle all the way through the canopy of trees to the sky overhead. Péist gathered himself and leapt, opening his wings to fly.

"You're doing what?" Ivar roared as the others heard for the first time the plan for Caymin and Péist to go back through the Portal.

"We only just got you back," said Cíana, grabbing Caymin's arm. "You can't."

"We must." Caymin looked at her.

"But why?" said Séana, looking distressed. "What on earth could be so important that you would risk being lost in the otherworld again?"

Caymin glanced at Enat, who said, "We cannot tell you that." She immediately held up a hand at the protests. "Not because we don't trust you. But this is something that only Caymin and Péist can do, something so potentially devastating to the entire world, that we cannot risk having Timmin or Angus learn of it. And we know how skilled they are at manipulating others' minds."

All those gathered in the meetinghouse sat silently, while Péist and Mactíre crouched outside the door.

"How will you find your way back?" Neela asked.

"We have a guide this time," Caymin said. "Mactíre will go with us."

"What about your bodies?" Méav asked.

"What do you mean?"

She threw up her arms. "Péist had to fish you out of the pond last time. Who's going to drag a great, bloody dragon out of the water so we can keep watch over your bodies?"

"*It was not necessary,*" Mactíre said.

They turned to him.

"*What do you mean?*" asked Neela as Diarmit whispered a translation for Garvan.

"Her body would have remained below the water just as it was here. In a suspended sleep. When we go through the Portal, we will be able to remain there until we return."

Ivar glared at him. "And you can promise you will return?"

Mactíre blinked. "I cannot. But if all happens now as it should, then we will return."

Garvan leaned forward. "If this thing you have to do is so important, how do you know Angus and this Timmin don't already know of it?"

Caymin looked at him. "We do not. We can only guess because they have not done anything with it."

"How do you know?"

Enat smiled grimly. "Believe me, we would all know if one of them did."

"What can we do to help?" Daina asked.

"There is nothing you can do to help us with our task," Caymin said. "But we would go with easier minds if we knew you were safe from Angus and Timmin."

"Why can't you do that?" Garvan looked around at everyone. "We don't know what Angus is doing since he attacked Caymin, and I don't believe any of you know where Timmin is. You said Timmin has been able to get into your minds, read your thoughts? Do you know for certain he doesn't already know what you're searching for?"

Enat looked at Caymin. "A fair question. Have you felt Timmin in your spiritwalks or pushing into your waking mind lately?"

Caymin shook her head. "I have not, but I cannot say he has not, and I do not remember."

Garvan spread his hands, saying, "Why don't you do the same to him?"

Eachna frowned at him. "What do you mean?"

"Is there some magic law that says you can't get into his mind? Find out what he knows? Same for Angus."

The mages all looked at one another.

"Mactíre said Timmin was near the Portal," said Ronan. "If he's going in and out of the otherworld, would it be safe to enter his mind there?"

"I don't know," Neela said. "This is beyond anything we've ever done before."

"We would need something of theirs, some connection, since they're not here to make physical contact," said Eachna.

"We have Timmin's belongings from his cottage," Enat said. "His books and scrolls. We could go back and retrieve clothing or bedding."

"And I have this." Diarmit reached into his tunic and pulled out a rough, carved cross hanging from a leather cord. "Angus told me his first abbot gave this to him."

Niall expelled a breath. "We don't normally invade someone's thoughts like this."

Méav glanced at him. "But these aren't normal times."

"Timmin is still one of the most powerful mages alive," Eachna said. "If he feels us, he'll be able to block us."

Enat turned to Gai. "You haven't said anything. What do you think?"

Gai sat, twirling his finger and making the candle before him dance. "Angus isn't a trained mage. He may not realize what's happening, but Timmin will. What if..." He glanced toward the door. "What if a wolf appeared in his spiritwalk? Mactíre has already been through the Portal. If Timmin is still there, watching, he'll have seen him. Could one of us join with him and get into Timmin's mind that way?"

The elders exchanged glances.

"Aye," Neela said. "I think it could be done." She turned to the wolf. "If you're willing."

Mactíre bowed his head. *"I am."*

As they had done the night Mactíre dragged Caymin back through the Portal, they all gathered together. It had been decided that two of the elders should be the ones to try and bridge the gap—Ivar to Angus, and Enat to Timmin with Mactíre's help.

The others cast a wider circle of fire and spell around them to prevent any outside incursion. They clasped hands to link their magic.

Péist placed his head in the circle, between Caymin and Ronan, to add his power.

Mactíre, Enat and Ivar all drank a potion and then lay down in the middle of the circle. Méav, Una and Neela placed enchanted stones and crystals on their heads and chests to guide them.

Ivar clasped the cross Angus had given Diarmit while Enat draped one of Timmin's tunics around Mactíre's neck and wrapped it around her own hand.

"What do we do?" Daina whispered as Ivar and Enat went into deep trances.

"Just keep feeding the circle," Una whispered back. "It's up to them now."

"Quiet," Eachna snapped, not removing his gaze from Ivar and Enat's faces.

Caymin waited anxiously as both Enat and Ivar sank deeper into their spiritwalks. Enat had watched over her the night she took the spiritwalk that showed her her true name, but she'd never been on this side of the trance, watching and waiting. Ivar scowled and Enat groaned as their spirits roamed. Next to Enat, Mactíre's legs twitched as if he were running.

The stars slowly wheeled through the sky as the mages fed the fire surrounding them, keeping watch as the three continued their journey. Caymin's body ached from sitting so long on the cold ground, but on and on they waited.

Night was half-gone before Ivar's eyes fluttered open and he sat up, looking around wildly.

"What did you see?" Neela asked.

"Shhh," Eachna whispered, watching Enat.

Her hand was twisting the tunic wrapped around Mactíre's neck. She tugged and pulled on it, so hard that she actually moved the wolf's limp body a hand's breadth across the ground.

"Do we need to bring them back?" Ronan asked.

Eachna pursed his lips. "Wait a bit. Give her a chance."

Séana handed Ivar a cup of water, and he drank deeply.

Without warning, Enat gasped and rolled over, wrapping her arms around Mactíre and pulling him to her. "Help," she breathed.

Hands reached out, grasping fur, as the mages combined their power to draw the wolf back to them. Agonizing moments passed before Mactíre stirred and opened his eyes, breathing heavily, his tongue lolling.

Enat sat up shakily and leaned over the wolf. *"Are you all right?"*

"I am." Still, Mactíre panted as he lay there.

"What happened?" Daina asked, handing Enat a cup.

She drank, steadying herself, and then said, "Timmin."

Caymin offered a bowl of water to Mactíre. He lifted his head enough to drink and then lay back down.

"He is powerful," Mactíre said. He looked at Caymin. *"He knows you have been in the otherworld, but I do not think he knows you have left it. He is seeking a way in."*

Caymin laid a hand on his shoulder. *"Does he know where to go? Does he know why we are going?"*

"No." Mactíre closed his eyes in exhaustion.

Enat turned to Ivar. "What of Angus?"

Ivar's brows knit in a scowl. "He is in Éire, in a village along the northern coast. He is seeking travelers from the far north, trying to learn more about dragons."

"Did he sense you?" Neela asked.

Ivar shook his head. "I don't think so. He wasn't guarding his thoughts at all." He looked at Péist. "He means to find a way to wrest control of you from Caymin."

Péist raised his head. *"Then that is his mistake if he thinks that Caymin controls me like a winged ox."*

"He does not understand the bond between us," Caymin said.

"That doesn't mean he can't stir up trouble by getting others to notice you," Ronan said.

"I don't like this," said Ivar. "It's too risky for you to go back through the Portal just now."

Mactíre sat up. *"We must. We cannot wait any longer. A thousand winters is long enough."*

CHAPTER 18

Co the Beginning

It felt almost as it had when first Caymin came with Enat to the mystical forest and met the other apprentices. They sat together, gathered around a fire, some one or the other of them playing absently with the flames, making them dance on the night air as they talked about nothing important.

Caymin sat with her eyes closed, her back to Ciana, who was combing and re-braiding Caymin's hair. In her lap, she held her bow—the one Enat had given her—as she plucked the string.

For a little while, she could imagine she was no more than an apprentice mage, just a two-leg girl whose biggest concern was mastering a concealment spell. For a little while.

"You're sure about this?" Daina asked.

Caymin opened one eye. "Sure about my bow?"

Daina gave her a grudging grin. "No. Sure about going."

"I am sure I must go," Caymin said. "I am not sure I want to go."

"And you still can't say why you must do this?" Una asked as she used a stick to poke the embers of the fire.

Caymin sighed and opened both eyes as she shook her head. "I cannot."

"Where's Péist?" Ciana asked, tying one of the braids with a leather cord.

"He is hunting. He does not wish to go to the otherworld hungry."

Gai looked at her. "Are you afraid?"

"Yes," she said, watching the firelight illuminate the contours of his face. "I am."

He held her gaze for long heartbeats and then looked down at her bow. "You can take this with you?"

"Eachna said I can. Things you wear or carry through the Portal can accompany you. It is how Mactíre was able to wear the emerald back and forth to find me."

Reaching forward, he lifted the bow, hefting it. Caymin tried not to look at the empty tunic sleeve hanging at his left side.

She tore her gaze away and cleared her throat. "Will you be continuing your studies here?"

"In a manner of speaking. Diarmit and I are going to travel north with Eachna and Garvan. We can still study with Eachna and perhaps earn our staffs someday, but for now, we can try to learn what Angus is doing."

Caymin glanced in surprise at Diarmit who flushed deeply.

"I want to try and make amends for the damage I've done," he said, averting his eyes. "I know Angus better than any. I think I can help."

"You're not the only one to make mistakes," Gai said.

"When are you leaving?" Caymin asked.

"We'll stay long enough to see you and Péist safely through the Portal, and then we depart."

They sat on in silence. Ciana finished her braiding. Caymin glanced around at them, her first two-leg friends, wishing things could stay as they were. The fire burned down, and they reluctantly got up.

Daina gave Caymin a hug. "We'll see you on the morrow."

Caymin turned toward Enat's cottage, and Gai fell into step beside her. They walked in silence for a way.

"It isn't your fault, you know," he said softly.

She did not need to ask what he was referring to. "Eachna said it was. And he is right. If it had not been for me..."

"If it hadn't been for you, Angus's warriors would be overrunning this forest as we speak, killing it, desecrating it. And I would still be sitting like a trained dog at my brother's side as we tried to figure out how to ransom my father."

He held out the stump of his arm, looking down at it. "I carry the scars of battle now. I used to fear it. I know I bluffed that I wasn't afraid, but I was. I'm not any longer. If I die in battle, I die for what I believe in."

He looked deep into her eyes. "You are the truest friend I've ever had, Caymin. I would fight to the death with you if need be."

Sudden tears pricked her eyes. "I hope it will not come to that, but if it does, I would be proud to fight with you by my side."

He smiled. "Good night."

No sooner had Gai left her than Beanna flew down to land on her shoulder.

"He is right. It is not your fault."

"It feels as if it is."

"It is not your fault Angus decided to take what is not his to take. It is not your fault that you were meant to bond with the worm. It is not your fault that you and he were destined for things you did not ask for."

Caymin didn't know what to say to this.

"I told you after you claimed your name that all felt how powerful you were," Beanna reminded her. "It was true then. It is truer now. You must remember this as you face whatever is to come."

Caymin smiled as she brushed her cheek against Beanna's breast feathers. "Thank you."

"I, too, will see you tomorrow." Beanna pushed off and flew into the darkness.

Caymin walked on and found Enat sitting in front of her cottage, watching the stars.

"A good evening with your friends?" she asked as Caymin joined her.

"Yes."

Caymin unstrung the bow and set it aside. "Gai and Diarmit are traveling north with Eachna and Garvan?"

Enat nodded. "Aye. The rest of us will stay here. We can continue training the other apprentices while they learn what they can of Angus's plans. He's still dangerous."

"You trust Diarmit?"

Enat gave a half-smile. "I can't say I trust him entirely, but I think he deserves a chance to redeem himself."

"Do all who make the wrong decisions deserve that opportunity?"

Enat glanced at her, eyebrows raised. "Why do you ask?"

Caymin sat with her head bowed. "We are about to go back in time to fight those who started the last dragon war. What if there was some reason we do not know for what they did? What if they ask forgiveness and a second chance? How are Péist and I to make that decision? What if we make things worse?"

"Ah." Enat leaned her head back and stared again at the stars. "I cannot answer those questions for you, Caymin, except to tell you that I believe there is a reason that you and Péist, creatures orphaned and damaged, were chosen for this task. Neither of you has a desire for power, and both of you have good hearts. I have faith that you will make the right decisions as you face them."

The fire was no more than embers when Caymin woke. Nearby, Enat breathed deeply as she slept. Silently, Caymin secured the knife Méav had given her to her belt and gathered her cloak—the one the badgers had taken the night they rescued her. She removed the dragon brooch Enat had given her before she fled with Péist's egg. Crouching by the red glow of the fire, she dipped her finger in the ashes and wrote on a scrap of parchment. With one look back at Enat, she gathered her bow and quiver and let herself out the door.

Walking quickly, she made her way to the stone circle where Péist and Mactíre waited.

"*You have the emerald?*" Mactíre asked.

Caymin withdrew it from under her tunic.

"*You said farewell to the badgers?*" Péist asked.

"Yes. I spent most of the day with them. And I had time with some of the others last night. I wish I could have said farewell to Méav and Séana."

"I think it best if we simply go."

"I am ready."

Mactíre led the way down the hill to a stream. He found a pool where large boulders had slowed the flow to form a partial dam.

"How am I to fit into that?" Péist asked doubtfully.

"This is where I entered to bring Caymin back. The entrance to the Portal is not like this realm. Size does not matter," Mactíre said. "But Timmin may be watching for us. We will need to be vigilant. We do not want to bring him through with us."

Caymin looked at the water. "I do not remember how I went through the Portal last time. I thought I was going to drown when Angus tied me and dropped me in the water. What will keep us from rising to the surface?"

"You went through the Portal because you had no choice," Mactíre said. "We intend to go through, so we must keep swimming with our destination in mind. The emerald will guide us. Trust it."

"That is easy for you to say," Péist said, still eyeing the pool of water dubiously.

Caymin climbed onto Péist's saddle and strapped the tethers securely. Mactíre leapt up, scratching with his back paws as Caymin helped to haul him into her lap. Péist backed away from the water, giving himself room to maneuver.

"Are we ready?" he asked.

"We are."

Caymin took a gulp of air and tightened her grip on Mactíre as Péist leapt into the air and dove into the pool.

The water was freezing. Mactíre was right. What should have been too small for Péist easily allowed him to enter. With powerful strokes of legs and wings, Péist swam deeper.

The emerald, despite its weight, floated out ahead of Caymin, pulling her toward a distant green light. With hand and leg pressure, she guided Péist. She held her breath until she thought her chest would burst. When she could hold it no longer, she gasped and found that she could breathe easily. Glancing back, she saw what looked like a wall of water, while the greenish stuff they glided through no longer felt like water.

As before, there came a point, she wasn't sure where exactly, when they were no longer underwater and Péist seemed to be flying through air. The emerald still guided them, along with Mactíre.

"Just there," he said as they neared a rocky arch.

Péist folded his wings enough to shoot through, opening them again on the far side of the arch. He spread his wings wide and decelerated to a landing. Mactíre hopped down and shook himself.

"What now?" Caymin asked.

"This way," he said, setting off at a lope.

Péist and Caymin followed him to the base of a mountain. Mactíre began to climb a trail worn into the rock.

Péist craned his neck. *"Up there."*

He spread his wings again and took off, flying circles, higher and higher until he was high enough to fly into the mouth of a cave.

Like their cave on Inishbreith, this had been built to accommodate a dragon. A wide hollow, filled with soft skins, provided a sleeping place big enough for a dragon larger than Péist. A separate bed was built along one side for a dragonmage.

Caymin loosened her tethers and climbed down. Péist immediately stepped into the hollow, circling several times before settling with a satisfied groan. Caymin walked deeper into the cavern.

"Whose cave is this?" she asked, spying a cauldron and bunches of dried herbs and flowers hanging from the walls. Shelves were filled with books and scrolls, and there was a table with candles and pots of ink and sharpened quills.

"It is ours now." Péist already had his eyes closed in contented comfort.

"He is right."

Caymin jumped, and Péist gathered to leap at the source of the voice. A light flared in the darkness at the back of the cave, illuminating a face—a face Caymin knew instantly.

Wordlessly, she walked toward the holder of the light, taking in every detail—skin smooth and pale as the moon, dark hair hanging over her shoulders, eyes large gray pools watching Caymin in turn as she approached.

"Aine."

It wasn't a question. Caymin knew her as surely as she knew her own name. Soft clicks of claws on rock announced Mactíre's arrival.

"The tunnel," Caymin said, and a flood of memory washed over her. She knew this girl, knew this place. But how could she?

Aine smiled. "Yes. We used the tunnel to get up here, since we cannot fly." Her eyes moved to Péist who had crept out of his bed to stretch his nose toward her. "Greetings, Péist of Caymin. It has been long since we have seen each other."

Caymin stood, transfixed, as she watched Aine place her forehead to Péist's. Aine straightened and led the way to a fire pit, already stacked with peat, and ignited it with a wave of her hand.

"Come and sit," she said. "I have food for you."

"*I have hunted. I do not need to feed,*" Péist said, settling in his bed once more.

Caymin joined Aine and Mactíre at the fire, where soft pillows cushioned the rock floor. Aine pulled near a woven bag stuffed with smoked venison, carrots, onions...

"And oatcakes," she said with a smile, holding one out to Caymin.

Caymin took it, shivering when her fingers brushed Aine's. Tentatively, she nibbled on the cake while Aine shoved the onions and carrots into the coals to roast them.

"This is good," she said.

Aine smiled. "That's what you always said."

"I do not understand," Caymin said. "I have gone to a realm in the otherworld, back in time to a life where my parents were alive, but it did not exist in the real world."

"Yes," Aine nodded. "You told me."

She raised her gaze to Caymin's. Gently, she reached out and touched a finger to Caymin's scars. "You said, in that realm, you had never been burned, but you also never found your power."

Again, Caymin shivered at her touch. "How are you here? Have we gone back in time in our realm?"

Aine pursed her lips for a moment, and Caymin watched the firelight gild the delicate contours of her face.

"Yes and no," Aine said. "Time is not a straight line. It twists and weaves on itself."

She reached over and pulled two frayed threads from Caymin's cloak. She laid one out straight on the stone floor, and made the other wriggle over top of the first.

"I know you come from here," she said, pointing along the straight thread. "But," she paused, looping the second thread back over the first, "you have come back to me here."

"We are in the otherworld?"

"Are we?"

"But we came to you through the Portal to the otherworld. Did we appear in your time in the real world as well?"

Aine tilted her head and smiled. "Which world is real?"

Caymin frowned.

Aine pointed to her threads again. "Imagine many, many such threads, each weaving and circling and meeting at different points and then going in different directions. Such is the nature of time. Each will feel real when you're there. That is why you need a tether to guide you, or you'll forever be wandering amongst the various threads."

"But, yes," Aine added as Caymin continued to frown. "You..." She glanced at Péist. "Both of you appeared in our time in the real world. My world."

"Before this?"

This time it was Aine's turn to furrow her brow. "I think so."

"How?"

Aine shook her head. "I don't know." She looked around. "This cave had been empty for as long as I could remember. I always felt drawn here, though I didn't know why. One day, you were here. You simply appeared. As I knew you would now."

She used a stick to nudge the carrots and onions out of the fire and left them to cool for a moment.

"Scolaí and Tuala are alive here?" Caymin pressed.

Aine bit her lip and nodded.

"*And all the other dragons are here, with their mages?*" Péist asked.

Again, Aine nodded. She kept her eyes lowered as she busied herself placing meat, carrots and onions on a wooden plate and passing it.

Caymin accepted it and ate a bit as she thought. Her head hurt and she felt dizzy trying to understand everything.

Aine likewise took a plate. "What do you know of the war?"

Caymin opened her mouth to answer, but then closed it and pondered. "If I tell you what we know of the past, as it happened in our realm, will it affect things in this one, or in our past?"

Aine chewed as she thought. "I think you asked me that before, and my answer is the same. I will not be here for the end of the war, so I don't believe anything you tell me can change the outcome."

Péist raised his head. "*What do you mean, you will not be here?*"

Aine met his gaze. "I have a task to play in this, as do you and Caymin."

Mactíre whined and crawled forward on his belly. He laid his head in Aine's lap. She smiled and gave him a bit of venison.

Caymin watched her. "The Méarógfola?"

Aine nodded, scratching Mactíre behind the ears. She took a breath and looked up at both Caymin and Péist. "You have arrived as the war is moving beyond Éire, reaching across the sea to the lands of the Britons and farther east to the Germanic and Celtic tribes. The other dragons and mages are being compelled by the Bloodstone to do Scolaí's bidding."

She suddenly looked around. The cave was empty save for the four of them. "I would have sworn..."

She whispered words and waved her hand in a circle. The air surrounding them shimmered as she sealed their conversation from any who might overhear. "Ríona and Ailill came to me. We have worked out a plan to steal the Méarógfola from Scolaí and Tuala. I have to get it away from them."

"Where will you take it?"

Aine stared into Caymin's eyes. "That I cannot tell you."

"But we need it. Ailill and Ríona have told us we must find it."

Aine smiled. "And you shall."

She got to her feet. "I must return before I'm missed. Stay in the cave until nightfall."

"And then what?"

She smiled and walked away into the darkness at the back of the cave. Mactíre followed her, leaving Caymin and Péist alone.

Caymin sat beside Péist in the mouth of their cave, waiting for nightfall. Throughout the evening, they had seen distant shadows in the skies.

"*Other dragons?*" Péist asked, watching with interest.

"*I think so,*" Caymin said.

They perched, looking out over unfamiliar terrain—wild, mountainous, with deep valleys below.

"*Where are we?*" Caymin asked.

"*I do not know. It does not look like Éire.*"

"*I agree. I have not seen mountains this high in Éire.*"

Péist scanned the scene beyond the cave, watching the other dragons soaring. Caymin laid a hand on his shoulder and felt him quiver.

"*You wish to join them?*"

Péist did not reply immediately but, at last, said, "*I wish to know other dragons. Ones that are not trying to lure me into the otherworld or kill us.*"

Caymin smiled wistfully. "*It would be nice to be with other dragons and mages. Do you think... this far in the past, could your sires be here?*"

Péist shivered again. "*I have been wondering the same thing.*"

She leaned against him. "*We dare not search for them.*"

"*I know.*"

Her heart ached for the sadness inside him. They sat on, each lost in thought.

"*Has it occurred to you,*" Péist said, "*that when Ríona and Ailill told us we must stop a war, they were not speaking of Angus?*"

Caymin thought about this. "*I have been so focused on Angus, that I have not really thought about our role here.*" She looked at him. "*I cannot remember Ríona or Ailill saying what happened to Scolai and Tuala.*"

"*Nor can I.*"

"Were they killed?"

"You mean, did we kill them?"

Caymin paused and then nodded. *"Yes. Did we kill them?"*

Just as the sun's last light faded from the west, a shadow, darker than the night, appeared, flying toward them. They backed out of the way as Ríona flew into the cave with Ailill strapped to her saddle.

Ailill unfastened the straps securing her and leapt down lightly. She ran to the entrance of the cave and cast a spell to seal it. In three strides, she closed the distance between herself and Caymin.

Grasping Caymin by the shoulders, she said, "Who are you?"

Péist snarled, and the sound reverberated within the walls of the cave. Ailill looked from the girl to the dragon and released Caymin.

"Who are you?" Ríona repeated.

"You do not know us?" Caymin asked.

Ailill's eyes remained narrowed suspiciously. "We only know that Aine told us to come here."

Péist stretched his neck toward Ríona. *"We are from—"*

"We are allies," Caymin cut in, stepping on one of Péist's toes in warning.

"Whose allies?" asked Ríona.

Caymin looked from one of them to the other. "Allies of those who oppose Scolai and Tuala. That is why Aine told you to come here."

Ailill went to the fire pit. Caymin followed while the dragons maneuvered around each other to settle close by. With a flick of Ailill's hand, the fire flared, lighting the interior of the cave. Her sharp gaze took in Caymin's limp. She gestured to Caymin to sit beside her. She grasped Caymin by the chin, turning her face back and forth, inspecting her scars. For her part, she looked much younger than the Ailill that Caymin had seen on her spiritwalks.

"Where are you from?" Ailill asked, turning to stare at Péist. "We have never seen a white dragon."

Péist, apparently having understood Caymin's warning, said, *"We are from a distant land. What is this place?"*

"This is an island far to the north of Éire," Ríona said. *"How do you know of us and the war if you are not from here?"*

209

"We heard of the conflict and came to offer our aid," said Caymin. "What is happening with the war?"

Ailill's shoulders sagged. "It goes poorly. Or well, from Scolai's point of view. He has used us to gain control of many of the lands to the east."

"Where is he now?" Caymin asked.

"*He and Tuala hide away in a fortress here on this island,*" Ríona said. "*How is it that they do not know of you?*"

"We only recently arrived," Caymin said. She leaned forward. "Is there anything you can tell us? Any weaknesses they have?"

Ailill scoffed. "Their arrogance is their biggest weakness. They think they are destined to rule all the world."

"*Why do they shelter here?*" Péist asked. "*Why are they not fighting?*"

"*Why should they?*" said Ríona. "*When they have us to do their fighting for them?*"

"Is there anything you can tell us that would allow us to help you?" Caymin asked.

Ailill looked her up and down, her eyes lingering on Caymin's crooked arm and leg. "What can a cripple and a young dragon do that we could not?"

CHAPTER 19

The Dragon's Lair

"I can't believe they left without saying farewell to us," Garvan grumbled.

Enat gave him a sympathetic pat on the arm. "She has had more farewells in her life than any young person should. I think she simply couldn't bear any more."

She stuffed a bag with a few more provisions. "I wish we had more to give you."

Eachna glanced up from where he was tying a sleeping mat and cloak into a tight roll to sling over his back. "You don't have much to spare. We'll make do and gather as we go."

Diarmit looked doubtfully at the meager food she had packed. "Will we?"

Garvan grinned and clapped him on the back. "A little fasting is good for the soul, boy."

Diarmit did not look reassured as Beanna flew to Garvan's shoulder. He gently took her in his hands and cradled her against his chest.

"Not this time, my friend," he said softly. "Eachna has Lorcan should we need to send a message back here. You've been through enough. Stay with Enat."

He handed her to Enat who likewise cradled her, stroking her feathers.

"*He is right, Beanna,*" Enat said. "*You have done more than enough.*"

Beanna clicked her beak. "*I will stay, in case you need me here. Not because the hawk can fly faster than I.*"

Enat chuckled as Lorcan blinked at them. She set Beanna down and went to Gai, who was standing off by himself as the others milled around in preparation for departing.

"You think she and Péist got to the otherworld safely?"

He looked down at the dragon brooch he held in his hand.

"I do," Enat said. "I'm not sure why I think so, but I do."

"And she really left this for me?"

"I told you. She left it, asking me to send it with you. For luck on your journey. It may help others up north to trust you more."

She took it and fastened it to his cloak, realizing how much he had grown. She reached up and pulled him into her arms. "May the gods and goddesses protect you on your journey," she murmured.

Gai endured the embrace stiffly at first, but then wrapped his arm tightly around her. "Thank you."

Neela stuffed some more oatcakes into the bag as Garvan shouldered it. "Remember, Angus knows both you and Diarmit. If he sees you..."

"We'll be cautious."

She held a bag that clinked as she handed it to Eachna. "This is what's left of the gold. Take it. You may need it to trade for food."

Eachna tucked it into his tunic and took up his staff as Gai and Diarmit both shrugged woven bags onto their shoulders.

"We'll send word as soon as we know something," Eachna said.

Enat approached him. They looked into each other's eyes, and a sort of truce passed between them. She placed her hands on his shoulders and pressed her forehead to his. "Travel safely."

Ivar gave Gai a rough one-armed hug but said nothing to Diarmit. Enat glared at him and went to Diarmit herself.

"Thank you for putting yourself in danger again," she said. "Take no risks. If you see Angus, watch him from a distance. He's still powerful, and he knows you well."

Diarmit nodded and followed the others as they left the village.

Séana came over to where Enat stood. "What do you think they'll find?"

"I don't know, but I know it won't be good," Enat said darkly.

Waiting until full darkness had fallen, Péist flew a wide circle around Scolaí's fortress. It was carved into a spire of rock situated on a large hill surrounded by almost completely flat terrain, so that any who approached would be seen from a distance. Tiny points of light could be seen, torches burning here and there, but there had been no sign of Scolaí or Tuala in the nights they had been surveying the enemy.

"Do you think they are not flying at all?" Péist asked, taking care to block his words from all but Caymin.

"I do not know. Tuala has to hunt."

"Not if they have kills brought to him."

Caymin had not thought of that. *"Why are they hiding, though? They have already proven how powerful they are. And they have the—"*

"Stop! Do not speak its name. We cannot be certain none may overhear us, despite our precautions."

"You are right. I did not believe it safe to mention to Ailill and Ríona that we knew of it. Part of its power might be to compel them to report to Scolaí and Tuala."

Another dragon came into view from around the far side of the fortress. Péist flew into the cloud cover.

"If they are all so busy fighting this war, why are there so many dragons and mages here?" he asked.

Giving up for the night, they flew back to their cave. Caymin climbed down and removed Péist's saddle.

"I must hunt," he said. *"I will go to the far side of the island."*

He took off again, leaving Caymin alone in the darkness. She stacked some turf in the fire pit and ignited it with her firestarters. She nearly jumped out of her skin when the firelight illuminated Aine's face.

"Why don't you use magic for that?" Aine asked from where she sat.

Caymin was still breathing hard from the fright she'd had. "I was taught to save my magic for when I need it."

Aine came closer and settled near the fire. "I've been waiting for you."

Her hair was gathered in a loose braid that hung down her back. Caymin hesitated and then sat so that her scarred side was hidden from Aine. She noticed for the first time that Aine's tunic and leggings were made of soft leather, worked with decorative stitching. She reached out to touch it.

"This must have taken many skins."

"It did." She in turn fingered the woven cloth of Caymin's tunic. "Did you make this?"

"No. We trade with others, those without magic, for what we cannot make."

Aine tilted her head. "What do you trade?"

"Healing potions and salves, enchanted stones, sometimes weapons and tools."

"How many of you are there?"

"It keeps changing," Caymin said. "And it depends on whether you are speaking only of two-legs. We have many winged and four-leg companions as well."

Aine eyed her closely. "Tell me how you got your scars."

Caymin turned away and played with the fire. "Have I not told you this story before?"

"You have. It's strange; some things I remember, while others I don't. If we spoke of them, I don't recall. But I want to hear it again, how the badgers saved you and made you part of their clan. It makes me feel as if I know them."

Caymin smiled and gladly told her of the night Broc found her and talked Cuán and the others into bringing the injured two-leg cub back to the sett. Aine laughed as she told of Broc trying to feed her earthworms. She listened raptly as Caymin told how she had healed Cuán after the wolves attacked, and how that bit of magic had led Enat to come searching for her.

"It sounds wonderful," Aine said softly when Caymin paused.

Caymin studied Aine's expression, watched the firelight on her pale skin, wishing she had more stories to tell, to keep Aine listening forever. "What about you?"

Aine's brow creased. "I don't understand."

"Are you an apprentice mage? I do not see a staff. Who are you studying with?"

"You don't know?"

"Know what?"

Aine sat back, hugging her knees to her chest. Just as she opened her mouth, Mactíre galloped up from the tunnel at the back of the cave, skidding to a stop near them.

"He is looking for you."

Aine leapt to her feet. *"Does he know how long I have been gone?"*

"I do not know. He is in a rage."

She looked down at Caymin. "I must go. I'll return when I can."

Caymin jumped up as Aine ran to the tunnel. "Wait!"

But she was gone. Mactíre padded to her, placing his head under her hand.

"Where did she go? Who is looking for her?"

He looked up at her. *"Scolaí."*

Caymin stepped back. *"She knows Scolaí?"*

"She serves him."

A storm raged outside the cave, rain slashing and wind howling past the mouth, as Caymin and Péist stayed safely within. Caymin sat hunched over a scroll, holding it to a candle so that she could read the account written there.

"What does it say?" Péist asked from where he lay curled up in his bed.

215

"Some is the history of dragons and mages, their deeds. Did you know that they saved entire tribes of two-legs by carrying them to safety during floods and by using their fire to stop skyfires from spreading?"

She lowered the scroll and looked at him. "How did we go from saving two-legs to destroying them?"

"Like Angus. Perhaps all it takes is one who becomes hungry for power and so it starts."

Caymin waved the scroll. "Two-legs used to seek their counsel. Even kings and queens did."

"Until Aolu. Riona and Ailill said it began with him, gathering the two-leg clans and seeking power of his own until he warred with Scolai and Tuala."

"Could we stop this before it started if we stop Aolu?"

Péist shifted his head. "We are not here to change the past."

Caymin frowned and rubbed her forehead. "I cannot remember what is past. Aine is with us now, yet remembers us from the past. It is too confusing. What is truly in the past? Are we not changing things simply by being here?"

"But it was already written that we were here, fighting Scolai and Tuala, while Aine got away with the..."

He left the word unspoken.

Caymin dropped her head into her hands. "What are we supposed to do? We have been here for nearly a fortnight—if time moves at the same pace here as in the real world—and we have not even seen them. How can we fight them?" She sighed heavily. "How can we defeat them if we do fight them? They are much older and more experienced warriors than we. What do we know that they do not?"

"I still want to know what Mactire meant when he said Aine serves Scolai," Péist said. "Can we trust her?"

Caymin raised her head. "Riona and Ailill trusted her enough to have her steal... it. If they trusted her, then I think we must."

As if responding to their names, a dark shadow in the sky approached and entered the cave. Water ran off Riona's scales as she walked deeper into the recess before Ailill dismounted.

"Now is the time," Ailill said from under a sodden cloak. She took it off and whispered a spell to dry it. She looked at them skeptically. "If you are to do anything it will be now."

"Why now?" Caymin asked.

"*And why are there so many dragons here if Scolaí is using you to make war to the east?*" Péist asked. "*I have seen them flying.*"

Ríona glared at him. "*That is what we have come to tell you. Tuala and Scolaí had called many of us back here to plan their next move. They are sending us now to the lands to the north, lands that have their own dragons who are not bound by the—*" She stopped abruptly and looked at Ailill.

Ailill sat at the fire, holding her hands out to the warmth. "You must know, through our own blind trust and foolishness, we are compelled to do as Scolaí and Tuala command. This will be horrible. No matter which side is the victor, dragons will die on both sides." She looked up at Caymin. "If you truly are what Aine says—the only ones who can defeat Scolaí and Tuala—it must be now, after we have left and will not be here to defend them."

"How do we draw them out? We have been flying, at night only, but we have not seen them." Caymin glanced at Péist. "At least we do not believe we have."

"No, you haven't," Ailill said. "Tuala is a bronze and Scolaí, well, you will know Scolaí when you meet him."

"*You said I was the only white dragon you have seen. Others must have seen us flying. Why have they not told Scolaí and Tuala?*"

"*They can only command us based on what they know, and those who have seen you wish to be free of this curse as much as we. They have kept silent as we have, hoping you are what Aine believes you to be.*"

Caymin looked from one of them to the other. "But you still do not believe we can help."

Ailill sat back and regarded her. "We have lived many hundreds of winters. We have great power, but we could not resist them. It is hard to imagine how you can do what we could not."

"You said that before," Caymin said, her eyes flashing. "But we are not the ones who gave away our free will to those who would use us for evil."

Ailill gave her a twisted smile. "Fair enough." She reached into her tunic and pulled out a piece of parchment. "This is a map of the fortress. Learn this, the patterns of the rooms and halls." She flattened it and pointed. "Tuala has his own chamber, but Scolaí is most often here." She indicated a multi-roomed wing. "If you can catch them separately, you will have a better chance of defeating them."

They spent time going over the various entrances to the fortress, where sentries would be posted, and the most likely ways in. As Ailill described the passageways and chambers, Caymin was able to picture them in her mind, as if she'd seen them before.

At last, Ailill stood and pulled her cloak over her shoulders. "We are off to the north in the morning. We may never see you again, Péist and Caymin." Her expression softened. "Take care. And if you succeed, the world will owe you a debt beyond measure."

As Ailill had said, the air was dotted the next day with the shapes of many dragons. The storm had passed by daybreak, leaving the sky a clear blue. Péist watched with longing as they flew to the north.

"*So many, and I will never know them,*" he mourned.

Caymin leaned against his shoulder, but she had no words to comfort him. They watched until the dragons disappeared from view.

"*When do you think we should enter the fortress?*" she asked.

"*If we go too soon, Scolaí may call the other dragons back to aid him. I do not wish to fight my kindred unless I must. I think we should wait until nightfall.*"

With that, he curled up in his bed, tucking his head under his wing. Caymin tried to read, hoping to find something, anything, that would help them defeat Scolaí and Tuala. She huffed impatiently as she tossed yet another scroll aside and then suddenly paused.

Ríona and Ailill had told them it was written that they would fight Tuala and Scolaí. Never had they said they would defeat them. She sat back, dumbfounded by that thought. Mayhap, their only role was to distract Scolaí long enough for Aine to steal the Méarógfola. Mayhap, she and Péist were never meant to defeat them, or even to live to return to their realm. They knew only that, once the Bloodstone was no longer in Scolaí's possession, the other dragons had been freed of its control. Not one had said that she and Péist were needed again beyond that task.

Péist did not stir, but she knew very well he had felt everything she had as she came to that realization. Together, they waited as sunlight and shadows shifted and changed the light within the cave. Her stomach rumbled, but she had no wish to eat.

At long last, darkness fell and Péist roused himself. Wordlessly, Caymin saddled him. When she was done, he lowered his head. She pressed her forehead to his, her hands on either side of his face.

"Whatever befalls us this night, little one," he said, "know that of all mages, I would have chosen you to bond with."

"And I you."

She checked her bow one last time, strapped her quiver to the saddle, and climbed up to tether herself to her dragon.

Péist walked to the entrance of the cave. Caymin closed her eyes as he spread his wings and dropped off the ledge. Immediately, his wings caught the air and he tilted, carving a wide turn. For long heartbeats, they flew together, reveling in the feeling of freedom, just the two of them in the dark. A sliver of a moon appeared in the east as they approached the fortress.

Remembering the map Ailill had drawn for them, they made for an entrance carved into a sheer rock face. Caymin nocked an arrow, prepared to meet sentries, but there were none. The entrance, as they neared, grew larger and larger, until they could see that it was wide enough for a dragon four times Péist's size. Enormous grates built of iron hung on either side, able to be swung closed if needed, but they stood open.

"Why have we encountered no resistance?" Péist asked as he cautiously flew in.

"I do not know." Caymin felt just as uneasy.

Péist flew until the huge tunnel they were in forked. He glided to a halt. Behind them, the rock vibrated and shook as a metallic clang reverberated off the walls. They raced back up the tunnel to find the grates had swung closed and were locked magically.

"It seems we now have no choice," Péist said.

He walked back to where the tunnel forked, neither of them in any hurry to see what awaited them. The passage to the left angled down into darkness while the right-hand one curved out of sight.

"*Do we stay together or split up?*" Caymin asked.

"*They know we are here. I think we should split up. I will go down to Tuala's chamber while you go to Scolai. If we can find them apart from each other, we may have a better chance.*"

Caymin unstrapped herself and slid down with her bow and quiver. She glanced back once as she walked away. "*I will see you soon.*"

For a two-leg, all would have been darkness, blacker than night with no stars or moon to light the sky, but to a dragon, not so. Péist saw the faint warmth of two-leg footprints on the rock. He followed them as quietly as he could along the corridor, following it down, down into the depths of the fortress. He saw the tiny heat-filled bodies of mice scurrying about, in and out of the crevices in the rock. He smelled the blood of a recent kill, dragged along the floor in the wake of the footprints and deposited at the end of the corridor. He felt a rush of air as the corridor, large as it was, opened into a much larger space. His eyes could make out the gray-on-gray edges of rock that showed him a cavernous chamber. The floor was strewn with bones and the putrid remains of carcasses. In the center was an enormous mound. It gave off waves of warmth, and was nearly twice his height. But as he stood there, he realized it breathed.

Tuala.

It could only be he. Péist was not normally reticent or shy about acknowledging his magnificence but, at that moment, he felt small and inconsequential. Tuala's hulking form dwarfed him. How in the name of all that was sacred was he to fight this giant?

He hunkered down, watching Tuala sleep and considering his options.

Through his link with Caymin, he had glimpses of her traveling through an upper corridor, smaller than this one, with torches every so often.

Péist extended his head farther into the cavern, looking around more carefully. As far as he could see, there was only one other entrance, on Tuala's far side. He could not remember where that passage led but, considering the locked grates behind him, hoped it led out of the fortress.

"Do you not think I know you are here, hatchling?"

The voice echoed inside Péist's head just as it did off the rock walls of the chamber. It was deep and rumbling and seemed to vibrate within Péist.

Slowly, the gigantic mound began to move. A sinuous neck uncurled as wings shifted and legs stretched. Péist stood paralyzed, as Tuala's great head swung around to fix him with eyes that seemed to pierce him with their yellow glow.

Tuala regarded him for long heartbeats, tilting his head as his neck twisted from side to side. Unable to move or look away, Péist stood as if his legs had grown from the very rock.

"Why do you come here all alone, I wonder? Ah... but you are not alone, are you, hatchling?"

Péist tried too late to block his connection to Caymin. Tuala laughed and the sound reverberated within the cavern.

"Two hatchlings. Thinking to defeat the greatest dragon and mage ever to live?"

At that, Péist drew himself up. *"You are not. The maddest, mayhap, but not the greatest."*

The spark of anger in Tuala's eyes momentarily lit the chamber. *"Who are you to speak to me thusly?"* He rose higher, looking down on Péist who fought the instinct to flee. *"You are nothing."*

"I am not. My mage and I will be your downfall."

Tuala gathered slightly, and Péist felt the strike coming. He lunged to the side as Tuala's jaws snapped the empty air where, just a heartbeat before, his head had been. Péist leapt into the air, his smaller size allowing him to maneuver within the chamber. He dove, striking Tuala's back with his talons before spiraling out of the path of the torrent of fire Tuala belched in his direction.

Like a sparrow harassing a crow, Péist flew circles, darting in to snap at Tuala's neck, his back. Tuala's scales were almost impenetrable—Péist's talons scratched, but could barely pierce them.

Tuala, for all of his bulk, was lightning fast with his strikes. His spouts of fire were enormous, scorching. Péist's inner eyelids closed reflexively, shielding his eyes as he flew through the inferno.

"*You are nothing!*" Tuala roared in rage as Péist harried him, snapping and attacking before darting out of reach.

Tuala suddenly stilled, and Péist, too, paused his attacks, as they both felt what was happening above them.

Tuala laughed again. "*And you will soon be mageless, you witless worm.*"

CHAPTER 20

REVELATIONS

Caymin's eyes fluttered open. Her heartbeat pounded inside her head as she tried to remember where she was. She only knew her body ached as if she'd been dropped off the edge of a cliff. A light flickered to her side, and she turned her head to see a figure hunched over a table, scratching away with quill and parchment. At her movement, the quill stilled and the figure rose. It loomed over her, and she blinked stupidly. The face came into focus. It looked vaguely familiar.

"So, you thought to slither into my domain and do what? Defeat me?"

She blinked again, looking up into eyes that pierced her—cold, gray as iron, set in a pale face framed by black hair. She tried to sit up, but was restrained by cords binding her to a wooden plinth. She had idea where her bow was and, as her hands groped along her belt, she found her knife was gone.

He paced around the plinth, staring down at her, his hands behind his back. "Who are you?"

Her mind cleared, and she tried to recall how she'd come to be lying here so helpless. She had been creeping up the corridor, toward

Scolaí's chambers, when she'd felt the sudden conflict between Péist and Tuala. Scolaí must have been alerted by it as well, because the last thing she remembered was a flash of green light.

He leaned over her now, staring deep into her eyes, and she felt him pushing into her thoughts. She squeezed her eyes shut, trying to block him. She'd never been able to do this properly. He pushed harder, and she instinctively repelled him with a shield charm. It was strong enough to push him back a little and, momentarily, worked in the opposite direction. Just for a heartbeat or two, she got a glimpse inside his mind.

His eyes widened for an instant, but he quickly laughed, the sound of it echoing around the chamber they were in.

He leaned over her again, leering down at her. "Who are you?"

She studied his face, his eyes. "It frightens you."

She felt a small surge of victory at the startled expression that flickered across his face.

"Nothing frightens me," he snarled.

"You lie."

Her words may have startled him, but the smile on her face infuriated him. His face twisted.

"What do you know of anything?"

She squirmed to keep him in her sight as he paced. "I know that it frightens you that we are here, and you do not know how. I know it frightens you that whatever power you think you have gained could be snatched away by those who oppose you."

He laughed again, but it sounded forced. "Tuala and I have no opposition."

"You are wrong. We could only have been brought here by those who oppose you."

He stepped nearer and grabbed her hair, twisting it painfully in his fist. "Who brought you?"

She looked up at him, trying to remain calm. "Surely, you were not always like this."

"Like what?"

"Evil."

He twisted his hand more tightly in her hair, lifting her face until she was almost nose-to-nose with him. "Do not presume you know me."

He slammed her head back down so hard, she saw stars for a moment. He stepped back. "Stay here and watch her. I wish to see what Tuala has to show me."

"Yes, Father."

Caymin wriggled around at the sound of that voice, searching for its owner. Aine stood nearby, watching Caymin with an expressionless face. Scolai's footsteps faded away, and they stared at each other.

"Father?" Caymin struggled against her bonds. "Scolai is your father?"

"Yes." Aine's voice was soft, her eyes guarded.

"You betrayed us," Caymin said, her eyes filling with angry tears.

"No." Aine stepped closer. "I have not betrayed you. You must believe me. You knew, in the past. When I realized you didn't here, I wished to tell you, but I didn't know how to say it."

Caymin continued to kick and fight. "How could Ailill and Ríona ever have trusted you? How could I?"

Aine rushed to her and knelt, placing a restraining hand on Caymin's forehead. "You must believe me. My task, my mission is still what it was. I am the only one close enough to do it. You and Péist must still fight them. This changes nothing."

Caymin felt as if a light inside her had gone out. In a voice barely a whisper, she said, "It changes everything."

Aine stood and backed away, her face once again impassive. With a wave of her hand, Caymin's tethers loosened.

By the time Caymin untangled herself and sat up, Aine was gone.

"Aine?" she whispered. "Aine!"

There was no answer.

Caymin ran from the chamber, back along the corridor to the one that led down to Tuala. She felt nothing from Péist, and that frightened her more than the fight she'd felt earlier.

She slowed as the other corridor descended. Her nose wrinkled as the scent of death and decay came to her on the damp air. Cautiously, she peered into a darkness blacker than the darkest badger sett, wishing she had dragon-vision.

Sudden light blinded her as Scolaí swept an arm and lit torches all around the chamber. A scream died on her lips when she saw Péist, his wings askew, lying pinned to the floor by Tuala's huge claws. The tips of his talons pierced Péist's scales, and drops of ruby-red blood shone on his white scales.

Scolaí looked at her with a cold smile. "Who summoned you?"

Caymin looked on helplessly as Péist squirmed. The bones littering the chamber floor under him crunched as Tuala increased his pressure.

"Tell them nothing, little one."

"Little one?" Tuala's lip curled. *"How fitting. Two little ones thinking to attack us in our own lair."*

Scolaí paced, smirking at her. Aine's resemblance to him was striking, and Caymin wondered how she hadn't recognized it immediately, but there was cruelty etched on his face that Caymin knew could never be on Aine's.

"I'll only ask one more time," Scolaí said. He gripped the air with his fists, and it was as if invisible hands picked her up and pinned her to the wall. "Who brought you here? Who has betrayed us?"

When Caymin still refused to answer, he reached under his tunic and pulled out a braided chain of silver. Suspended from it was a tear-shaped stone, smaller than Caymin's palm. At first, she thought it was black, onyx mayhap, but as it moved in the light, it glowed a deep, deep red. Blood-red. She gasped as Scolaí moved closer to Péist.

"I don't know if this works the same way if the blood isn't given willingly, but we shall find out," he said softly as he crouched. "First you and then your mage."

This time the scream did erupt from her, filling the chamber, tearing at her throat. Her power surged within her as it never had before, and she dropped back to the floor as the power of Scolaí's spell was shattered. Focusing her strength and anger, she raised her hands as she leapt forward. Scolaí was thrown across the chamber. His head slammed against the wall, and he slid to the floor, unconscious, blood trickling from his ear. She turned her fury on Tuala, her teeth bared, growling and snarling as if she would tear his throat out. He released Péist, backing away as he snarled in return.

226

Péist scrambled to his feet, reaching out to touch his wing to her. The contact amplified her power and it blazed, out of her control. She flung her hands outward, hitting Tuala with the full force of what she had conjured just as he released a volley of flame. Her spell rebounded all of it back at him. She jumped, scrabbling at Péist's saddle with hands and feet.

"Go!"

Péist took advantage of the wall of flame separating them from Tuala, and he flew into the tunnel he hoped would offer them escape. Wings taut, he arrowed through the twisting passage, back out into the night. She had no idea how long her spell would last but, behind them, she heard Tuala's roar of fury and frustration.

Péist landed heavily as he flew back into their cave. He stumbled, nearly throwing Caymin into the wall. She clambered down and ran her hands over him, feeling warm, sticky blood. With an impatient flick of her hand, she produced a ball of flame and bent closer to inspect his wounds. She felt sick at the sight of four punctures where Tuala's talons had pierced Péist's scales, ripping a couple of them off, leaving raw, bloody patches where all should have been white and smooth.

A sudden movement behind them made her whirl about, ready to hurl flame at the intruder, but Mactíre ran into the light.

"*We must leave this place,*" he said, panting.

"*We cannot,*" Caymin replied. "*I must heal Péist.*"

"*There is no time. They are coming. Searching for you. They do not yet know you have been staying here, but they will find you soon. We must leave.*"

"*He is right,*" Péist said. "*I can fly. Gather what you need and let us depart.*"

Caymin hesitated just a moment and then quickly gathered her cloak and a couple of scrolls. She didn't allow herself time to mourn the loss of her knife and bow—both gifts, both precious to her. She and Péist were alive. That was the only important thing for now.

She climbed back into the saddle, strapping herself in this time. Mactíre leapt up and settled in Caymin's lap as Péist trotted to the ledge and took off.

Mactíre directed them away from the fortress, to a dense stand of forest. Caymin felt Péist's pain, and laid a hand on his neck, giving him some of her power to help sustain him. He landed awkwardly in a clearing. Mactíre jumped down as Péist stumbled again.

"This way."

He led the way through the trees to a place where a wall of vines grew thickly, looking very solid. He pushed through and disappeared. Caymin dismounted and walked up to the vines. Parting them, she saw that they covered the entrance to a tunnel.

Again, she conjured a ball of white flame to light the way as she and Péist followed the twists and turns down into the earth. This tunnel was unlike the others. It looked to have been formed naturally and was just barely large enough for Péist. Tuala would never fit.

At last, it opened into a cavern large enough for Péist to maneuver. He dropped, panting. Caymin looked around and saw that there were provisions—food, candles, wood and turf. She lit several candles, and the cavern was illuminated enough to see that there were also a few beds. Mactíre dropped to his belly, tongue lolling.

She took off Péist's saddle. *"We must heal you."*

"No. It will take too much of your energy. You must conserve it. You may need it."

She laid a gentle hand on his neck. *"What I will need is you. Whole and able to fly with me."*

The slap of running footsteps on rock made them both jump. Péist arched his neck, prepared to breathe fire, while Caymin held her hands at the ready to cast a spell of protection.

"Stay," came Aine's voice from the darkness. "'Tis I." She stepped into the light.

Caymin watched her warily. "Why are you here?"

Aine ignored the challenge in her voice. "I brought these." She set Caymin's bow, quiver, and knife down.

She lit the fire and began warming water in a cauldron over the flames.

"I found this tunnel and chamber long ago," she said, avoiding Caymin's eyes. "This is where Ailill and I met to make our plans. Ríona could not fit here, but she kept watch. We laid many spells of concealment and protection on this place. I don't think Scolaí can find us here."

"Do you not mean 'Father'?" Caymin asked.

Aine paused at the accusation in the question. "He has never been a father to me," she said softly, keeping her eyes on what she was doing. "He sired me, from one of the young women who served him. He would have ignored me completely had he not sensed the power in me. He knew I could be of use to him then, and he fostered my magical training." She raised her gaze at last to meet Caymin's. Her gray eyes were hard, and Caymin saw a bit of Scolaí in them as she said again, "He has never been my father, though I was forced to call him such."

With the cauldron of water warmed, she dipped a cloth into it and used it to sponge away the blood covering Péist's side. He grunted in pain as the cloth rubbed against the raw spots where his scales had been ripped away.

"Now, we can see what we're healing," Aine said softly. "I'll help you."

Caymin stepped up, laying her hands on Péist and pulling her magic up. As before when she had done this, her hands glowed as if on fire. The cords of her neck stood out and her eyes rolled back as she drove energy deep into her dragon to heal the puncture wounds. Aine laid her hands over top of Caymin's, adding her power. For many heartbeats, they worked together to heal his wounds.

"Stop." Aine pulled on Caymin's hands. "Stop. It is enough. He'll be all right now, and you're losing too much strength."

Caymin slumped to the floor. Aine dipped some of the hot water into a cup and added some crushed herbs. Moving her hand over the cup, she whispered words of power.

"Drink this," she instructed, pushing the cup into Caymin's hands.

Caymin hesitated a moment but then closed her eyes and drank. The potion warmed as it went down her gullet, the herbs and enchantment sending renewed energy to her exhausted body.

Péist touched his snout to Caymin. *"Are you all right, little one?"*

"I am." She laid a reassuring hand on his jaw. *"Rest."*

He stretched out full on the floor, allowing his body to regenerate. Caymin sagged against him, drinking more of the potion.

Aine retrieved some smoked venison. "Eat."

She also sat with food and drink as Caymin gnawed on the meat.

Caymin glanced at her weapons. "Thank you," she said, gesturing in their direction.

Aine nodded. "You'll be needing them."

Caymin drained her cup and sat back. "I thought... I did not trust you. Can you forgive me?"

Aine looked into her eyes for several heartbeats before saying, "There is nothing to forgive."

"Why do you serve him?"

Aine smiled bitterly. "Because I must." She shrugged. "It has allowed me access no other has."

She reached into her tunic and pulled out a braided silver chain. Caymin gasped when she saw it.

Péist gave a lurch as he sat up. *"The Méarógfola?"*

The stone pulsed red in Aine's palm, as if it had a heartbeat of its own. She nodded, looking at it as she would something dead, something foul. "Scolaí was still unconscious and Tuala was walled off by your spell. I decided I would never have a better opportunity."

Caymin gaped at her. "But that means..."

"Yes." Aine let the stone swing from its chain. "It means, while I possess it, I control the dragons and mages whose blood it contains."

Caymin held her breath, watching Aine as she regarded the stone. Its bloody glow reflected off her fair skin, and she looked very like Scolaí.

"But..." Aine closed her hand over the stone, and her face was once again her own. "I know what I must do."

"Can we not destroy it now?" Péist asked.

Caymin glanced at him. "Yes. We have been told we must. Why can we not do it now?"

Aine hesitated a moment. "You may try."

She set the stone on the cave floor and stepped back. Péist gathered his fire and loosed a torrent. When it burned away, the stone lay unscathed.

Caymin pulled her power up and flung the full force of it at the stone, trying to pulverize it into nothingness. Still, it lay there, untouched.

"I don't think it can be destroyed by ordinary means," Aine said quietly. She picked the stone up and draped the chain over her head as they sat back down.

Caymin huffed in consternation. "How then?"

Aine met her gaze. "That is something you will need to learn. I don't know the answer." She reached into her tunic and pulled out a small piece of wood. She took Caymin's hand and pressed the wood to her palm.

Caymin held it up. It looked like a bit of twisted root. "What is this?"

"You'll need that."

"Why? When?"

Aine smiled. "You'll know when. And why. When the time is right."

She looked at them sadly. "I must leave now. Scolaí and Tuala will both be in a rage. There can be no going back. I must take this and flee. You need to leave as well. Mactíre can guide you back through the Portal."

Caymin and Péist turned to each other. Caymin lowered her eyes as a silent understanding passed between them.

"*We cannot leave yet,*" Péist said. "*We must engage them long enough for you to get away.*"

"You can't!" Aine grabbed Caymin's arm. "You don't know what they're capable of. I've never seen any others defy them as you did. I don't know how..." Her eyes were wide with fear. "Your power, in that chamber... They thought you both too young to be a threat. They won't make that mistake again. The next time you encounter them, they will kill you."

Caymin, rather than feeling more frightened upon hearing those words, felt instead a sense of calm. "We know what we must do. You and the Bloodstone are the most important things. We cannot risk it falling back into their hands. If you do not get away, all is lost."

Aine's eyes filled with tears. "Never," she whispered, but her throat caught for a moment. "Never will I forget you."

She leaned forward and kissed Caymin's cheek. Her tears splashed onto Caymin's skin. She pushed to her feet and ran from the cavern.

Mactíre whined as he watched her go. Caymin pressed a hand to her cheek.

Gai stared in wonder at the village below them. It sat perched on the side of a river that emptied into a sheltered lough.

Eachna pointed. "At the far end of the lough, it connects to the sea."

Gai had thought the village within and around his father's fortress was large, but this was larger still. A few boats bobbed on the river as fishermen hauled nets loaded with wriggling fish out onto wooden docks. In the distance, other boats were coming in.

"How will we know if Angus is here?" asked Garvan.

"People notice Angus," Diarmit said. "He likes to call attention to himself."

"If he uses any magic, I'll be able to sense it," said Eachna. "But if he doesn't, we'll just have to look and ask."

He squinted at the sky. "It's past midday. Let's split up. If any one of us finds him, don't interact with him in any way. We only want to find out what he's up to. We'll meet back here at dusk. I think we'd better spend our nights away from others."

Eachna sent Lorcan to fly on his own, and the four of them scattered as they descended the hill into the village.

Gai wore his cloak fastened with the dragon brooch at his neck, so that it draped loosely over both shoulders. Few people seemed to notice him as he walked. Apparently, they were accustomed to strangers and thought nothing of this one. He was surprised by the number of fair people he encountered. Their blond hair and strange language marked them as northmen. He paused at a blacksmith's stall, pretending to be perusing a table filled with knives. The workmanship was exceptional, with fine scrollwork on the hilts and a keen edge on the blades. He looked up to see the smith, a muscular man with blue eyes and full blond beard, eyeing him.

"Nice work," Gai said, holding up one of the knives.

"Thank you."

Relieved that the smith spoke his language, Gai said, "You're from the north?"

The smith nodded. "From Daneland."

Gai looked at the forge, a sturdy stone hearth sheltered by a wooden structure. "You live here?"

The smith grinned. "I do now." He gestured behind him to where a pretty woman sat, working leather with tools to make sheaths for the knives. "I came ten winters ago on a ship. The others took what they wanted and went back. I found what I wanted and stayed."

The woman didn't glance up, but her cheeks reddened as the smith chuckled.

Gai smiled. "Are there many of you, from the north, living here?"

The smith shrugged. "A fair few. Many go home, but most of my village was wiped out by the plague in my father's father's father's time, and we're scattered now."

"But you're not here to pillage or fight?"

The smith put his head back and laughed. "Boy, do I look like I want a fight? We've three little ones to feed. I'm not after going on raids." He shrugged his massive shoulders again. "There are those who do come to raid, though. They know to steer clear of this village. Those of us who decided to stay just want to live in peace."

He stepped over to the table and hefted a sword. The pommel was worked with silver in intricate knots. Gai leaned in for a closer look.

"Is that a dragon?"

"Aye." The smith looked pleased. "Here."

He tossed it to Gai who caught it with one hand. The smith stared at the stump that had reflexively reached forward from under Gai's cloak. Gai felt his cheeks burn, but ignored the stares from the smith and his woman. He brandished the sword. It was beautifully balanced, even with one hand. He lifted it to inspect the complicated knotwork of the dragon curled around the pommel.

"Do you know the stories of dragons from your homeland?" he asked.

The smith scratched his beard, eyeing the brooch on Gai's cloak. "I only know a few. But there is one, a fellow named Elfred, who knows most of the old stories."

Gai tried to keep the excitement from his voice as he asked, "Where can I find this Elfred?"

The smith pointed toward the river. "He has a cottage near the water. His boat is painted with a dragon on the bow. You can't miss it."

"Thank you," Gai said, handing the sword back.

The smith frowned as Gai turned to leave. "Wait." He reached under the table and held out a knife.

Puzzled, Gai looked at it. The handle was worked with the same knotted dragon as the sword, and the leather sheath had a similar pattern.

"Keep it."

Gai shook his head. "I can't accept this."

The smith held up a hand. "You take that. Elfred will know you're a friend by that. It'll bring you luck."

Gai blinked down at the knife. "Thank you."

The smith waved toward the river. "Go on with you, then. Go find Elfred."

Gai grinned and left with a last nod of thanks. He wandered down to the water, where it seemed most of the fishing boats were back. Some had masts, but most had only oars, the boats themselves low-slung and long. He spied one that had a colorful dragon painted on its prow.

An old man with a white beard was sitting on the dock nearby, cleaning an enormous mess of dead and dying fish. Gai couldn't help wrinkling his nose at the smelly pile of entrails he was tossing aside. Birds were gathering over the discarded bits, squabbling noisily as they flapped and hopped around, tugging at the slimy remains.

"Are you Elfred?" he asked.

The old man continued working, but glanced up. He eyed Gai, taking in his rich cloak and fine leather boots. His gaze fixed on the brooch. "Who's asking?"

Gai squatted down. "The smith sent me." He suddenly realized he hadn't even gotten the man's name.

Elfred squinted at him. "Tarik sent you?"

Gai nodded and held out the knife, trying not to grimace as Elfred took it with hands covered in fish blood and scales.

He handed it back. "What do you want?"

"I want to know what you can tell me of dragons."

Elfred's bushy eyebrows went up and his blue eyes brightened. Obviously, this was a topic to his liking. "Dragons, eh?" He pointed to the brooch. "Seems you already know some."

"A little, but I'd like to know more."

He tossed a fish at Gai. "Put that new knife to work, boy."

Gai gave a resigned sigh and undid the clasp at his throat. Elfred paused only for a heartbeat or two, his eyes narrowing as Gai removed his cloak and sat back down. He pulled a scrap of wood near and pressed his foot on it to hold the fish steady as he began to cut along the fish's belly.

"Tell me about the last dragon war," he said.

Wind whistled in Caymin's ears and rain stung her face as Péist shot through the air, Tuala and Scolaí in pursuit. Tuala might have been huge and sluggish inside the confines of his cavern, but he was surprisingly agile in the sky—a miscalculation that had almost immediately cost Caymin and Péist their lives when he matched Péist turn for turn in their first skirmish.

All day, they had fought, the mages firing spells at each other while the dragons performed their own war dance in the air. Tuala used his size to his advantage at every opportunity, driving into Péist as a falcon takes a sparrow.

Still, Péist's smaller size was to his favor as he suddenly twisted claws-up in the air and fanned his wings to decelerate. As Tuala's momentum carried him past, Péist raked his belly, his white talons leaving bloody gashes in the bronze scales, while Caymin shot an arrow, which found its mark at the soft place where wing met scales.

Péist and Caymin fell like a rock for a few heartbeats as Tuala roared in pain and fury. Coiling mid-air, Péist righted himself and flew toward a nearby mountain shrouded in cloud. They took cover in the mist. He clung to the rock, breathing hard. Caymin started to pass some of her energy to him.

"No. You have already depleted much of your own fighting Scolai." He panted. *"We only need occupy them long enough for Aine to escape."*

Caymin hoped she had escaped, because she wasn't sure how much longer she and Péist could evade the older mage and dragon.

As if reading her thoughts, Scolai's voice came to them, "You think to escape us by hiding in the fog, like cowards? There is no escape! Your fate was sealed from the moment you showed yourselves. None can stop us. And we will retrieve the Méarógfola from you before we leave your carcasses for the carrion-eaters to feast upon."

Péist took one last deep breath. *"Are you ready, little one?"*

Caymin leaned forward to press her cheek to his neck. *"Ready."*

Péist loosed his hold on the rock face and pushed away. He flew out of the concealing cover of the clouds and almost directly into Tuala's tail. The larger dragon whipped his tail, catching Péist's wing with one of the spikes. Péist roared in pain as the leathery expanse of his wing flapped feebly.

The sudden imbalance made it impossible for him to maneuver quickly. He flapped hard, trying to outpace Tuala, but the bronze talons reached out, grasping for Caymin. They caught her around her trunk. She stabbed with her knife, jabbing it into Tuala's claw. He howled in pain, but did not loosen his grip. His great wings beat, and the tethers holding Caymin to the saddle dragged Péist along with him.

Caymin looked around wildly. "Go!" she said as she slashed the tethers.

"NO!"

But Péist's protest was too late. The last strap was cut, and Tuala suddenly veered away with naught but Caymin's slight weight in his clutches.

Péist flapped awkwardly, but Tuala sped away with Caymin dangling from his claw. She twisted, trying to look back at him, but Tuala's talons dug into her stomach and back.

"Go! Save yourself!" she called.

Péist flapped faster to close the gap. "Ready yourself!"

Caymin only just had time to realize what he intended when he loosed a volley of white-hot fire and caught one of Tuala's wings aflame.

Scolaí cursed and quickly extended a shield of his own to extinguish the fire, but the damage was done. Tuala's charred wing had holes in it. He tilted at the sudden lack of air resistance on that side, and his talons opened reflexively, leaving Caymin to tumble toward the earth.

Péist streaked after her, but Tuala dove, catching Péist from above. In his fury, he drove Péist toward the ground as Caymin fell.

In the distance, other dark shadows flew toward them through the rain and mists.

Caymin could only watch helplessly as Tuala grasped Péist by the neck, forcing his head upward, as he opened his maw. Scolaí yelled something triumphantly. Just as fire erupted from Tuala's throat, Caymin hit the earth and all went black.

CHAPTER 21

BROKEN AND UNBROKEN

Broc hunkered down beside the stream, her nose twitching as she turned her head this way and that, sniffing the damp earth where scent held. Enat sat next to her, her arms wrapped around her knees. Beanna rested on her shoulder.

"Can you feel anything?" Beanna asked.

"No," Enat said. *"I keep hoping I will sense something from them."*

Beanna hopped down to join Broc on the bank. *"And you are sure this is where they went in?"*

Broc glanced at her. *"You have asked me that each time we have come here. As I told you before, we had their scent to this place. Not beyond. This is where they entered the other realm."* She sniffed again. *"There are still traces of their scent."*

The water in the pool swirled as the stream flowed in and hit the boulders that clogged the exit, forcing the water back upstream and creating a deep eddy.

Beanna waddled up to the edge of the pool, peering in. *"If they die there, will their bodies come back to us?"*

"I do not know." Enat sighed. *"I have never known another who went to the otherworld."*

238

Broc sat up and placed a paw on Enat's leg. *"How long will you wait?"*

Enat smiled and stroked her head. *"As long as it takes."*

Caymin woke to the buzz of many voices, some spoken, some unspoken. She hurt everywhere. She kept her eyes tightly shut, willing herself not to wake to the pain she knew was waiting for her, but her mind would not sink back into oblivion. Reluctantly, she opened her eyes to find Ailill leaning over her.

"Don't try to move yet. We've set your bones and helped the mending along, but you've still a long way to complete healing."

Caymin blinked up at her, trying to remember what happened. Her eyes snapped wide open, and she sat up, ignoring Ailill's warning. Gasping at the stab of pain from her back and leg, she nearly passed out again.

Ailill pushed her back.

"She does not listen, does she?"

Ríona came into view, her enormous black snout snuffling as she nudged Caymin's hair.

"I will stay down," Caymin said weakly as her head pounded with each beat of her heart. "But what happened? Where is Péist? Did Aine escape?"

"Aine escaped," Ailill said, beginning with the last question first. "She got away with the Méarógfola, else we could not have returned."

Caymin's sluggish mind tried to keep up. "You are here. And you are injured."

Ailill nodded and glanced down at her arm, bound to her chest with a bandage. "Yes, child. We're here. With the Bloodstone no longer in Scolaí's possession, we were freed to come back and fight them."

Caymin frowned. "Help me to sit up." She struggled to sit back against some pillows. She panted through the pain of moving.

"We arrived in time to see Tuala and Péist fighting as you fell."

Caymin remembered and gasped again, but not from pain this time. "Péist! Tuala had him. Did he get away? What happened to them?"

She looked around wildly, expecting to see Scolaí's cold eyes and Tuala's enormous bronze head over Ailill's shoulder.

"They are no longer a threat," Ailill said, laying a calming hand on Caymin's arm. "There were too many of us who returned when the Bloodstone released us."

Caymin frowned. "What do you mean? Are they dead?"

"*They have been banished to a realm in the otherworld where they can do no harm,*" Ríona said.

Caymin pressed her fingers to her forehead, where it pounded painfully as she tried to remember. Was she still in the otherworld, or in the past? Which was which?

"But people can enter and leave the otherworld," she managed at last. "How do you know they will stay there?"

Ailill held a small piece of dark gray quartz in her palm. "This is the only way to find the realm to which they were banished. The only tether."

Caymin fumbled under the neck of her tunic and withdrew the leather cord holding the emerald. "And this was the only tether that could bring me to this realm. Aine and Mactíre held it for us. If you kept a tether to Scolaí and Tuala, someone else may use it to find them and release them."

Ailill smiled as if Caymin were talking gibberish. "That won't happen."

Caymin opened her mouth to argue, but then thought of something. "Péist." She looked around. "You did not tell me how he is. Where is he?"

Ailill looked away, and Ríona lowered her head.

Caymin's heart stopped. "Is he...?"

"He's not dead," Ailill said quietly.

Caymin stared at her. "Then what?"

"*Tuala's fire,*" said Ríona. "*Scolaí cast a spell that prevented Péist from protecting himself. His eyes... He is fireblind.*"

Caymin blinked, certain she hadn't heard properly. Dragons had inner eyelids to protect them from fire. Her thoughts must have shown on her face because Ailill repeated, "He couldn't protect himself. Tuala's fire caught him full in the face, with his eyes open. We've tried to heal him, but..."

"I must see him." Caymin got to her feet and nearly went down as her leg refused to hold her. "Help me."

Ailill wrapped her good arm around Caymin's waist, nearly picking her up, as she hobbled. Ailill led her from the chamber where she had been lying, and Caymin realized they were in Scolai's fortress. Dimly, she was aware of the stares from other mages and dragons, but she had no interest in any of them at this moment. Ailill helped her into a dark chamber where Péist's white body glowed in the gloom.

With a strangled cry, Caymin broke free of Ailill's arm and stumbled the last few steps to her dragon. Falling to her knees at his side, she leaned against him.

"Péist! Péist, I am here."

He didn't remove his head from under his wing. He didn't acknowledge her at all. Behind her, Caymin heard Ailill's footsteps retreat, leaving them alone together. She shifted, panting in pain, to sit, still leaning against him.

For long heartbeats they sat, neither speaking. At last, Péist said, *"You should go, little one. I can feel the pain from your broken body. You need to rest."*

"I will not leave you. Will you not let me see you?"

Slowly, Péist withdrew his head from under his wing. Even in the darkness of the chamber, Caymin saw that his once-beautiful green eyes were scarred, as white as the rest of him.

He lowered his head to press his forehead against hers.

The fortress was abuzz with activity—dragons and mages coming and going. Where just a short while ago, Péist would have given almost anything to be among them, to fly with them and speak with them, now he stayed in the chamber that had become his. Others hunted for him—like Tuala, he thought bitterly—leaving deer and elk carcasses for him to feed on.

He could hear some of what they said as they made plans to try and repair the devastation they had wreaked under Scolai's power. He listened to the whispers about what a shame it was that Tuala had made him fireblind. Péist wanted to rage at them that that did not make him deaf, but he didn't have the energy even for that.

It was strange. If he had known of fireblindness before, he would have expected it to be nothing but blackness, but it was not. His world had become one of perpetual mist or fog—all was gray, impenetrable.

Caymin was the only one he would speak to, but rarely did he even do that. When he heard her enter, her limp more pronounced now, he usually pretended to be in a sleep-trance. What could he say to her? What could he offer her now? She was bonded to a dragon who could not fly, could not hunt, could not be a dragon. Sometimes, he wished Tuala had killed him.

He lay there, pondering the future—a future that stretched out into eternity. Nearby, mice scratched along the rock floor of his chamber. He heard spiders crawling up the walls. He sensed the nearby heat of others—two-legs and dragons. In some ways, it was like his night vision. But... there was something else. Something that had been there, a shadow among shadows, present even before the final battle with Scolai and Tuala. He had sensed it before, but paid it no mind, as there were so many strange things here in this realm. But now, now it showed itself more plainly, or mayhap he was only more aware of it in his current state. He could not tell what it was, whether it was friend or foe. It simply was.

His stomach rumbled with hunger, and he wondered when his next kill would be brought to him.

There was no day or night in his chamber, so he had no way of marking time, but his hunger became more insistent. Still no meat came his way. He raised his head, sniffing the air, hoping someone would notice his restlessness. When more time passed and none came, he got to his feet. As he took tentative steps, he stumbled over something. He sniffed. It was a sleeping mat. It smelled of Caymin, from when she slept near him. He tilted his head, listening. She hadn't been to him for a long time—a day or more? He sensed her, but could not tell where she was.

"*Caymin?*"

There was no response. He took more steps, stretching his nose out in front of him, sniffing and feeling his way. He kept bumping into walls.

He called again. "*Caymin!*"

Still no response. His heart began beating faster. What if he was alone there? What if all the others had left? What if Scolaí and Tuala had found a way to come back, and the others had left him behind?

Péist stumbled again, bumping into a wall and changing directions. He roared in confusion and fear.

"*I am here.*" Caymin's uneven footsteps came running into the chamber. "*I am here.*"

She leaned against his shoulder. He lowered his head to press his jaw against her.

"*Where were you? I was alone and no one came.*"

She withdrew and placed her small hands on either side of his face. "*It is time.*"

"*Time for what?*"

"*Time for us to fly again.*"

He pulled away from her. "*I cannot fly.*"

"*Yes. You can. Your eyes were damaged, but your wing is now healed. We need to fly.*"

He turned away. "*And how am I to see where I am going? Will I be tethered to another dragon and led about?*"

"*I will help you. You can see through me, and you will learn to see differently. And you will hunt.*"

He whipped around, and his tail crashed into something. He ignored it. "*Hunt? How am I to hunt?*"

"*The same way you used to hunt at night when you could not see.*"

Her calmness infuriated him. "*You, none of you, can know what this is like!*"

"No. We do not. But you and I must face the future as we are."

He stood still for long heartbeats. "I am frightened."

She came to him again. He felt her hands on his neck, and he lowered his head.

"I know you are frightened. I am, as well. But this is something we must face together."

When he said nothing more, Caymin moved away from him. A moment later, he felt his saddle settle into place on his back. She tightened the cinches and then climbed up. Her slight weight was comforting. She must have repaired the saddle because she fastened her tethers and then guided him into a passage out of his chamber, using their connection and her hands on his neck to guide him.

The passage opened onto fresh air. He stood breathing it in, feeling sunlight warm his face. He turned his head this way and that, sensing the wind currents moving over his face, the emptiness of the air just one step farther. Taking a deep breath, he spread his wings and let himself fall.

"But don't you see?" Gai said as he and Diarmit walked alongside Eachna and Garvan. "The stories Elfred told me—the dragon and dragonmage who started the last war—that has to be why Caymin and Péist went to the otherworld."

Eachna glanced at him. "Could be."

Frustrated by their lack of interest, Gai pressed on. "He said the war simply ended. The ones who started it just disappeared. There was no victory. There was no account that says they were killed, and surely someone would have written of it if they had been. That must mean they can come back."

"If Angus has heard those stories, he'll try to learn more about them," Diarmit said.

"Boys, those are just stories," Garvan said. "They've had a thousand winters to grow and become more fanciful. Who knows what the truth is anymore?"

Gai and Diarmit shared a frown and stomped along behind the older men as they traveled. There had been no sign of Angus in Elfred's village. The northmen who had settled there were simple fishermen and tradesmen. Since Elfred knew more of dragons than any others in that village, it seemed certain Angus would have sought him out if he'd gone there. If he had it in his head to stir up more trouble, he wasn't likely to find any amongst those villagers. Eachna had been told of another village where raiders sailing from the north often put in for fresh water and supplies, and they figured Angus might have made that his destination.

"What exactly are we thinking we'll be doing if we do find this lunatic?" Garvan asked as they strode along.

Eachna snorted. "We could always kill him. It would save a lot of trouble."

Garvan stopped. Eachna looked back with a sardonic smile.

"You're too good to take a life?"

Garvan studied him. "I've killed. In defense of another and not deliberately. I won't be party to a murder."

Eachna tilted his head. "Even if killing this one could save countless others?"

"If it comes to that, I'll think on it." Garvan walked on, leaving the others to follow.

Gai fell in behind. He'd watched that interaction with keen interest, as he'd asked himself the same question. He still didn't know what his own answer would be.

Caymin sat on a high ledge, watching Péist fly with Ríona. Her own heart soared to see him, matching the black dragon, spiral for spiral, banking on the air currents washing up from the valley below them, diving until he nearly brushed the treetops with his tail as he pulled up. His confidence and trust of his other senses had grown so that he was hunting for himself again. She sighed.

"You are thinking of leaving us."

She twisted around to see Ailill standing beside her. She looked back out at the flying dragons as Ailill lowered herself gracefully to sit.

"It is time," Caymin said. "Péist can fly and hunt again."

"And you?"

Caymin did not look at her. "What do you mean?"

"You are not whole."

"I was never whole. A more crooked leg does not matter."

"I wasn't speaking of your body," Ailill said softly.

Caymin said nothing. She glanced over and saw that Ailill wore the quartz crystal on a cord around her neck. She pressed her fingers to her own tunic and felt the emerald there—the thing that had brought her to Aine and to this realm. Sewn into the hem of her tunic was the piece of wood. Her only connections to Aine.

"Is it safe to wear that openly?" she asked.

Ailill lifted the crystal and looked down at it. "Why do you worry so? They're safely banished. None will help them escape." She looked over at Caymin. "Are you so afraid of them?"

"Yes." Caymin searched Ailill's eyes. "Are you not? Péist and I barely survived. We would not have if you had not returned. You and the others could not defeat them when they had the Méarógfola in their possession. What if they do escape and find it again?"

Ailill didn't attempt to hide her amusement. "That will not happen."

Caymin frowned. "You can be so certain?"

Ailill shrugged. "Yes."

Caymin turned away, her jaw tight.

Ailill got to her feet. She placed a hand on Caymin's shoulder. "Do not worry so."

Barely had Ailill departed than Péist flew to her. The wind from his wings buffeted her as he landed.

"You are flying well," she said.

"Yes."

He hunkered down next to her, turning his face this way and that to sniff the air as the wind shifted. *"It is time."*

"Yes."

"Would you wish to remain here? Without her?"

Caymin's head snapped around. "What do you mean?"

"I felt the pull of your heart. Toward Aine. Would you have taken her as your mate?"

Caymin blinked back sudden tears. "When I first saw her, in the cave, it was as if I had known her for all time. It makes no sense. Why would I feel that?"

"Perhaps being destined to love her is no different than being destined to bond with me."

"What about you? If we go back, you will be alone again. The only dragon."

"I have thought of that," Péist admitted.

"I would stay here if you wished to."

He nuzzled her hair. "Thank you, little one. But we do not belong here."

A fresh current of air blew in their direction, and Péist raised his head to sniff. "What now?"

She looked up at him. "What do you mean?"

"We were to stop a war. We stopped two."

She pondered. "We have not found the Bloodstone. It is still out there, wherever Aine hid it, waiting to be destroyed."

"True, but if none have found it in a thousand winters, will they after all this time? Can you and I not simply live in peace?"

Caymin sighed. "That would be nice. Where would you like to go?"

"Back to Inishbreith?"

Caymin's first thought was that she would have to leave the badgers and Enat yet again, but it was not fair to Péist to stay where he could not fly freely.

As if reading her thoughts, he said, "The two-legs near the forest and in other parts of Éire know of me now. I think it only a matter of time before some clan leader thinks to try and claim me for his own as Dughall attempted."

Caymin recognized the truth of his words.

Péist rested his chin against her shoulder. "Would the badgers come with us to Inishbreith? We could take them easily. They could build a new sett there."

"We could ask them. And we could fly back sometimes. It is not so very far."

"*And Beanna? Do not tell her, but I miss her.*"

Caymin chuckled. They sat together for long heartbeats, both of them lost in thought.

Caymin leaned against him. "*Forever is a very long time.*"

CHAPTER 22

AN UNSETTLED PRESENT

A nearly full moon lit the night sky as clouds scudded by her. Caymin gathered the few things she'd brought with her: her cloak, her bow, quiver and knife. She also tucked a couple of scrolls inside her tunic where the emerald still hung about her neck. She didn't know if they could go with her back to the real world, but she intended to try. She fingered the bulge in her tunic where Aine's sliver of wood was secured, wondering where it would lead them.

"Are you ready?"

Péist stood, saddled and ready to go.

Mactíre trotted to them. *"I am going with you."*

"Are you sure?" Caymin asked as she tied her bow to the saddle.

He sat on his haunches. *"I have done what Aine asked me to do. I have waited for you, given you the emerald, helped you to help her steal the Bloodstone. My task here is finished. I would return with you, and go to lie with my ancestors when my time comes."*

She laid a hand on his head. *"We are happy to have you with us."*

When all was ready, Caymin fastened her tethers and Mactíre

scrambled up in front of her. Péist walked to the entrance to his chamber and spread his wings.

"*Are you certain you do not wish to say farewell to Ríona and Ailill?*"

Caymin hesitated, twisting to look back toward the inner chambers of the fortress. "*I think not. I do not think they will even notice we have left. And if we see them again in a spiritwalk back in our realm, who knows what they will remember?*"

Péist leapt into the sky. With Mactíre's guidance, they flew back into a green-tinged, watery world. Above them, Caymin saw a tiny circle of light. Upward, Péist flew or swam—she wasn't sure which.

With an enormous splash, they burst from the pool in the stream. Péist clawed his way onto the bank and stood there, breathing hard. Mactíre jumped down and shook the water from his coat. Caymin shivered as she ran her hands along her limbs. They felt a little slimy, like the rocks under the water.

The same large moon floated overhead. From the forest near them came a rustling and a soft grunt as a badger waddled into view. He stopped abruptly at the sight of a wolf standing there. He arched his back and hissed.

Caymin unbuckled her tethers and hopped down. "*Cuán! It is only Mactíre. Oh, it is so good to see you.*"

She dropped to her knees and held him as he whickered his pleasure.

"*We have been watching for you, little one.*" He looked warily at Péist and Mactíre. "*For all of you.*"

Mactíre tilted his head. "*You have nothing to fear from me, as we are all friends of Caymin.*"

More badgers trotted out from the underbrush. Broc was accompanied by her young cubs, now old enough to hunt for themselves. They all climbed up into Caymin's lap, nuzzling her and grunting contentedly.

"*We should go to Enat,*" Broc said.

"*It is late,*" Caymin said. "*She will be sleeping.*"

"*She has been waiting with us. She would want us to wake her.*"

A loud flapping of wings announced Beanna's arrival. "*Little one!*" She landed on Caymin's shoulder. She looked up at Péist and froze for a moment. *"We are glad to have you all back among us."* She flew up to land on Péist's back. *"You, as well, worm."*

Péist reached his head around to sniff her. He snorted, ruffling all of her feathers. *"It is good to be back."*

Caymin went to him and took his face in her hands. His milky white eyes stared sightlessly at her. She pressed her forehead to his, words unnecessary.

"I will go to the circle of stones to rest," he said.

Beanna fluffed her feathers back in place. *"I will go with him."*

Caymin watched them go, then turned toward Enat's cottage with Mactíre and the badgers accompanying her.

As she neared the cottage, Enat came out. Upon seeing Caymin, Enat rushed to her, enfolding her in a tight embrace.

"Oh," she breathed in Caymin's ear. "I've been waiting for you. Come inside and we'll get some dry clothes for you."

A few moments later, dry and warmer, Caymin sat at Enat's hearth, drinking a hot cup of healing tea with Mactíre and all of the badgers lying at her feet.

Somehow, word spread and, soon, everyone was awake and gathered in Enat's cottage to welcome the weary travelers back.

Méav held her tightly. "Tell us everything, little badger."

Caymin glanced at Enat, who said, "I imagine they can't tell us everything."

Ronan pulled Caymin to sit on a stool at the hearth while the others sat on the floor. "All right, then tell us what you can."

Caymin opened her mouth but then shut it as she thought for a few heartbeats. "I can tell you that we, in the otherworld, went back in time to the last dragon war."

She smiled as Daina and Ciana both clapped hands over their mouths, but Ivar glowered.

"You didn't bring any of those monsters back with you?"

Enat stilled Caymin's retort by laying a hand on her shoulder and saying, "I think it safer to say, that the fact that we've not had dragons here for the last thousand winters is because Caymin and Péist went back."

Séana gasped. "You stopped the last war?"

"We... helped."

"Where's Péist?" Niall looked around as if he expected to see him in a corner of the cottage.

Caymin's face crumpled as she fought tears.

Neela put her hands to her cheeks. "He didn't die?"

Caymin shook her head, her chin quivering. Mactíre whined and laid a paw on Caymin's thigh.

He turned to Neela. *"He was injured. He is blinded."*

Cíana whispered to Daina, who still could not speak without speaking.

"What could blind a dragon?" Una asked quietly.

"Another dragon," Ronan said.

Enat squeezed Caymin's shoulder almost painfully. "He did come back with you?"

Caymin nodded. "He and Beanna went to the circle of stones to rest. He has had to learn how to use his other senses to fly and hunt. I had hoped, when we came back to this side of the Portal... but he is still blind."

All were quiet for a while, the crackling of the fire the only sound.

"We should let you rest as well," said Neela, getting to her feet as a signal to the others.

With more murmurs of welcome, they filed out. Neela came to Caymin and gave her a hug. "We are so grateful, to both of you, for what you've done."

Caymin wrapped her arms around Neela and then pulled back with an intake of breath. She looked up at Neela and then laid a hand on her belly.

Neela beamed, laying a hand over top of Caymin's, and whispered, "The others don't know yet. Not even Ivar."

Caymin smiled. "I will not say anything."

With a last squeeze, Neela left with Ivar, who was waiting for her.

"We will leave you for now, little one," said Broc.

The badgers waddled out to resume their hunting for the night.

"I, too, must hunt," Mactíre said. *"I will see you soon."*

Caymin rested a hand on his head for a moment. *"We would not have succeeded without you, and we would never have returned here. Thank you."*

He blinked up at her and then padded out into the night. Enat shut the door behind him. She waved her arm and whispered words to seal the cottage so that none could overhear.

Joining Caymin at the hearth, she asked, "You succeeded on all counts? The Méarógfola?"

Caymin nodded wearily. "We could not destroy it. It was taken somewhere safe. Scolaí and Tuala were banished to another realm in the otherworld."

Enat's sharp eyes studied her. "But not before they hurt you as well as Péist."

Caymin stared at the fire. "We were not strong enough. We could not defeat them. We only distracted them while the Bloodstone was taken. If Ailill and Ríona had not returned with the other dragons, they would have killed us."

"You didn't expect to return."

Wordlessly, Caymin shook her head.

"They used you."

Caymin looked up at the anger in Enat's voice.

"Ríona and Ailill. They used you to do what they could not."

Caymin nodded. "We realized that was our role. The Méarógfola was the most important thing."

Enat closed her eyes for a moment. "Not the most important." She stood. "Come. You need to rest."

She led Caymin to her old bed and wrapped a warm blanket over her. "Sleep. You're safe now."

Gai and Diarmit stared in wide-eyed wonder as they walked through another village situated on a sheltered harbor. The atmosphere of this one was immediately different. There were no women or children visible, at least no women kept as mothers or mates. Every man carried at least one weapon. There were many more northmen gathered here, and they all spoke their own language.

They'd arrived at midday and decided to split up and search for any sign of Angus.

"Remember," Eachna said to Diarmit, "he knows you. Let Gai do the asking if you think you're getting close to him."

As they walked, Gai kept a tight grip on his sword under his cloak, and Diarmit made himself look as big as possible. Drunken brawls seemed to break out around them every few steps. With a repulsed expression, Gai stepped around pools of vomit and urine.

"Why are they all looking at us?" Diarmit whispered.

Gai glanced around and realized he was right. They obviously stuck out as not belonging there, judging by the stares—some hostile, some cunning, and others...

"Boys."

They both started to find themselves facing two women who were eyeing them as a wolf eyes a sheep. The women's eyes were darkened with charcoal, and some kind of red colored their lips. Diarmit's eyes darted down to the open lacing of one's gown, exposing an ample pair of breasts.

The other woman with flaming red hair licked her lips and put a hand on Gai's chest, looking him up and down and fingering his fine cloak.

"You look like you need some company," said the first, her dark hair a wild nest around her head. She stepped close enough to Diarmit that her breasts brushed against his chest.

Diarmit froze, his eyes locked on the vision before him.

"Like what you see?" she said, reaching around his waist.

She suddenly screamed.

"Drop it," Garvan growled, squeezing her wrist until she winced and loosed her grip on Diarmit's knife.

Diarmit jumped back, patting his hands on his belt. He snatched his knife up from the mud. His cheeks burned a fierce red as Garvan released the woman.

"Get out of here!" he barked, and the two women scurried off.

He rounded on the boys. "What were you thinking? Don't you know they would have stolen everything you have on you before you knew it?"

He grabbed them each by the scruff of their cloaks and dragged them around the corner of a squat stone building.

"Stay here and stay out of trouble."

Diarmit seized his arm. "What are you going to do?"

Garvan gave him a crooked grin. "Where there was one monk asking questions, they might not think too much of another doing the same."

Gai watched him disappear into the swirling mass of men shouting, laughing, stumbling, fighting.

From the safety of their quiet corner, the boys watched the village. The buildings here were a mix of sturdier stone that looked as if they had been standing for a long time, and many newer, hastily built structures that looked as if the first good storm could blow them over.

Few fishing boats bobbed in the harbor. Instead, larger boats sat heavy in the water, with both masts and long rows of oars on either side. Their prows sported carved figures—wolves, eagles... and dragons.

Gai pointed. "I think we may have come to the right place."

They hunkered down to wait, pulling some food out of their packs. The sun was sinking low in the sky when Eachna found them.

"Do you feel any magic from him here?" Diarmit asked as he gnawed on a strip of smoked fish from the last village they stopped at.

Eachna shook his head. "I don't. There's much going on here, but none of it magic."

Daylight was fading by the time Garvan returned.

"Any luck?" Eachna asked, handing him a bit of bread.

"Oh, yes." Garvan gave him a satisfied smile. "Angus was here. First, he tried converting a few of them." He turned to look back over his shoulder to where two men were pushing each other over a woman who didn't look as if she cared which she went with. "You can imagine how well that went over."

His expression darkened. "But, what they told me was that when he started talking dragons, he got the ear of one man in particular. A raider by the name of Haldor. He got passage on Haldor's boat, headed back to the north."

Gai's mouth fell open. "If he convinces them there's a dragon here, they may send a whole fleet of raiders."

Garvan nodded. "That's my thought."

Eachna's eyes narrowed. "Where would they land? These northmen won't want to march for days and days. They'll stay at sea and put in closest to where they want to be."

The two men scuffling over the woman fell to raining fists on each other.

Eachna got to his feet. "Let's get out of here. I'll send Lorcan back with a message to the others, telling them what we've found out."

Caymin's back ached as she bent over, helping to plant. Spring's warmth fell gentle on the land, with soft rains to coax everything into life.

"You don't need to do this," Neela had said to her when she arrived at the clearing where the rows were dug into the earth, waiting.

"I want to."

Since there were no new apprentices now to do the planting, all the mages had gathered to get the work done. Working together, they got the planting completed in one day.

"This was more fun when we were watching you lot mess it up with magic," Méav recalled.

Cíana laughed. "Then we had to do it all over again the next day."

Enat chuckled. "Every group thinks they can get away with that."

Ivar finished his row and hurried over to Neela. He took her bag of seed from her. "I'll finish this. You should rest."

She shook her head. "I don't need to rest." But she, too, straightened to stretch her back. Her belly had a gentle swelling now. She rested a hand on it as Ivar took over planting the turnips.

When they were all finished, they walked back toward the village.

"You're limping again," Séana said, laying a hand over Caymin's shoulders.

"I always limp," Caymin said with a forced smile.

"I mean more than you used to."

Caymin shrugged. "I am just tired."

She felt tired. And broken. And old.

Séana seemed to understand all that Caymin didn't say. She squeezed and said, "I know you're still healing. Both of you. We're just glad you returned to us."

She released Caymin and walked on to catch up with Méav, while Enat sidled up next to Caymin.

"Neela and Ivar seem happy," Caymin said.

"Aye." Enat smiled. "I can't remember if we've ever had a babe born here among the mages. New life will be welcome. We've had precious little to celebrate of late."

Caymin glanced at her. Enat looked worn and much older than Caymin remembered before.

Enat caught her. "We've both of us been through a lot. And we're not recovering as I'd hoped we would."

They waved good night to the others and veered toward Enat's cottage. Caymin stirred the fire and put a kettle on while Enat prepared some porridge. There was a companionable silence as they worked. Before long they sat with bowls of porridge drizzled with honey and cups of hot tea made from some of Enat's herbs.

"Where is Péist?" Enat asked as they began eating.

"Resting at the circle of stones." Caymin ate a bit. "It is hard to believe it will be Bealtaine soon. It seems long ago that I was learning of these things for the first time."

"Much has happened since you came here."

"Will Una go through her trial for her staff this Samhain?"

Enat nodded. "She should've done hers last Samhain, so yes. The others still have some studying to do."

"Will you reap this spring?"

Enat considered. "We've spoken of it. We should offer a place to the apprentices we had to send home. The immediate threat of Angus is over for now, but we don't yet know what his intentions are. It might be safe to bring new apprentices here for training but, to be honest, I don't know if I have another long journey in me just yet, and Ivar won't let Neela out of his sight." She sighed. "Never have we gone this long without new apprentices to train."

Caymin looked out through the open door at the gathering darkness. "Things are changing."

"What do you sense?"

"I do not know how to explain it, but the forest feels... lonely. Emptier. As if part of it has left."

"What of you?"

Caymin turned back to Enat. "What of me?"

"You've been partaking in your studies here with the others, but you've Péist, something no other mage has. Do you intend to try for your staff as well?"

Caymin pushed her porridge around with her spoon and didn't answer immediately. "I do not know. I have been studying because I need to get stronger with my magic. I have relied too much on Péist to help me. I had not thought beyond that."

"He has been flying and hunting?"

Caymin nodded. "He has. For many days after he was blinded, he would not talk to me, would not do anything. I think he wished Tuala had killed him."

She felt Enat's gaze, studying her, but she kept her eyes lowered and ate a bit more.

"What would you have done if he had?" Enat asked.

Caymin bit her lip, surprised by how fresh the feelings of despair were. "I do not know. It would have been difficult to go on without him."

"And so you feel you rely too much on him."

Caymin didn't respond.

"You share a bond unlike any other."

"He wishes to go... where we can live alone," Caymin said softly. "Back to where we went after he hatched."

Enat could not hide the look of disappointment that flashed across her features. "You would go?"

"For him, I would. He does not feel he can fly freely here. Already, the two-legs outside our forest mark his flights. He thinks soon, clan leaders like Gai's father will try to capture him."

"He's probably right." Enat sighed heavily. "I will miss you dearly. Both of you. I cannot pretend otherwise, but we can ask no more of you. I worry, though, that you will be alone."

Caymin glanced up. "I think Mactíre and Beanna will come with us. And the badgers." Her brow furrowed. "Have you..."

"What?"

Caymin hesitated, knowing how Ríona and Ailill would react, but then said, "All is changing. The forest. Fewer people believe in the old ways. You have said it is harder to find young ones with power. Have you ever thought about... Would you come with us?"

Enat sat back. "Well, now, that's a thought. I assume you're speaking of a place known only to dragons and dragonmages. Something I will ponder."

A long silence stretched between them.

"Something else makes your heart heavy," Enat said at last.

Caymin pushed the last of her porridge around with her spoon. "How old were you when you met Sorcha?"

"I..." Enat paused. "I had earned my staff, and had made my way back toward my village. I was maybe twenty winters or more."

"And how many winters did you have together before she died?"

"Nearly fifteen. She caught a fever tending to a sick child. She stayed with them too long and was very ill by the time I found her. I could not heal her." Her voice caught, and she coughed to clear her throat. "That was when I came here to teach others."

Caymin raised her eyes to meet Enat's and saw the pain there—a pain that time would never diminish.

Enat held her gaze. "Why do you ask?"

Caymin blinked and looked back down at her bowl. "There, in the otherworld, a thousand winters in the past, I met someone. Aine. It was she who had to steal the Méarógfola and hide it."

Enat waited.

A tear dropped onto Caymin's hand. "When I saw her, it was as if I had always known her. I knew her face. I knew her voice. I knew her heart."

She raised her face, and tears ran down her cheeks. "She was Scolaí's daughter. I said horrible things. But she saved us. She stole the Bloodstone, and she got away. Else the others could not have come back to fight. But now, she is lost to me again. How could I have felt such a bond with her? A thousand winters separate us."

Enat's own eyes shone with tears as she smiled. "I don't believe time can ever stop the pull of the heart. I don't know if you'll ever see Aine again, but I do believe she came into your life for a reason. Trust that, Caymin."

Caymin rubbed the heel of her hand against her chest, as if she could rub away the pain there. "I do not understand these feelings."

"I think most of us never understand love; we only feel it. 'Tis not just two-legs who feel it. What is it that brought Broc and Cuán together? The heart makes its own magic—the strongest magic of all."

CHAPTER 23

SHADOWS AGAIN

Péist turned his head this way and that as he soared low over small stands of trees and open fields. His nose tested the air, his ears were attuned to any rustling of brush below him, and his altered vision sought any sign of heat from prey. A stag suddenly bounded out from under the trees, as if he could outrun a dragon. Péist dove, claws extended, and snatched him mid-gallop. With a quick twist of his jaws on the stag's neck, he ended the deer's life quickly.

He thanked the spirit of the stag for sustaining him.

He had no idea if other dragons did that, but his bond with Caymin had taught him to appreciate the sacrifice other four-legs made to keep him fed, especially since his blindness. It had been humiliating to have to be fed by others, and he knew he would never again take for granted the ability to hunt for himself.

Flying to a remote hilltop with his kill, he fed. He had not quite finished when he heard approaching voices. Growling his frustration, he gobbled a last mouthful and took off again before the two-legs drew near enough to see him.

The two-legs who lived within his hunting range had become accustomed to seeing him fly at night and, more and more often, they were marking him, trying to get near enough to see the dragon close-up. He was finding it difficult to hunt and feed undisturbed. These two-legs were only curious and meant him no harm, but before long, others would come who were not simply curious.

He knew Caymin was loath to leave the forest and the mages, but they would have to depart soon.

He flew back toward the forest, in no hurry to land. He soared over the dense trees, wings twitching as he adjusted to catch the air currents blowing gently through the night skies.

Something small and fast flew by under him. An owl or hawk. He paid no attention. He banked and made his way to the stone circle where Beanna was waiting for him.

Caymin's eyes fluttered open. All was dark and still, but something had awakened her. She rose from her bed and looked back to see her body still lying there. Enat was likewise in her bed, breathing deeply. With a resigned sigh, she opened the door to find the mist she knew would lead her through this spiritwalk.

Following the path laid out for her as the mist parted just in front of her, she listened, but there was no sound.

"*Péist?*"

There was no response. A quiver of uneasiness ran through her. On and on she walked until, at last, the fog lifted, and she found herself on a familiar hill overlooking a broad valley. Fully expecting to see Ailill or Ríona, she was puzzled to find herself alone. She sat down and waited, watching other dragons flying in the distance.

Just as she got to her feet, thinking she should walk on, Ríona flew to the hilltop with Ailill on her back.

She eyed them curiously, as she hadn't seen them since she and Péist left the otherworld. Ailill dismounted, looking much as Caymin remembered—silver threaded throughout her hair, a harder set to her eyes and mouth—not as young as she had appeared in the otherworld, a thousand winters in the past.

"Why is Péist not here as well?" Caymin asked by way of greeting.

Ailill grabbed her by the shoulders and looked her over sharply. "You've been there. You went back."

"Yes." Caymin felt an inexplicable anger rising inside her. She pulled loose from Ailill's grasp. "We went back and did what none of you could. Tuala blinded Péist. But you knew that and said nothing."

Ailill had the grace to look somewhat ashamed, but Ríona said, *"What would you have had us say, Caymin? Would you and Péist have wanted to know ahead of time?"*

Caymin dropped back to the ground without answering.

Ailill sat beside her.

"Why have you called me here?" Caymin asked.

Ríona settled her great bulk, with a soft rustling of her wings as she folded them. *"Something has happened."*

Caymin looked from her to Ailill and back again. "The Méarógfola?" she asked with a sinking heart.

"No. It has not been found." Ailill glanced at Ríona. "At least not that we know of. We believe we would know immediately if it were in another's possession."

"What then?"

Caymin stared hard at Ailill, and her eyes drifted down to Ailill's slender neck. Her empty neck. She pointed. Her mouth opened, but no sound came out. At last, she rasped, "Where is it?"

Ailill could not meet her eyes.

Caymin's chest heaved with her shallow breathing. "The quartz. The tether to Scolaí and Tuala. Where is it?"

"It has been stolen." Ailill closed her eyes. "I'm sorry."

Caymin's mouth gaped for several heartbeats and then she snarled, her teeth bared. "You are sorry. The tether to our enemies has been stolen. After you swore to me that they could never escape. And you are sorry."

She pushed to her feet and paced, limping back and forth. She stopped and turned to face them. "Who took it?"

"*We do not know, little one.*" Ríona lowered her head to fix Caymin with one golden eye. "*We do not think it happened here.*"

"What do you mean? If it did not happen here, then where?"

Ailill said, "None have been here except those dragons and mages who came here with us. But we think it is probable that another came with you to the past, and stole it from us in the otherworld."

"But who could have gone with us?"

"*You are certain no others were linked to you when you went through the Portal?*"

Caymin closed her eyes and groaned. "Timmin. He was linked to Mactíre earlier, when we were trying to learn where he was and what he was doing. Could he have used that link to follow us in?"

Ailill nodded somberly. "He could have."

Caymin frowned and pressed her fingers to her eyes. "But you had it. Here, when we were here with you before, you had it. I remember wondering what it was."

She dropped her hands and looked to them, hoping this was a terrible mistake.

"Yes," Ailill said. "Three mornings ago, here, I woke and it was gone. I have never removed it from my neck. For all these winters, I have safeguarded it. It could only have happened in the past, and now our present is altered."

Caymin collapsed back to the earth, numb. "They will come back."

Above Caymin, the circle loomed, its ancient stones standing, covered in lichens and moss. The sun, just rising high enough to hit the stones, threw long shadows. The immense age and power of this place never failed to press itself upon her when she entered, almost as if it made the air heavy. Péist lay within, his head raised to the sky, his eyes closed as he hummed.

Beneath him, Beanna lay in a similar pose. She looked around at Caymin's approach. She got up and waddled toward Caymin as she sat on the ground next to Péist.

Caymin smiled wistfully, watching Beanna. She looked like a miniature Péist, with her white feathers.

"The worm has gone into one of his trances." Beanna hopped up into Caymin's lap.

Caymin laid a hand on his side, but he didn't respond. *"How long?"*

"Since he returned from hunting in the night."

Beanna cocked her head to fix Caymin with one eye. *"You are upset. What has happened?"*

Caymin stroked the sleek feathers on Beanna's back. *"The enemy we helped defeat in the otherworld–the ones who started the last great dragon war–may have found a way to escape."*

"They may return to this realm?"

"Yes."

Caymin leaned against Péist and waited, her heart filled with dread at the thought of having to tell him what she knew.

The golden light of the sun gleamed against Péist's scales, creeping down his neck as the sun rose higher in the sky. He stirred, and Caymin sat up.

Lowering his head, he turned his sightless eyes in her direction. She reached out to lay her hand on his jaw.

"You know?" she asked.

"Yes."

She didn't know what to say.

"Why did they not kill them when they had the chance?" Péist asked bitterly.

Caymin was about to reply when they heard running footsteps and panting. Beanna flapped away, and Caymin jumped to her feet, hands out, ready to defend them.

Enat ran into the circle, clutching her side. She leaned over, gasping for breath, her other hand braced on her knee.

Caymin ran to her, laying a hand on her back. "What is it?"

"Lorcan." Enat had to pant for a bit longer before she could continue. "Lorcan flew in with a message from Eachna. Angus found a raider from the north who was interested in hearing about a dragon in Éire. He has sailed with them to the north. Eachna thinks they may return with an entire fleet of raiders."

She straightened. "Looking for you, Péist."

Caymin's jaw clenched. She backed away from Enat and picked up a stone. Screaming in frustration, she hurled it as hard as she could.

Enat waited as Caymin stood there with her eyes closed. "Péist and I were called to Ríona and Ailill in a spiritwalk last night."

Enat stepped nearer. "What did they want?"

Caymin shook her head, her fists clenched, unable to talk.

"*Ailill kept a crystal,*" Péist said. "*A tether to the realm where Tuala and Scolai were banished. It was stolen from her three nights past.*"

Enat's eyes flashed. "Who stole it?"

"*They do not know. But—*"

His head snapped up. "*The shadow.*"

"What shadow?" Caymin asked, looking up at him.

"*It was there, in the otherworld. I sensed it before the final battle, always a shadow among the shadows. After I was blinded, I felt it more, though I could not say why. I thought it just one of the many strange things about the otherworld.*"

Caymin's shoulders slumped. "I think Timmin used his link to Mactíre to follow us through the Portal. If he is the one who stole it and uses it to help them, Tuala and Scolai could return."

"*You should leave, now,*" said Beanna. "*Fly away. Go back to Inishbreith.*"

"Yes." Enat laid a hand on Caymin's shoulder. "Go. You have both done more than enough."

Caymin turned. "I asked if you would leave with us."

Enat's eyes shimmered as she shook her head. "I can't. I have to stay and help."

Caymin nodded and turned to Péist. He pressed his brow to hers.

"Nor can we leave," Caymin said at last.

"*We have no choice now,*" Péist said. "*We must find the Méarógfola.*"

On the other side of the mystical forest, heavy fog hung over a lake so still, it looked solid. Birds called to the morning. Swans glided across the surface of the water, barely making a ripple in the stillness.

The mist began to shift, writhing and twisting though there was not a breath of wind. Honking an alarm, the swans took to the air. Ripples formed as something moved under the surface of the lake, making the water lap against the shore. A figure rose out of the depths, shrouded by the fog. Wading onto dry land, Timmin combed the excess water from his long beard with one hand. With a grim smile, he opened his other to look at the crystal of smoky quartz lying in his palm.

THE END

Character & Pronunciation Guide

Ailill – (ah LEEL) – dragonmage, bonded to Ríona

Aine – (EN ya) – girl mage from the otherworld

Angus – (ANG gus) – fanatical Christian monk

Bardán – (BAR dawn) – a boy in the otherworld, Caymin's friend

Bealtaine – (BELL tān) – Celtic summer festival, traditionally May 1st

Beanna – (B'YAWN nuh) – crow, friend to Caymin, Enat, and Péist

Broc – (brawk) – badger sow, Caymin's badger mother

Caymin – (KĀ min) – orphan, rescued by badgers, dragonmage to Péist

Cíana – (KEE ah nuh) – young mage apprentice

Cuán – (KOO awn) – badger boar, Caymin's badger father

Daina – (DĪ nuh) – young mage apprentice

Diarmit – (DEER mit) – young mage apprentice

Dughall – (DOO gull) – Gai's father, king of the Eoganacht clan

Eachna – (AHK nah) – mage to the Eoganacht

Éire – (AIR uh) – Gaelic for Ireland

Enat – (Ā nut) – mage, teacher

269

Eoganacht – (OH ga naght) – Gai's clan

Eoghan – (OH in) – Caymin's father

Fergus – (FER gus) – new mage

Fionnair – (FYUN air) – Caymin's mother

Flann – (Flăn) – Gai's brother

Gai – (GĪ – like the English word 'guy') – young mage apprentice

Grián – (GREE awn) – girl in the otherworld, Caymin's friend

Ian – (EE in) – Caymin's little brother in the otherworld

Imbolc – (IM molg) – Celtic spring festival, traditionally February 1st

Inishbreith – (IN ish breth) – island where dragon young hatched and grew

Ivar – (EE var) – mage, teacher

Lughnasadh – (LOO nuh suh) – Celtic harvest festival, traditionally August 1st

Mactíre – (mac TEER) – wolf, Caymin and Péist's guide to the otherworld

Méarógfola – (MARE og fōla) – the Bloodstone

Méav – (māv) – new mage

Neela – (NEE la) – mage, teacher

Niall – (NEE ull) – new mage

Osán – (Ō sawn) – female giant elk, mate to Ríordán

Péist – (Pesht) – white male dragon, bonded to Caymin

Ríona – (REE ah nuh) – black female dragon, bonded to Ailill

Ríordán – (REE ur dawn) – male giant elk, mate to Osán

Ronan – (RO nan) – new mage

Samhain – (SAH win) – Celtic winter festival, traditionally the night of October 31st to November 1st

Scolaí – (SKUL lee) – dragonmage, bonded to Tuala

Séana – (SHAWN uh) – Méav's mate

Timmin – (TIM min) – mage, teacher

Tuala – (TOO ah la) – bronze male dragon, bonded to Scolaí

Una – (OO nah) – older mage apprentice

Urard – (OO rard) – scribe of the Eoganacht clan

CHAPTER 1

CONFESSIONS

The night air was mild, filled with the scents of summer—trees full of leaf and growing fruit, mosses and ferns and other things that grow low to the ground, all full and lush with the frequent rains. The badger stopped to dig, her long claws raking the soil to unearth several grubs and worms. She ate and trundled on, her nose twitching busily as she hunted.

A shadow passed overhead. She looked up to see a dragon silhouetted against the stars.

"All is well, little one?" she called.

Another shadow leaned over the side of the dragon. "All is quiet, Broc. We have seen nothing amiss."

Reassured, the badger resumed her foraging. All had been quiet for the past moon, but Caymin and Péist insisted on flying nightly, patrolling the expanse of the protected forest, keeping watch for any sign of danger.

Broc stopped to sniff the air herself and realized it wasn't quiet at all. She heard mice and voles rustling through the underbrush. She saw smaller shadows pass overhead as owls glided by on silent wings. She had nothing to fear from them, but she heard small cries as sharp talons found their prey. She jumped as a fox trotted out of her den.

"*Greetings, Sionnach,*" said Broc.

"*Greetings, Broc.*" The vixen sat and tilted her head.

"*Your young are healthy and growing?*"

"*Yes.*" The fox raised her nose and sniffed as a gentle breeze tickled the air. "*The hunting will be good tonight.*"

She glanced to the sky. "*The winged worm and your two-leg cub have seen nothing?*"

"*No. But we know danger is coming.*"

The fox looked at her again. "*The entire forest knows it.*" She twisted her head and gave a small bark. Eight young foxes tumbled out of the den, playing and wrestling with one another.

Broc was grateful her own young were grown and hunting for themselves now. "*Good hunting.*"

She waited until the foxes disappeared into the forest, and then she moved on. Sionnach was right. The forest was waiting. Every four-leg, every winged one knew something was coming. The two-legs who guarded the forest had done what they could to add protections. Whether they would be enough, and what the dangers might be, they could only wait and see. For now, she needed to find more grubs.

Péist glided down and landed within the circle of standing stones. Caymin unfastened the tethers that secured her to his saddle and climbed down. He crouched so that she could pull the saddle off, and he stretched out on his side.

"*I think I might be tired enough to rest now,*" he said. "*You need to sleep, as well, little one.*"

She laid a hand on his jaw. "*I know. I will see you later.*"

She left him and walked through the forest, her limp a bit more pronounced than usual. Her leg ached, and the scars behind her knee pulled after spending half the night astride her dragon. As she walked, she listened, her head twisting this way and that, attuned to every sound, every rustle, every voice of the four-legs and birds around her. A sudden flapping of wings made her jump.

"*I did not mean to startle you,*" said the white crow who landed on her shoulder.

Caymin took a deep breath. "*It is not you, Beanna.*"

"*I know. The worm is the same. He is ready to breathe fire at every bug that crawls out from under a leaf. You are both wary.*"

Caymin scoffed. "*Wary. Yes, we are wary.*"

Beanna cocked her head. "*I know it is more than that.*"

They walked on through the forest for a bit.

"*You believe they will return?*" Beanna asked. "*The ones who hurt you?*"

"*I know they will.*"

"*The rest of us will help in any way we can. You are not alone.*" Beanna gave her ear a gentle nibble before taking off into the night.

Caymin was glad to see that the cottage was dark. She carefully opened the door, hoping to let herself in without waking Enat, but when she stepped inside, it was to find Enat sitting at the hearth.

Her silver hair glinted in the light thrown by the peat fire. She held out a cup. "Here. Drink this. It will help you to sleep."

Caymin sat on a stool next to Enat. "Then you should be drinking some."

Enat smiled and poured hot water into a second cup. "I am."

For many heartbeats, they sat side by side watching the flames as they sipped their tea.

"The forest is safe?" Enat asked pointlessly.

"Yes," Caymin replied, just as pointlessly. They both knew that if anything were wrong, they would not be sitting there drinking tea.

Sleep didn't come easily to either of them these nights. Caymin often heard Enat whimpering in her sleep. She knew Enat's spiritwalks must be filled with the horrors of the torture she had endured at the hands of Angus when she'd been his captive. As bad as Enat's spiritwalks might have been, Caymin suspected her own were worse. Every night, she relived the battles she and Péist had fought against

275

Scolaí and Tuala in the otherworld—losing battles against a mage and dragon much older and larger and battle-hardened than they.

She felt herself falling to the earth while Tuala's huge claws grabbed Péist. Through her link with Péist, she saw the fire building in Tuala's maw, the flames erupting from his throat as Scolaí uttered a spell to keep Péist from protecting his eyes just before all went dark. And every night, she lunged up in bed, certain she was fireblind. But when her hands flew to her face, her eyes, all she felt was her own old scars from the fire when she was a baby.

She knew Péist revisited those horrors himself, though they never spoke of it.

"Caymin?"

She started at the sound of Enat's voice and the touch of her hand on her shoulder. Words were unnecessary as they looked into each other's eyes.

Caymin tore her gaze away and focused once more on the fire. "Where do you think Timmin is now?"

Though they had had this conversation many times since Bealtaine, they were no closer to an answer.

"I wish I knew," Enat said.

"If he has the tether to finding the realm Scolaí and Tuala were banished to in the otherworld, what is he waiting for?" Caymin shoved up from her stool and paced. "It has been over a moon since we were told the tether was stolen. If he is going to release them and bring them back to this world, I would rather he just do it."

"I have been thinking on it." Enat leaned forward to prod the flames with an iron poker. "When he does bring them back, my guess is they won't attack this forest first."

Caymin paused her pacing. "Where then?"

Enat used the poker to draw a shape in the ashes. Caymin recognized the outline of Éire.

"Even a dragonmage and dragon would have a difficult time penetrating our protections."

Caymin sat back down. "Yes. Péist and I could not get through when we returned. We needed your staff. I do not think Scolaí has one, but Timmin does. He can let them in."

"But Timmin, ultimately, wants to protect places of magic. I don't think he has any wish to destroy or attack this forest. He wants to drive the Christians from Éire." Enat frowned at her rough map. "If I were them, I think I would begin by terrorizing those in far-flung parts of Éire, forcing them to cower and swear fealty to us, to those with magic."

"You say 'us' as if we are with them."

Enat smiled grimly. "Do you not think the believers of the Christ, like the ones who followed Angus, will believe that we are allied with them? In their ignorance, they will put all who practice magic, who keep the old ways, together. They will not distinguish between us, and Timmin and Scolaí. And if Scolaí and Tuala begin by burning and destroying, as they did in the past, there will be outright war."

Caymin stared at her, knowing she spoke the truth. Her brief interactions with Angus's warriors after their skirmish in the mountains had taught her how narrow their views were.

"I wish Garvan were here," she said. "A monk who believes in magic and knows that we are not evil could help us to reach out to them."

"But he isn't," said Enat. "I've been thinking on this, as well. Angus and his warriors are not a threat to this forest for now. If I'm right, and Timmin and Scolaí begin their attacks elsewhere, we are wasting our time sitting here waiting for an attack that is unlikely. I believe we should send a few mages out to warn the people and try to win their support now, while you and Péist begin your search for the Méarógfola."

Caymin stared at her. "But we do not know where to look."

Enat met her gaze and held it for long heartbeats, until Caymin looked away. "Is that the only reason you hesitate to leave here?"

Caymin didn't respond.

Enat reached out to grasp her arm. "'Tis natural to be afraid, after what you both went through, Caymin. If I could wish it different, I would, but I believe you and Péist are destined to battle them again. As you search, you should attempt to make allies of your own, before Timmin unleashes Scolaí and Tuala on the rest of Éire."

Caymin bit her lip. "When do we tell the others there may be another dragon and mage loosed on this world?"

"Soon," Enat said with a sigh. She took Caymin's cup. "I think we should both try and get some sleep."

A soft rain fell as Caymin made her way to the village housing the only other two-legs in this mystical forest. There were no signs of anyone stirring in the boys' or girls' cottages. Ivar and Neela were living together in his cottage now that Neela was four or five moons away from giving birth. That left Neela's cottage for Méav and Séana. Smoke was rising from the chimneys of both, and their doors were open, the windows unshuttered.

She peeked into the first to see Ivar kneeling at the hearth, stirring a pot. He glanced up as her shadow darkened the door.

"Greetings," she said. She glanced around. "Where is Neela?"

He waved an irritated hand vaguely in the direction of the latrine. "She's up six times a night. Which means I'm up six times a night."

Caymin watched him for a moment, his huge body and shaggy black hair and beard reminding her, as he always did, of a bear.

"Well, good morning to you."

Caymin turned as Neela came up behind her. She took Caymin's hand and pulled her into the cottage, out of the rain. Ivar jumped up and guided Neela to the table.

"Sit," he said. "I've nearly got the porridge ready."

Neela gave Caymin a knowing smile, letting Ivar fuss. "Have you broken your fast?"

"I have," Caymin said. "I am going to the meetinghouse."

"We'll meet you there in a bit," Neela said. "We're going into the forest to work on the elements today."

Caymin frowned. "But that was the first thing we learned."

"And therefore the first neglected."

A short while later, Neela paced among the apprentices as they practiced: Caymin with water, Daina with earth, Cíana with fire, and Una with air.

"All of you can now easily manipulate the elements when they're lying in front of you," Neela was saying. "It's not so easy when you're trying to call them up from wherever they may be around you."

The rain had stopped, but the skies were still heavy with it. Sunlight burst in scant rays through the clouds as Caymin struggled to summon water.

Neela stepped close. "Find it," she murmured in Caymin's ear. "Bring it to you."

Caymin raised her hands and twisted them in the air, as if she were grabbing something solid. Water trickled from her fists into a clay pot lying at her feet.

"Good," said Neela. "More."

She walked on to Cíana, who was having a more difficult time drawing fire from the wet air. Over and over again, she was able to conjure balls of flame to sit in her palms, but when she tried to pull larger fire from around her, nothing happened.

"When there's fire in the sky, it's easy," Neela said, moving over to stand behind her. "You can call it to you, aim it, direct it—if you're strong enough. But remember, lightning can kill you if you're not careful. This..." She reached over Cíana's shoulder to guide her two hands. "This is more like coaxing the fire forth."

She merged the balls of fire floating in Cíana's hands, molding them with her own, adding to them until the flames shot up into the sky.

"Take it," she breathed, handing the tower of fire to Cíana, who took it, moved it, twisted it into a knot.

Daina stood off to the side, on a small island of earth, while all around her, she had moved the dirt to form a rampart encircling her.

Una called the air, forming a small whirlwind that danced around her, picking up small sticks and stones and leaves from the ground. With a sweep of her hands, she flung her wind at Daina's wall of earth, toppling it, and encrusting Daina in dirt.

Daina stood, sputtering, as she looked down at herself. "Why did you do that?"

Una gave a tight-lipped smile. "You're the one who hasn't mastered air. If you're going to play in the dirt, you need to make your walls more solid, else anyone can breach them."

Caymin watched, a fountain of water frozen in mid-air. She knew Una resented having to practice with them.

Neela deftly stepped in between them. "I think that's enough for today. Your next lessons will be to learn the names and movements of the stars. Your days and nights will be mixed up for a bit, so try and get some sleep the next two days." She looked Daina over. "Since you've a need for a bath now anyhow, it might be a good day for you all to visit the bathhouse."

Una turned on her heel. "I already know the names of the stars, and I don't need a bath."

Daina's face, under the dirt spattered across it, was a furious pink. "Why must she take her anger out on us? It's not our fault Niall got to take his trials last Samhain and she didn't."

"I know," Cíana said sympathetically as the three girls made their way toward the bathhouse. "It rankles her more that after we all got sent away, Angus and his warriors never even threatened this forest. But it doesn't help that Niall is here. Seeing him walking around with his staff every day is like salt in a wound."

"That is my fault," Caymin said.

They entered the bathhouse and stripped out of their clothing. Even in summer, the spring water that fed the bath was icy. Caymin dipped a toe in and shivered before jumping in to join the others.

Daina rose from under the water looking much cleaner already. "Why do you feel guilty?" she asked.

"It was Péist and I who brought Niall here to take his trials last Samhain," Caymin said as she scrubbed Daina's back.

Daina turned to look over her shoulder. "But Niall was here. Una wasn't. It was Méav who helped him prepare. That isn't your fault."

As the girls took turns scrubbing each other's backs, they compared the changes in their bodies. Cíana and Daina both had small breasts beginning to form, while Caymin's body lagged behind.

Daina shook her head. "You'll always look like a boy."

"Not a boy," said Cíana. "Just a tough girl most wouldn't want to take on when she's angry. Ask Ivar."

They giggled, remembering how Caymin's magic had thrown Ivar across the sparring yard when she lost control.

Caymin could feel Cíana's fingers gently working over the old scars covering most of the right side of her body. Cíana undid the thin braids in Caymin's hair so she could wash it. "What are Niall and Ronan doing anyway?"

Conversation halted for a moment as all three went underwater to rinse their hair.

"They're probably at the sparring yard," said Daina when they emerged.

They pulled their clothing into the water and washed it while they were there.

"That's all we can do," Cíana said. "Spar and practice and wait."

"But what are we waiting for?" Daina asked. "No one will tell us."

Cíana glanced at Caymin, and then stared harder. Caymin felt her cheeks burn.

"I told you," Daina said triumphantly. "She does know something."

They each took Caymin by a shoulder and turned her to face them. She looked from one to the other.

"Enat says it is time to tell all of you," she began. "But do not say anything to the others until we tell them all together."

Daina and Cíana exchanged worried glances at Caymin's cautious tone.

"This doesn't sound good," Cíana said.

Péist flew down to the village. He felt the sun's warmth disappear when he dropped below the shadow line of the trees. The two-legs were gathered around a fire burning in the pit in the center of the dwellings. He could see the heat of their bodies encircling the warmth of the fire. Their conversation ceased upon his arrival.

"*Greetings to you,*" he said, speaking so that all could hear.

"Thank you for coming, Péist," Enat said.

He settled next to Caymin and, a moment later, heard the flapping of Beanna's wings as she flew to perch on his back. He twisted his neck around to sniff her as she settled with a soft rustling of her wings.

"Over a moon ago," Enat began, "when Caymin and Péist returned from the otherworld, you knew that they had gone back a thousand winters in time to the last dragon war. Some of you guessed that Péist had been blinded by another dragon. It's true. Caymin and Péist fought Scolaí and Tuala, and then other dragons and mages returned to join in the fighting. It has always been known that the others were victorious, but it was never written what happened to Scolaí and Tuala. Our young friends were both injured in the battle, and we know now that Scolaí and Tuala were banished to another realm in the otherworld where they have been exiled all this time."

Péist turned to Ronan's voice as he said, "Why do I have the feeling you're about to tell us they're no longer there."

Caymin stirred. "We do not know if they have been freed. But someone has stolen the only tether to the realm where they were banished. We believe it was Timmin who stole it."

"What tether?" came Ivar's voice. "And why are you only now telling us of this?"

Péist felt Caymin's hesitation. *"We must tell them, little one."*

She laid a hand on his foreleg. "The dragons and mages who survived the war exist still. We have been in communication with some of them," Caymin said.

All around him, Péist listened to the startled exclamations of the humans and knew that Enat had been right. If these two-legs were upset to hear this, others would be panicked, like the sheep on the islands off the coast who ran off the edge of the land into the endless water when he was hunting.

Méav's voice broke through the clamor. "Where are they?"

"We do not know," Péist said.

"Are they in the otherworld?" Méav pressed. "Were they with you there?"

"Yes," said Caymin. "And no."

More unsettled muttering broke out, and Enat said, "Hush. Let them speak."

"They were in the otherworld, in the past," Caymin said. "But we have also communicated with two of them in our spiritwalks, in the now."

"Where?" asked Neela. "Can they come to help?"

"*We do not believe they are here,*" said Péist. "*Nor are they in the other-world. After the war ended, and two-legs no longer trusted dragonmages and dragons, they retreated to a place where they could live in peace and cause no further conflict.*"

"Ailill and her dragon, Ríona, have been guiding us in our spiritwalks," Caymin said. "It was Ailill who guarded the tether to the place of banishment, and it was they who told us it had been stolen."

Ivar's size made him easy to recognize as he stood. "So you're telling us that Timmin or someone else has a key to releasing the dragon and mage who started the last war? And they could come back here to our world?"

"Yes," Enat said. "That is what we're saying."

"And why has it taken you more than a moon to tell us this?" Ivar demanded again.

"*We hoped there was some mistake,*" Péist said. "*We hoped Ríona and Ailill would tell us that Scolaí and Tuala were still safely imprisoned. But they have not.*"

"That's why you've been flying every night," said Séana from where she sat next to Méav. "You've been making sure we're safe."

"Is there anything else you haven't told us?" Niall asked.

Péist bowed his head, but he and Caymin said nothing. A profound silence settled over them all.

"What is it?" Neela asked.

"There is something else, but we cannot tell you any more about it," Caymin said. "You must trust us on this."

"Trust you?" Ivar paced outside the circle of two-legs sitting around the fire. "You're about to bring back the worst threat our world has ever known, and you want us to trust you?"

"Caymin and Péist aren't bringing them back," Neela said.

"It's because of them that this is happening!" Ivar shouted.

"Stop," Enat said. "It's because of Caymin and Péist that we've known a world that hasn't been ruled for the last thousand winters by a mad dragon and mage. It was only their intervention that prevented Scolaí and Tuala conquering all the known lands back then and ruling them to this day."

Péist turned in the direction of Méav's voice as she said, "If the other dragons and mages came back to fight them, why would Tuala and Scolaí have taken over? What prevented the others from revolting against them back then?"

There was a soft gasp from Séana. "That's it, isn't it? The thing you can't tell us. It's the thing that prevented the others from resisting them until you went back."

"*We cannot say more,*" Péist said.

"No more need be said," Enat insisted. "Caymin and Péist have risked their lives repeatedly for us, for Éire."

"Are we just going to sit around and wait for them to return?" Méav asked.

"What do you want to do?" asked Una, her voice shrill. "We're not leaving the forest again, are we?"

"No," said Enat firmly. "You will go through your trials this Samhain. And we need some of us here to protect this forest, but Méav is right. I don't believe we should sit and wait. We should spread out across Éire and prepare the people for what may be coming."

"Who would believe this?" Cíana asked. "I wouldn't if I hadn't seen Péist for myself."

"No," said Ivar. "We should stay together. That way, we can combine our power to fight them."

"They blinded a bloody dragon," Ronan said. "What do you think we're going to do? Together or separately?"

"We can fight them," Enat said. "They are not invincible, but people must band together to defend themselves."

"Wouldn't it make more sense to wait until this Scolaí and Tuala actually make themselves known?" Neela said. "You've defeated them once already. They may not be eager to fight you again."

"We did not defeat them," Caymin said quietly. "We only delayed them. If the other dragons and mages had not returned when they did, we would be dead."

Péist lowered his head to rest his jaw against her arm.

"I have been thinking on this, too," said Enat. "Those of you with staffs will be best prepared to battle and protect, should it be necessary. What if Péist flew you to different parts of Éire?"

Caymin jerked. "No!"

"*Calm yourself, little one,*" Péist said. "*Enat and Ciana are right. Showing myself to other two-legs may help to convince them the threat is real.*"

He felt Caymin's consternation as Enat continued.

"I know it will be difficult for you to be apart, but it's the quickest way to get us to different regions. That way, the people could see for themselves that we speak the truth. I'm certain tales have been told that there is a dragon here now. Too many have seen him. We would then have you spread out in places where we could communicate no matter where they might show themselves. Word could easily be sent back with birds, and the rest of us could go to help, or defend this forest as needed. If Scolaí and Tuala do return, and especially if they do so with Timmin's help, who knows where they will attack. We need allies."

"But will they attack?" Daina asked. "They've been locked away for a thousand winters. If they are freed, mayhap all they will want is to live in peace."

Péist snorted. "*You have not faced them. They will not want peace. They will want vengeance. I am willing to do this.*"

Enat stood. "Then it's settled. Let's begin preparations. Lessons for the apprentices will have to wait for a bit. We'll need to decide who goes where."

Caymin sat alone inside the hollowed-out trunk of an uprooted tree. It had been her first place of refuge when she had come to the forest with Enat, a badger-child unaccustomed to two-leg ways. The tree was so large, Ivar could have stood inside it without crouching. Outside, rain poured in a steady rhythm, but inside the tree, all was dry.

Péist was flying Ronan north to find Fergus and tell him all that had occurred since the battle with Angus. From there, Péist would take Ronan west and leave him to organize the people in that region. Through her constant link with him, Péist was able to reassure Caymin that all was well. They had encountered no resistance.

"*Seeing me, the two-legs here have been willing to believe another dragon may come,*" he had told her. "*I think Enat was right. They must see to believe.*"

A shadow moved through the curtain of rain, and Caymin tensed, ready to throw up a defensive spell.

"Caymin?"

She relaxed at the sound of Méav's voice. "Yes."

Méav walked in, shaking rain from her cloak. Despite the mildness of the summer morning, the damp was enough to chill. She took her cloak off and ran a hand over it, whispering words to dry it.

"Enat thought you might be here, little badger," she said as she sat.

Caymin hugged her knees to her chest. "I am not a little badger anymore."

"You'll always be that to me." Méav flicked her hand to light up the gloomy interior of the tree. "You miss him." She set a small blue flame alight.

"I do not like being apart from him."

Méav nodded. "It's good of both of you to do this. I think it's necessary to let people see we've an honorable dragon in our midst."

They sat in silence for a bit.

"Enat is reading everything she can find about the dragon wars," Méav said.

"That is wise, since we will soon be fighting another."

Méav reached across the space between them and laid a hand on Caymin's arm. "You won't fight alone."

Something snapped inside Caymin, and she yanked her arm away. "Is that so? Are you hiding a dragon somewhere that I have never seen? Or Enat? Or Ivar? If not, I think Péist and I are the only ones who will be fighting them when they return. You and the forest and all of Éire will simply be tinder for Tuala's fire!"

She shoved to her feet, her chest heaving. "You do not know... None of you know what it was like."

Méav stared up at her.

"I did not ask for this." Caymin turned away, ashamed of the tears that stung her eyes. "I am not a warrior."

A heartbeat later, she felt Méav's hand settle on her shoulder. "But you are, Caymin. You are one of the bravest people I've ever known. You don't fight for foolish things like land or because some petty king orders you to. You fight to protect those you love, the places you care about. There is no greater reason to fight. I know you're frightened. You would be foolish not to be. You and Péist have faced something none of the rest of us can imagine, but I know, when the need arises, you and Péist will do what needs to be done. And we'll stand with you, doing whatever we can."

For a moment, Caymin was afraid Méav was going to pull her into an embrace, and she knew she wouldn't be able to hold her tears back if she did. But Méav simply squeezed her shoulder and sat back down.

"Séana was right," Méav said. "About the thing that kept the other dragons and mages from rebelling back then. There was something, wasn't there?"

Caymin sat as well. She nodded wearily. "We must find it and destroy it."

"Destroy it? Why?"

"It is too dangerous. If it is found, anyone who held it could control all the dragons and mages, just as Scolaí and Tuala did during the last war."

"But..." Méav's eyes narrowed as she thought. "You said you've been in communication with some of them in this day, but you don't know where they are. If this thing, whatever it is, were to be found, they could be brought back here?"

Caymin nodded again. "That is what they have told us."

"Then you must find it," Méav said, leaning forward and grabbing Caymin's arm again.

"I just told you that. We must destroy it."
"No." Méav's voice was hard as she squeezed. "You and Péist must find it, and then you must use it."